BLAZING THE SUN

CAMERON LAMBRIGHT

BLAZING THE SUN

Cameron Lambright

-INCANDESCENCE PRESS-

This is a work of fiction. FICTION! The old adage applies: "Please don't sue, he's not talking about you." Names, places, etc... resemblance, etc... entirely coincidental, etc, etc.

INCANDESCENCE PRESS
www.incandescencepress.com

Original Cover Art and Design: Soheil Hamidi Tousi

For those who dreamed to win, and those who lost.

C H A P T E R 1

SAMSON FORD LEANED ACROSS THE wings framework of his
ship and tightened down its bridging bolts with an old
steel wrench. Racing ships filled the hangar bay around him,
bright and gleaming in their stripes. His hands were strong
and had the texture of work. Crowds of spectators watched
from stands of seats. Mechanics and pilots scrambled across
the hangar floor. They were almost as strong as him. All of
them were. They used force wrenches and robot assistants,
they didn't work at it. Not old steel wrenches, not work by
hand. It didn't seem fair. He smiled.

"Is that all checked out?" his mechanic, Ben Johnson,
asked from below.

Samson climbed down the side of the white, cylindrical
ship and dropped onto the hangar deck. His old, black pilot's
suit had a red 'V' painted on its back. Something stank. Ben
slid out from underneath the ship and flipped up a pair of
goggles. His jumpsuit was streaked with oil and ash, and the
ends of his salt and pepper beard were singed.

"You should be more careful with your welding," Samson said.

Ben smiled.

"I'm always careful. Hurry up and get strapped in."

A hum filled the air minutes later as the enormous hangar doors slid slowly open. Samson watched from the pilot's
bubble on the front of his ship as they cleared the deck. Most
of the younger mechanics on the floor had blue skin. A faint
shade of blue, that was the style now. He looked at his own
tanned, brown hands. The blue skinned mechanics were all
tall and symmetrical.

A bell echoed through the hangar. Samson switched on

his engine cells, and twisted his hands muscularly around the control wands, anxious to get into space. He was tall too, and symmetrical. He glanced at the pilot in the ship beside him. The man was older, his skin was purple, dark. His hair and eyes were milky white. He looked back at Samson curiously, and finally gave him a thumbs up. Samson ran his eyes over the man's ship and looked back up to watch the hangar door.

A rocket arced out into space. He watched it intently, unblinking. It burst into shimmering quicksilver three miles out that splashed across the void, and the vertical take-off ships exploded through the hangar door. Samson's ship rose more slowly, and shook when it finally crossed the field barrier into space. The main pack accelerated away from him.

His thrusters hummed and Samson picked up speed, he could feel the sound vibrations leveling out. The other racers stopped pulling away and started getting closer. Saturn turned below them. A great, golden ball, the lines on its craquelure surface appeared and melted into each other gracefully, and the famous rings hung about it like a halo. He kept accelerating, thrusters whistling. His ship was screaming speed, it pressed into his back. Other racers began to disappear behind him as if they were stopped.

He caught up to the main pack as they were entering the first obstacles, a series of hoops that snaked in a giant spiral around Saturn's rings. A crush of ships cornered through the hoops tightly, nudging each other, jockeying for space. There was a collision, and two long, silver, cigarette racers spun out of the pack, burning. One of them exploded. The other drifted down towards Saturn's endless fluidic gas.

Samson flew past, above the pack. He sent his ship into a cartwheel and spun end over end around two close-linked rings, passing them from an impossible angle.

"Jesuschrist," a pilot said on the com.

The crush of engines opened and spread apart as ships in the front of the pack rushed to catch up to him. Samson coursed forward, waiting to regain full consciousness from the maneuver. He focused stubbornly through tunnel vision. Decelerometers on either side of him vented steam.

"Nice move, kid," the weathered voice of August Martins said on the com. "I haven't seen flying like that in years."

Martins swooped down from above and tried to crack Samson's cockpit open with the plated base of his ship. Samson dove too, fending off the collision, and Martins jockeyed past him into the lead. The two ships slalomed through the rings as if they were tethered together.

"I didn't think they'd give an old man like you a ship that fast, August," Samson said, trying to avoid the engine wake of Martins' V-shaped, blue and white racer.

"You don't know a lot of things," Martins said, and angled his exhaust fumes into Samson's path.

The other ships began to catch up with them as Martins continued jockeying Samson out of position, preventing him from accelerating through the hoops. They cleared the final corner inside the swirling rings of Saturn, and dove towards the horizon of the planet. Samson's ship snapped across the surface like a crack of pearly lightning, and Martins struggled to keep pace.

"You're too close to the planet, you'll burn out your GCU," Martins said on the com.

Samson ignored him and sunk into a tight turn that would take him across the top of Saturn's atmosphere. He switched off his Gravity Control Unit and felt the lurch of the planet's mass pulling him forward. He accelerated into it. Martins followed above, in a wider turn, a safer one. Samson opened up his throttle. His ship could take the turn tighter than Martins, he would have a shorter flight path and gain more boost from the planet's gravity. It would be impossible for Martins to catch up.

As his ship approached the apex of its turn, Samson gritted his teeth unconsciously. Saturn came closer and closer. The trajectory on his sensors predicted disaster, it would be close. It always was close, that was what made him a winner. High above, Martins' racer changed its course to intersect with Samson's path. Samson held steady and watched the edge of the planet. Saturn came closer. Martins angled down at him and activated the last charge in his thrust boosters. Saturn came closer. The blue and white racer plunged at Samson's ship like a diving falcon. He tried to slip out of its way. He was too close to the planet. Martins was on him. His ship shook with a tremendous crunch, and Samson raised his arms over his head instinctively against the impact.

Sandy darkness swirled around him. Saturn's clouds. He hit his brakes and looked at his sensors. Martins' ship expanded its turn and accelerated away. Bastard. Samson pulled up slowly, back into an orbital path around the planet. The wings framework of the ship seemed to be intact, he could feel it funneling the gaseous atmosphere and forcing it behind him. Two more ships sped past above and whipped expertly around the planet. Samson lit a booster and switched on his GCU. A few minutes later, as the booster began to fade, he craned his neck and made a visual survey of the damage. The wings framework, the honeycombed cylinder of tiny wings and rotors that surrounded the ship, was intact, but two of the bridging bolts had been torn off and it was out of alignment. He breathed a sigh of relief and spun the ship in a barrel roll as it continued to accelerate back up to speed. His heartbeat slid back into his chest.

Samson's ship was fast. He caught up and passed the two racers again. With the throttle open and engines shrieking in protest, he accelerated through the finish line at the space station where the race had begun. He came in second. Martins had finished at least two minutes in front of him.

That night, after the awards ceremony. After being held back from attacking August Martins. After being escorted out of the hangar, and after being told that the Racing Board would wire him his second place winnings the next day. And after being told that a fee would be deducted from his winnings by the Racing Board for causing a scene... A bellboy delivered a handwritten note to Samson's hotel room.

"Can't a robot do your job?" Samson asked the rose haired, green eyed, freckled boy.

One didn't see freckles very much. Freckles were rare.

"Can't a robot do yours, sir?"

"No."

"They don't use robot helpers in nice hotels, sir," the boy said, as if this should have been obvious. "It's low class."

"Did your parents give you those freckles?"

The boy touched his face.

"Are you mocking me sir? Just take the note please."

Samson took the note out of the boy's hands and apologized.

"It didn't work out the way they wanted. My parents–" the boy said uncomfortably. "Something went wrong."

"A lot of people have freckles where I come from," Samson said.

"That must be a shitty place, sir. I'll be going now, then."

"Oh, right."

The boy was holding out his hand and Samson grabbed some coins off the hotel nightstand and and gave them to him.

"Thank *you* sir," the boy said, and turned back into the hall.

"It's not so bad, you know," Samson called through the closing door. "Women like a man who is different!"

The door slammed shut and he walked over to the bed and slid onto it, with his back against the headboard. He folded open the note the boy had given him, which had 'Samson Ford' scrawled in pen on the outside.

Nice race today. Please meet me for a drink tonight in the hotel bar, I'll be there from 9PM-10PM. A friend of mine wants to meet you. I hope you are not still moping about losing the race, or afraid to come have a drink in public.

Samson stared at the signature on the paper, trying to make it out. He crushed the note in his hand and threw it into a waste basket beside the bed. *Augustus Martins.*

C H A P T E R^2

THE HOTEL BAR WAS DIM and smoky, like a speakeasy in an ancient mobster film. Plush brown leather and oak, burgundy upholstery. It had a big, open, four sided bar. A worn out man in an ancient suit stared vacantly at spinning holographic projections against a wall near the door as his last credits trickled away. Samson stepped past him and saw Martins sitting at the bar. Beside Martins sat a young woman with a frozen yellow daiquiri. She looked up expectantly and made eye contact with Samson, then looked quickly back at her drink, poking at it with a cocktail umbrella.

Samson sat down on the other stool beside Martins, then his feelings got the best of him and he grabbed Martins violently by the collar.

"You tried to kill me, you son of a bitch."

The bartender turned around and watched. Martins didn't react, but slowly pulled Samson's hands away and straightened out his collar. His frizzy, African hair was already grey; for a racing pilot, he was old. His shirt was old fashioned, skin faintly silver, eyes green. Martins had never been a great racer, but had always been a good one. He was an old fox in the game, he knew all the tricks.

"That's just racing, don't take it so personal," he said, with the faintest hint of a smile. "I want to introduce you to my friend, Lisa. Lisa Maui."

Martins indicated the girl beside him, and she reached out tentatively to shake Samson's hand. He began to brush her away, but looked up and her face seemed innocent, ingenuous. Bright eyed, and apprehensive. She was blushing. He changed his mind.

"It's nice to meet you, Lisa," Samson said, shaking her hand. "I'm sorry, we had a collision during the race today. I hope I haven't bothered you."

"I saw your race," Lisa said. "It was good."

"Oh, thanks."

She looked at her drink again and pursed her lips.

"Where did you get your ship?" Martins asked. "I don't think I've seen another ship like that before."

"You never have?" Samson said, suddenly more interested than angry.

"No, it's an unusual ship. The framework is a different design, it reminds me of some of the prototype stuff they're coming out with on Earth. Hard angles, and vortices. I hope I didn't break it."

"No."

"Could I get you a drink?" the bartender asked, catching Samson's eye.

"Do you have a decent bottle of Chianti?"

"Tuscan wine?"

"Yes. Anything gallo nero would do."

"I'll check and see, sir."

"Thank you."

Lisa watched Samson curiously.

"What's gallo nero?"

"What is it?" he said.

"Yeah, what is it?"

"Tuscan wine."

"Oh," she said, and looked back down at her drink.

"So, where did you get the ship?" Martins asked insistently.

"You've really never seen a ship like her?"

"No, never. I mean, it's a cigarette racer, obviously, but not the same structure. The engine placements are different, pentagonal, and inverted. And the framework, of course. Plus — what's it made out of?"

"The frame is a curium alloy."

"Curium?"

"Yes."

"Where did you get it?"

"Believe it or not, it was a junker. I bought it for scrap and rebuilt it."

"It's really curium?"

"It's hard to work with, believe me."

Martins looked skeptical, and smoothed out the crease in his collar again. He finished the last of his drink.

"Well, it's a beautiful ship. I have to be leaving. See you in the races."

He walked away quickly, and Samson slid over to sit beside Lisa. She stirred her drink with the cocktail umbrella.

"Do you, uh, do you know Martins well?" Samson asked.

The bartender came back with a dusty bottle of wine in his hand. He held it out proudly.

"Gallo nero, 2310. What do you think?"

Samson eyed the bottle.

"A bottle that dusty might be more than I can afford."

"No. 100 credits. We just don't get many Chianti drinkers, it's not expensive. We have a little bit of everything downstairs just for special customers like you."

Samson smiled and assented.

"I have to buy a new booster for my ship, you see."

"Ah, you're one of those pilots. Look out for those pilots," the bartender said, winking at Lisa. "They're all rascals you know."

"Thanks," Samson said, sipping the wine. "Thanks, it's good."

"I don't know him well," Lisa said abruptly, "just from the races. I work for the Racing Board, I'm an intern. That's how I know you."

"Oh, and I thought I had my first fan."

Samson smiled at her. Lisa met his gaze half-way and swallowed.

"I'm a fan..."

"Martins almost killed me in that race today, did you really see it?"

"I know."

She stirred her drink with the umbrella again.

"But, like, that's racing isn't it?" she said. "I'm sure it wasn't personal."

Samson watched Lisa curiously, as if he were just now seeing her for the first time. She was a pretty girl, young. Perhaps twenty-two. She had an English style face, with an urchin nose. The faintest hint of freckles on her cheeks, but none that one could readily pick out. Her hair was a curly, reddish brown, grown long down her back. Her eyes were big, with enormous pupils. They shifted from green, to silver, to blue, like tiny haloes reflecting off the edges of a round, black shield. He looked at her body, it was lean and pert, athletic. Average height. Her hips were nice. She was wearing denim jeans that fit her figure flatteringly. The skin peeking out above her jeans was shiny and smooth.

He looked up again quickly, back to Lisa's face, and her eyes were watching him. She was blushing again, and looked down. Samson reached out to take her hand, but she pulled it away.

"You're funny," he said.

"Why?" she asked, leaning away from him, not looking up.

"Well have you ever had someone almost kill you?"

"No."

"It wasn't an accident, you understand, he knew there was a good chance that I would die."

"Yeah."

"I take it personal."

"But August hasn't won a race in a long time," she said, still looking down. "You shouldn't be mad at him."

"I am mad."

"Let's change the subject, can we talk about something else?" she said, looking up at him again.

She drank a sip of her melty daiquiri. Samson finished his glass of wine slowly and poured another.

"I don't have that much time, what do you want to talk about?"

"Well, like, you got second place, that's something to be happy about, right? You made a lot of money."

"I need a lot of money."

"Oh, come on. It's the best finish you've had since you moved up to the Silver Circuit."

"That's true. How do you know that?"

"I love racing. Besides, I work for the Racing Board."

"Right," Samson took a heavy drink from his wine glass.

"Well, I have to go," Lisa said suddenly, standing up and walking half-way across the room. "Maybe I'll see you at another race sometime!"

She ran out the door before he had a chance to say anything in reply. Samson exhaled an exasperated whistle, wondering what she had been after, and looked down at the glass in his hand.

"Could you cork this bottle for me, please?" he said to the bartender. "I'm going to take it with me."

As he stood up to leave, Samson noticed Lisa's melted daiquiri. She had hardly drunk any of it. He lifted her drink and gulped it down, then smiled at himself, picked up his wine bottle, and walked towards the door.

"Nice race today, stranger," a woman called from across the room.

Samson tipped his hat to her, but didn't stop.

"If you do that again you'll probably die," she said quickly, before he could reach the door.

He turned and looked at the woman. She was sitting by herself in a dark alcove along the wall, he could barely make her out.

"What do you mean?"

"That inverted cartwheel with your thrusters open and vectoring down, you're lucky you didn't blow out your atmosphere."

He walked over to the alcove and stood with his hands on the little table, trying to see who the woman was. She was black haired, pale, white skinned.

"Well, you're right about that," he said, "but my ship has some adjustments to compensate for the blowback and protect the atmospheric systems from pressurizing."

"I hope you don't mean force panels," the woman said dismissively.

"What's wrong with force panels?"

She looked up and down at him like an appraiser, and smiled.

"Look, don't you want to sit down?"

He set down his Chianti and sat opposite her in the little booth, rubbing his hands on the leather bench.

"I don't know if I want to, but I will. How do you know so much about racing?"

"I know so much about a lot of things," she said, and winked at him.

"Y– You're the most brazen woman I've ever met!"

"Oh, surely not. Besides, only with my brain. Not with my body, I can assure you."

"Well, what's wrong with force panels?"

"90% of the manufacturers fudge on their ratings. And they don't protect against shearing forces. Also, they substantially destabilize in a gravity control field. You're lucky to be alive."

Samson looked at the woman curiously. He picked up a box of matches on the table and lit the old fashioned candle in the center of it. The woman watched him with magnificent confidence, as if he were putting on a show for her.

"Lean forward," Samson said, "I want to see your face in the light."

She leaned forward and turned her face at an angle to let him examine it. Her features were perfect, but subtle. Her skin tone was pale and natural. It had an exquisite, milky richness. Her face was unblemished, and her thick hair shimmered like cracked obsidian. Her eyes were impenetrable. Samson leaned back, and she leaned away again.

"Your eyes are very dark."

"Do you always talk about a woman's eyes?"

"They're unusual. Dark eyes aren't that popular."

"They're making a comeback."

"And your eyes are different, they have a quality I haven't seen before."

"Oh?"

"Anyway, I really don't know you, do I."

"But I know you," the woman said mischievously, "you're Samson Ford."

"Of course, you saw me race."

"Of course."

"Well what's your name, then?" Samson asked.

"Stephanie."

"Stephanie what?"

"Just Stephanie."

"You don't have a last name?"

"Do you want to have a drink? I could call the waiter to come uncork that bottle for you," she said, and sipped at the unmixed, amber liquor in her glass.

"I can–" Samson began to say and pulled out the cork with his hands, swigging it from the bottle. "I'll just drink it like this."

Stephanie laughed.

"I want to see your ship," she said.

"My ship?"

"Yes, I'm not in love with you. I want to see your ship."

"The cartwheel today was great, though, wasn't it?" he said, changing the subject.

"Oh, it was beautiful. I haven't seen a move like that in years. Mind you, Killian Gideon could do that any time if he wanted to."

"Killian Gideon. He could not."

"He's the best."

Samson hit his hand angrily against the table, and some of Stephanie's liquor sloshed out of her glass.

"He *was* the best," he said. "Now I'm the best."

Stephanie smiled at him.

"You've spilled my drink."

"I'm sorry," Samson said, mopping it up with a napkin.

She drank the rest of what was left in the glass.

"You are very good. You might be able to become the best. Eventually."

"Oh, thanks."

"Are you going to let me see your ship, or what?" she asked, leaning forward flirtatiously until Samson could see the long line of her neck sloping down into the top of her chest and the tops of the buttons in her shirt.

"I haven't decided yet."

"Your ship is very unusual," she said, leaning back again.

"Yes, I've already heard that once tonight."

"Where did you get it?"

"I'm not sure I trust you," he said, taking another swig from the bottle of wine.

"I don't trust you either," Stephanie said, rubbing an unusual green and metal ring on her right hand. "I just want to see your ship."

SAMSON DID FINALLY TAKE STEPHANIE to see his ship. After he had finished his Chianti and they had talked about ships and racing for another hour. He was surprised when she stood up – she was tall, as tall as he was. Her body was beautiful, perfect. Like an archetype of woman. Not overstated like the models and working girls, not too much. She moved with a kind of exceptional elegance, like a superior being. He had never seen anything like her. Or maybe he had just had too much to drink. He looked down at his feet skeptically as they walked to the hangar.

"Am I drunk?"

"I doubt it," Stephanie said, looking at him affectionately.

"I feel drunk," he said, putting his arm around her shoulder.

"You're not drunk," she shrugged his arm off. "You're just lonely," she elbowed him in the ribs, "or something like that."

Samson caught his breath.

"Maybe I'm in love."

"You're not in love," Stephanie said, and laughed.

They walked into the utility hangar and Samson pointed to Ben's Junket, which the racer had already been loaded onto.

"I've never met a beautiful woman before who knows so much about ships," he said, as if in explanation.

"You haven't met enough women."

"Oh, so you know a lot of women who are experts like yourself I guess?"

"I know me."

"What's your last name?"

"It's just Stephanie, you know, like the Brazilian racers. Just one name."

Samson caught Stephanie tightly by the arm and stared at her with a hard stare. Few men could meet his gaze when he leveled hard eyes at them.

"Listen, I'm liking you a lot so far, and that's why I'm being nice. Tell me who you are and what you want. This isn't a game. If you won't be up front with me then you should leave."

Stephanie tried to twist out of his grip, but could not. She stared into his eyes, angrily.

"My name is Stephanie. I don't have a last name, but I can give you my com code if you want it. I do freelance work as a mechanic because I like ships and racing. I don't have to do it, I do it for fun, usually for friends of mine," she stepped forward and pushed Samson back a step with her shoulder. "Some of the teams I've worked on are Star's Hawk in the Copper League, and Racing Centauri. You can look me up."

Samson let go of Stephanie's arm, and started to mumble an apology. She slapped him hard across the face. He couldn't believe how fast she was. His eyes stung from the blow, and she was crying.

"Hey, what's going on?" Ben called, jogging towards them across the slate paneled hangar floor.

"You're an asshole," Stephanie said and walked away with quick strides of her long legs.

"Hey. Hey, Stephanie I'm sorry," Samson ran after her. "I'm sorry. Please don't go. You can look at the ship. I'll show you anything you want. Please. I was really enjoying your company. I'm sorry. Forgive me."

She finally stopped and turned back around, sniffing, staring daggers at him, but relaxing.

"I'm sorry, Stephanie. Look, I do want to look you up. I've never met anyone like you before. Can I still get your com number? I want to keep in touch with you, anyway. Like, you don't understand, you're right I was an asshole, I didn't handle that well, but, like, racing is a dirty business. You must know that. We have some enemies. I'm just a bit paranoid. I'm sorry. Forgive me, ok? Come look at the racer, I want you to see it."

He held out his hand and Stephanie finally reached out and shook it. He caught her hand between both of his and squeezed affectionately before letting go. Ben watched curiously.

"Ok, Samson. Show me your racer. I want to see how the engines are set."

"Ok. Great. I'm sorry. Yeah, the engine placement is really unusual. You'll find this interesting."

Samson introduced Stephanie to Ben, who greeted her politely.

"Did you see someone over there?" Ben asked, staring at the hangar exit.

"Someone?" Stephanie said, looking back. "It's just us I think. I didn't see anyone else outside. It's pretty late, even if this place operates 24 hours, I think most people are in bed."

Samson led Stephanie inside the Junket and showed her the racer. The bridging bolts were still torn off, and it looked out of sorts from the damage of the race.

"You took quite a hit today," she said.

Ben was shocked to discover how much Stephanie knew about ships. He warmed to her immediately, and they were almost instantly like old friends. Stephanie examined the ship like an expert mechanic would, and Ben was excited to show her each and every detail of the construction and design. Samson, though he had done much of the rebuilding work himself, could barely keep up with the technicalities of their discussion.

At about 4 am, Stephanie finally bid goodbye to Samson and Ben, and walked out of the old space carrier. She was exhausted, but exhilarated. Samson's racer was in many ways unlike any she had seen before, and she had enjoyed the company of the two men immensely. They were like kindred spirits, she thought to herself. Just as she was leaving the hangar, she remembered an article she had recently been reading about booster coils, and wondered how the coils on Samson's racer were designed. She ran back to the Junket to take a quick look.

"Samson? Ben?" she called softly, as she opened the door.

Snoring echoed through the metal hull, and Stephanie hushed herself. She tiptoed back to the racer to have a quick look at the architecture of the coils.

Samson sat on the bridge of the Junket, staring out the window at the other ships on the hangar floor. Huge bulk transporters and passenger ferries, several that needed the full hangar doors to open for entrance and exit. He thought about Stephanie, and felt bad for grabbing her arm and upsetting her. She seemed to have forgiven him. He wished he could take it back. Outside, an open topped car filled with men in suits drove across the hangar floor. Samson wondered where a woman like her had come from. What environment had created her. She seemed almost superhuman.

The car was driving fast. Samson looked down at it again. The men were all carrying guns. It screeched to a halt right in front of the cockpit windows, and all five men raced for the Junket door.

"Oh shit," Samson said, spilling coffee on himself and lurching forward to the cockpit controls. He sealed the door and switched on the engines, warming them up. The Junket shuddered, and a low rumble shook the hangar floor.

"Open the door, you fuck!"

Gunfire outside proved the hostile intent of their visitors,

and Samson could hear bullets bouncing off or burying themselves in the door and hull.

"Open up, or we're gonna blow the door!"

Ben rushed into the cockpit.

"What the hell's going on?"

"Mob," Samson said.

"Mob?"

Samson hit the throttle and the Junket lurched into the air.
A gangster on one of the wing panels slid off and fell precariously to the ground. From below, one of the gangsters opened
fire with a shoulder cannon. Samson twisted the ship to one
side, throwing Ben against the wall, and continued to rise.

"Don't stand there, strap in and get online and get the
door open for us!"

The side entrance for smaller ships was unmanned and
automatic. Ben punched in the authorization code to open
it, and they escaped into open space.

As they cleared the hull of the space station, Stephanie ran
onto the ship's bridge.

"What the hell's going on? Put me down!"

CHAPTER 3

B EN AND SAMSON STARED AT Stephanie in disbelief, and she gasped as she looked out through the bridge window into space. She was clutching her arm, and had a lump on her head.

"Oh, shit, are you ok? Take over the wheel, Ben."

Samson leapt out of his seat and put his hands around Stephanie's shoulders protectively. She flinched away from him.

"We have company," Ben said, voice thick with adrenaline. "Get strapped in, and hurry."

A blast shot exploded under the ship's hull, and Ben canted them into an evasive split-S. Samson caught Stephanie and cushioned her as they were thrown against the wall of the ship.

"What are you doing? Take me back to the station!" she screamed hysterically.

Another cannon shot exploded near them and shook the Junket. Samson pushed Stephanie into the nearest seat.

"Hurry and strap in. What are you doing here, I thought you left? Are you ok?"

"You gotta get them off me, Samson," Ben said urgently.

"Are you ok, Stephanie? Strap in, damnit!"

"You have to put me down on the station! Are you guys crazy?" Stephanie screamed, but strapped in reluctantly as the Junket shook again.

Samson sprinted down the halls to his racer. He cursed at the torn bridging bolts, but climbed into the cockpit and warmed his engines while strapping himself in.

"You gotta get them off of me, Samson. They're going to sink us here," Ben said on the com.

"Roger that," Samson said, suddenly feeling alert and confident. He primed the racer's engines as the Junket's bay doors slid open, and blasted out into the vacuum of space.

A trail of short-range space fighters were right on the Junket's tail. They could have already sunk it if that was what they wanted to do. They must be trying to disable it. One of the fighters had a large cannon, but most of them were only equipped with small arms. Samson flew straight at them like an angry bolt of lightning, scattering the group as each ship swerved to avoid collision.

He swooped across the bow of the cannon ship, nudging it into an awkward spin that sent its engines into a cough. The smaller ships circled carefully, each lining up their sights to shoot Samson down without hitting their friend. Ben flew steadily away with the Junket at full throttle. Stephanie unstrapped and hurried to the windows, watching the scene now unfolding below.

Samson dove evasively before any of the fighters could line up a careful sight on him, and looped around them in a tight, infuriating corkscrew. The fighters lined up behind him, chasing, trying to lock onto his six, determined to shoot him down. The cannon ship still spun awkwardly, engines sputtering, unable to right itself without steady engine power.

He opened up his throttle in a long spiral dive across the inkiness of Saturn's back. Shots exploded behind and to the side of him, but the pilots could not lock onto his path. The big planet was lit up beautifully at its edges, and bits of sun reflected around on the backs of its rings.

"Go Samson!!!" Stephanie yelled anxiously on the deck of the Junket, as it cruised farther and farther away. "Oh my God. Damn, he's good. You guys are crazy, Ben. Will he be ok?"

"He's better than good," Ben said, looking back at Samson and the space fighters, darting through space in the distance like mosquitos. "He'll be ok. The only thing I'm worried about is that racer is still damaged, though."

She caught her breath.

"Are we going as fast as we can?"

Ben nodded.

"Samson will distract them until we can get completely out of their range, that's the plan, right?"

He nodded again.

Stephanie sat back in her chair and clenched her fists.

"Well, just make sure you're at full throttle. This is crazy."

Ben laughed.

"Hurry up, Samson," he said into the ship's com. "Your woman is worried about you."

"Oh shut up," Stephanie said.

Samson pulled up into a tight Immelmann turn, and cut like a scythe through the path of the space fighters. Four of them spun away, but the other was too slow, and Samson dodged neatly around him as their ships almost collided. Then he hit his boosters and coursed around the space station in a long, silver loop. He looked down at it as he passed, the huge chunk of rock and metal orbiting Saturn. Station 16 – Pegasus. It was one of the uglier stations. It didn't open up onto Saturn the way you would like. From up here it looked bubbly and lopsided, like black and silver spit floating through space. He raced back at full speed to catch up with the Junket, leaving the fighters far behind.

Stephanie waited anxiously for him to get back to the ship. She breathed a sigh of relief when Samson came onto the com and gave an all clear. But as soon as he was safely on board she was only angry and suspicious.

Samson stumbled back onto the bridge covered in sweat.

"Where the hell are you guys taking me?" Stephanie demanded, pointing her finger at him.

C H A P T E R⁴

THE OLD, RUSTY JUNKET SPUTTERED through blinding sunlight on its course towards Mars. It was a tubby, whale shaped ship. Outlined on the side, where paint had long ago peeled away, one could make out the name 'El Marja', but everyone called it 'the Junket', 'Ben's Junket', or, more critically, "Ben's junk." Ben started calling it Junket because the ship reminded him of an old Chinese sailing vessel he had seen in a museum. And he didn't want to call it 'junk'. He took a kind of pleasure in letting the outside of the ship rust away, but inside it was well maintained.

Stephanie sat with Ben and Samson in the ship's little dining room, sipping a mug of tea.

"Why the hell are you going to Mars?"

"We have to go somewhere," Samson said.

He tried to explain their predicament. It wasn't easy. The more he talked, the more ridiculous he felt.

"Look, basically, I got into a fight and beat up some gangsters. And now, they want to kill me."

"You already said that."

Stephanie slid back along the table bench until her back rested on the ship's hull.

Samson stared at her apologetically, wondering what else he should say.

THREE WEEKS BEFORE, SAMSON HAD been sitting in a little bar outside the race courses at Punaho Delta. It wasn't a big race, but he had won it, and was treating himself to a bottle of celebratory champagne. Everyone in the bar would have recognized Samson's ship, but only a few recognized him in person and lifted their drinks or applauded as he walked by. That suited him perfectly. He had never been anxious to be in the spotlight. He chatted with the bartender and downed a few glasses of bubbly, waiting for Ben to get back from depositing the money. These little race tracks liked to use cash, it was shady. He would feel much better once it was converted and safely on their cards. Ben took 30%. That was their agreement from the beginning. Samson would have given him more if he had wanted it, he didn't care. They always spent most of the money upgrading and repairing the ships, anyway.

Samson watched himself in the mirror behind the bar and smiled. He toasted himself.

"Don't go getting vain on me," the bartender said.

"Here," Samson said to the man, reaching forward to grab another clean glass from behind the bar and filling it with champagne, "have a drink with me."

The bartender coughed and took a step back. Two men were standing behind Samson, and he smiled at them in the mirror, but they weren't smiling. One of the men was smaller than him, and the other was larger.

"You cheated, you son of a bitch," the smaller man said, and Samson turned his stool around to face them.

"Oh get out of here, what are you talking about," he said lightly, holding out the bottle of champagne. "Have a drink."

The larger man ripped the champagne bottle out of his hands and smashed it on the floor. Everyone in the bar stopped.

"You cheated," the smaller man said again. He had copper skin and sported a thick moustache. "You cost me a lot of money today, do you know that?"

Samson stopped being friendly and stood up. The goon pushed him back into the stool. Samson's eyes flashed darkly, and he slowly turned his head to look at the smaller man, who had started smiling. Without warning, Samson slammed his hand up into the big man's face, burying his first two fingers completely in the man's nostrils. He squeezed and wrenched at the goon's nasal passages, as the man bent his head back to try to relieve the pressure. The smaller man stood frozen, startled, while the goon started coughing up blood and vomiting, suffocating and panicking. He wrenched his face away and fell backwards across the floor.

The smaller man drew a gun, and Samson spun to the side as he fired. The bullet hit the wall and the bar went mad. People dove under furniture or sprinted for the exits. Samson was in a frenzy and caught the man's gun in both hands, crushing it with his grip to stop the action and pushing it up towards the ceiling. Bang. Blood dripped from Samson's hands, but the action had stopped and the gun was jammed. The big man stood up off the floor, coughing red and holding his face. Samson kicked him in the temple as hard as he could, and the man fell back to the ground. He reached for Samson's ankle and Samson stomped into his temple, still wrestling for the gun with the smaller man. The goon collapsed with his tongue hanging out, blood puddling around his mouth. Samson wrenched the gun out of the smaller man's hands and kicked him in the testicles The man doubled over, but came back up with a knife.

"Who do you think you're fucking with?" Samson screamed ominously, in a kind of animal hysteria.

He grabbed a bottle off of the bar and started beating the man with it, easily avoiding the knife thrusts, laughing humorlessly. He smashed the man's knife hand hard with the bottle, and the blade went skittering across the floor. The little, moustachioed man suddenly looked afraid. Samson kicked his legs out from under him and sunk his toe into the man's head. He was breathing heavily, exhaling spit. His heart felt larger than his chest. He kicked the two men on the ground, over and over again, in the ribs and hips, in the knees.

"How dare you fuck with me?" he screamed incredulously,

eyes going crazy. "You fucking idiots. I'm the right hand of the devil! You got that?" He kicked the men again and again. "The right hand of the mother fucking devil, you fucks!!!!!"

"What's happening here?" Ben shouted, wading through overturned furniture at the bar's entrance.

The bartender's eyes were huge, and shifted back and forth. Ben caught Samson in a bear hug and dragged him away.

"So, I don't know," Samson said sheepishly. "They attacked me, and I think I hurt them pretty bad. We hoped they would just blow it off, but one of the guys was a mob boss or something, and they're trying to kill me."

Stephanie tilted the last drops of tea into her mouth and set her mug down. She leaned her head back against the ship and closed her eyes.

"Let's talk about something else," she said.

"I'm actually, I'm gonna go to bed," Ben said, yawning extravagantly. "It's been too long of a day for me. I'll see you guys tomorrow, err, in about eight hours or, anyway. Good night."

"Ok, Ben, good night," Stephanie said, and looked at Samson.

He slid back along the bench opposite her, until his back was resting against the hull, too. Stephanie closed her eyes again.

"Aren't you tired?" he asked. "Just let me know and I'll show you to your cabin and get you situated with everything. We have some new mechanic's jumpsuits if you want to wear one of those and wash your clothes or something. That's– I mean, you're welcome to wear some of my clothes, or anything. Just let me know what you want and I'll see what we can do. I feel really bad about you being stuck here with us, I want to make you as comfortable as possible, that's all. So, you're the guest here, so make yourself at home and everything."

She opened her eyes again and looked at him, completely awake.

"It's going to be a problem for your racing career if you have gangsters following you around trying to kill you," she said.

"Yeah..."

"It's not like they have to search hard to find out where you're going to be."

"Yeah, I know. It's. Like, that happened three weeks ago, we were hoping they would– I don't know what we're going to do."

"Sorry," Stephanie said. "Ok, different subject. Where did you learn to race?"

"That's... a long story."

"We have time," she said. "Or do you need to get some sleep, too? You're probably exhausted."

"No, no. Well, let me ask you a question first then, where did you learn how to work on ships?"

"Oh," Stephanie said, "well I don't want to tell you, it's like asking the story of my life."

"Same."

She laughed. Samson turned facing her and stretched his feet out until they were resting on the opposite bench, just touching her leg. Stephanie smiled and squeezed his foot affectionately.

"Well what is your goal in racing?"

"What is your goal as a mechanic?"

"I asked you first," she said quickly.

"I asked you most recently."

Stephanie pushed his feet off the bench, but didn't stop smiling.

"I don't have a goal," she said, "I just love ships and do it for fun. It's more of a hobby than a job. There isn't any outcome I'm trying to reach. I'm a good mechanic and I make a bit of money that way working for friends when they need an extra hand. It's good enough."

Samson couldn't help feeling that she was holding a lot back.

"So, what is it that you want out of racing, what are you trying to accomplish?" she said.

He slid down the bench until he was lying on his back with his legs hanging off the end. Until Stephanie couldn't see his face, and he was just looking up at the ship's ceiling.

"It's not so much that I have a goal. I love flying, racing. I'm damn good at it. My reflexes are better than other people, it's like, I have an instinct about the movement of the race that other people don't have. A situational awareness. I just want to see how far I can get, how good I really am, you know?

"It's not so much a goal, but more like a dream. I want to race in the Solar Regatta. That would be the greatest. Just to have done it, pushing that envelope against the sun, what do you think?"

"Oh, it's the most amazing race, unquestionably. I worked the hangar on the crew of a Solar Regatta ship once."

"At the Solarium?" Samson asked, a hint of awe in his voice.

"Yes, at the Solarium, of course."

"Was it as beautiful as they say? Right in front of the sun, practically touching it. I've never gotten to go there, it always looks so magical when you see it. On tv or whatever."

"Oh it's, the sun is amazing, and there are some incredible viewing galleries, and architecture and stuff. But, it's just a big casino, Samson. It's not that different from the satellite on Saturn, really, just more expensive. The people there are all super-built. Really artificial. It's something to see once, but the race is the main thing."

"How did your team do?"

"Oh, he finished. We were all really happy. We didn't have a ship that was competing for any honors, just to finish the race. That was eight years ago now, I was just young still. Twenty-one, I guess. Well that's the problem, only 50% of the racers survive. It's so dangerous. You shouldn't dream of a race like that!"

Samson laughed.

They talked for hours, until neither one could finish a sentence. About the Solar Regatta, the Solarium, racing, about life. Each trying to pry too much into the other's past, each trying not to reveal too much of it. Finally, Stephanie stumbled into her cabin bunk, locking the door behind her, and Samson wandered off to bed.

Ben sat on the bridge the next morning and watched Mars come slowly into view. He sent out a signal requesting space clearance, and waited for the all clear. It was just a formality. He had been born on the red planet, and it always felt like coming home.

A signal from the security station came through on the com.

"Number 293-HC-5721 you are not cleared for this airspace, copy."

"What?"

"Number 293-HC-5721 you are not cleared to enter Martian airspace, please reverse course immediately. Copy."

CHAPTER 5

"WHAT DO YOU MEAN I'M not cleared for this airspace?"

Ben brought the Martian officer up on his holo-screen. The officer looked annoyed.

"Your ship is on our ban list, sir, please turn around and go back wherever you came from."

Ben slowed the Junket to a halt.

"There must be a mistake," he said mildly, "are you sure it is this ship?"

"Two, nine, three, dash, capital H, capital C, dash, five, seven, two, one."

"Well what are we supposed to have been banned for?"

The young man frowned and a supervising officer walked over and stood behind him, watching the screen.

"I don't know, sir. You'll have to get in touch with the Flight and Security Administration, but right now you have to leave."

"Let me talk to your supervisor," Ben said, pulling at the ends of his beard.

The senior officer bent down and peered through the holo-screen.

"I'm right here. Your ship is on the ban list, you must leave Martian airspace at once."

"That doesn't make any sense," Ben said. "We're *from* Mars. This ship is based *in Mars*. We haven't done anything that could possibly get us banned from Martian airspace. We've just been to Saturn on a race and are returning back to our home port!"

Samson stumbled onto the bridge, with Stephanie not far behind him.

"What's all the shouting about?"

"It's just a misunderstanding," Ben said quietly.

"Excuse me, ensign Halil," the supervising officer said, motioning the younger man out of his chair. He peered into the holo-screen at Ben. "Repeat your ship number for me please, sir."

"293-HC-5721," Ben said.

"293-HC-5721, small space freighter. Crew capacity four to six, 19 tons cargo capacity for EEM liftoff, 32,000 cubic meters standard volume. Formerly titled 'El Marja'. Universal Space Registry renewed August 12, 2315."

"That's right," Ben said.

"Yes sir, your ship has been banned from Martian space. Please leave our planet's vicinity immediately."

"WHAT??"

Ben punched the key panel in front of him.

While Ben and Samson argued with the Martian space officers, Stephanie stood up and quietly exited the bridge. She tiptoed down the metal corridor to her cabin, ducked through the pressed steel door, and locked it behind her. She could still hear them shouting angrily in the background.

She sat down on the bunk and opened up her purse, withdrawing from it a small grey card. The card was the size of a standard computing card, but was slate grey and featureless. It even had the texture of slate. She ran her finger along its edge and the card lit up. After a moment, a man appeared on the face of the card, as if it were a video screen.

"Madame," he said graciously.

The man was dressed formally in an expensive business suit. He had walnut skin and africanesque features. His eyes were amber-grey. He was sitting in an immaculate office, with massive windows behind him that looked out onto the bright lights of a huge metropolis. It could have been Hong Kong or

Chicago. It could have been Pum Daarit on Mars. He smiled at Stephanie through the screen with a hint of concern on his face.

"Hello," she said quickly. "I'm on board a ship outside Mars, designated 293-HC-5721, and they are denying us entry."

"I'll straighten it out right away. I trust your health is well?"

"Of course I'm fine. Handle this immediately, please."

"Of course, Mistress."

"Sorry to be short. Send me a note telling how everyone is doing. Thank you."

Stephanie ran her finger along the card again, switching it off. She slid it back into her purse and zipped the purse shut.

On the bridge, the situation was deteriorating.

"We have a code 3 in sector C17, please respond immediately," the officer said into a handheld com.

"No you don't have a code 3," Samson shouted, "you fucking idiot. I want to speak to the FSA administrator on duty!"

"Leave now or your ship will be seized," the Martian officer said icily, reaching forward to switch off the com link.

"We don't have fuel!" Ben said quickly.

"That's not my problem, sir," the officer said, and the screen went black.

Samson turned around and saw Stephanie walking back onto the bridge, smiling. She caught his eyes and her expression shifted to a frown.

"Have you been watching this?" he asked.

"No, what's happening?"

"They won't let us into Martian airspace."

Stephanie peered out through the bridge windows blankly. The red planet looked like a giant glass bowl from this perspective, lit up and glowing from the inside. She breathed a sigh and sat down in her chair.

"I really need to get back to that space station, Samson. This is becoming like a kidnapping."

Samson's eyes bulged.

"It's not kidnapping!"

Stephanie laughed. Ben tapped the com button again and again, trying to re-establish a link with the Martian security. In the distance in front of them, silhouetted against the backdrop of the planet's daytime surface, a dark speck slowly grew.

"We've got company," Ben said suddenly, and pulled back on the ship's throttle, reversing course. "Warship, S-class. Can you believe that? That termite sent an S-class warship after us."

"Get us out of here," Samson said nervously.

"They probably know you have a kidnapped girl on board," Stephanie said. "They're probably on a rescue mission to save me."

Samson twisted back to glare at her while Ben turned the Junket completely and opened up its throttle, accelerating away from Mars.

"This isn't funny, Stephanie," Samson said, "we don't have enough fuel to make it to any other planet. We're going to end up adrift."

"Oh, I think it's funny," Stephanie said lightly, in a conciliatory tone. She stood up and stepped behind Samson's chair and squeezed his shoulders with both hands. "I'm sure it will be ok. You two seem to have a knack for landing on your feet."

Samson touched her hand and held his breath. Stephanie kissed him on the top of the head and retreated back to her seat. She stared at him, looked down demurely to avoid eye contact, and stared again whenever he looked away. The warship was fading behind them, it had been content to ward them off. Ben piloted out towards the deeper space of the Solar System, wondering where to go.

Suddenly they received a faint signal from Mars. Ben

brought it up on the screen and the same Martian space officer appeared before them, grainy in the distorted hologram. The officer's face had turned white.

"I'm sorry, sir," he said quickly, before the link grew too faint, "your ship has been cleared to enter Martian space. There has been a terrible mistake, please forgive me."

Ben slowed the ship to a halt.

"What?"

"I'm sorry, sir! Please return. Your ship has been cleared to enter Martian space. It was a terrible misunderstanding, I promise you it won't happen again. I hope you won't take it personally, we're just trying to do our jobs here, we're only human after all, sir. It won't happen again!"

"We don't want any trouble," Ben said. "We weren't trying to cause any trouble, we only thought there was a misunderstanding and we don't honestly have enough fuel to get to another planet right now."

"Oh now, sir," the officer said again, and his hands were trembling, "there won't be any trouble I assure you. You are cleared for Martian airspace 100%. Please return and feel free to land or orbit at your leisure."

"Oh... Ok. We'll just come back to Mars then. Uh, I guess that's all, then?"

"Of course, sir. I'll leave you to your business. I'm sorry again, and please just let us know if we can be of any assistance to you."

"That's all right. Thank you very much."

Ben cut off the com.

"What the hell was that?" he said, looking at Samson.

Samson stared at the blank com screen, completely mystified.

SAMSON AND STEPHANIE STOOD AT the counter of an interplanetary terminal on Pum Daarit. The man behind the counter was short and pudgy. His skin was mottled tan and he had acne on his face. Stephanie smiled at him politely, and he seemed uncomfortable.

"50,000 credits for the express, sir," the ticket agent said, avoiding eye contact.

Samson blinked a few times.

"You said 50,000 right?"

"50,000 for the express, sir. It leaves at 2:30U and reaches Sat-16 in twenty hours."

"Ok," Samson said, frowning.

"Or you could take the ferry this weekend, sir. It does take a week, but it's not a bad trip."

"No," Samson said slowly. "No, we need the express. We'll do that. One adult passenger, please."

He slid his card through the scanner and put it back into his pocket. Stephanie touched his arm lightly.

"Are you sure you can afford it?"

"It's not a problem," he said, wrapping a hand around Stephanie's waist and pulling her against him. "I know you're anxious to get away from me."

"Thank you, sir. Your receipt is on your card," the ticket agent said. "I hope you will have a nice trip, Ma'am. It's right around the corner, the shuttle will board in just a few hours."

"Thank you," Stephanie said, "I'm sure I will."

"It's not that, Samson," she continued, as they walked away, "I just really need to get back as quickly as possible. All my things are there, hopefully, still in my hotel room. My friends were worried to death, but they should have gotten the message I sent by now. I have a lot of business to take care of, you know. I wasn't planning to fly to Mars this week."

"I'm sorry," Samson said, and kissed her on the cheek.

She pulled away from him, but smiled. They walked around the terminals and trading stations, watching the ships and crowds of people. Stephanie took the opportunity to buy a change of clothes at a little boutique. Red shorts and a ribbed silk, short sleeved blouse. She modeled them for Samson outside the dressing room.

"What do you think?"

"You look beautiful. Very stylish."

"Oh, stop lying. They're terrible."

"They aren't."

"Well, they're just in case. If the shuttle gets delayed or has to stop somewhere or something like that. I can fit them in my purse."

"At least you're traveling light."

"Oh, yes, thank you very much for making that possible."

"I'm so glad we've had the chance to spend this time together," he said dryly, and Stephanie laughed.

At the terminal, before she left, she hugged him and promised to keep in touch.

Samson threw his card onto the hotel night stand. He didn't want to think about how many credits he had left. He picked the card up again and started to plug it into the room's terminal, but changed his mind and dropped the card back down onto the table. He pulled off his shirt and pants and dropped onto the bed in a heap, falling asleep immediately.

He was flying in the Solar Regatta. He was piloting a little, cloud shaped ship. Stephanie sat behind him, in the navigator's seat. It seemed like the sun was all around them and would make their ship evaporate at any moment. Samson was blinded by it. He wondered where the other racers were.

"I can't see. Where are we?"

"Just keep your eyes open," Stephanie said.

"Are there any other ships? I can't see!"

His ship cruised forward, neither slow nor fast, drifting away from the other racers. Ben was behind them in the Junket.

"Why are you flying so slow?" Ben's voice came through on their com. "I have to pass you, Samson, or I'm going to get caught on the slingshot."

Samson punched at the com, but none of the buttons were familiar, he reached for the ship's control wands, but couldn't find any.

"This isn't a racer," Stephanie said coldly, "you have to actually fly it."

"What's wrong with our sunscreens? I can't see," Samson said tensely.

"There's nothing wrong with the sunscreens. Open your eyes."

He opened his eyes as widely as he could, and the blinding white heat burned into his retinas until he screamed. He closed his eyes again and continued to see white, as if the raw, unfiltered sun were permanently imprinted on his brain.

"It's no good, you'll have to fly," Samson said desperately.

"I can't fly, Samson, I don't know how."

He turned around to look at Stephanie. He turned his face to where he thought she would be. As if he could make eye contact without seeing her.

"Take your goggles off," Stephanie said. "That's why you can't see."

Their cloud was evaporating. Stephanie smiled at Samson as if she were in love with him. He didn't know how he could see her smiling when he couldn't see. He felt along his face and there were goggles there, so he pulled them off. They sunk down through the blue ocean. Stephanie was gone. Samson looked around him, marveling at how the cloud could exist within the water. He wasn't wet. A ship flew past above him with a hook on it that almost tore his own hull open. Samson grabbed his control wands and opened up the throttle.

He punched up the com and tried the public channel.

"Stephanie? Stephanie? Are you there?"

"Aaahh! Samson!" Stephanie's voice wailed grainily through the com. "The sun's too bright. I'm burning up! The ship's melting. Get us out of here. Get us out of here! Noooooooo!"

Her voice rose into an animal scream and disappeared.

Samson plunged his ship straight down through the water, deeper and deeper. The other racers laughed at him. Everything was black around him. He was accelerating. Why was this ship going so slow, it must not even reach 10,000 km/hr. He hit every button that he could think of that might be the boosters. He dove deeper, holding his breath, choking on the water, it ran into his nose. He held his breath desperately, trying not to drown.

A GROTESQUE SOUND OF TEARING hinges bruised the air. The hotel door twisted awkwardly on its bolts and crashed to the floor. Samson leapt out of bed, pale and sweating, and staggered back against the wall with his arms up in front of him. An enormous man was standing on top of the broken door. He was more than a foot taller than Samson and more than twice as broad, as if an unusually short and muscular man had been precisely enlarged. He had red eyes, short, scrubby blonde hair, and was wearing athletic clothes. There was something strangely unnatural about him, even aside from his size. His features looked designer, but were mixed up and uneven. He had acne, and was extremely hirsute.

"Put on your clothes and come with me," the man said in a deep, grinding voice.

Samson, now fully awake, sat back down in his bed and pulled his pants on slowly. He looked up at the big man again, as if to confirm that he was really there.

"It's very rude to barge into another man's motel room like this," he said, sliding his card into his pants pocket.

"Hurry up."

"If someone needs to talk to me, there are more polite ways to arrange a meeting."

The large man took two steps into the room, until he was one enormous arm's reach away from Samson who was still sitting on the bed.

"I'm only going to tell you one time to leave," Samson said menacingly. "Leave now. If you want to talk to me you can call on the hotel phone."

"Shut up and put your shirt on!"

Samson sprung forward across the tile floor, feinting with his hands and aiming a kick at the big man's testicles The man stepped backwards and caught Samson's wrist easily with a crushing grip that was nearly strong enough to break the bones. Samson leapt into the air to encircle the big man's arm with his legs, but the man allowed him to execute this lock and held Samson's entire body up with just the locked arm. He spun and threw Samson heavily against the wall, then caught his wrist again and dragged him out of the room.

"Fuck you!" Samson screamed.

In the hall, two men with suits were waiting. One put a gun in Samson's ribs.

"Please cooperate, Mr. Ford. Our orders are to kill you if necessary."

The big man led the way in front of them, and they marched Samson quickly down the hall and through the cramped little lobby of the hotel.

BEN WALKED ALONG THE SIDEWALK a block away from Samson's hotel. He was carrying a double scooped ice cream cone, and enjoying it thoroughly. He smiled at the strangers on the sidewalk. He wondered how Stephanie's send-off had gone, and wished her good luck. He inhaled the warm, dusty air of the Martian summer so that it mingled with the flavors of the ice cream and brought back memories of his childhood. He always enjoyed coming back to Mars.

A commotion at the entrance of the hotel distracted him, and he stopped and stood on his tiptoes to see what was happening. A huge man pushed people on the sidewalk out of the way and opened the door to a long, black sedan. It looked like a government car, there were no markings on it. Two other men shoved Samson into the back of the car.

"Hey!" Ben shouted, spilling his ice cream scoops as the men jumped into the car and it sped away.

Lucho Gonzalez' casino circled the planet of Mars in a perfect, low, geostationary orbit. Its enormous glass dome faced the planet's surface, creating the effect that the surface of Mars was the casino's sky. Iron, dusty red, snaked with blue, and a lush green that spread out along the edges of the blue. It was a beautiful effect, ever changing with the Martian weather. Ships streamed into and out of the casino's hangar doors. Business was good.

The casino was famous for a track of sand and gravel that encircled its perimeter. The synthcat track. Gamblers came from every corner of the Solar System to bet on the races, tourists came just to see the cats. Synthcats were a genetic hybrid of the ancient cheetahs, horses, fish, and greyhound dogs. They were leggy, whip-like creatures, with shimmering, mottled fur. They raced with a special intensity, on instinct alone. They didn't need anything to chase. As soon as one started forward, the others would try to beat it. Even when they were cubs. Once led onto a track, they quickly learned the start signal and the finish. A synthcat would continue to scramble furiously for the finish even if its knee had buckled and leg collapsed in half. They could be vicious, too. They might attack a dominant cat during the race just to stop it from winning again, out of animal spite. Unpredictable. The gamblers loved them. Betting rackets on every planet were anxious to get in on the action, to broadcast the races, but Lucho Gonzalez refused to allow it. He had a monopoly, and was afraid of losing control. The exclusivity kept people streaming in. Besides, the casino was a nice place to gamble. It had all the usual fare, the roulette, the craps, the holographic slot machines – even blackjack and poker. It had real dealers, good looking dealers, ones with some synthetics in their DNA. It had over-plush hotel rooms where a gambler could sleep for a song. Working girls and boys. It had everything.

Ben stepped onto the casino floor and scanned it, trying to look inconspicuous. His beard was trimmed and he was wearing a suit and tie. He guarded a small stack of chips in front of him with his free hand, trying to act out the part of a tourist. He was already nervous, so it was easy. He walked over to a roulette wheel where the croupier was barking out numbers and drawing a crowd. It was an old fashioned roulette wheel, a real wooden job. Maybe even hand made. The croupier seemed to take childish satisfaction from spinning it, as if it were his favorite thing to do. He spun it hard and the wheel whirred mechanically in a blur, then slowed down and the ball finally bounced across it and chose a number.

"32, red!"

Ben took half his stack of chips and set them on the table. A long bet. A real tourist's bet, he thought to himself.

The wheel spun again, furiously, and Ben looked up at the stairways and balconies that fronted onto the main floor. He tried to make note of the security, the goons and the cameras. He tried to distinguish between the public and private areas of the casino. The people around him were shouting and clapping, and he wished that none of them had won.

"Your winnings sir," the croupier said, pushing a large pile of chips in front of him.

"What? What's this??" Ben asked, startled and suspicious.

"Your winnings, sir," the croupier said again with a smile, as if he had seen it all before. "11, black."

The people around Ben quieted and smiled curiously.

"Go on, don't act so surprised!" a man said loudly, and slapped him on the back.

"Oh. Oh, yes, of course. Excellent! Thank you very much."

Ben scooped the chips into his arms and walked away from

the table quickly, like a bandit. Everyone laughed.

He dropped the chips onto a tall cafe table, sat down on a stool, and began stacking them. A pretty, dissolute looking girl walked over and sat down at the table beside him. He glanced up and pulled his pile of chips closer, then relaxed when he got a good look at her. She couldn't have been more than eighteen years old. A child. She smiled at him nervously, and he groaned inside.

"That's a lot of money you won, mister," the girl said blankly.

"Yes, it is," Ben said, stacking faster.

"You made a great bet."

"It's only luck," he said dismissively.

"I wish I knew more people who made good bets. More people who really knew what they were doing in life, you know?"

"Not really, no," he said.

"I mean," the girl continued, sucking in her breath, "what are you going to do tonight? Are you going to party or something? You seem interesting. Maybe I can party with you or something."

Ben looked up at her again. Heavy eye make-up. Why did the sorry ones always wear heavy eye make-up? He would have bet that her eyes were pretty underneath it. They probably had dark lines under them. She was a pretty girl, with rosy, copper skin and straight, white hair. He was tempted for a moment, and disgusted with himself.

"Don't you think I'm a little bit old for you to be partying with?" he said, and stood up holding the large tray now full of neatly stacked chips.

The girl stood up too.

"I'm not hung up about age," she said, and held out her hand. "My name is Melanie."

"You should be," Ben said, in what he hoped was a gentle tone, and turned and walked away.

"Hey, where are you going?"

He stopped and turned his face half-way towards her. There was an enormous looking goon in the corner opposite them, standing guard outside a column with an elevator shaft in it. The elevator opened up and the casino floor manager walked out. He wore a shiny, black tuxedo with pale, blue highlights, pearly buttons, and a blood red scarf. A real character, a legend – sort of an attraction unto himself. Apparently. Ben had seen pictures of him in the casino brochures.

"To watch the synthcat races," he said, turning his body back, half-way around, out of politeness.

"Oooh," Melanie said, running to catch up with him, "can I come? I love to watch the cats."

"You can go where you want, I think," Ben said without stopping, angling toward the large viewing gallery at the track's starting gate, where most of the betting took place.

"You're terrible," Melanie said, taking his arm, "don't you like me at all?"

"You're not a working girl are you?" he said, "Because if you are then you're wasting your time."

"Of course not!"

Melanie seemed a little bit hurt by this, but didn't relinquish Ben's arm. They walked up the stairs and sat down at one of the tables looking over the track. The cats milled about below, waiting to go into the blocks for the race to begin. They were beautiful, and alien. Ben had never seen them in person before, and was surprised by the appearance of a brown and violet cat with stringy fur, that the other cats seemed to be wary of. He felt the impulse to place another large bet, and made a snap decision not to bet any more at this casino.

"Aren't you going to place a bet?" Melanie asked.

"No."

She finally let go of his arm and slid back into her chair, away from him.

"Well, you're not far away from a working girl are you," Ben said, not looking at her, "living this kind of life."

"What kind of life? You don't know me."

"A casino groupie kind of life, or whatever you want to call it. That's not far off is it?"

"So?"

Ben looked at her carefully, and thought he saw something in her eyes. Something deep down, a kindness. She reminded him of Samson. Not a lot. Just in a faint, shadowy kind of way. Somehow like Samson, when he was young and lost. Ben's stomach turned over.

"I just think you could do better with your life, that's all," he said seriously. "How old are you, 17? You look fucking worn out already. You're living no kind of life."

"I'm 18," Melanie said quietly. "What's your name?"

"Ben, sorry. It's Ben. Look, I'm not trying to insult you. You remind me of a good friend of mine. A guy that I helped to get out of a hard place when he was young. I don't think I can help you, but you can help yourself."

"Yeah," Melanie said distantly.

"You could start by hitting on men your own age!" Ben said loudly, and people close by turned to look at them.

"Oh, they're so boring," Melanie said, smiling again, and blinking at him flirtatiously.

"Just stop it," he said, chuckling. "You're terrible."

The synthcats were lined up in their boxes and the race began with the striking of an enormous metal gong. Gamblers and spectators all around them shouted excitedly and cheered on their favorites. Ben and Melanie watched the cats begin and then lost interest.

"Why don't you get off this casino?" he said. "How long have you been here?"

"I don't know, a few weeks I think," Melanie said dismissively. "It's all a blur."

"Well, it shouldn't be a blur. Why don't you let me buy you a ticket back to Mars."

"Mars? Ugh," she said, sticking out her tongue.

"Well, where then? Earth? Do you have somewhere to go on Earth? Somewhere a bit more wholesome than a gangster's casino, maybe?"

Melanie laughed, she slid forward in her chair again and hugged Ben's arm, resting her head on his shoulder.

"Oh, you just want to get rid of me, lover."

He sighed, and maintained his posture stiffly.

Only a few hundred meters away, but deep within the private offices of the casino, two hard-men dragged Samson forward and threw him down onto a black ceramic floor. His hands were handcuffed behind him and Samson twisted heavily onto his shoulder with a thud, barely protecting his head from the impact. One of his eyes was black and swollen shut. He looked up at an enormous desk at the end of the room in front of him. The room was big, and lined with couches. Behind the desk was a glass window that looked out into the stars. Sitting in the desk was Lucho Gonzalez, the owner of the casino. A gangster who was short and had a moustache, who Samson had seen once before.

He stood up from his desk and walked forward.

"No, no. Take his cuffs off, it's ok."

Samson stared up at Lucho through his one eye while the goons unlocked his cuffs and lifted him to his feet. Lucho looked the same as he had then. Except he had two shiny metal butterfly bandages on his face. Samson thought he might have hit Lucho there with a boot. He couldn't remember for sure. The big goon was nowhere to be seen.

He rubbed his wrists and stepped forward into the middle of the room. Lucho leaned back casually against the front of his desk.

"So, this is the great Samson Ford, the big racing pilot. Well, not big, but people say you're real talented. Big tough guy, a real character. I always wanted to meet you, you know. Oh, wait – we've met before."

"What do you want me to say?" Samson said evenly, although his lip was badly split.

"Oh, there's nothing you can say, Samson Ford," Lucho said, with a faint smile on his face. "You've already said what you had to say. You've already had your chance to say. You've already said."

Samson turned around and left Lucho to look at his back. He watched the two goons behind him. They stood in front of a big, ebony, double door, looking on grimly.

"I'm not mad at you, Samson Ford," Lucho continued. "You're a big, tough guy – why, you're the right hand of the devil himself. You can't help the way you are. I'm not mad at you at all."

He laughed. Samson turned back around.

"Can I sit down on one of these couches?" he asked. "I'm tired."

"Oh sure, sure. Sit down. Make yourself at home," Lucho said, chuckling. "No, I'm not mad at you, Samson Ford. Not mad at all. It's just, the way I see it, you owe me now. You almost killed me, after all. You owe me a lot. So that's why I brought you up here, so I could tell you what you owe me and what you are going to do for me."

Samson sat down on one of the couches. Lucho walked forward until he was closer, but not close enough for Samson to lunge at him.

"I don't take revenge, Samson Ford," he said, placing careful emphasis on every word. "I don't take things personal. I only take payment due. That's why I've been successful in life. That's why I'm the best."

Samson watched him warily.

"So, this is the plan," Lucho continued. "You're going to work as my slave for the foreseeable future, as one of my racing jockeys. You'll be fitted with a device which will prevent you from ever leaving. But don't worry, if you win enough races, I might choose to let you leave in as little as five or ten years. I probably won't, but I might. And if you don't win races, well, I'm sure we'll be able to find some kind of use for you."

He walked back behind his desk and sat down, shuffling papers in front of him. The two thugs moved forward slowly, and Samson stood up and faced Lucho, letting them take him by the arms.

"If that's the plan then you're a fairer man than I thought, Lucho," he said evenly, turning to be led away.

"Oh no, that's not all," Lucho said, standing up again. "That's just the long term plan. Put the cuffs on him."

Samson pulled angrily against the gangsters' arms, but they were both very strong. They forced his wrists behind his back into the cuffs. Then each one rested a heavy leg on top of Samson's shoes, pinning his feet to the ground. Lucho walked forward, grinning, and for the first time Samson noticed that he looked quite strong too. His limbs had a muscular kind of spring in the way they attached to his body. Like a chimpanzee.

He punched Samson in the gut while the guards held him. Slowly, carefully, focusing all of his strength. He hit Samson in the gut again. He hit him in the liver. In the spleen. He hit him with each fist. With one and then the other. He bruised Samson's organs. He hit him again. Samson coughed and sputtered. Lucho kept punching him, as if he were a heavy bag. As if this was a workout. Samson coughed blood. His legs were jelly, but the two goons held him in the air. Lucho kept punching. He spit in Samson's face, and punched him, and rubbed the spit into Samson's swollen eye, and punched him again. He kicked Samson in the stomach He hit him again. Samson vomited blood and Lucho leapt backwards as it splashed onto the floor. He laughed. He punched Samson again. He kicked him. Samson couldn't see anything. The goons held him up. He hit Samson again. He hit Samson again. Lucho mopped the sweat off of his brow and slapped Samson hard across the face. The face didn't move. He hit Samson again. He kicked him. He hit Samson again.

CHAPTER 8

BEN TOOK THE SHUTTLE TICKET from the clerk and passed it to Melanie. She examined the ticket, looking disappointed.

"It leaves tomorrow," she said.

"The sooner the better," Ben said. "This place is miserable. I'm getting out of here tonight. Hopefully."

He patted Melanie on the back and stepped away from her.

"Now I have some business to take care of. Maybe I'll see you around down here tonight or something. But don't forget to catch that shuttle tomorrow."

"No, wait."

Melanie followed him stubbornly, like a lost puppy looking for an owner. He didn't have the heart to be mean to her, and he couldn't figure out how to make her go away. She ignored all his protestations, and they wandered around the casino awkwardly, with him analyzing the space station's layout and security, and her analyzing him.

"You don't really have any business to take care of, do you. You're just trying to get rid of me," she would say, and Ben would wander down another hallway or take an elevator up to another balcony and try to figure out which areas were public and which led to the private headquarters of Lucho Gonzalez and his gang.

Finally he got impatient and selected a random corridor that he had seen some goons emerge from. It was a narrow, carpeted hallway tucked in behind a bank of slot machines. The slots were busy, busy, with tourists and grandmothers and long faced gambling addicts reaching out again and again into the projection, tapping the spinning dials and trying to get them to stop at the right place. He ignored the "employees only" sign and started casually down the hall.

"Hey, where are you going?" Melanie said, stopping in front of the sign.

"I'll be back in a minute, I have to find the bathroom."

"There's no bathroom down there."

"I think there is."

Melanie watched him disappear around the corner, then slowly wandered off to see if she could refund the shuttle ticket for some cash.

Samson's eyes cracked open and slowly began to focus. He watched a cloudy light above him. It seemed like he was seeing it through frosted glass. He was laying on something. A bench? He felt it with his hand, it was upholstered and lightly padded. Some kind of bunk. He slid slowly up against the wall, and turned until his shoulders and head were propped on it. Everything hurt. The room was coming into focus now. It was some kind of cell.

"Hey, you're awake," said a friendly male voice from across the room.

Samson shifted his eyes to look in that direction, but his neck was too stiff to turn his head. He could see now. He was in a little holding cell. There were bunks along the walls. A toilet and sink. It was white, uncomfortable and bare, but not grim as far as jails went. A large, reinforced door with a red light above it was apparently what was holding them in.

"Hi yourself," he said hoarsely, and winced.

"You got it pretty bad," the man said. "You must have really made them angry."

"Yeah."

"Don't worry, you'll be ok. They'll want to make sure you're healthy and have a full recovery if you are going to race ships for them. Lucho's doctor is actually quite good. First rate, in fact. They'll have had him look over you and make sure you'll be ok, repair whatever needed to be repaired. Ruptured kidney maybe."

"Maybe."

"You can't turn your head, can you?" the man asked politely. Not with compassion, but friendly curiosity.

"No."

"Oh, well I'm sorry," he said and moved to the bunk in front of Samson, so that Samson was facing him. "This is better here, now we can see each other."

"Thanks."

The man was wearing a white mechanic's jumpsuit. He was of average height and build, but had distinguished features. His hair was metallic silver, and he had arched eyebrows and an inquisitive face. His skin was pale, very faintly blue, and unblemished, and he had long, articulate fingers. His eyes were the color of honey and clashed with his hair. Some eccentric intellectual family, Samson thought. He tried to push himself up into a sitting position, but it was too painful. He caught his breath and tried to relax.

"My name's Ken," the man said. "Kenichi Iwahara. What's your name?"

"Samson Ford."

"Oooh, Samson Ford. You're a very talented young pilot. I heard they had found someone good."

"You follow racing?" Samson asked skeptically.

"Of course. I'm a racing engineer. A ship's engineer, technically, but racing ships are my specialization. And my passion."

"It's just that," Samson continued, "I've done ok and everything, but I haven't raced in big enough races for a lot of people to know me yet."

"Oh, don't be so modest Mr. Ford," the man said, "people in racing know you, believe me. Your maneuvers in that Sat 16 race were quite extraordinary. Some of the journalists have even noticed now. You're one of the 'ones to watch'."

"Do you know what time it is?" Samson asked. "Oh, and call me Samson."

"Ok, Samson. No, I have no idea. That's one of the reasons this place is so miserable."

"What are you in here for?" Samson asked.

"Oh, I made them mad again. You know, the usual. Not like you. They stuck me in here for a few days to make me humble. It's good, because then they brought you here. And we get a chance to talk without anyone else around. That's lucky, isn't it? Can you believe they don't even have cameras in here? I was surprised, but it's true."

Kenichi spoke rapidly, but with unusual precision, as if everything he said meant exactly what he had wanted to say. Samson recognized it as the speech of a highly technical mind matched with an emotional personality. Kenichi knit and unknit his fingers as he spoke, and gesticulated with them in little, rapid movements, like the darting of a humming bird. For a prisoner or indentured servant, his eyes were remarkably bright.

"What did you do in the first place? To become Lucho's slave, I mean," Samson asked.

"I had a gambling debt that I couldn't pay," Kenichi said, and his eyes suddenly seemed like mirrors.

Samson noticed an odd bracelet around Kenichi's ankle. It was bulky, metal and plastic, and held up his pants leg. A glowing indicator light on the side indicated electronics.

"Is that what they're going to put on me, too," Samson said, motioning slightly with his arm and regretting it, "to prevent escape?"

"Oh, probably," Kenichi said, and took the anklet off. "I deactivated this one years ago."

Samson blinked in surprise.

"How long have you been stuck here, Ken?"
"Twenty years."
"Twenty years?!"
"It was a big debt," Kenichi said simply.
"Fuuuck that."

THE ENORMOUS GANGSTER WHO HAD broken down Samson's hotel door strode across the main floor of the casino in a track suit and walked quickly up some stairs. His red eyes and patchy blonde hair seemed to frighten people. He turned down a hallway to the casino's fighting gym. The gym was a big, mirrored room with heavy ventilation, filled with punching bags, mats, weights, treadmills, and a couple of fighting rings. And a couple of dozen lean, muscular men. It was a real fighter's gym, filled with professionals and amateur hard men. Filled with mashed, lopsided faces and cauliflower ears. A good doctor could fix those things, but most of the fighters couldn't afford one.

"Heya, Scamp," the gym owner said as the big man ducked to walk through the sliding glass doors.

"Hi."

He walked back to the locker room and stripped down to shorts and a tank top. His muscles might have been carved from stone. For such a big man, the muscle definition looked strange. He walked back out into the gym. Other fighters paused and hushed their conversations as he approached, then slowly picked them up again after he passed. Scamp sat on a bench and wrapped his hands with stretchy, yellow hand wraps. A full wrap could barely cover one of his enormous hands. He chained the wraps together and used three at a time.

A gargantuan heavy bag hung from two of the metal beams in the gym's ceiling. It was more than twice as large as the other, normal heavy bags. Its heavy chain was made from steel as thick as a man's fingers. None of the other fighters bothered with this bag, it might have been put there just for Scamp. He lit into it with incredible fury.

Scamp punched and kicked the heavy bag in a frenzy, deforming it and lifting it with each blow. His red eyes seemed to sparkle, to glow, angrily. It was easy not to notice that he feinted, ducked, and moved around the bag with balletic footwork like a seasoned professional. Some of the other fighters stopped their workouts and watched him in awe. Each punch or kick was enough to lift the bag through the air. Not to hold it to the side against the pull of the chain, but literally to lift it up, until the chain was slack, until the bag fell back down with a crash and Scamp struck it again.

He circled the bag for thirty minutes, slamming it continuously with punches and kicks, until the floor was covered in a dark ring of sweat. The bag finally tore open, and sand poured out of it onto the wet floor. Scamp slapped at it in disgust.

"Anybody want to spar?" he asked loudly, but the other fighters only looked at the ground.

He pulled a towel off of a rack on the wall and mopped the sweat from his face, then draped it on his shoulders, which were wider than the towel, and walked out of the gym.

BEN TURNED THE CORNER AND walked down the hallway quietly, trying to look casual. He was glad that Melanie had not followed him. He walked past a pair of waiters carrying trays full of shots, and smiled at them as they passed. He turned another corner, past the kitchen, and wandered into an elevator. The elevator went up a floor and opened. A goon in a suit was waiting to get on, and Ben stepped off. The goon eyed him suspiciously, but didn't say anything, and the elevator closed up behind him. Ben kept walking, wondering what he was doing, what he could accomplish this way.

He walked past a common room with tables and a large holographic tv. Several men were sitting in the room, drinking and laughing. He stood outside the door, and tried to listen to their conversation.

"You fucking idiot, what do you know about it?"

"It's big in racing now. They can make your reactions faster. I'm telling you, this is the next big thing."

"Yeah, there's always something. It's always a big merry-go-round, the big merry-go-round of life. There's always some idiot anxious to buy."

"Fuck you."

"Look, I'll tell you what. If that stuff was all they said it is. Look, there is this racer, Samson Ford. I just read an article about him. The dude is a fucking lunatic on the course, he flies maneuvers nobody has ever seen before. He does fucking spins and turns that are supposed to kill you. All the morons are excited about it, saying he's going to be the next big thing. Now get this: The dude is a fucking normal. A normal! He's a fucking normal."

"Bullshit."

"I got it on good authority. He's a normal, a child of the fucking Magdalena cult, no less."

"And you call me an idiot."

"Hey," a voice said roughly in Ben's ear. "Should I know you? What are you doing here?"

SIMON OKUNLE STARED INTO THE muddy coffee in his paper thin, bone china cup. His amber-grey eyes were impenetrable. He inhaled the steamy aroma, and smiled appreciatively, then set the ancient silver spoon down on its silver tray. Phillipe Bloodworth sat opposite him, a small, wrought ebony coffee table between them. Bloodworth hadn't touched his cup. His eyes were on the sun, fixed on it – unblinking. It was so close, as if you could step into it. The windowed wall here was so transparent, as if it wasn't there at all. As if you had stumbled into someplace you were never supposed to be. Someplace that you weren't supposed to be while being alive. When the Sun cast out an incredible arm of fire, it was like witnessing the beginning of the universe. Or the end of it. These were the things that Simon Okunle thought, but Bloodworth stared at the sun as a kind of act. Because that was the way he thought he should behave in this situation. Because he thought it would make Simon more comfortable. He wasn't entirely wrong.

Phillipe Bloodworth was a fat man. Conspicuously unstylish. He fancied himself a sort of fashion throw back, a reverse trend setter, independent, but his clothes and bearing smacked of something else: the smug complacency of wealth and power. Arrogance. His hair was dark, greying, combed back severely with old fashioned grease. His face betrayed the meticulous shave of a well practiced slave wielding a straight razor. His eyes were an old fashioned pale blue – aggressive, intelligent, and distant all at once. And faintly mean. He picked up his coffee and sipped it, without adding cream or sugar.

"Have you considered the possibility of a merger between our companies?" he asked casually.

"Of course."

"Well. And what does your owner think about the idea?"

"Our owner is very conservative."

"I don't understand how you have managed to keep his identity a secret," Bloodworth said, watching Simon closely from the corners of his eyes. "I say 'he', but of course, it's more than likely that your new owner is a woman."

"That's certainly possible," Simon said, sipping his coffee.

They were on the Solarium, sitting in a private club called the Icarus Club. It was incomparably exclusive. A large, subdued space punctuated by exquisite furniture and priceless art. A favored meeting place of presidents and kings. There were never enough patrons here to interrupt one's sense of privacy. It had been a trusted location for well over a century. The entire far wall of the Icarus Club was a windowed viewing port that looked out onto the sun. One could sit bathed in the glory of the sun while only a few feet away the room was dim and quiet. It provided exultant solace, a punctuation mark to an experience which was not meant for punctuation. Its walls had heard the conversations that shaped history. Its tables had borne witness to meetings that decided the fates of planets, of the whole Solar System. Once upon a time, of the sun itself.

The little table between Simon Okunle and Phillipe Bloodworth had taken decades to carve. It was made from a single block of fine-grained ebony, and covered in intricate bas-relief sculpture depicting ancient Greek legends. The table had been submerged in chemical resin for twenty years, impregnated with the sealant until it was virtually indestructible. Its surface was flecked with silver and gold. The Greek heroes' eyes were tiny, mercury diamonds. Mercury diamonds were supposed not to exist.

"I cannot understand this secrecy, Simon," Bloodworth was saying. "I was a good friend of Baron de Rothschild. We used to sit at this table together. For that matter, we restructured the Solar System together. Here. Sipping this coffee. Staring at the sun. It is difficult for me to conduct so much of my business with Rothschild's without ever meeting with your firm's owner!"

"I'm sorry, Phillipe," Simon said smoothly, "that is not in my control. Our new owner is secretive and uncompromising."

"It's ridiculous," Bloodworth said, showing irritation. He wiped sweat off of his forehead and tried to relax his features.

Simon set his cup down and stared at the sun impassively. The raw light seemed to suit his walnut skin. He was attentive to Bloodworth, polite, friendly – and totally impenetrable. A picture of diplomacy.

"There's another matter I wanted to discuss with you," Bloodworth said pregnantly.

"I thought there must be," Simon agreed, picking up his coffee again.

"We're putting into motion a plan to bring final closure to this naturals problem. To put it to pasture once and for all, so that everyone can move forward without conflict."

"Legislation?" Simon said skeptically.

"Exactly. The time has come, Simon. We've become the majority. For a hundred years past, we've become the majority. It's time to separate the inferiors and place them on planets and colonies of their own. A quarantine. They don't belong in our society, and we don't belong in theirs. This much has been obvious for centuries, but now we have the power to do for them what they could never do for themselves."

"You have the votes for this? On every planet?"

"On the planets that count. The rest will fall into line, eventually. We'd like for Rothschild's to be with us on this initiative, Simon. We would consider your support invaluable."

"But you are prepared to go it alone?"

"We won't have to go it alone, man! This legislation will be popular, it's not a question of whether it will pass. It's a question of who is standing at the gates and taking credit for this revolution, it's a question of who will partake of the rewards. You have the power to make our job much quicker and easier, and we want to cut you in on the deal."

"I have to be honest with you, Phillipe," Simon said carefully, "I have never been a proponent of this sort of legislation. And I cannot see that there is a problem here requiring solution. I can understand the aesthetic virtues of the new Solar System you want to create, but from my point of view you're trying to fit a problem to your resolution. You have a grand vision for the future, but at Rothschild's we're more short sighted. We view the Solar System in terms of profit margins and market share alone. From a markets point of view, this preoccupation with genetic superiority is a waste of time."

"You're wrong, Simon," Bloodworth said with genuine passion in his eyes, and pounded his fist on the table. "You don't know how much you are wrong."

"You may be right, my friend, but we have discussed these merits before."

"Think it over again, for my sake," Bloodworth said beseechingly. "Consider all the angles, not only business. This thing is coming to a head, and we want our best partners there, marching into the future with us, not lingering behind."

"I will discuss it with our owner, of course."

"Excellent."

Their security teams met them outside the doors of the Icarus Club. Bloodworth walked Simon to his waiting space transport, and they discussed each other's well being politely. At the private gangway they embraced as old friends, and wished each other well. Simon and his security detail walked quickly onto the ship.

As soon as the cabin doors had closed behind him, Simon became a fury of business. He ordered the captain to return them to Rothschild's headquarters at maximum speed, and ordered his chief aide to begin immediately with the work of blunting Bloodworth's legislative initiatives.

"I'll get started on it at once, sir."

"Any word from our owner?" Simon asked, in a tone of concern.

"Not since the last message, sir."

"Impetuous child," he said to himself quietly, and the ship took off.

BEN LAY ON THE BED in a huge, opulent suite, and stared up through the windowed ceiling at the surface of Mars. He was still wearing his suit and tie. This room was what he had spent his roulette winnings on. It, and Melanie's ticket. And he had a little bit left over still. He thought about Samson and his skin crawled. He imagined what they were doing to him, horrible things. Samson was here, somewhere on this station. He must be. And what could he do about it? What was he even doing here? He'd have better luck with the police.

Ben sighed.

Lucho Gonzalez was protected by the police. He owned the police here. Fucking gangster. Ben rested his hand on the tiny gun inside his jacket pocket. It had taken some work to smuggle it in. He wondered what he was doing, what this was supposed to accomplish. His skin crawled, and he fought back tears.

He stood up and left the suite, looking disheveled, tie hanging loose around his neck. He walked downstairs and wandered the casino floor. He squeezed up to the roulette table and placed another big bet on 11, black. The wheel spun and spun. The ball skittered around it nervously and finally dropped. He didn't win.

"No luck today, Ben?" said a familiar voice, and a woman gently touched his arm.

It was Stephanie.

C H A P T E R ¹⁰

THE CELL DOOR BURST OPEN and Scamp walked in. Ken was pointing to his anklet intently. He pulled his pants leg down to cover it. Samson was on the opposite bunk. Sitting up now. The swelling on his face had gone down a little bit and the bruising had spread.

"Don't worry Sam, you'll get one of those soon enough," Scamp said coldly. "We just happen to be out of them right now."

He stepped back out into the corridor.

"Well? Get up, let's go. You too, Ken. I'm supposed to start showing our friend Sam the ropes."

Samson stood up gingerly, and they followed Scamp down a long, industrial corridor, hurrying to keep up.

"Don't try anything. I've got permission to kill you, Ford. And I wouldn't mind doing it, believe me."

"What are you doing working as a goon for this gangster?" Samson asked, as if they were old friends.

"Are you talking to me?" Scamp said, turning to walk sideways and glare.

"Someone like you could do a lot of cool things," Samson continued sociably. "It seems like a waste."

"Yeah, like what? Walk faster."

"You could be a prize fighter," Samson suggested, "you could be a champion. Easily."

"Well, let's just say I don't meet their requirements," Scamp said, an edge of bitterness in his voice.

He led them into a small ship hangar.

"Your racer is over here."

"What, your blood is bad?" Samson asked curiously.

"Something like that, kid."

Scamp pointed Samson towards a beat up cloud bouncer

with an old style, top mounted cockpit on it. There were half a dozen other ships in the hangar, and several pilots and mechanics on the floor working.

"Is it? You and I are the exact opposite then," Samson said, trying to keep the conversation going.

Kenichi followed them quietly, head down, saying nothing.

"How's that?"

"Didn't you know? I'm all natural. I was conceived."

"No shit?" Scamp stopped.

"Yeah, I grew up in the Magdalena cult."

Scamp looked at Samson again as if seeing him for the first time. He scanned him from head to toe, looking at his bone structure, his features, skin, eyes, hair, the way he carried himself, at his hands and feet. Quickly, but with intense focus.

"You know, that's hard to believe," he said coldly, "you're too excellent to be a product of conception."

"You know, the thing they say about natural breeding," Samson told him, trying to mirror Scamp's speech patterns, "is that it's a big lottery. And they say even though most people don't win, a few people do. And when they win, they win big."

"Yeah," Scamp said, walking up to the ship and resting his big hand on its hull. "This is the ship you are going to be flying. I can't let you in it until we get you fitted with an anklet."

Kenichi stood back away from them, always trying to keep Samson between himself and Scamp.

"Are they really going to keep me here ten years?" Samson asked bluntly.

"Maybe longer," Scamp said. "If you want some advice, try to make friends with Lucho. He's a forgiving man; he didn't kill you, after all. If you want to become one of his regular pilots, instead of his slave pilot – he might look favorably on that after a few years."

Samson continued trying to ingratiate himself with Scamp

and finally convinced the big man to let him look at the ship's controls. Kenichi sat watching them on a bench beside the ship, looking depressed. Scamp climbed up onto the side of the ship and let Samson climb up after him. He always made sure he was close enough to Samson to grab him. Samson peered into the open cockpit and chatted about the controls. He said they were old fashioned, and talked about the differences in the newer ship controls. Scamp watched him nervously, stopping Samson every time his hand went near to the ship's power or engine ignition switches.

"Watch this," Samson said good naturedly, and Scamp watched him intently.

He flipped a small metal switch on the side of the control panel, and rolled into the cockpit at the same time. The cockpit hatch snapped violently shut, knocking Scamp backwards onto the concrete hangar deck. As Samson powered up the ship, Scamp leapt back to his feet and wrenched at a heavy power cable on the ship's belly. The cable tore away, spitting out showers of sparks and fire. The ship dropped abruptly back to the ground and Scamp was nearly flattened under its fin. He stood up again slowly, but the expression on his face was angry and unfazed.

Samson switched quickly to the ship's auxiliary power, and the ship leapt back into the air. He turned it slowly, as Scamp reached up to grab hold.

"Sorry, mate, this is going to hurt," Samson said, with genuine regret.

With immaculate skill, he dropped the ship down a foot through the air, just onto Scamp's head. It was enough to knock the big man abruptly to the floor. To leave him helplessly unconscious. But probably not to kill him. It left a significant dent in the ship's lower hull.

Kenichi stared at the scene in open-mouthed amazement.

The other pilots and mechanics were shouting, or just watching from a distance, but none of them wanted to get involved. Samson popped the hatch open and lowered the ship back almost to the ground.

"Well, Ken, do you want to come with?"

C H A P T E R 11

STEPHANIE AND BEN SAT AT the casino bar. It felt familiar to them both, it was the kind of bar you would find on all the little space stations and moons that held races. The walls were banked with holographic slot machines. It was leathery. Expensively furnished, but somehow cheap at the same time. They poured heavy, generous drinks in these bars, always giving you more than you had paid for. Ben sipped at a glass of Scotch on the rocks and Stephanie drank cognac.

"I wouldn't have figured you for a cognac drinker," Ben said, watching Stephanie's perfect white fingers on the glass, and her peculiar green ring.

"Really?"

"You seem more of a vodka martini sort of girl."

Stephanie chuckled.

"Oh no, not for me. I'm definitely a cognac kind of girl."

"I don't think I've ever met a cognac kind of girl before," Ben said, and rubbed at a stain on the counter with his finger. "Cognac is an expensive drink. You're lucky I won big at the roulette wheel yesterday."

"Is it?" Stephanie wondered.

"It's 50 credits a glass, think about it."

"Oh, I guess you're right. Sorry. Well, I can pay for it."

"No, no," Ben said, "don't worry about it."

"How's Samson doing?" Stephanie asked, and her bright, dark eyes betrayed the eagerness of the question.

"Not good," Ben said, and downed the rest of his Scotch.

"What?"

"I don't think he's doing too good. He might not even be alive right now."

"That's not a funny way to joke."

"Let's get a table over there," Ben said, motioning to a booth against the wall.

He ordered another drink and they moved. Stephanie watched him intensely, she had a kind of presence about her when she focused on something, as if she could see and understand everything in the world. As if she had X-ray vision, like in an old comic book, but not only the ability to see through things, to see through people. Through their ideas and personalities. Through their emotions, and intent. As if she could see through circumstances, and actions, and events, right through to their underlying structure, and really understand them. As they walked over to the big leather booth, it occurred to Ben that she was really a very intimidating person.

"What's wrong with Samson?" Stephanie said quietly, sliding around close to him.

"The other day," he said, "on Thursday. Late that afternoon, after you had left on your shuttle, Samson had gone and gotten himself a hotel room to crash, and I had finished docking the ship and finally gotten back down to the surface. And I went to go find him to see how he was doing, to hear how things had gone with you and everything."

"Yes?" said Stephanie impatiently, eyes narrowing.

"Ok, so I'm walking down the street in front of Samson's hotel, and there is a commotion up ahead in front of the building. You know, on Pum Daarit the streets are really busy, there's a lot of pedestrians, and I was craning to see over people's heads and see what was happening. And some huge fucking goons dragged Samson out of the hotel without a shirt on and threw him into the back of a car and drove away."

"What?"

Ben was crying, he coughed to steady his voice. He clenched his fists.

"Yeah, for real. So I tried to run after them, but they were gone. The car was unmarked. I asked around and nobody knew anything about it, most of the people on the street hadn't even noticed anything happen. The door to Samson's hotel room was all smashed in, and the police came, but they just acted weird. Like they weren't taking it seriously or something. The people at the hotel just seemed to think Samson must have been a scum and they were happy to be rid of him."

"The police didn't care?"

"They, like, they opened an investigation and stuff, but I just got a feeling from them, like they were going through the motions."

"Ok."

"I knew it must have had something to do with that gangster that was trying to kill us back on Sat 16, I mean, obviously. So I started looking the guy up and asking around, which Samson and I didn't really do before. We just figured he was small time or something, you know, neighborhood loan shark or something. We weren't that worried about it, we didn't think he would come all over the Solar System to get revenge."

"Samson just beat this guy up in like a bar fight?"

"Yeah. No. Sort of. It's like, it wasn't just a bar fight, they had money on the race and they said that he cheated, then they started fighting and the dude pulled out a gun and tried to shoot him. Samson went completely berserk – like, he didn't want to tell you how it was. He went completely, totally apeshit on those guys. I dragged him out of there as soon as I got to the bar, but those guys were fucked up really bad. I was afraid they were going to die, but we didn't wait around to find out."

"Wow. Ok, so? Who's the gangster?"

"Ok, so I started looking into it, and I found out it is this guy named Lucho Gonzalez."

Stephanie's eyes widened.

"He's apparently really big time," Ben continued, "he owns this whole space station, and he has a lot of influence with the Martian police. That's why they weren't really helping, because after the first guys showed up to do the reports the police just stonewalled me."

"You're sure it was Lucho Gonzalez?" Stephanie wondered.

"Yes."

"And that's why you're here."

"Exactly. Hey, what are you doing here anyway, Stephanie? I can't believe how quickly you travel around."

"I looked up your ship's docking numbers," she said honestly. "I had a friend with some access and he found out you were—"

A massive crashing sound shook the space station, and there was screaming and commotion on the casino floor. Ben and Stephanie ran out of the bar to see what was happening, people all over the floor were pointing at the glass dome. Far up above them, an old, battered racer floated over the casino dome in a cloud of broken polyglass and debris. The ship's stern was almost completely smashed in, and it appeared to be non-functional.

Warning sirens went off around the casino, and a pleasant woman's voice filled the air, "There is a pressure leak in wing three. There is a pressure leak in wing three. Wing three is being statically sealed."

Casino patrons stampeded in every direction. The synthcats became confused by the commotion and stopped racing. They milled about on the track, and one of them even ran backwards and hunkered down in its cage in the starting blocks. A mob of gambling addicts went berserk, at first confused and not understanding why the race had stopped, then screaming that it was a fix and rioting, fighting with employees and each other, hurling the gallery furniture onto the track. One man in a tan suit and Lincoln hat charged out onto the track and was eventually attacked by the cats.

The battered racer above the space station twisted helplessly as if it were caught on a wire. It did a barrel roll and two men inside fell awkwardly against the cockpit glass.

"Holy shit, that's him," Ben said, and sprinted away.

Stephanie chased after him, stretching out her long legs, but he trailed away in front of her.

"Wait! I'm coming with you!"

C H A P T E R

BEN RAN DOWN a long casino hallway and turned left. He went up some stairs and then down another set where an elevator shaft was mobbed with people. He pressed though the crowds, down a large corridor, while Stephanie struggled to keep him in sight. Everything looked different with all the commotion – crowds of people running in every direction, hysterical. He paused to try to get his bearings.

"Hi Ben," a friendly voice called. He turned around.

Melanie was sitting on a bench along the wall behind him. Her face was cleaner, she had washed a lot of her make-up off. She waved at him with a smile, and seemed to be enjoying the commotion.

"Where's Hangar B?" he asked urgently.

"It's just – take a right here, and then another right, it's right there. But you–"

"Thank you!" Ben said, and sprinted for the hangar.

Stephanie had caught up and was just behind him. Two mobsters with guns in their hands charged down the corridor a few seconds after her. They stopped in front of Melanie, looking left and right.

"Hey, did you see where that guy with the beard went?"

"He asked me about hangar D1, I told him to take a–"

"Right!"

They ran down the opposite hall, and Melanie grinned. She watched the people streaming down the corridor, walking quickly, starting to jog, nervous. She laughed at the ones who sprinted, red faced, at full speed. She especially laughed at the fat ones, and the ones who were angry. She felt sorry for the families with children. She hoped someone else would come along to ask her which way to go and how to get to where. It suddenly occurred to her that she should get a job at the casino, and she wondered why she hadn't thought of it before.

"LADIES AND GENTLEMEN, THIS IS the casino manager speaking. Everything is being taken care of, there is no cause for alarm. Please remain calm and return to your normal activities. We apologize for the disturbance. A small ship malfunctioned and crashed through the gate of one of our private docking bays, but there was no loss of station pressure and that area has been statically sealed. No one has been hurt and the casino will resume normal operation immediately. Again, we apologize for the commotion. We will be serving free drinks at the bar and will be handing out free 20 credit chips to every patron on the casino floor during the next hour. I repeat: everything is under control, the casino will resume normal operations immediately. We will be serving free drinks at the bar and handing out free 20 credit chips to every patron on the casino floor during the next hour."

People in the hangar stepped back out of their ships and looked at each other, wondering what to do. Ben clicked his card to open up the rear loading platform of the Junket and sprinted onto it without pause. He ran to the bridge and flicked on the engines. Stephanie burst onto the bridge behind him as he was entering the code to seal the ship.

"What are you doing? Get off my ship!"

The ships controller clicked onto the com.

"Hey, El... Marja. Why are you turning your engines on?"

"Uh, sorry," Ben said quickly, "a little malfunction."

Stephanie sat down and strapped into the co-pilot's seat.

"Well turn them off, you're not cleared to fly. We're locking this hangar down right now."

Ben looked up and he could see the big hangar door sliding closed. He glanced at Stephanie again, but she was already bringing the ship's anti-gravity online.

"Shit."

"Don't be an ass, you might need me," Stephanie said.

"El Marja you are not cleared to fly. I repeat, El Marja you are not cleared to fl– Look out!!"

The Junket leapt forward through the air. A warning siren sounded and red lights flashed around the hangar. The hangar door stopped abruptly as the Junket accelerated towards it and snaked through the opening that was left. A ship waiting outside the hangar flashed its lights at them angrily.

"You fucking idiots. Who's piloting that fat hunk of junk?" a pilot's voice demanded.

"Hey Ben," Samson said on the com, his voice was crystal clear and relaxed.

"Samson!"

"Hey, I've got you on a secured line. Our com is alright. You can switch off the public one."

"El Marja, you are in breach of safety regulations, please halt your ship immediately and–"

Ben switched off the public line.

Above the glass dome of the space station, a casino tug was trying to grab Samson's ship with its powerful robotic arm. Samson used the gravity controls to rise and fall out of the arm's path, but he was buying time. The arm was close to catching him already.

Ben's Junket floated into view, it was moving fast.

"Hit your brakes, Ben. Open the cargo port and roll the ship so I can float up into it. I don't have any engines at all."

Ben reversed his engines and slowed to a smooth glide. He rolled the Junket into position above the broken racer with Samson and Kenichi in it. The cockpit of the racer was designed to have one occupant, and Kenichi crouched awkwardly against the glass, hoping Samson knew what he was doing. Samson turned down the anti-gravity, pulling them up towards Mars. The coppery red planet loomed over them, as if it were balanced on their little ships. Samson floated the battered racer into the Junket's cargo bay door, but it stopped abruptly. Half-way in. He turned the anti-gravity down more, and there was a grinding sound, but they didn't move. The tug had got them.

Ben tapped his control panels.

"We have company," Samson said grimly, as two police cruisers floated up over the far edge of the dome.

A hatch opened up on the Junket and its main robotic arm slid out into space. It spun and twisted, snapping open and closed at the end like a snake.

"What are you going to do with that?" Samson asked.

Ben looked over, and Stephanie was operating the robotic arm.

"What are you doing?" he said.

"What?" Samson said.

Stephanie gazed intently at the viewing screen, where cameras mounted on the robotic arm allowed her to control it. The arm twisted precisely, and took hold of the tug's gripping arm just behind its pneumatic hinge. Stephanie hit the pressure pumps and the Junket's arm locked down tight. She pushed it forward and the tug's arm cracked. With a final flourishing twist, she tore the tug ship's arm clean off at the broken joint.

"Holy!" Samson said, as his ship suddenly lurched into the Junket's hangar bay.

"Get us the fuck out of here!" Stephanie shouted, breathing heavily.

A small armada of police and security ships descended on them like a cloud.

C H A P T E R 13

When Samson burst onto the deck, Stephanie sprang forward to hug him. He stepped back as if she were a ghost, but then squeezed her politely.

"Oh, you didn't know I was here, did you," she said, and ran back to the co-pilot's seat.

"Jettison that hunk of shit," Samson said to Ben. "I don't want Lucho saying I stole his ship, too."

He looked a mess. His face was bruised up, and where it wasn't bruised it was grey. He hadn't showered in a long time. Kenichi stood bewildered at the back of the bridge, a crease from the edge of the ship's cockpit still imprinted on his face. Ben barely looked at them. He was trying to steer the Junket through a cloud of little security ships and past a couple of big tugs that were grabbing at it. Samson hurried to the control panel and brought up the com. Lucho came on immediately, sitting in his office, in full hologram.

"You can't get away, Samson."

"Look at all those journalists filming down there, everyone's watching, what do you think about that?" Ben said.

"Fuck you."

"Ok Lucho, you beat the shit out of me and locked me in your jail. Why don't we call it even or something," Samson offered.

"I've contacted the Martian space control, Lucho," Ben said. "You better pull your ships off or this is going to blow up in your face. Everyone's watching. Your casino has a reputation to uphold, doesn't it?"

"You're dead! You're all fucking dead! Every one of you! I see you there Ken, you fuck. You're DEAD!!!!"

Samson cut off the com.

"A pleasant fellow."

LUCHO'S SHIPS BEGAN TO DRAW back, and Ben piloted the Junket at full speed away from the space station and away from Mars. He wasn't even sure where he was going, he just wanted to get out into deep space where Lucho couldn't track him, then they could decide what to do.

"I'll be ok," Samson said as Stephanie pressed him with concern. "Anyway, it's good to see you, Stephanie. You're, uh, I didn't– I guess we have a lot of stories to trade tonight."

Kenichi still stood at the back of the bridge looking nervous.

"Tell that guy to sit down," Ben said.

"Hurry up and strap in, Ken," Samson said, and motioned towards a couple of empty seats. "Guys, this is Kenichi Iwahara, a ship's engineer."

Stephanie's eyebrows raised ever so slightly at the name. She squinted at Kenichi as if her vision had blurred and she was trying to see him better.

THEY SAT TOGETHER THAT EVENING on the metal benches of the little dining table next to the ship's kitchen. Samson sat beside Stephanie. The Junket piloted itself towards Earth through the bright vacuum of the inner Solar System. It was where their next race would be, and any work they needed to have done on the ship could be done on Earth. Samson had finally been qualified for the open class racing league after his impressive performance on Sat 16.

He stirred at a brown puddle of sludge in his bowl, scooped it into the air and drizzled it back through the air with a wet 'plop, plop, plop'.

"I really have to apologize about the food," Ben said, glancing at Stephanie. "I haven't had a chance to get the ship re-stocked properly, with all the insanity the past couple of weeks."

"It's ok," Stephanie said politely, "it's just food."

"It's better than what I usually eat," Kenichi said with a smile.

"Lord, man, what do you usually eat?"

"Oh, water and a crust of bread. Sometimes gerbil gizzards."

"Gerbil gizzards?"

"Yes. I hadn't known before that gerbils had gizzards. But, apparently, some do. Samson wouldn't eat them. They probably aren't natural gerbils. You really don't want to see what they look like raw..."

"Oh God," Stephanie said, and put down her spoon.

"...But you'd be surprised, you get used to it."

Kenichi looked at Stephanie for a moment, with a puzzled expression on his face.

"Oh, I apologize," he said. "It's manners, too. I haven't been in an environment where you use manners very much. Not for a long time. I'm sorry madame, you'd be surprised what it can do to your brain, being a slave for so long."

"Don't be sorry," Stephanie said. "You're doing fine."

"Lucho had Ken imprisoned working on his ships for twenty years," Samson said.

"Twenty years??" Ben spat out his gruel.

"Yes, I'm simply not as brave as our friend Samson," Kenichi said, and his face turned red. "I became used to the life there, in a way, and it never seemed worth the risk to try to escape. As with most people, I prefer to not die."

"I'm not that bothered about death," Samson said, and smiled winningly.

Stephanie choked back a laugh.

"That's terrible, Ken," Ben said. "I don't even know what to say."

"Oh no, don't say anything."

"Lucho's coming after us, though," Samson said.

"Lucho only operates in and around Mars."

All three men turned to stare at Stephanie and she looked down and swallowed another spoonful of gruel.

"How do you know that?"

"Oh. I used to have some syndicate friends. Lucho isn't very popular in the rest of the Solar System. A lot of the other gangsters would like to see him dead. It is weird that he went after you on Sat 16, though."

The three men continued to look at her curiously, wondering who she was. And each of them observed to himself what a beautiful woman he was looking at. The starry night of space shone in the window behind her, and sparkled in harmony with her bright, dark eyes.

"Although, Sat 16 is really a backwater shithole," Stephanie continued. "I don't think he would come after you on any planet or on any major moon. Other than Mars, of course."

She looked down.

"You guys are all staring at me."

Ben cleared his throat, and Kenichi quickly apologized. The men looked away, except Samson, who reached over and squeezed her knee. She smiled at him.

"Anyways, I'm exhausted," Ben said, yawning convincingly. "Why don't you let me show you a bunk where you can stay, Ken."

When they were alone, Samson slid up against Stephanie on the bench, so that his leg touched hers from hip to ankle. She looked down tensely, and purred.

"I'm so glad you're here," he said, "I was afraid I wouldn't see you again."

"I'm glad too," Stephanie said. "I'm so glad you're ok! I was just at the casino hoping to run into you guys and I found Ben and he started telling me about how you had been kidnapped and everything. It was scary. Ben was really shaken up. I don't think you know how much this affected him."

"I'm glad you were both there to rescue me," Samson said softly, and smoothed her hair back carefully until it was pressed behind her ear, revealing her face in full profile.

Stephanie's skin was pale and milky, perfectly smooth, and unblemished. It was perfect. She was perfect. He kissed the hinge of her jaw, and breathed deeply, intoxicated by the smell of her, and breathed out softly against her neck. She trembled.

"You, uh, you're not very much like anyone else," he said, leaning his head against hers and rubbing her arm. She squeezed his hand.

"You're not very much like anyone else, either. You're – were you really conceived?" Stephanie asked curiously, leaning away so that she could look into his eyes.

"Yes."

"Yes, I can see that, you don't have any," she tilted her head and looked up and down at him, she ran her hand through his hair, "any designer stuff in you. But you're still exceptional. You're like a natural superman."

"Nobody's a superman," Samson said defensively.

"No, you're right. It's an awful expression."

He tried to catch her eyes, to stare into them, to see into them, through her, to the depths of her, into her heart to make it stop beating, to see her eyes change suddenly and realize that she was his. But her gaze was just as strong, and she stared back just as hard, as if she could see his soul, and she was such a magical creature, he wondered if she really could.

Samson turned more towards her, and pulled at her waist to squeeze her body up against him. He ran his hand up and down the arm that was away from him, rubbing and caressing it affectionately. He rubbed past her wrist and put his fingers on the little green and metal ring that she always wore on her right hand.

Stephanie flinched, and slapped his hand away. Samson's fingers stung, and he slid back away from her, confused. She looked shocked. Her face turned red, and she could hardly look at him. She felt out with her other hand and gripped his warmly, as if in apology, but kept the ring hand tucked under her leg.

C H A P T E R ^14

KILLIAN GIDEON SLAPPED THE SIDE of his ship angrily. "Where is this Samson Ford that I've heard sooo much about? Wasn't he supposed to be at this race? And yet he's not here."

Killian was tall and broad. He was physically perfect. Literally, perfect. His features were beautiful, strong, and inhumanly symmetrical. His body totally unblemished, except for an occasional small racing scar one might discern on his forearm, for example, or the side of his neck. His skin was white. It wasn't pale skin, not like Stephanie had, not the kind of skin popular among parents who wanted their children to have a natural, elegant look. It was white like paper, like processed milk. Perfectly white. And thick, and opaque. He was completely hairless, from head to toe, and his eyes were violet. He was wearing a black, designer racing suit. The spectators in the stands around them had gone insane as soon as he stepped out onto the ceramic ships' platform. The women, especially, screamed and swooned over him.

"Samson Ford. What a name. He's probably afraid of you, darling."

Killian's companion was a famous model named Cindy. She was nearly as tall as he was, blonde and exceptionally, sexually, beautiful. She wore a matching black jumpsuit that hugged her exquisite curves with affection, and followed behind him like a nervous puppy. Killian mostly ignored her, but in a careless way that somehow implied ownership.

"It's very possible he would be afraid of me. He certainly should be," he said, not looking at Cindy but at his ship. She stood two steps behind, respectfully. "But from what I've heard he's not smart enough to be afraid. Can you believe, he's a normal. A normal, racing in the open class. It's hard for me to believe, that's why I wanted to see him. Of course, it would explain why he is too stupid to be afraid, they don't tend to be very smart after all. They're basically just unusually smart monkeys, aren't they. Think about it. What's the difference? Between them and the animals at the zoo? They have little intelligence, and less self control. They're mere products of nature that evolved from little bugs in the water."

Killian laughed heartily at this observation of his, and rubbed one of the shiny advertising decals on the side of his racer. It was a cigarette racer like Samson's, but where Samson's ship had a perfectly cylindrical wings framework, Killian's was more of a rounded, teardrop shape. It looked more cutting edge, less traditional. The honeycomb structure of Killian's wings framework was also less complex than the one on Samson's ship – one could follow the patterns of the wings and funnels easily, while on Samson's ship the pattern seemed almost random, totally impenetrable. Killian's mechanics ducked around him meekly, clambering over and under the ship, performing the necessary safety checks, making sure that it was ready to race. He watched what they were doing from the corners of his eyes, but, more than that, he trusted them.

"Can you believe some scribbler said he believed Samson Ford would beat me in a race?" he asked incredulously, glancing at Cindy for the first time.

"I don't know why you even bother to read those reports, honey. The people who write them are idiots."

"Samson Ford could beat you," said Lisa Maui cheerfully, standing in front of Killian and holding out a compu-tablet with the pilots' forms on it.

"Who says?"

"I do. I've seen him race. He's fast."

"My times are better than his on every course he's ever run," Killian said dismissively.

"You should see how he flies. And his ship is also... I dunno, I just think he could beat you."

Killian laughed, in high amusement. He took the tablet from Lisa and began filling out the forms. Her jaw dropped as she watched his hands. They moved with unbelievable speed and precision. As if he were an industrial machine that had been made to fill out these forms as quickly as possible. He barely glanced at the tablet, but penciled in neat little checks and letters, more quickly than most people could type.

"What's your name?" he asked.

"Lisa."

Killian handed the tablet back to Lisa, and she walked away without saying anything else. He watched her walk away, smiling happily, with a sort of twinkle in his eye.

"What a little bitch."

"Compose yourself, Cindy," he said distractedly. "She's a nice girl."

He stood in front of his ship and closed his eyes, imagining the race ahead, playing it out in his mind like a recording. His arms reached forward, back and forth, twisted, and his hands clenched, and he punched at buttons in the air with his fingers. With his eyes closed. It was like shadow boxing, like a pianist drumming their fingers precisely on a table, warming up. He was like a machine, and, somehow, also like an animal. There was something raw and uninhibited about him. Something almost out of control. Many of the other racers stopped and watched him. They couldn't help themselves. Many of them were like an inferior version of him, and felt it profoundly. And loved or hated him for it. He was the one that had come out of the oven perfect. The one whose mix had been exactly right. The others, they might have been burnt a little on the bottom, or they might not quite have had enough flour, or a touch too little yeast, or perhaps they had been baked at a moment when the atmospheric conditions weren't quite just so. With Killian, everything had gone right, everything had fallen into place, he was the ideal condition, the model. Cindy breathed heavily as she watched him, barely able to control herself. When she stood close to him and watched him work like this, her eyes became damp with tears, and she blinked through them without the slightest hint of embarrassment.

Killian leapt up to the railings of his ship, and scrambled up and stood on top of it.

"Lisa!" he shouted loudly, and she turned around. "Do you know Samson Ford?"

"Well, sort of. Yes."

"Watch what I do in this race. Tell Samson what he missed."

"Ok," Lisa said quietly and looked down, uncomfortable with the attention.

When the race began, everyone was surprised to see Killian languishing in the middle of the pack. His ship was going slow. Cindy held her breath.

"Killian Gideon is well back, he had a slow takeoff," the announcer said excitedly. "He's forty or fifty ships behind the leaders, really right in the middle of the pack. He might be having trouble with his ship."

KILLIAN TURNED SPINS and weaves in the middle of a huge racing pack. The closest ships edged away from him. He spun a corkscrew around one ship, then pulled forward and arced up into a full 360-degree nose hook around another. The pack spread out nervously.

"Fuck you, Killian," a racer said on the public com.

"No, fuck you, Jared," Killian said, "fuck you very much."

The race course took them in a loop around a small, black moon. The moon sparkled with lights from little colonies on its surface, like a black diamond under a bright light that sparkles in defiance of itself. Killian loved this moon. He wanted to give them a show. The course played to his strengths. It was an intricate flying course – hard turns and loops, accelerations and decelerations, filled with bottle necks and opportunities to crash, few straightaways. The first time Killian had flown this course he had won the race by half an hour. If it had been made for him it would not have suited him better.

A girl racer flew in front of him, and Killian edged up against her tail, until his ship was touching it. It always amused him that they let women race. He wondered what it would be like to be a man and lose in a race with a woman, and thought of the many men in this race and laughed. Most of them had experienced that, he realized. They weren't even men. They weren't even much better than the monkey people like Samson Ford. He watched through his cockpit and saw the girl looking back at him nervously, and enjoyed the fact that she was afraid. She swerved, trying to lose him. Losing speed. She was losing her position in the race. He kept his nose right on her, right up against her tail. If she hit her breaks it would kill them both. He thought he could anticipate it if she did, but didn't think she would risk it. He could just see her left hand on its control wand, clenched tensely. He wondered what position she was trying to get. Obviously a woman wouldn't dream that she could win this race. He laughed at the thought. What did she dream about, what did she aspire to? Tenth place, maybe? Was that her dream? He laughed again. Everything was funny today. He was in a good mood.

"Get off me," came the woman's voice tensely.

He edged up against her ship until he was applying pressure to her, ever so slightly turning her off course, sending her out around the path, out of bounds of the race. She tried to push back against him without losing control.

A bright red ship hurtled aggressively at Killian, boosters flaring. He saw it just in time and dove as it clipped across the top of his framework, chipping a splash of paint out into the vacuum. The collision would have killed them both.

"Kiss my ass you weird, white, freak," Jared said, and looped gracefully through the obstacles.

The female racer lit her boosters into a straightaway and disappeared into the main pack.

"Oh, you're trying to ruin my fun, Jared, that's not very nice," Killian said mildly on the com.

He focused himself and sped through the obstacles acrobatically, cutting the corners ever so close. Accelerating and decelerating in perfect time. Plunging through Gs that would overwhelm a GCU and tear most racers out of their skin. His ship was better than most. He ignored the pain and flexed the muscles in his body magnificently, for minutes at a time, to keep the blood flow even and primed into his brain. He flew at the edge of his ship's capacity for flight, right at the point where it would break. It creaked and whistled angrily. He passed other racers as if they were idle spectators that weren't even part of the competition.

He hooked a ship on its engine as he spun past it in a tight corner. Deviating ever so slightly from his flight path to ensure the perfect contact. He caught its vulnerable central control panel square with the metallo-ceramic guard rails around his frame. It was a small, white, V-shaped ship. It looked like four pyramids glued together, with yellow racing stripes and a side-mounted cockpit. It seized up on impact and tumbled down into the moon. The ship's pilot jettisoned his cockpit before hitting the moon's atmosphere. The cockpit pod drifted slowly down towards the moon, blinking out a yellow and red SOS pattern.

Killian flew past the girl pilot he had been harassing earlier, and waved politely as he passed.

"Racing is a man's sport, miss," he said on the public com, and laughed hysterically.

"You're a dick, Killian," someone said meekly.

"Oh, be quiet."

Jared had gotten far ahead, near the front of the pack. They were more than half-way around the moon now. Killian turned past another ship as it was hitting its boosters, and nudged its tail, sending it hurtling at the moon. The ship clipped one of its stabilizing fins on the edge of an obstacle as it plunged, and the fin tore off violently, trailing an explosive spray of atmosphere. The cockpit jettisoned before the pilot even had time to cut his boosters, and the ship exploded violently in the top of the moon's atmosphere, like a splash of fire.

"I– I'm ok," the ship's pilot gasped into the com as his cockpit pod sank quickly towards the moon. "I'm only 50% oxygen with the backup. I need help, hurry."

Killian laughed again, and twisted through another obstacle and hit his boosters into a big loop through a few more. He passed several racers.

"The only way they could help you is by taking away your racing license," he said, as the disabled racer coughed into the com.

Jared was up ahead of him now, in an old fashioned red ship that was shaped like a hawk. It had golden highlights on it, and was well sponsored. Killian had never liked Jared. He guessed that Jared had never liked him. It was so stupid for someone not to like him. He was obviously superior. Only irrational jealousy could prevent them from liking him. He was better than Jared in every way, Jared should try to look up to him and learn. Instead, Jared had always tried to give him a hard time. It was as if he thought he was Killian's equal. It was stupid.

Jared was at the front of a small line of racers, and the race leader was about ten ships in front of that. Killian slid into the back of the tight line of ships, maneuvering so that the other ships would cloak him and Jared wouldn't see that he was there.

"Where is that Killian prick?" Jared said. "Tell me if he's coming up behind us."

The pilot in the ship in front of Killian looked back and stared directly at him. Killian made eye contact with the man and shook his head warningly.

"Hey, I think he might be back here, Jar," one of the pilots said.

"Where is he? I don't see him."

They were flying in a tight, corkscrew loop that would take them through four obstacles in a smooth pass. Killian suddenly cut out of the loop and accelerated straight at Jared's red, hawk racer. He could see Jared look up in surprise at the unlikely angle. It would take him out of the course and he would have to circle back, losing time. Jared tried to dive out of the way. He was too slow. Killian's timing was perfect. His ship slid into Jared's tail and he hit his jump boosters on the point of impact, throwing the ship headlong into an obstacle wall. The red hawk racer exploded. Jared didn't have time to scream.

Killian plunged out into space and circled back to repeat the obstacles. The crowd back at the racing stadium went wild. It had been such a bold move, and executed so perfectly. People around the Solar System, watching on their holo-screens, screamed and cheered. It had taken everyone's breath away, such a beautiful, devastating attack. The fans in the stadium chanted Killian's name. They cut it short and chanted, "Kill! Kill! Kill!" and laughed. Gamblers held up their tickets happily, showing that they had placed a bet on Killian to kill another pilot in this race. "Oh dear," the race announcer said, "and that's another one done by Killian Gideon. Jared Illich, number 13. That's an unlucky number, number 13. And if you can believe it, that's the 13th pilot that Killian has killed in his racing career. Assuming he gets officially awarded the kill, of course, which I'm sure he will...."

As the racers sped back to the ceramic racing platform perched at the top of the big space station, Killian stopped playing and raced to the front of the pack. He was neck and neck with a small cigarette racer that had led most of the way, but in the final stretch Killian's ship was simply faster and he squeezed into the lead to win the race.

The crowd on the racing platform held up huge banners in Killian's honor. "Killian Our Hero", and "Gideon Superman", and "UNSTOPPABLE!" with a cartoon drawing of Killian's racer.

Lisa happened to be standing on the platform nearby when Killian landed. He noticed her as he climbed down out of his ship, but didn't look at her. He kissed Cindy in a long, open mouthed kiss, and massaged her buttocks as he kissed her. And waved to the crowd at the same time. They cheered hysterically.

Ten minutes later, Killian climbed the steps to the podium to accept the first place trophy. He held Cindy close to him, like a favorite toy. She smiled emptily, as if her brain were gone. He never let go of her. He held her with one hand and shook the chairman's hand with the other. He picked up the race trophy and held it aloft with one arm, while massaging her right breast vigorously. She smiled dimly, and her face was red, and her eyes were spacey as if her mind were somewhere far away, somewhere that was only for her. Fireworks exploded above the platform and a rain of confetti fell onto them, and the crowd thundered their applause.

As they walked across the huge ceramic tiles, Killian saluted the crowd perfunctorily with the trophy. Cindy's eyes stared straight ahead, while her body perked up to display itself through the tight jumpsuit. Killian massaged her ass uninhibitedly as they walked along the edge of the stands to the exit.

"GRUEL AGAIN?" SAMSON SAID AT breakfast, but shoveled it into his mouth.

"Until we can restock at Earth," Ben said, standing in the little kitchen across the ship's corridor from the table. "Don't complain."

"Who's complaining?"

Stephanie sat beside Samson, but away from him. Her eyes were lined, and she seemed drained, but her behavior was impenetrably neutral. Samson could feel the space between them like it was an object. A creature with a life and intention of its own. It felt tense, and cold. He made eye contact with her and she smiled an embarrassed smile and looked away. He wanted to stretch out and touch her, to show how he felt. To destroy the space that separated them, and let her feel the warmth he felt for her. The warm feelings. The space seemed to push him back. As if it was powerful.

"I really like this gruel, it's extremely nutritious," Kenichi said. "Have you examined the ingredients? I was looking at some of the labels a little while ago, it's very well made. The company, Ni-Shi-Oh, has an excellent track record and man-ufacturing practices. I remember when this kind of food was invented, they said back then that if you ate only this for your entire life it was extremely healthy and would increase your life expectancy by an average of ten years. As far as I know that data has never been controverted."

He looked around at the three of them, and there was an awkward silence, as nobody else thought of anything to say in response.

"Please forgive me, sometimes I talk too much."

"No, not at all," Ben said. "I did know that you could live on this stuff, but I was never too sure how healthy that would be."

"I don't think I would trust those studies," Stephanie said.

"Oh you're right, there was almost certainly a degree of self-interest involved, most studies of this type are commissioned by the companies which sell the products that the studies are meant to justify."

"Yes," she said.

He looked at Stephanie admiringly, and she looked down and ate her food.

Conversation turned to their plans going forward. Stephanie was unsure how long she could stay with them. She didn't say exactly what she needed to do, but left it implied that she had business to take care of. She had a vague way about her that discouraged further inquiry.

"So, we're going to go to Earth and race in the next race, we already missed the one last night," Samson said. "Earth should be safe, and we'll try to figure out what to do about Lucho while we're there. What are you going to do Ken?"

Kenichi scooped a spoonful of gruel into his mouth and tapped on the table. He looked out the window beside him for a moment, but his eyes were distant, as if he didn't see the brilliancy of space that shone at them through the glass.

"Do you have some family to re-unite with or something like that?" Samson offered helpfully. "There must be a lot of people who have missed you all these years."

Kenichi glanced between Samson and Ben.

"Perhaps I could stay on with you, as part of your racing team," he offered tremulously. "I'm a ship's engineer, I'm a very good one. I would like to repay you for rescuing me."

"Don't even worry about that," Samson said. "It wasn't any extra effort to take you with me, I was happy to do it. I would have felt guilty to leave you behind there."

"Thank you," Kenichi said. "You are too kind. I would still like to offer you my services as ship's engineer, I would like to stay on and help your racing team. I believe I can be an asset to you."

Samson and Ben glanced at each other. Stephanie looked at Kenichi with the same quizzical expression from when she had first met him. As if she had seen him before.

"Well, that's— I'm sure you're a good engineer," Ben said. "But we don't really need an extra man right now. Samson and I are just barely scraping by ourselves most of the time, we're really operating on a shoe string and all our money goes back into the ships."

"That's good, that's the way I like to operate too."

"Well, and the racer, besides the mechanical work, you know we're going to be racing open class races now, and it's about time. Samson's racer is really a technical ship, it's really state of the art. We can do the mechanical work, but anything major that has to be done – there's only a few shops in the Solar System we can take it to that know what to do with it."

"Please let me look at the racer," Kenichi said, sliding out of the bench and standing up. "Then I can tell you whether I would be able to be helpful or not."

"But Kenichi, my friend," Samson said, watching him curiously, "don't you— I mean, you've been locked up in Lucho's dungeon for twenty years! You must have friends and family who have been wondering about you all this time."

Kenichi's face turned red.

"I would prefer to stay on," he said. "I have nowhere else to go."

Samson led Kenichi to the end of the corridor and unbolted the blue steel door to the ship's hangar. He led the way into the darkness as the hangar lights slowly blinked on overhead. The darkness turned to a grey and the white cigarette racer materialized in front of them. The grey filtered away into a natural, bright light.

"Th– This is impossible!"

Kenichi ran across the hangar floor to the racer. He looked back and forth at it, up and down, holding his breath, eyes wide. He peered under the ship's belly and ran his hand along the wings framework. Samson tilted his head sideways, as if Kenichi's behavior would make more sense viewed from that angle. Kenichi scrambled on his hands and knees between the ship's hull and the wings framework, and opened up a circuit panel and shouted happily. He crawled back out to the hangar deck and sprinted back to Samson in ecstasy.

"What's going on?" Samson said as Kenichi grabbed him by the shoulders.

"This is my ship! This is my ship!"

"What?"

"Don't you understand? You're flying my ship! I made her. She was my masterpiece. I made her!"

He sank to the floor and wiped at his eyes.

"Woah, are you alright? Easy there," Samson said, catching Kenichi's shoulders when his legs buckled.

Kenichi sat on the floor and shook his head, grinning.

"Samson Ford! Samson Ford! Don't you see? I thought I would never see her again. I thought I'd lost her. She was my masterpiece. Oh, she was so beautiful," he held his arms out. "And she's there! By some miracle she's there. She's so beautiful. It's beyond comprehension. It makes a man want to believe in the god. I'm here, and you have my ship, and now I can work on her again and finally finish the job. You don't understand. Where did you get her?"

He was bawling.

"You built *this* ship?" Samson asked skeptically.

"Every inch of her," Kenichi said. "Every inch. Tell me

where you got her. I have to know. I absolutely need to know!"

Samson sat down on the hangar floor beside Kenichi and stared at his racer re-appraisingly. He looked at Kenichi coldly, analytically, evaluating him.

"It's true!!" Kenichi screamed in impatience and exasperation, and stood up and ran back to the ship and started examining it again, and laughed happily.

Stephanie and Ben came out into the hangar, curious to see what the commotion was. Samson walked behind Kenichi, beginning to smile himself now. Beginning to appreciate what fate had done for him.

"I found her in an old junkyard, Ken," Samson told him. "Almost ten years ago. I was doing some little local racing things, jet bikes and stuff like that. I took all my race winnings and bought the old racer immediately. On the spot. God, I couldn't believe it. And Ben was already working with me by then, acting as my manager and mechanic, and we just went to work on the ship whenever we had time. It took us three years to get her flying again."

"It's so amazing. You got her flying. You got her flying!"

That night, after Kenichi and Ben had gone to sleep, Stephanie pulled Samson into her cabin conspiratorially. It was a tiny little room.

"Come here, you have to see this."

She had her card plugged into the cabin terminal, and had been doing research.

"Sit down. Listen to this. I knew I recognized him from somewhere:

" 'Kenichi Iwahara, better known as Yakuza Ken, was a noted spacecraft engineer who worked for several top racing teams at the end of the 23rd Century. He is most famous for being implicated in a series of professional racing scandals that destroyed his career.' "

"Yakuza Ken," Samson said. "I've heard stories about Yakuza Ken. Like, racing legends sort of stories."

"I know," Stephanie said, "and look at the picture, from a trial on Earth in 2293. It's him."

The picture on the screen was twenty-five years old, it was grainy and in black and white, but it was unmistakably Kenichi. He had a massive beard, his eyes were sunken in, and he was in a prison suit, but it was him.

" 'Kenichi Iwahara was born on Earth in Old Town, Tokyo, in 2265. His mother, An Ji Iwahara, and his father, Joseph Iwahara, were both engineers who worked for Toyota corporation. Kenichi was a child prodigy and graduated from the Tokyo University Engineering Academy at age 15, the youngest ever to have done so. He was remarkable not only for his youth, but for the fact that he had made valuable new contributions to the field of engineering while he was still an undergraduate, an accomplishment rarely recorded among similar child prodigies in history. Among young Iwahara's inventions was a simple quantum field thruster, the first proto-type of which he developed while working in the Engineering Academy's Advanced Space Technologies lab when he was only 14 years old. This was the first quantum field thruster to achieve pseudo-perfect efficiency, and is the basis for most engine thrusters currently being manufactured. The patent rights on Iwahara's quantum field thruster caused a minor scandal, as Tokyo University appropriated the patent claim under a 'work for hire' doctrine, and Iwahara himself saw little or nothing of the estimated 500 trillion credits income that the patent generated. Throughout the rest of his career, Iwahara denounced Tokyo University bitterly, and claimed they had been a hindrance to his development as a scientist.

" 'After graduating from Tokyo University, Iwahara focused his attention on spaceship racing designs. Several prominent engineers and scientists criticized this as being a waste of his talents. Iwahara was one of the leading proponents of the 'cigarette racer' design, and helped to establish this design's dominance in space regattas and mixed races. Iwahara initially attempted to form his own independent engineering firm, Iwahara Race, Ltd., but this company quickly folded due to financial incompetence and mismanagement. He then worked for a series of racing teams as chief designer and lead engineer, including Bugatti-Oddo, Ponichach, and Hermes Unlimited. Iwahara's race designs were often revolutionary, and the racing teams he worked for were consistently ranked in the top 5 during his time with them. In his final years with Hermes Unlimited he was matched with the legendary pilot Bibi M'Beki, and the Hermes team dominated open class racing during this time, winning the Earth Grand Prix three times, the Martian Regatta once, the Saturn-Jupiter Loop three times, and the 2292 Solar Regatta, among other races."

Samson was standing up, staring at the holo-screen impatiently, wanting Stephanie to go faster.

"Ok, but what about the rest of it?"

"Calm down," Stephanie said, and ran her finger through the projection, scrolling the text. "Here:

" 'Iwahara's career came to a shocking halt when he was implicated in a series of high profile racing scandals. ...gambling against his own racing team. ...sabotaging his own ship, causing a spectacular crash in which the young pilot, Gabriel Jiminez, was paralyzed from the waist down. ...In 2294 his trial was dismissed on a technicality and Iwahara was set free.'

"Now get this: 'Shortly after being freed, on January 15, 2294, Iwahara boarded a shuttle in downtown Tokyo and was never seen again.' !"

"Holy–"

"It's. Hold on."

The computer prompted them with an urgent signal and Stephanie brought it up. The Junket's present course would cross paths dangerously close to a large transport ferry in about two hours. Samson reached out to select 'OK' for the small trajectory change. Stephanie caught his hand before he could push the button.

"Wait. Computer, give us a readout on that ferry please."

The screen flickered and an image of a large passenger ship appeared in front of them, along with a full technical readout of the ship's registry data and itinerary.

"It's bound for Mars," she said conclusively. "Samson, I need to board that transport. I have to return to Mars right away."

"What?"

"I can't really explain. I'm going to go to the bridge and try to bring them up on the com to arrange a passenger transfer. I need to get back to Mars immediately. I didn't want to say anything, but now that there's an opportunity to do it I have to take it."

"Are you kidding?" Samson was incredulous, almost angry.

Stephanie was already jamming her few belongings into her purse.

"I'm not joking, I have to go to Mars."

She pulled her hair back into a neat ponytail, and looked at herself in the mirror. Rubbed her face and smoothed out her clothes. Samson touched her arm.

"Stephanie, a passenger transfer in deep space, on no notice– Even if you can get them to agree to it, that's going to cost a fortune."

She grabbed his hand and pulled him out the door.

"Come on!"

"Stephanie, this is crazy. And we can't afford the credits to pay for it, it's just not possible."

"I'm not asking you to pay for it, I wouldn't ask you to do that. All I'm asking you to do is dock with their ship so that I can transfer over."

She stood at the com, punching it up again and again, trying to contact the passenger ferry.

"I hope they're paying attention."

"Is it something we're doing, have we somehow made you uncomfortable?" Samson wondered, grasping at straws. "What could be this important that you have to do a deep space ship's transfer at an hour's notice?"

"It's nothing like that, I just can't explain it to you," she said, looking him in the eyes. "I have business to take care of, I should have been back in Mars and never gone to the casino at all."

"Don't say that. I'd probably be dead if you hadn't come."

Stephanie didn't hear him, she was clicking at the com board frantically, and steering a collision course for the ferry. Each time the ferry re-adjusted its course to avoid them she adjusted the Junket's flight path to match.

"This'll wake them up."

"What's going on?" Ben said, stumbling onto the bridge in his pajamas, and yawning.

"I don't know. Our friend Stephanie has apparently gone mad."

"Oh, shut up," she said.

Kenichi came onto the bridge, too.

An hour later, after Stephanie prevailed in an intense argument with the ferry's captain and agreed to pay a truly exorbitant boarding fee that made all three of the men's jaws drop, the Junket and ferry docked in deep space. It was a huge ferry, seating 10,000 passengers. Docked at one of the ferry's passenger ports, the Junket looked like a barnacle stuck to the side of an ocean liner. A slurping sound shook the Junket's corridors as the two ships established an atmosphere seal.

"Goodbye Ben," Stephanie said, and hugged him.

"Goodbye Kenichi," she shook his hand warmly, and Kenichi's gaze followed her with infatuation.

"Goodbye Samson, I'll see you again sometime."

She hugged him tightly, but Samson barely returned the embrace.

"Don't be angry at me," she said, walking away from him and turning back again. Her dark eyes flashed with dew.

"No, I–"

The Junket's door slid open and Stephanie ran through without waiting, waving behind her as a ship's steward on the other side said, "Hurry please. Through the doors. As quickly as you can." The door snapped closed again, and with a sucking sound the atmospheric seal was broken. The gigantic ferry released its lock with the Junket and plowed ahead immediately, turning on four enormous booster panels that left a long trail of blue lines through the vacuum of space. The Junket drifted slowly across the blue booster tracks and seemed to bob up and down, suddenly a very small, lonely ship drifting in a very large universe.

THE UNITED EARTH CONGRESSIONAL ASSEMBLY met twice a year in Rio de Janeiro to debate and vote on planet-wide initiatives. Its 500 delegates convened in a large, bowl-shaped chamber that resembled a miniature, indoor, football stadium. Only delegates were allowed to enter the floor of the stadium, but the viewing balconies above them seated approximately 5,000 visitors. Perfect silence from the balconies was maintained technologically, with an invisible, mono-directional sound barrier that separated the visitors from the delegates below. Each delegate wore an identical black gown, except for the Chief Delegate whose gown had golden highlights sewn into it. The Chief Delegate stood in the center of the bowl, and acted as administrative officer for the Assembly. Three days before, he had opened debate on Universal Law #9727F7, the "Quarantine of Genetically Primitive Persons Act".

"Ilya Muntari, you are recognized to speak," the Chief Delegate announced soberly, as debate continued.

A tall man with thick, red hair, true black skin that vanished against his robes, and bright pink eyes stood up. His smile displayed straight, impossibly clean, ivory teeth.

"Thank you, Chief Delegate. My fellow delegates. As always, it is an honor to be able to speak in front of this august body.

"As we discuss the contentious issue before us today, it is important to remember history. To remember that our fathers discussed this issue. That our grandfathers discussed this issue. That our great grandfathers discussed this issue, so many years ago. Every generation has been called upon to act. Every generation has felt the need and heard that same clarion call," scattered delegates booed and hissed, but he ignored them, "that same clarion call that we all feel today. To act, to do. To solve the problem in front of you instead of setting it aside. This is the difficult thing that confronts us today, the great challenge. To solve, once and for all, a centuries old problem, and to solve it in a way that is beneficial and just to all men.

"Yes, my friends, we have heard the speeches from each other, the pros and cons, but I have always felt what is so often lost in the shuffle when it comes to this issue, the thing that so often disappears within the rhetoric of debate, is that everyone stands to gain from the legislation in front of us. Everyone will benefit from this legislation, every man, woman, and child on this planet. And doubtless, in the Solar System as well. You see, the dividers among us, to my mind, this is the way it seems to me, that the dividers among us try to cast us against each other. They try to say that this legislation is in one group's interest and against another group, they try to say that the interests of our two great, but divergent classes of people are mutually exclusive. Those of us with superior genes can only benefit from a harm to those of us with inferior genes – we are told. But it is a lie!"

"You lie!" another delegate snapped, angrily.

"Please sir, wait until I have finished. As I was saying, there are hearts among us who burn with a passion that is very much like hatred, that burn with a passion against another group of people, that rejoice at the division amongst us. They say that those men with inferior genes can only benefit from the harm of men with superior genetics. In other words, we are meant to believe that we are at each other's throats. We are meant to believe that this legislation is one dimensional and benefits the superior men against the inferior, natural men.

"But that is a lie! It is the interests of the natural man that lie at the very heart of the legislation before us. Ladies and gentlemen, we have been selling ourselves short. This legislation is truly visionary, and is carefully crafted to be of benefit to all."

A large section of the assembly grumbled and hissed, some members standing up and holding out a thumbs down gesture in the air.

"Consider," Muntari continued, "please my fellow delegates, consider the perspective of an ordinary, natural man or woman. Consider their position in our modern society. Imagine getting up every morning, and going to work, and being surrounded by people who are better than you. Who are smarter than you, who are taller and stronger than you, better looking than you, people who exceed your capacities in every way. But they have feelings the same as us. It must be incredibly discouraging for them. Put yourself in the shoes of a natural man. Or a natural woman. Imagine her getting up every morning, and working so hard to put herself together, to make herself up and try to approach the modern standards of beauty, but it is impossible for her. And she walks through the crowded streets and sees the people more beautiful than her, and feels her inferiority so palpably, so painfully. And she is treated as an inferior. Oh yes, we treat them with scorn, don't we. We try not to, we try to be kind hearted people, but it is impossible, even on a purely unconscious level, for us to ignore the fact of our own superiority. We lose our temper when they mix up our dinner order, or when we get into a taxi and one of them cannot find his way to the address we want, and we have to explain the street layout, as if they were children. We're horrible to them, but we can't help being born the way we are, and it is a beautiful way to be. And they can't help being born the way they are, and there is nothing wrong with the way they are born.

"The problem is putting our two societies together. It is bad for them, and it is bad for us. They suffer under a constant burden of inferiority and discrimination, and we are held back as a people by the weight of their natural inadequacies. The solution of separation is measured to be equally beneficial both to them and to us.

"It is a simple matter of quarantine," Muntari continued in his understated, patrician voice, and the booing and grumbling grew to a climax. "It is a simple matter of quarantine, my fellow delegates. Although I would suggest that quarantine is too loaded of a term, far too negative of a term. It is a simple matter of partitioning. This is not unprecedented in the history of man. We have two groups of people who are each better off separated from each other than they are mixed together. We have two groups of people who are each better off being on their own, than they are being with the other group. It is within our power to implement this separation in a way that is civil, fair, and beneficial to all involved. This is our moment in history, our chance to form a better world for *everyone*, and it is imperative that we act. The issue, the difficulties, the negative emotions on every side of this issue, can only grow. It is only through action that all of us, natural born and the rest of us alike, it is only through our action here, in this legislative session, that all of us can move forward into a better future. Together – but apart.

"Thank you."

He sat down and the rest of the delegates stood up, cheering wildly or shouting and castigating him angrily in a wild cacophony of human emotion. The Chief Delegate pounded his gavel again and again, "Order! Order, I say! Order!"

"The Gentlewoman from Riyadh, Rahima Bernstein, is recognized to speak."

A very tall, very thin woman, with intricately knotted black hair, stood up. The skin of her face was a bright, soft, shocking yellow, her lips were white, her fingers long, with long white nails that seemed to catch and reflect light, and her eyes were a crisp, intimidating green. The visitors in the balconies, nearly all of them journalists or foreign dignitaries, sat on the edges of their seats, holding their breath.

"I've no interest in Muntari's dissembling!" Bernstein shouted angrily and without introduction. "And I won't stand on protocol or propriety! My people send me to get a job done, not to speak quietly out of two sides of my forked tongue. There's one thing I agree with Muntari about, and that's that separation is necessary, but there is one big problem with his theories and natterings on – the naturals are still going to breed! They're reproducing faster than we are. It's only because they're so weakly formed, unproductive, and inherently self-destructive that we have even been able to surpass them in population. These normal women are cranking out one or two babies in a year, filling our planet up with imbeciles. And I don't see how foisting them off on some other part of the Solar System is any kind of solution at all. We need to deal with the problem. We need to deal with it now. I've been saying this for years, there is one solution, it's the only rational solution, and it's the simplest solution: forced sterilization of anyone who was naturally born. We can solve this problem in one generation, and it's not even a difficult problem to solve. No more double talk! No more forked tongues! I'll say what we all feel, and I'm not ashamed of it: We need sterilization, and we need to implement it now!"

"But will you vote 'yes' on the current bill?" another delegate shouted.

"Order. Order."

"Will I vote 'yes'? I haven't decided that yet. My point of view is that this bill has been introduced abruptly and is being jammed down our throats, regardless of its merit, which may be great. We've had no time to put the bill into proper order, and it has one huge flaw that I'm already aware of, which is the absence of a sterilization provision. I don't know what kind of idiots are drawing up legislation like this, but if you stab someone in the back you had better be damn sure they can't come back to haunt you ten years later. As daft as they are, normals can still be very crafty, and forcibly deporting five billion of them without doing anything to put a permanent end to the breeding problem in the first place is asking for trouble. So that's my answer, we need to get this legislation back into committee and create a solution with real teeth that bite!"

"Thank you. Thank you. Polite and well measured as always, Delegate Bernstein."

"I only speak the truth, Your High Holiness, as always."

"Yes, thank you, Rahima. No need to be sarcastic."

A tall, distinguished looking gentleman with natural, coppery skin stood up. His eyes flashed a sharp, shocking blue, and his hair had the greying edges of the old school.

"Yes, Delegate Gregory, you are recognized."

"Thank you, sir. My fellow delegates. I am deeply disturbed by what we have been witnessing here these past few days. By the spectacle we are making of ourselves. The spit and vinegar, the vehemence, the antipathy. I say, I am deeply disturbed!"

"Why don't you go home then, old man," Rahima Bernstein shouted angrily.

"Order. Order."

"This is precisely what I am talking about," Matthias Gregory continued, "the disintegration of the dignity of this august assembly. We have become unworthy of ourselves. We have become a mockery of ourselves. We have become a raging, emotional, unthinking mob of animals. And why? Why is it? What has caused us to diminish ourselves so?

"It is precisely because of the piece of legislation before us. Legislation which is wholly unworthy of the attentions of this honored body. 'Quarantine of Genetically Primitive Persons' – what nonsense. This hate literature has no business here, among civilized and educated people. And I can assure you, that if it had not been pushed through strategically in the midnight hour, four days before the session was to end, I would have prevented this bill from ever reaching the floor in the first place."

The delegates booed and hissed, and cheered, and shouted at each other to sit down.

"Setting aside for a moment the fundamental question of human rights and dignity," Gregory continued, "let us consider the question rationally. Let us consider the realities of attempting to remove half the population of our planet and relocating them to a colony in a distant part of the Solar System.

"There is a pragmatic difficulty, right from the beginning. The expenses we are talking about are enormous. Even if the colony is already in place and freely available, as Phillipe Bloodworth dubiously claims, think of the pragmatics of the problem. To transport five billion people across the Solar System? The expense would be astronomical. There would be rioting, there would be armed rebellion among large groups of our natural citizens, and make no mistake, plenty of so-called superior men and women would join them. There would be massive collateral damage associated with such an endeavor. And that is the best case scenario. In the worst case, it could result in the total destruction of our society.

"And why? Why do we do this to ourselves? What is the purpose? These natural born men and women do no harm to our society. They work and are productive, just like the rest of us. We wouldn't know how to live without them. And no, I don't get angry when I have a waitress who is natural born and she mistakes my order, any more than when I have an accountant with exceptional genetics whose mistakes cost me two or three million credits! And that has happened to me more than once. Everyone makes mistakes, my friends. We are not immune. The criticisms that I hear of our natural born citizens are mere stuff and nonsense. It is like the smart older brother trying to throw the slower, younger brother out of the family. Because he might be slower, that doesn't make him worthless. There are many genetically enhanced citizens among us who are smarter than many other genetically enhanced citizens among us, but that doesn't mean that we throw some of them under a bus, or lock them away in a closet and claim that they are unworthy to share our oxygen. The idea is preposterous, it is a product of the basest human emotions, emotions that should have been stamped out centuries ago. But, we are all human, we are all weak, no matter how much we tinker with our DNA, the fact remains. We cannot overcome ourselves."

"Speak for yourself," another delegate shouted.

"Let us remember, my friends, that we are, all of us, every last one of us, we are all descended from natural born men and women. We are all the product of natural born men and women. They are our ancestors, we are their descendants, their children, and in hating them we are only hating ourselves."

"We're all the descendants of apes, but that doesn't mean we should marry them to our daughters!" someone shouted, and the amphitheater erupted into chaos.

LATER THAT DAY, WHILE THE debate continued, Phillipe Bloodworth appeared as a guest on Earth's most popular news program. He stared into the camera gently, selling himself, ingratiating himself and his words into the hearts and minds of the viewing public. He was remarkably, silky smooth.

"Look," Bloodworth said, "I've got fifteen good friends who are natural born, and all of them are tired of the tension and just want themselves and their own people to have a place of their own. They say, 'Let us live in peace, and let them live in peace.' There is just no need for all this consternation.

"Now, way out there, orbiting Uranus, in one of the nicest, most peaceful corners of the Solar System, is Oberon, that's the second largest moon around Uranus, it's about one eighth the size of earth, and it's a moon that I happen to own. We've been doing mining there for the past two centuries, but I had a better project in mind for Oberon. For the past fifty years, starting when I was just a young man, we have been terraforming that little planet, and it's just a pristine, beautiful place to live. You wouldn't believe it. Here, look at the pictures. Just look at them. And anyone can look this up. Space travelers flying by have been begging to know how they can get there, how they can visit, but that's not what it's for. I've been building it up for the greatest humanitarian project, the greatest humanitarian gift in human history. A whole, beautiful planet. A whole place for the natural born to move to and call home.

"You just can't ask for better than that, you can't even dream of it. Hell, I'm getting thousands of calls and messages a day from genetically superior people all over the galaxy who want to settle on Oberon. People are begging me to settle on Oberon. But I've set it aside for our natural born citizens, to be a home planet of their own, and I really mean that, I'm giving it away, this is part of the legislation, the natural born citizens will own Oberon and be completely free—"

A woman's hand waved to change the channel on the wall-panel holo-screen in front of her. The screen flickered and changed back to live coverage of the debates.

"He's so horrible, Simon," she said with disgust.

"He is an important business partner, Mistress," Simon Okunle said, getting up from a terminal that was set into the carved mahogany table in front of him. He bowed politely and walked out of the room.

"I wish he wasn't."

The Rothschild heir sat with her back to the terminal table, in an ancient, high backed chair that was covered in royal emblems and insignia. Her arm pointed out lazily from the side of the chair, revealing long white fingers that escaped a sleeve of exquisitely draped, gold-bonded, silk fabric. The room was a large den, or study, and its floor was covered in a soft, thick carpet of vicuña wool. Vicuña wool was supposed not to exist anymore. Priceless art work decorated the wall, paintings of Van Gogh, Rembrandt, Da Vinci, Majiz. The walls were gilt gold and intricately embroidered. Several servants and aides waited at the peripheries of the room, permanently at the Rothschild heir's disposal.

"Here is your tea, mum," a young woman said affectionately, and passed her a fine china cup and tray.

"Thank you, dear."

"Oh, mum, don't call me 'dear', you embarrass me," the woman said, blushing.

"No, you're my friend, Cylla. Don't be that way."

The young maid smiled brightly and set the tea tray down on a beautiful, polished walnut table. Everyone in the room was relaxed and comfortable. They adored the Rothschild heir, loved her. They had grown up with her, or they had watched her grow up. They had been treasured family friends. Mentors and confidants. The children of her mother's servants. They worshipped her.

On the holo-screen, a short, metallic skinned man was filibustering the Assembly. He read from the ancient Bible, page after page.

"Why do you boast in evil, O mighty man? The goodness of God endures continually. Your tongue devises destruction, like a sharp razor, working deceitfully. You love evil more than good, lying rather than speaking righteousness. You love all devouring words, you deceitful tongue. God shall likewise destroy you forever; He shall take you away, and pluck you out of your dwelling place, and uproot you from the land of the living."

"You speak of the god?" a man shouted incredulously, "Sit down and stop embarrassing yourself!"

"The righteous also shall see and fear," the speaking delegate continued, refusing to yield the floor, "and shall laugh at him, saying, 'Here is the man who did not make God his strength, but trusted in the abundance of his riches, and strengthened himself in his wickedness.' But I am like a green olive tree in the house of God; I trust in the mercy of God forever and ever. I will praise You forever, because You have done it; and in the presence of Your saints I will wait on Your name, for it is good."

The Rothschild heir sipped her tea, and pulled nervously at her beautiful, shining, black hair.

"I'm so proud of Arthur," she said, "he is fighting so hard for us."

"Mistress," Simon said, returning, "if a vote is allowed, it seems a strong possibility that the measure will pass."

C H A P T E R 18

SAMSON CLOSED AND SEALED A circuit panel on his racer and ducked out from between the wings framework and the ship's hull. He began cleaning out a dirty evacuator housing, but paused distractedly as commentators on the radio announced that another speaker was taking the floor at the Assembly. Kenichi was on a ladder, making internal modifications to the thrusters' valve architecture with a quantum cutter. Ben pushed Samson aside and tore away at the crusty build-up in the evacuator with a big metal spoon and scrub brush.

"Forget about it, Sammy," he said, "don't even think about it, focus on the race. We're not tied down to this shithole planet anyway."

"Yeah."

Samson walked back to the front of the ship and began checking the gas intakes around the cockpit canopy. He rested his hand on the bottom of the ceramo-metal glass dome, and spit on the floor. After a long pause, he went and turned off the old radio.

Late the next morning, when Samson stumbled out of his cabin and into the kitchen, Kenichi greeted him with an excited smile.

"'Morning Ken."

"Samson, did you hear the–"

"Stop."

"What?"

"Is it about the Assembly?"

"Yes, there was a phil–"

"Stop!" Samson interrupted loudly. "I don't want to hear about it. I'm not thinking about it until after the race."

"Oh, of course," Kenichi said meekly, "please forgive me, I didn't mean to be distracting you in any way."

"No, don't apologize. It's not a problem, I'm just telling you. Let's all forget about it until after the race, that's all."

"Certainly. That's the best idea," Kenichi agreed.

Samson sighed and mixed together a bowl of fruit, oats, nuts, and milk.

"Ah, real food," he said.

Kenichi was rinsing dishes in the sink and putting them back in the ship's little metal cabinets.

"Did you know that people used to drink cow's milk? Milk from a cow, like a cow you get beef meat from, that used to be the standard form of milk that everyone drank."

"That's disgusting," Samson mumbled, chewing furiously.

"It's weird, isn't it? But human breast milk used to be produced much differently than it is today. It wasn't really produced at all, just some of the women would feed their babies at the teat. Like this, you know," he said, holding an imaginary infant to his breast. "And so they would basically produce just enough milk for their one infant, and no more, so it was actually considered very taboo for any adult to eat human breast milk, it had a kind of sexual aspect to it."

"Weird," Samson said, staring at the milk in his cereal and slurping up a spoonful of it.

"Yes, in a weird way that is actually how the milk industry that we have today developed. Back when genetic engineering started to become really useful and more common, there was a group of sort of, like, they would have been considered sort of sexual deviants I guess, there was this group of people in ancient Japan and they had this fetish about hyper-lactating women. And so when the genetic engineering technology started to get really good, there were a few of these guys who were quite wealthy, and they had these women born with hyper-lactational breasts. And these women had all this breast milk, and it was a classic case of the old American saying to 'make lemons out of lemonade', no, I'm sorry, that's not what the saying was. But, anyway, these poor women who had been given these breasts that would produce like, a gallon of milk a day, per teat, just started selling it, and it created a market. You know, milk is the most healthy food that human beings can possibly eat, even still today with all of our sciences and synthetic nutrition. It's another example of how we're all really just idiots bumbling around blindly like ants in this big universe. So then this huge industry eventually developed, but you know the cow's milk industry was a huge thing back then and there was–"

"Ken," Samson said, stopping him. He had been staring at Kenichi for a while, waiting for him to pause for breath.

"What?"

"Let's focus on the race, man."

"Oh, yes of course. I apologize."

THE "EARTH-MOON SOLO GRAND PRIX" began at midnight in the outback of Australia. The race was always held on a clear night during a full moon, and occasionally in the past weather conditions had caused a delay in the race until the next moon cycle. This night, the moon shone so brightly that they could see its silver rays pierce down through the floodlights that illuminated the racing concrete. Thousands of satellites spun past in the sky above Earth, as if all the heavens were in motion.

Samson slid his fingers into his chest pocket and ran them over the beads and cross that he always carried when he was racing. He tried to say the rosary.

"Our Father in heaven, who art, Hail Mary, mother of Jesus, and the Christ, and forgive us our sins in heaven, and..."

He sighed, and squeezed the cross tightly, until its corners pressed into his skin. He resealed the pocket and flexed the control wands in front of him, back and forth, methodically, creating tiny, intricate patterns in the air. He switched on the engines and prepared for take-off. The racer rumbled behind him.

Lisa Maui had signed him into the race. He was surprised to see her. He had almost forgotten about her, everything had been so crazy. She was a cute girl, there was something endearing about her. Something that made you want her to like you, not like with a charismatic person, but more like the way you want a family member to like you, only she wasn't a family member. He liked her eyes, they were crisp, and her irises were like thin, beautiful haloes that radiated from the edges of expanded pupils. He wondered if her eyes had been made to be that way, or if that was just the way they happened to be. The color, of course, would have been made. They always chose the color. Lisa's eyes had a color shifting quality.

Samson shook his head, surprised at how distracted he was. He thought she must be prettier than he had realized. But they were all pretty, all these manufactured girls. All these excellent girls, genetically modified women. They were all beautiful, that had been the strangest thing to him. It had been the most difficult thing to adjust to.

He pulled his mind back to the race. The passages through the moon would be dangerous. Pilots died in this race every year. He wanted to avoid the other racers as much as possible, to not take any risks. His ship's speed would be enough to win if he could make good time through the moon. It wouldn't matter which path he took. Kenichi was confident about his modifications. They were only small changes, tiny adjustments. Samson and Ben had watched Kenichi closely. The changes couldn't have done much harm, in the worst case.

He flexed the control wands again, and the racer shifted back and forth on its landing. He visualized the start of the race, avoiding the main pack, passing them on the straightaway, the passages through the moon. This was his first open class race. He visualized the loop back, the jockeying at the finish. If Kenichi was right then his racer would be the fastest one on the straightaways. He visualized victory.

The starting flare shot up into the sky, and Samson watched without blinking. It splashed apart high above the concrete plateau, in an enormous red cloud. He held the control wands tensely. An explosion echoed across the Australian desert and the red changed instantly to green. Samson shot horizontally over the concrete, cutting the air across the horizon. Most of the racers rose vertically. He gained speed and pulled into a sharp, accelerating loop that took him up to the front of the racing pack alongside the fastest ships. Another racer spun at him and Samson weaved out of the way naturally, as if there were invisible waves that were carrying his ship, that were carrying all the ships, and he had gotten in front of a wave and it was pushing him.

He accelerated towards the moon and the other racers punched in their boosters to keep up. Few of them noticed that he hadn't used his boosters. The ship was fast. In a cigarette racer, with the cockpit on the very front of it, with the pilot floating out in a bubble of glass and seeing everything around him, the ride was like being strapped onto the tip of a rocket. It was exhilarating A few of the ships passed Samson with their boosters, but he stayed close behind them, conserving his own for emergencies, or for the final straightaway.

The surface of the moon came into view in front of them, cratered and corrugated, lined with tracks from the lunar mining trucks. The little planet had been practically destroyed long before technology for terraforming was developed. The mining and research colonies here were meagre, miserable, enclosed in small glass domes. The moon had been stripped bare, its earth-facing surface protected by statute, but its dark half eviscerated viciously. The mining tunnels had sunk into the surface and never stopped, not until they ran through to the other side, until it was a hollow shell. Like some ungodly anthill had been plucked from the outer universe and set down here in space, networks and tunnels running everywhere, from one end to the other, from every end to the other, and in the center, where so many tunnels met, were incredible caverns that had been hollowed through the centuries. The "deep sink", the central cavern within the core of the moon, was more than 50 miles wide. It hadn't quite hit the center of the core, it was set off to the side a matter of degrees. As with everything else about the moon, it had been done imprecisely and rapaciously, as soon as it was barely possible to do.

The racers circled around to the moon's pole, like hornets raiding an enemy nest, and rushed into the planet through the old mining shafts. The mining shaft entrances were brightly lit, but after that it became dark. The pilots switched on lights, or flew by wire using their sensors, and tried to avoid the rocky ceilings and walls, and the natural pillars that ran through the caverns. If a pilot turned down a wrong tunnel and hit a dead end there was a good chance he would explode against the rocky wall before he could realize what was happening. Each pilot had a plan of which tunnels and shafts he would take, but there were so many of them, millions of tunnels, and it was easy to become lost or turned around, to fly down a wrong tunnel, or to follow a pack of racers down one without thinking. Most of the tunnels led in the same general direction and would eventually take you to the other side of the moon, but some of them did not. One year, ten racers had followed the race leader into a dead end and every one of them had died, ships completely destroyed. The explosions had shaken the whole moon. A navigational computer could solve the problem for them, but pilots were not allowed to have one on their ships.

Samson rolled past a rocky pillar and dropped into a narrow tunnel. He plunged through the maze without regard to his own safety, like a kamikaze pilot in the ancient war. He watched his clock. He believed he was still on his chosen course, but in the dark of the mining caves it was difficult to be sure. He could judge his progress by the time. How long it took him to reach the deep sink, how long it took him to reach the other side, how long between caverns, this would give him a gauge to judge his progress, and if he had taken a good course.

The walls of the tunnel disappeared and he burst into the inky blackness of the big sink. He could recognize it from his sensor read-outs, from the size. A few mining trucks still crawled along the cavern walls, emitting pinpricks of light from the distance, like stars in space. Samson swung left around an enormous stalactite, noticing it just in time. He pulled up higher into the cavern. Other racers darted around the cavern like fireflies, or, with more purpose, like photons streaming through a hyper-gravity tube.

Most of them were behind him.

"Slow down, kid, you're getting ahead of yourself," Martins' voice came through on the ship-to-ship com.

"Who let you into open class again, old man?" Samson said.

"The same people who let you in."

The far wall of the big sink came crashing towards him on the sensor screen. As Samson got close to it the tunnels became little bumps on the line. He aimed for one in the middle, hoping to hit the biggest tunnel, which would take him straight through to the other surface. The tunnel he went into curved wildly, and Samson could barely keep the racer off its walls. It twisted like a snake, dropped, and rose. He flew on instinct, on situational awareness, raw, seeing nothing but the dusty grey, stoney walls flashing past. He accelerated. He had to make hard time to keep up with whichever racers had hit the main tunnel. A rocky outcrop tore one of his lights off, and the racer teetered wildly as it plunged into another large cavern. Samson held steady and the ship flattened out. He knew where he was. It was a straight shot to the other side now. Ten minutes. 10,000 km/hr. He accelerated. 20,000 km/hr. He screamed past a more cautious racer in the tunnel. Five minutes.

The long, white, cigarette racer exploded out of the moon and into the light, like a missile emerging from its tube. Samson pulled into a tight arc back towards Earth, and opened his throttle completely, until the ship seemed to compress him. It seemed to explode through him, to accelerate forever. He shifted his eyes with difficulty and scanned his panels. Three racers in front of him. He could see two. The third was dark, a dark grey ship. He couldn't see it. He continued to accelerate. He was gaining.

He punched up his boosters, he had saved all of them. The racer lurched forward precipitously. The relativity effect began to overtake him. Space seemed to bend, to warp, the passage of time took on a different character. It was indescribable, like a dream that you can't remember. He tried to increase the cockpit's kinetic and gravity shielding. The GCU was already maxed, it was hissing. The whole ship started ringing with an absurd resonance. It seemed to shatter his mind, to burst open his skull, as if his whole body would explode in a gush of liquid onto the cockpit glass. The other racers were falling behind him, he could see the grey racer now. It was falling behind. He was nearing the Earth's atmosphere, he had to slow down.

Samson eased off the throttle and punched up his reverse thrusters. It seemed as though he had three hands. His mind was numb, fuzzy. He needed to slow down. The Earth atmosphere flamed around him magnificently. He should have been hot. He couldn't feel the heat. Thermal shielding. He couldn't finish a thought. Friction. Friction. The button. He was in space, floating, bombarded by a low wave, a whooshing, as if he were trapped in some enormous speaker, some enormous low speaker, some giant, 2 Hz speaker that moved ten million cubic meters of air. His muscle memory took over, and he landed the ship in a daze.

C H A P T E R ¹⁹

Ben and Kenichi supported Samson between them, and half carried him across the concrete. The sun was rising on the horizon and touched their shoulders. They were all in costume, acting out their parts in the production. Two mechanics in greasy singlets carrying a pilot in his racing suit away from his ship. Samson's black racing suit with a red 'V' on its back was appropriately dramatic. Spectators cheered several hundred yards away. The dark grey ship had gotten second place, and drifted slowly to the ground to land. An orange suited medical team drove up in a little, flashing car and jumped out.

"What a race, folks!" the race announcer's voice echoed across the concrete and desert. "What a race! I'm not sure I've ever seen anyone fly that fast. I don't know how he survived it. I think he could barely land. Can you believe it? His first open class race, too. Samson Ford, what a pilot!"

"Is he ok?" the lead medic asked. "What's wrong?"

"I'm ok," Samson said weakly. "It's just a bit of relativity effect."

"Why don't you let them take a look at you, Sammy," Ben said.

"No. I'm ok," Samson repeated, pushing the medics away and taking his hands off of Ben and Kenichi.

"Ok, calm down," the chief medic said. "Just let us know if it starts to get worse. And congratulations!"

His legs were wobbly. He focused on standing up and waited for the medical team to drive away. They watched him apprehensively, and he tried to smile and wave, but couldn't. He was so nauseous. The medical car finally pulled away to check on another racer who had just landed. Samson sank down onto his butt as Ben and Kenichi reacted too slowly to catch him. He rolled onto his back on the concrete, smiling, with his arms stretched out wide as if he could lay there forever.

"We won it," he said. "Did we really win it?"

"We won it."

"I'm not surprised you're feeling sick, Samson," Kenichi said, "you were moving quite fast up there. You set a new record for this course, in fact. Is this the first time you have experienced relativity sickness?"

"Yeah," Samson croaked, blinking up at him.

"I wish I could experience it," Kenichi said wistfully. "Very few men ever have. Less than 100, in fact. Who have lived through it, I mean. You pushed it too hard, that was very dangerous. You're lucky the racer didn't lose integrity."

Samson sighed and tried to push himself up. He rolled onto his side and vomited. Ben slapped him on the back and pulled him to his feet.

"Come on, kid, you have a date with the winner's podium."

He had run into Lisa after the race. Their hands touched as she was handing him the pen for the forms tablet. He liked the feel of their hands touching, it felt comfortable, it felt surprisingly relaxed. Samson had wondered, casually, what she was doing that evening, and they ended up planning a date. He slapped aftershave onto his face, and flexed his muscles in the mirror. He was surprised how nervous he felt. He was glad that most of the racers were leaving their ships in the race hangars and he didn't have to go clean up until tomorrow.

"You're looking good," he said to himself, and flexed again. "You're the race winner, the champion. You got a lot of money in your pocket. You got a cute girl to go out with tonight. Haven't seen any gangsters. Your life is pretty good."

He smiled and turned his head back and forth, irritated

with the slight crookedness of his teeth.

"Perfect teeth aren't so great," he said, dropping the towel off his waist and appraising his full masculine glory. "Women like something a bit different. Something with a bit of character. She knows where you come from, she knows you were born to a woman. That's not bothering her. Maybe she even likes it. Something a bit different, something a bit special. I can be special."

He walked out into the hotel room and chuckled at himself. He'd rented a nice room. Nothing too expensive, but quality. A large hotel, with good security. He'd used a false name at the front desk. He pulled on his cotton underwear, and did some shadow boxing in the big room, and wondered at the relativity effect. It was so strange, it was almost like he couldn't remember it. As if the indescribability of the experience had prevented it from sticking firmly in his brain. He thought about Lisa. She was just an intern. She was kind of young. She might be too young for him. He thought about how young was too young, and hoped she wasn't.

He was sorry that Killian Gideon had missed the race. Killian was supposed to be there. Lisa hadn't said anything to Samson about Killian, but he was disappointed not to get to race against the racing circuit's premiere pilot. He had beaten Killian's record on the Earth-Moon Grand Prix. He had beaten it by three seconds. It was a record that was not expected to be beaten for the foreseeable future. Maybe that's why he didn't come. Killian had raced a perfect race to set that record, it was a famous race. He hadn't had any reason to run that race again.

Samson slid his card into the hotel terminal. 6,000 new messages. He had been getting 500 a day since the write-up which named him as a "pilot to watch" and outed him as a natural. Now 6,000 in the past twelve hours. He didn't want to think about it, and pulled his card out without checking them.

Samson and Lisa met at "Wonder World", a local amusement park. He found her in front of the gates. Waiting for him, sitting on a bench. He was wearing denim jeans and a black synthetic shirt with padded leather elbows. She wore a ribbed yellow t-shirt, and summer shorts that showed off her legs. She was made-up nicely, like the date was important to her. Not too much make-up, but as if time had been spent on it. Her eyes took him in brightly, but she looked down, as if uncomfortable. Samson kissed her on the cheek.

"I think I dressed too warmly," he said, smiling, and Lisa agreed.

The Australian air was hot and dry. The sun was only beginning to set, and the air on the horizon shimmered around the big park. Behind the fence were incredible machines. Powered roller coasters that skated on magnetic rails at 300 km/hr, and plunged riders deep underwater in a bubble of air. Gravity spring platforms that bounced ten thousand feet to the sky and floated slowly back down. An enormous, blue ferris wheel where every car was softly padded and equipped with zero gravity. The biggest attraction of all was a massive, gravity shielded dance hall. A giant neon man and woman, at least a dozen meters tall, floated end over end above the hall invitingly.

As soon as they met, Lisa wanted to apologize for the vote at the assembly, on behalf of Earth. She told Samson that the filibuster was still going, which surprised him, and that she was sure it wouldn't pass. It was the last subject he wanted to get caught up in on their date. He challenged Lisa to a race to the dancing pavilion.

"A race? Are you serious?"

"Of course, you have shorts on," he winked at her. "You look great in them, too, by the way."

"Thanks. I don't think a race – go!" Lisa squealed a high pitched, girlish squeal, and took off running ahead of him.

Samson was an expert at maneuvering in zero-G. The dance hall was a natural environment for him. He spun through the air frenetically, matching the pounding rhythms; he drew everyone's attention. For Lisa the zero-G was more novel. She moved awkwardly, tensely. The more he showed off, the more tense and awkward she became. Samson slid affectionately through the air around her, trying to help her relax, and they danced for a while. At the first convenient opportunity, Lisa dragged him back outside.

"You don't like the zero-G?" Samson wondered.

"No, it was nice. Just, let's do something different now."

"Ok," he agreed and put his arm around her as they walked through crowds of excited vacationers.

Lisa's shoulders were tense, she didn't relax into him. He rubbed her shoulder with his hand gently. She shrugged him away.

"What's wrong?"

"Nothing's wrong."

Her face was red.

"You're funny, Lisa."

"Let's go over here. Why am I funny?"

She led him towards a small, old fashioned building, with incandescent lightbulbs shining through its windows.

"I don't know, I don't mean in a bad way. You're just somehow different than most girls I've met before."

"Well, different is good right?"

"Of course. Where are you leading me to?"

"Let's go in here," Lisa said, opening the door. "This place is more my style."

It was an old fashioned soda fountain. Like the ones in the ancient movies. Lisa ran through the entrance and picked a red leather stool at the counter. She spun the stool in a circle, and stared at the menu on the wall with a big smile, deciding what she was going to have. Samson sat down beside her. There were only a few other people there besides the two of them. The man behind the counter, in a little white hat, seemed excited to have customers.

"The soda fountain, eh," Samson said.

"I know, isn't it great?"

Lisa grinned at him, and turned her stool back and forth until her knees bumped up against his leg, and looked away from him coyly.

"Why do I get the feeling you've been here before?"

"Oh, I haven't. It was on the map."

"Ah."

"What?" she said, laughing.

"Nothing."

She ordered a cherry and vanilla sundae. Samson looked at the menu on the wall. It was an old, white board with rails and black sliding letters on it.

"What's a 'rootbeer float', is that good?"

The man behind the counter nodded.

"Oh, that's the best. Wait, I want that," Lisa said. "No, wait, no cherry and vanilla sundae, I'll stick with that. Cherry and vanilla sundae."

"Give me the rootbeer float, then. Whatever that is."

The man behind the counter smiled at them and began mixing up the drinks.

"So, are you excited to tell me about yourself?" Samson said rakishly.

"Are you excited to tell me about yourself?" Lisa giggled.

"Most indubitably."

She giggled more and they stared into each other's eyes.

"Well, tell me," Lisa said.

"Ok. Hey, how old are you, anyway?"

"Nineteen."

"Nineteen?" he sounded surprised.

"Yeah."

She watched his reaction nervously, but also with amusement. The man at the counter set their drinks down, and Lisa took hers and sipped at the straw, eyes peering up at Samson at the same time.

"Nineteen. Well, I'm 27, are you sure I'm not too old for you?"

"It's ok," she said, and her eyes twinkled. "Hey, I have a question for you."

"Ok."

"How's your rootbeer float?"

She grinned mischievously, and Samson reached over and pulled her stool closer to his, and they watched each other's eyes, and each other's bodies, and their ice creams. They talked about racing, and Lisa talked on and on about ships, and her internship, and she seemed nervous and excited, and her face flushed, and she wouldn't look away from his eyes, but she wouldn't stop talking. Samson kept waiting for her to pause, for the moment he could swoop in and kiss her, she was so warm and attractive in the yellow light of the ancient style light bulbs, she was so bubbly and bright, he felt like he could just lean against her, just wrap his arms around her, and it would be the most natural thing in the world. She talked on and on about racing and her internship, she talked quickly, as if her mind were buzzing, as if she were focusing really hard on keeping talking.

Samson thought of Stephanie, how different she was from Lisa, and the thought irked him, and he tried to push her out of his head. Lisa paused in thought and he leaned forward to kiss her, and she looked frightened and ducked away, blushing fiercely.

STEPHANIE SHUFFLED THROUGH A TRAY of bolts in a dusty space hangar. She was wearing a worn out mechanic's suit and fiddling with an old racing frame that was unattached to any ship. A holo-screen on the wall behind her blared incessantly, giving endless updates of sports news. She cut and welded the frame distractedly, and pounded its bent iron rails into shape with a force hammer. The highlights of the Earth-Moon Grand Prix came on the television. Stephanie stopped her work and watched. She cringed at Samson's aggressive flying through the tunnels, and at the racers blowing up. Four of them had died. When Samson's racer hit its top speed and flew past the race leaders she gasped and applauded. At the end of the segment, Samson stood at the top of the podium, holding up the trophy and doused in champagne, with Ben and Kenichi on either side of him. Stephanie cheered them as if she were there, and smiled more happily than any of the three.

PHERICAL, BLUE, STEEL ROBOTS FLOATED through the night sky above a little island in the Earth's Pacific Ocean. They scanned the air and water meticulously, laser cannons and quantum burst missiles primed, ready to annihilate any threat or unwanted intruder. Any airship or submarine, or warhead, or tiny robotic fly. The little island below them disappeared beneath an enormous castle, engulfed by it. The castle was made of cubes. Great, black, obsidian cubes. Piled on top of each other, blending together. Tiny, obsidian cubes that could barely contain a room, cubes one hundred stories high that could contain a thousand. A harbor on the island ran up against the edge of the castle. An enormous ship hangar hung out over the land and into the water. Under the water, endless windows allowed the castle's inhabitants to relax and watch the living sea. Deep in the earth beneath the island, deep beneath the ocean's deepest floor, was a bunker, a perfect shelter that could shield its inhabitants from any natural disaster or conceivable act of war. Where they could live comfortably for fifty, even one hundred years. The rapid elevator down could bring them there in less than ten seconds. This great, cubic, obsidian castle was one of mankind's most impressive structures. One of the wonders of the world. It had never been photographed. It was unknown.

The master bedroom in the obsidian castle was larger in volume than most office buildings. It was a huge, cavernous room. Its ceiling was one-way mirrored glass, invisible from below, as if it were always open to the sky. As if the whole room were an enormous courtyard. It was the bedroom of a man who hated to be enclosed, who hated to be limited in any way. Who had always craved bigger, craved more, who had always striven for greater and grander, who had never been satisfied. Who wanted the space that he owned, even the space where he slept, to recede into the distance, to disappear on the horizon as far as the eye could see. For the space that he owned, that he possessed, for what was *his* to be limitless and neverending. The floor was covered in black tiles and ancient mosaics that had been taken piece by piece from archaeological sites all over Earth. In the center of the room was a huge bed, raised on a dais, with mirrors and cameras that floated in the air and could be lowered over it or made to disappear. Fifteen meters away was a bath area enclosed with beautiful screens. There was also an enormous, floating holo-screen that could be drawn to anywhere in the room with a motion. The room was punctuated by exquisite rugs, fine furniture, and rare curiosities, but mostly it was open space, wide open space, and never crowded. Small humanoid creatures cleaned and maintained the bedroom on a continuous basis. It was the bedroom of a man who was more than extravagant, more than ambitious – who was sick.

Phillipe Bloodworth paced his bedroom floor in an old, silk bath robe and pajamas. He mumbled to himself angrily as the wall sized holo-screen, ten or fifteen meters away, showed live footage of the filibustered assembly. Arthur Amati had grown exhausted and collapsed, but an allied delegate, Fei Han Amoretti, had risen from his chair with miraculous timing, and resumed the filibuster immediately. He had been speaking for hours. His lips moved voicelessly on the muted screen.

"Filibuster. Filibuster. Who told you to fuckin' filibuster? Fucking pricks!!! I'll have your children's godamned tongues removed. Filibuster me? Who's running you? Who's got your fucking ear? Who's got their hand down your fucking pants – fucks!"

He spit and hissed as he talked. One of the little creatures – like a man, but shorter and bent over, but with fur. Like a monkey, but like a man. With a tail. With half a beak instead of a normal mouth. One of the little creatures, that was sort of like a man, approached him nervously, carrying a tray of wine.

"...bought you off you shit for change sons of bitch. Who's your fucking master, I know you didn't do this on your own. Who's against me? Filibuster! You know what it cost to have this vote happen today? Necks I had to fuckin' tweak to get the bill voted on immediately, you fucking idiots. If not tomorrow morning it holds over 'til next session! Hundred and fifty years to get this vote – you – fuck – ing – scum!!!"

His fists were clenched and white.

"M-master," the little creature said nervously, holding up a gold tray. "Please have a drink, master. A drink will be good for master."

Bloodworth picked up the glass of wine angrily, then slammed his fist into the tray sending it flying from the creature's hand. The wine bottle shattered across the floor. The creature crouched and whimpered. He pounded on it with his fist and stamped on its toes with his heavy foot, and kicked it in the ribs. He slapped it across the face three times, hard.

"No, please master, please. I'm sorry. No. Oooh! Please," the creature begged pathetically.

Bloodworth splashed the glass of wine in his servant's face.

"What do you want me to do, throw you out in the street?!" he screamed into its tiny, pointed ear. "You want me to order you a ticket straight to Hong Kong, where monkey-man is the favorite dish?! You know what they do to crossbreeds out there, don't you??"

"No sir, no sir," the creature scampered away crying, bleeding.

"Simon Okunle could have stopped this," Bloodworth continued, fuming. "With Simon Okunle behind us too, it would have been a lock. But no, fucking Simon has to be high minded. Piece of shit! It's someone like Simon who's behind this, who's preventing me. It's some enemy. Some goddamn back stabbing meddler."

The live coverage on the holo-screen had cut to hourly news highlights, and Bloodworth motioned to switch on the volume.

"Amazingly, the instant Amati collapsed from physical exhaustion, fellow delegate and close political ally, Fei Han Amoretti, rose and was recognized to speak on the floor. He has maintained the filibuster for the past seven hours, and appears determined to continue until the Assembly automatically recesses tomorrow morning. Several delegates, in interviews outside the Assembly Hall, have expressed a desire to change the Assembly meeting rules at future sessions in order to prevent filibusters like this one from happening again.

"Also in the news today, the Earth-Moon Grand Prix was held last night, marking its fiftieth anniversary. That's right, there have been fifty Earth-Moon Grand Prixs, if you can believe it, since the race was first held sixty-three years ago. In the earliest years of the race, the Grand Prix was not held annually, hence the sixty three years. The race last night was won by a young pilot named Samson Ford, one of the brightest stars in the next generation of racing jockeys. And wouldn't you believe it, this same Samson Ford is a man who was naturally conceived, with no genetic enhancements at all. In fact, he is reputed to have been a child of the notorious Magdalena cult.

"How do you like that, Bob? Perhaps those naturals aren't so inferior after all."

Bloodworth's eyes nearly exploded from their sockets. "WHAT????"

CHAPTER 21

THE MORNING AFTER THE RACE, news reports were grim and alarming.

"The United Congressional Assembly went into official recess only a few hours ago, after an historic filibuster of the 'Quarantine of Genetically Primitive Persons Act'. Two delegates opposed to the act were successfully able to block a vote, including Arthur Amati who spoke for nearly three days before collapsing from exhaustion. The next Assembly will meet in six months and is sure to pick this legislation back up, with proponents swearing they will pass it within the year.

"And we are receiving alarming reports from all over Earth today that security forces are harassing naturally born citizens, perhaps even forcing them into quarantine camps in preparation for the implementation of the quarantine bill. These reports are still unconfirmed and we are not clear about the exact details, but we have received several convincing video recordings which seem to show natural born citizens being harassed or imprisoned this morning. We will be showing those videos during the next hour and will keep you updated as more information becomes available."

"OUR INFORMATION HAS IT LISTED that you are a naturally born person, is that correct?"

"What does that have to do with anything?" Samson asked.

"Please answer the question. Interference with the duties of Earth Security Agents is a violation of the law and punishable with a minimum five years jail term."

Two men stood in front of him in black suits and dark glasses. They were each wearing a conspicuous earpiece. A crowd of race organizers and hangar workers had formed a little circle around them, jeering the security agents, outraged.

"Yes, I'm naturally born, so what?"

"Please don't be belligerent, sir. Naturally born citizens on Earth are being re-settled in preparation for the implementation of Universal Law #9727F7. You are required to leave Earth or be escorted to the new settlement area for natural born persons."

An angry grumbling echoed from the crowd of mechanics, custodians, race organizers, and pilots that had gathered around the Junket. The two security agents were sweating and watched the crowd apprehensively.

"Don't you know who that is? That's Samson Ford!" a man shouted.

Lisa pushed her way through the crowd.

"Why don't you leave them alone you assholes!" she yelled, and ran up to Samson. "You can stay here as long as you want, Samson. I can't believe these guys. Who do they think they are?"

"Mr. Ford, you have to leave the planet now or we will escort you to the new settlement. There is no other option. Which is it going to be?"

"But that legislation hasn't even passed yet," Ben said in exasperation.

"We have our orders."

"Let's leave this place anyway," said a tall, thin, awkward looking man standing next to Samson. "We don't belong here."

An unmarked black car flew into the hangar and landed nearby. Four more black-suited security agents got out.

The Junket puttered through space on a course for Saturn. At least they had been able to retool and resupply before getting thrown off Earth, Ben thought. He still couldn't believe it. He sat on the bridge of his ship and watched the three other men on board as they discussed the legislation and events. An odd bunch. He watched Samson's brother in his old fashioned clothes. Natural born, alright. He wasn't like Samson at all, his face was misshapen and scarred from acne. His hair and eyes a dull brown, skin uncolored, pale and thin. He could never pass as anything but natural born.

"They're right, Samson," Theodore said, "we don't belong among them, and they don't belong among us. We might take issue with their methods, but on principle they are not wrong."

"That's so ridiculous, I can't believe you believe that," Samson said to his brother impatiently.

"You know I believe that, don't pretend it's a surprise. You should believe it too. If you pause to think about it, perhaps they have done you a favor. You have been running away from your life for so many years. This is an illustration of where you belong in life, where your home is. They threw you out, because you don't belong there. You, we, don't belong among their kind. We belong with our own, that is simply the nature of humanity."

"Don't start at me with that Magdalena bullshit, Theo. I don't believe in it, and we've been through it all before."

"Look, they threw you out of their planet! Did I throw you out of their planet? No. They threw you out of their planet, and that's the way it is. Don't reject the lessons that life throws right into your face."

"I never realized that the Magdalena Cult held these prejudices so strongly," Kenichi said. "If I am hearing correctly, is it true that a man who has had modifications to his DNA would not be allowed into the Magdalena settlements?"

"In the first place, sir," Theodore said hotly, "the Church of the Magdalena Revelation is not a cult. And you are correct, genetically modified people are not generally allowed within our settlement zones. We believe that naturally born men and women should separate themselves from the genetically modified aberrations that have begun to fill up the Solar System. It is important to have an uncorrupted, natural gene pool. The genetic modifications are a tragedy and will end in disaster. It is crucial to the survival of mankind, and proper in the eyes of God, that a natural, untampered-with strain of humanity continues to exist and multiply."

"Do you mean that even naturally born people who have ancestors that were genetically modified would not be allowed to enter the Magdalena settlements?"

"Of course. It doesn't have anything to do with how you were born, it is all to do with bloodlines and DNA. Being birthed by machines is unnatural and disgusting, but that is not the fundamental problem."

"That's fascinating," Kenichi said, "I have never heard these arguments before."

"Well, your media is controlled by corporations and their intention is to keep you uninformed," Theodore said patronizingly.

"Try not to be so rude, Theo," Samson said. "These are my friends."

"It is not my intention to give offense, and I do apologize if I have done," Theodore offered.

"What's the difference if a person's DNA is one way or another?" Ben said. "We're all human beings. We all have consciousness and free will, and that's all that matters. There's no need for all this divisiveness."

"What about the monkey men?" Theodore countered.

"That's different."

"It's not different at all, it speaks to the fundamental issue—"

"Monkey men were an abomination, they're illegal everywhere in the Solar System," Ben interrupted him. "They don't even exist anymore."

"They do exist! They're available on the black markets and

being bred in private. Not only monkey men, men of every conceivable variety. You must know that."

"It's rare," Ben said.

"They don't usually survive, of course," Theodore continued. "The experiments are quite horrible. But there are many thousands of them in the Solar System, perhaps many more than that. They say there is a whole colony of beast men on one of the mining outposts on Pluto, but I haven't been able to confirm that story for certain yet."

"Well, so what then? If they have consciousness and free will they're human beings too as far as I'm concerned."

"Oh, but do you want their DNA in the mix, do you want the beast to merge with the man? Do you want them marrying your daughters? Then it becomes a different story."

"It doesn't become a different story. As for their DNA, if it is mixable then it is close enough to human that I'm not bothered by it. If some women fall in love with a beast man and want to marry him, then more power to them. He's a human being with feelings and a soul, isn't he? He must be.

"Look, there are retarded people, even among the genetically engineered, and they are accepted as human beings, so why shouldn't these beast men be? Some of them are as smart as any of us, according to what I've read of history. One of them had a high IQ and got a PhD from Harvard University on Earth."

"He was gifted a PhD," Theodore said, "it was not one that he earned. They made a special exception for him, because it fit their social opinions at the time. If he had been a normal man, if you go back and look at his records, I assure you, if he had been a normal man he never would have been admitted into Harvard University, not that it was such a great school anyway, even back then the reputation far outweighed the reality with that infamous institution."

"That doesn't matter, the point is he was smart. And the

point is, even if they're dumb as rocks, if there are women who love them then more power to them. There are women who love retarded men, there are women who love men with all manner of genetic aberrations and deformities, these monkey men, by all accounts, were or are conscious creatures, creatures with intelligence and free will, creatures with feelings and empathy, like all the rest of us."

"They are beasts, Ben, it is amazing to me that you can try to logic your way around that."

"Don't be so arbitrary!"

"They were not created by God, and that is a fact which you can have no answer to."

"I don't know anything about God," Ben grumbled.

Theodore watched him silently with something like pity on his face.

"It's just sort of ironic, isn't it," Samson said, directing himself to no one in particular. "I mean, that natural born human beings would be rejected from Earth. Not from Mars, or from Venus, or one of the moons of Saturn, or any other place, but from Earth. When you think about human beings hundreds of years ago, developing these new sciences and technologies, trying to build a better future. And their children's children's children are disgusted by them, are disgusted by what they are, or were. Find them foreign and inferior. The descendants that they created want all the men like them to be thrown off of the planet.

"It's like Earth, the birthplace of civilization, the birthplace of life – the birthplace of humanity and all the rest of it. Earth is rejecting its natural born children. The children that created civilization, are being thrown out of civilization. The planet which should be their natural home is casting them aside. Isn't that strange?"

THAT NIGHT, ALONE IN HIS bunk, Samson slid his card into the terminal and checked his messages. He ignored the thousands of messages he had received from strangers. There was a hologram from Stephanie. She peered into the camera and smiled nervously.

"Hi Samson, I'm so sorry I had to leave abruptly like that. I've been so busy, and I wish I could have messaged you sooner. I saw your race and it scared me, you fly too aggressively, winning is not worth dying for. I would really be upset if something happened to you. But you flew beautifully. I'm sorry, I mean, congratulations!

"I'm so sorry to hear about this disgusting bigotry that is happening on Earth, I hope you've not been caught up in it. You should stay away from Earth until it blows over, and they don't deserve you there anyway if they are going to behave like this. I don't know how you must feel about it, but don't let it put any hate in your heart.

"Well, I have good news, I'm going to be working at the race on Titan, so I should see you there, right? I hope I will, and I want to see you race against Killian Gideon, someone needs to clip his wings and put him in his place. I can't think of anyone better than you to do it, and when you beat him it will really set an amazing example to prove the bigots on Earth wrong.

"Ok, I hope you're not mad at me. Take care."

Samson played the message over again and watched Stephanie's face, her body. Regretfully, longingly. His stomach turned over and his chest swelled up with warmth. He wondered what she was doing, and why she was so difficult to him, so secretive, why she pushed him away.

He had also gotten a note from Lisa.

Dear Samson, I hope you're ok. That was so ridiculous what happened when you guys had to leave. I'm so mad. If you need

She was as hard to understand as Stephanie, in different
ways. He wanted to see her again, but didn't want to hurt
her. He couldn't tell how well she liked him, he couldn't tell
what she was feeling. She was young, maybe she didn't know
herself. She had gone to a lot of trouble to meet him in the
first place, maybe that meant something.

The next message, he was surprised to discover, was a
hologram from Killian Gideon. Samson wondered where Killian had gotten his private address. The message came up and
Killian's purple eyes leered at him through the camera from
inside a beautiful living room. Killian was dressed in braided
black leather clothes and appeared ready to go out for a night
on the town.

"Hello Samson Ford,

"I wanted to congratulate you, that was an exceptional
race you flew in the Earth-Moon Grand Prix. You experienced
the relativity effect, didn't you? It's an indescribable feeling,
I'm sure you'll agree. Well, my hat is off to you, young man.
Beating my record was not a small accomplishment, I never
would have believed someone with primitive genetics would
be able to do it. You're an unusual pilot.

"You take a lot of risks. I hope you don't die before we
get a chance to meet. I want you to race against me. I want to
give you the opportunity to see how a real master pilot flies.
Maybe you can learn something, even though your capacity
for learning is relatively limited. Bye."

C H A P T E R 22

IT HAD TAKEN A CENTURY TO terraform Titan, Saturn's largest moon. Half again as large as the Earth's own moon, Titan had been a hostile mess of ice, volcanic activity, and heavy gases. It had been one of the few planetary bodies in the Solar System with a heavy atmosphere, ten times more dense than the natural atmosphere of Earth. Today it was a paradise. It was always Spring. An endless expanse of rolling green and lines of blue. Turf fields, not plains. Not long wild grasses. Genetically modified grass turf that grew to a height of exactly four inches and no higher. Just this turf covered most of the planet. Of course there were other plants – trees, flowers – made possible by the Earth-sized, mirrored sails that floated through the far reaches of Saturn's orbit and multiplied the big moon's exposure to solar radiation. But mostly it was turf. Rolling, rolling, endless fields of perfect green. It was like some lunatic's extravagant pastoral fantasy. A planet sized, undulating, grass lawn. The endless turf was punctuated and divided by clear waters, rivers mostly, some lakes, an occasional sea, perfectly clean. From their source, at least, perfectly clean. And, of course, there were cities. Beautiful, expensive cities where only the rich had ever lived. Without the faintest hint of smog, only clean air. It was from Titan that humanity rediscovered what cities looked like without smog. Visually. There were no roads, of course. Anti-gravity was already old technology by the time Titan was re-formed. There was never any need for roads.

The racing ships did not meet Titan's pollution control standards. But, every few years the people of Titan held their big regatta, and allowed the racing ships in, and threw their lavish, excessive party. And afterward the little planet sucked in its collective breath, and tightened its belt, and lived cleanly again for a year or three, until the next big extravaganza, or the next regatta, whichever came sooner.

Samson walked with Theodore through little alleyways, broad paths, and courtyards. The race this year was from Pollonia, the second largest city on Titan. It had a population of about ten million people, though only five percent of those were naturally born. Theodore cut an unusual figure in his brown plaid, moleskin clothes, long moustaches, and deerstalker hat. He was angular and awkward, his arms hung motionless at his sides when he walked. He could have passed for a scarecrow, and was taller than even most of the genetically modified men. There was little tension between the two populations here, and people smiled at Samson and Theodore politely as they passed. It would be a lovely place to live. Even Theodore thought so.

Samson managed to buy Theodore a direct ticket to Neo Vega at the shuttle station. The big city out on the edge of the Solar System. From there, he would be able to travel to the Magdalena territories easily. Theodore could have bought the ticket, he had a budget, but Samson insisted. He was flush with cash after winning the Earth-Moon Grand Prix.

"You don't belong out here, Samson," Theodore said regretfully.

"I know you think that, but I do."

"You know they're going to send me back for you again. You know what this looks like for me."

"I hope they send you looking for me again soon, Theo, it will be good to see you."

"I get paid to find and recover the lost sheep. Do you know how it looks for me when I can't even recover my own brother?"

"I'm sorry, Theo."

"It's bloody embarrassing! And every time I get home

without you, Mom and Dad look at your old pictures and cry. You know that, don't you?"

"Don't do that to me, Theo."

"Well let that image roll around in your head a little bit and think about it. We need you back there. There are a lot of pretty girls back home looking for a husband like you. Everyone misses you and wants to see you again. You don't know how it is, everyone remembers you and wonders why we're not good enough for you."

"Give me a hug, Theo," Samson said emotionlessly. "I'll see you when they send you out again, if I don't get back to visit sooner."

The two men embraced, and Samson clapped Theodore on the shoulder, and turned around and walked away.

"We need you at home, Samson," Theodore called after him, but Samson didn't look back.

As Samson walked away, Theodore glanced self-consciously at the other people nearby. A man in a coffee shop across the street was watching Samson intently. The man walked outside and followed the same path where Samson was walking, about a block behind him. He was a very tall man, with yellow hair. Even taller than Theodore. He was a huge man. He seemed like he was trying to act inconspicuous. Samson disappeared around a corner, and the man following him turned at the same corner and disappeared. The paths and alleyways were crowded. It occurred to Theodore that Samson wasn't watching his back because of him. Because he was getting away from him, from his brother. So his guard was down. Or that maybe it was.

He looked at his watch, and jogged down the street to make sure of what was happening. He turned the corner and saw Samson a few blocks down, and the man a block and a half behind him with an old fashioned paper newspaper, holding it up as if he were reading about something. Samson turned the corner and the tall man seemed to speed up, to walk quickly, until he got to the same corner and turned there himself. The man was huge, people moved out of his way nervously on the paths. Theodore chased after him.

The main racing hangar was several miles away from the shuttle station and Samson appeared to have decided to walk. He turned and twisted through the dense, vertical, peculiar city. The tall man followed him block by block, from a distance, trying to appear inconspicuous, trying to duck into a shop or doorway whenever Samson seemed like looking back.

Theodore ran up behind the tall man angrily.

"Excuse me, sir," he said, tapping the man on the shoulder.

"I'm busy," the man said with a brusque wave, and without looking back. "Leave me alone."

"What are you doing following my brother, sir?" Theodore said insistently, and poked his long index finger into the man's shoulder.

The big man spun around. His eyes were a shocking red, like the lenses that people wore for costume parties, but somehow more disturbing, more real.

"What? I'm not following anybody, what are you talking about?"

"You are following my brother, sir. Samson Ford. I've been watching you."

"You're crazy," Scamp said. "What are you bothering me for? Leave me alone."

He tried to walk away from Theodore, still in the direction where Samson had gone.

"Who are you, sir?" Theodore said in a loud voice that may as well have been a shout. "And why are you following my brother?"

Everyone nearby turned to stare.

"I told you, I'm not following anyone," Scamp said guilt-ily. "Now leave me alone if you know what's good for you."

"Tell your mother to leave you alone."

Scamp whirled angrily, and the other people on the path ran to get out of his way.

"What did you say to me?"

"Haven't you heard that expression, my good man? I said tell your mother to leave you alone."

People gasped. They were beginning to draw a crowd now. Samson was long gone.

"Listen to me, you little shit," Scamp said, stepping close to Theodore and raising a fist. "If you say something like that to me again *your* mother is going to have to fly out here and identify your corpse today."

Theodore stared into Scamp's eyes appraisingly.

"You poor bastard, you're not even all human are you?"

"WHAT?" Scamp's eyes bulged.

"I'm sorry, my friend, I didn't mean that as an insult. You have my sincere sympathy."

"Are you trying to be clever, mate?" Scamp said, beginning to shake with anger.

Two local police officers were pushing their way through the crowd of pedestrians.

"What did they mix you with, my friend?" Theodore said pointing his finger, voice rising to a shout, "Was it BA-BOON?!"

"You're a dead man," Scamp barked, with an inflection that had very little resemblance to the human voice.

He caught Theodore by the collar, lifted him into the air and threw him into the ground like a small child. Theodore landed on all fours and scrambled away, snatching his hat off of the ground as he did so.

"Here, stop, what's going on here," the officers shouted,

rushing in front of Scamp, who threw them both aside.

Theodore sprinted through the crowd.

"You're a baboon!" he yelled for good measure, holding his deerstalker hat onto his head and running away as fast as he could.

Scamp chased after Theodore, but both police officers shot the big man in the back with stun guns and he collapsed to the ground with a percussive "slap" of flesh on pavement.

BEN MET SAMSON TENSELY WHEN he finally got back to the hangar. After walking a few miles through Titan's tranquil, rolling grass, Samson had been feeling refreshed.

"Hey, I'm glad you're back. Did Theo get off ok?"

"Yeah, I guess. We got him on a direct shuttle out to Neo Vega."

"Good. Good. Walk over here with me for a minute, Sammy."

They walked out along the edge of the hangar, away from all the pilots and mechanics rushing about.

"Listen, there was someone here earlier," he said, "asking about you. Claimed to be a journalist. I have a bad feeling about it, something wasn't right."

"Lucho?"

Ben scanned the hangar warily.

"I don't think so. This guy was high class. Real smooth. A bit scary."

"Scary?"

"I don't know why, but he was. He kept asking about the Magdalenas."

"Samson? Ben?" Kenichi called from a distance, waving at them. He jogged over, looking grim. "Hey, you guys need to come see this. There's something– it's not good, come look."

He led them quickly back to the racer, which was in a tent

near the middle of the hangar floor. He had taken the gravity control unit out and it was sitting on a floating tray.

"Look at the GCU, notice anything strange?"

Samson ran his finger over the little blue cells of the GCU.

"Get to the point, Ken," Ben said impatiently, watching the hangar around them through the tent's open side.

"Look between the cells. Here, use this magnifier," he said, handing Samson a glass magnifying panel.

"Holy shit."

"See the cuts? It's been tampered with."

"What's wrong with it," Ben asked, walking over.

"I don't understand when someone could have done it," Kenichi said. "We've hardly left the racer alone, and there are always people around here, other pilots and mechanics, and the hangar's security staff as well."

"This is—"

"What the fuck—" Ben said, examining the tiny cells curiously. "It's cut exactly along the cell seams."

"It is cut," Kenichi said affirmatively, "there is no possibility that this happened on accident."

Samson's card buzzed and he took it out of his pocket. It was an unlisted account calling him.

"Hello," he said coldly, answering it.

"Samson?" It was Stephanie. "Samson, this is Stephanie. Is something wrong?"

"Stephanie! Oh, it's good to hear you, sorry," he said, stepping away to talk to her. "No, it's ok, well, things are kind of weird here, actually. My racer has apparently been sabotaged."

"Sabotaged? How could that happen, you guys haven't left it alone have you?"

"No, one of us has been watching it. Ken has been watching it a lot. It's strange. I mean, it's a weird job, too. You wouldn't believe this one."

"You should transfer over to my friend's hangar," Stephanie said. "It's a private hangar, it's just us here. It's not far away."

"Could we do that?"

"Of course."

"Could we do that right now?"

Stephanie laughed.

"Of course, as quickly as possible. I'm sending you the hangar coordinates as we speak."

"Stephanie, there is– I mean, there might be someone after us here," Samson said reluctantly, suddenly worrying about her.

"This will be a lot more secure than the main hangar over there at the racing stadium. Just get over here before anything else bad happens to you, I'm worried now."

"Yeah. No, don't worry, we're moving immediately then. Thank you Stephanie."

"I can't wait to see you," she said, and they hung up.

He walked back over to where Kenichi and Ben were talking about the GCU damage. Ben was still on edge, watching out across the hangar floor while they talked.

"..very sophisticated job. I don't even know how someone would make cuts like this. It's sheer luck that I even found it, this would have destroyed the GCU as soon as it was stressed above approximately three or four standard gravities."

"We're getting out of here," Samson said, resting his hands on the GCU.

"Yes, you can't race like this, Samson," Kenichi said. "It's not at all safe. It will take time to repair."

"I'm not pulling out of the race!" he said incredulously, as if Kenichi had lost his mind. "We're moving hangars. Stephanie is working at a private hangar nearby, it's her friend's hangar, she said we can move there."

"Good, let's move," Ben said, and began packing their gear immediately.

"You can repair it, though?" Samson asked.

"I can repair it," Kenichi said. "But can I repair it before the race? I don't know. Maybe not. Maybe."

"I knew you could. " Samson said positively. "You're the best."

"Maybe not, Samson!" Kenichi protested, but Samson was already installing the GCU unit back into his ship.

C H A P T E R 23

{AMSON TIGHTENED DOWN A COUPLING on his racer. He
didn't really need to do it, it didn't actually tighten any
farther. It was just for the sake of his nerves, and for good
measure. Three hundred or so racing ships, spread out on the
tarmac, stretched around him and merged in the distance with
the rolling grass fields. There were spectators in the distance,
too. Great stands of them. He could make out a banner with
his name on it, and cheering washed through the air as pleasant, energizing white noise.

"Everything's locked tight and double checked, Sammy,"
Kenichi said.

"It won't fail will it?"

"Samson," Kenichi repeated his name more formally. "You
should bow out of this race and wait for the next one."

"Ben wouldn't even come down," Samson said, half to
himself.

"Ben is right. Have you ever seen what happens to a pilot
when the GCU fails while he is torquing around a planet?
Because I have."

"Not pretty, eh?"

"It rips the bones out of your skin!"

"Don't worry, Ken, I trust you," Samson said incorrigibly.

"I'm telling you, it could fail at any time."

"Got it. We've been over this. I'm racing today. I have to.
Anyway, going out in a blaze of flames and glory on the back
of a detonating fusion cell isn't a bad way to die."

He climbed up into the cockpit and strapped in. He felt
against his chest pocket, tracing the outline of the cross and
beads. It always made him feel better, more confident, just to
touch the cross. He thought it was strange, because he didn't
actually believe in it. But it made him feel better, anyway.

Kenichi was on the ladder, double checking the cockpit locks and glass and hinges. He made sure Samson was secured properly in the harnesses.

"Hey, Ken."

"Yes?"

"Say a prayer for me, ok?"

"Say what?" Kenichi asked, as if he didn't understand.

"A prayer. Say a prayer for me on this one."

Kenichi laughed.

"A prayer?" he said. "I didn't even know that's how it was pronounced."

"That's how it's pronounced."

Racers across the tarmac began warming up their engines. The sound slowly crescendoed into a massive roar that seemed to shake the little planet. Samson brought his engines online and prepared to seal the cockpit.

"Hey, Ford!"

He cocked his head to the side, listening.

"Hey, Ford! Hey, kinderfuck!"

Samson's face turned red. He twisted in the harnesses to see over his shoulder and it was Killian, standing on top of his racer imperiously only a few ships away, shouting above the roar.

They made eye contact, and Killian sneered. He stuck his thumb out and dragged it across his neck in a throat cutting motion, then laughed mirthlessly. Samson tried to shout back, but the engine noise drowned him out. He began unstrapping his harnesses, but Kenichi pushed him back down into the seat.

"Ignore him, Sammy. He's not so great. Focus on your gravity stresses and not blowing the control unit. Let's survive this race today, ok?"

Samson pressed the wooden cross into his chest tightly, and Kenichi climbed down off of the ship and pushed the floating work platforms away.

"Hail Mary, Mother of–The Lord Jesus, he maketh me to lie in cool waters. I shall not want. Be thou our vision, O Lord, and lead us not unto temptation, for God created the heaven and the Earth, and He gave His begotten Son for whosoever shall believe in Him..."

STEPHANIE MADE THE FINAL CHECKS on her friend's racer while he warmed up his engines. It was a crescent shaped, blue racer with huge engines and an old fashioned, top mounted cockpit. It had no wings framework like the cigarette racers did. She looked across the racing tarmac at Samson's ship, fifty meters away, and watched him intently. He seemed to be talking to himself, or meditating, or both. She had been so busy, she had barely had a chance to talk to him since he switched hangars. Samson and Ben had been busy, too. She hadn't even heard what the sabotage that happened was. There would be time to talk after the race.

"Hi Stephanie!" Lisa shouted, walking past. She followed Stephanie's gaze over to Samson's ship. "Did you hear what they were saying?"

"No, what?"

"I think they said Samson's gravity unit could fail."

"You know Samson?"

"Yeah–"

"Wait, did you say the gravity unit?" Stephanie interrupted.

"Yeah. Is that bad? I really want him to beat Killian."

"The gravity *control* unit?"

"I think so. I have to run."

"If his gravity control unit fails he will *die*!" Stephanie shouted over the din, in a voice caught between anger and alarm.

"What!? No, I probably just heard it wrong. Samson said he can race anyway. I gotta deliver these papers. Good luck Stephanie!"

Stephanie waved as Lisa broke into a run to get out of the racing area. Her pilot looked down at her with irritation etched across his face. She stood with her brow knit and watched Samson's ship. His cockpit was already closed and sealed. Ben was nowhere to be seen. Finally she remembered her own pilot. He gave her a quizzical look, and Stephanie pulled her face into a smile and motioned him with two thumbs up. She pushed the work platforms away from the ship and walked quickly to get out of the take-off zone.

The race began and Killian rocketed into the lead, leaving most of the other racers trailing immediately. Samson accelerated more slowly. Very slowly. He was near the bottom of the swarm of racing ships disappearing up into the sky. Stephanie kept her eyes on his ship, maintaining an intense focus.

"Why is he going so slo– Oh no. He wouldn't."

CHAPTER 24

$\int$ AMSON CRUISED LOW OVER THE endless lawn, picking up speed, passing other racers. He gained slowly on the pack leaders. He had to be careful not to pull too many Gs against the planet's gravity. Green blurred away below him, and occasional lines or spots of blue flashed past. He passed more racers until most of the other pilots were behind him, but on the lead pack he gained slowly. They were almost all cigarette racers. Here, in atmosphere, the wings framework of the cigarette racers gave them an enormous advantage over other ship designs.

Lore Giesling, the mathematician who had discovered the wings framework, was considered one of history's great geniuses. It was the first perpetual motion device, and had revolutionized physics two hundred years before. Giesling had pioneered a new class of 'intelligent' algorithms to model fluid dynamics. He modeled wings, fans, funnels, jets and vortices, and spheres and footballs, and bits of string, spinning through a gas or liquid. His algorithms had grown and learned, until they were creating billions of new object designs each day – sometimes incredible new innovations, but mostly boring ones, broken ones, designs that were useless. Many trillions of useless and mundane results for every one that was slightly interesting. He developed other algorithms to comb through the endless random designs and find the interesting ones, the anomalies that promised something new. One day they had found it: 'WOW'. His computers had called it 'WOW'. He almost fell out of his chair.

WOW was a succession of thousands of wings and funnels, fans, thousands of surfaces, holes, bumps, ridges – it looked like a mess. WOW. It was a sort of wing that multiplied Bernoulli anomalies as it moved through the air, into a cascade of forces on top of and against each other; it put an order to the profound instabilities of the fluid flow, the unmanageable chaos of turbulence. The net effect was an object that wanted to accelerate as it moved through air, that was actually propelled forward by the fluid that it was moving past. It was an airplane that could fly forever. It would continue to accelerate with no added power until it hit its terminal velocity, at which it would cruise, steady, thrown forward by the atmosphere around it, rebounding back from that atmosphere and stopped from accelerating more.

Cigarette racers were racing ships built within a cylindrical wings framework. Their main advantage, as racers, was that they gained extra thrust from the bernoulli cascade when they were flying in atmosphere. Even in space, racing ships often had to fly through gaseous clouds, or obstacles that contained atmosphere. Cigarette racers dominated the open class racing circuits, although in some races, such as the Solar Regatta, the framework provided little real advantage and was added weight.

Samson was gradually closing the distance on the leading pack as the ships circumnavigated the surface of Titan to complete the race's first stage. The unique wings framework of his ship, a key innovation of Kenichi's design, made him faster than them. He could see them on the horizon, approaching the first of the race's famous hoops. High speed trains carried giant rings on a winding, cross-country course at 1,000 km/hr. Each pilot had to fly through all the rings, so depending on the pilot's approach and timing the course could be shorter or longer. Samson watched the lead pack slip through a little ring in the distance like a tiny, liquid line. He gauged the train's path and aimed for an intersection, still accelerating. The lead pack had reached the hoops early, before they could be navigated with maximum efficiency, and this would also help him catch up. He passed another ship that was trailing the lead pack.

"You're too slow, Martins," Samson said, opening up his com.

"Go to hell."

The first hoop grew bigger and bigger, but not quickly enough. An optical illusion from so much speed gave the effect of an impending crash, a feeling one never quite got used to. Samson smiled at the queasiness in his stomach. In fact, the hoops were 25 meters in diameter, large enough for even the largest racers to pass easily through. His own racer was five meters in diameter, and he slid through the inside edge of the ring gracefully, without altering his acceleration. A city in the distance buzzed with air traffic from the crowds of people that had come out to see the race in person. If he had not been moving so fast, Samson could have seen crowds picnicking and celebrating on the ground.

BY THE END OF THE first stage of the race, Samson was just behind the leading pack of racers. Killian was just in front of them. His ship was painted a bright pink and covered in exotic decals. Samson glanced at the few, forlorn decals on his own racer as the ships in front of him pulled to vertical and rocketed into space. His sponsors didn't even pay him, they just provided parts and service. He had thought that after his recent successes sponsorships would come pouring in, but for some reason they had not. *For some reason*', he italicized the words in his mind. He switched on his GCU to enter zero space and slowly ascended through the atmosphere of Titan, pulling a long loop and losing time. The GCU hummed, or something hummed, or not even a hum – a fuzzy, high pitched sound, like static from an ancient radio. He hoped it wasn't the GCU. He ran a systems check and everything seemed fine. The racer curled into space and Samson pulled vertical, drawing relatively few compensated-Gs as he exited the atmosphere.

He opened up his throttle and hoped the ship was fast enough to make time again on the lead pack, and hoped that Killian was showing off and holding them back.

As Samson cruised through space, the ship pressed hard against his back, just a few Gs. It was like being in the womb. He could cruise like this for days, just accelerating. He could sleep like this. He ran another scan on his GCU and worried about the problem. It wasn't the failure of the GCU, in general. That, by itself, would only mean the end of his race and a mildly uncomfortable trip back to Titan in a zero-G cockpit. The problem was *when* the GCU would fail: when it was most stressed. This was when nearly all GCU failures occurred. It would mean instant death. A GCU might easily be compensating 50 or 100 Gs during a gravity ascent. During a gravity slingshot it could be 1,000. If the unit suddenly failed, all of that force would instantly load onto the pilot and his ship. His body would burst, like a balloon in a vacuum, or have the bones ripped out of it and crushed against the windshield. The ship would have a good chance of coming apart, too.

GCU failures were a rare event, Samson had never seen the consequences of one up close, or even on a visual record. The units were solid state now, very robust. They might reach their limit and the pilot would start experiencing gravity effects beyond which the GCU could compensate, but it wouldn't just fail. They might lose power, but the power loss would be gradual, from wear over a period of time, not sudden. A sudden GCU failure was most pilots' worst nightmare. They feared it more now than the pilots did years before, when GCU failure had been a real problem. They were haunted by a demon that they knew of but were never confronted with, that they never had to encounter face to face. In their imaginations, it loomed large.

Samson was different, he was less afraid to die. The thought of being splashed around the cockpit didn't bother him at all, he just didn't want it to happen today. He wanted to win more races first. The leading pack was far in the distance, tiny specks on the windshield of his cockpit. He felt certain that he would die racing ships, he had no illusions about it. He just didn't want to die today. He increased his acceleration until it was uncomfortable. He had no delusion of invincibility.

The Titan Regatta's second stage was a straight flight to Saturn's third largest moon, Iapetus. Pilots then had to fly through a series of checkpoints in Iapetus' ice canyons before circumnavigating the surface and flying back to the finish line at Titan. Iapetus was a funny looking moon, half black and half white, like a rock that had been partially frosted – a giant, stony cupcake. It had virtually no atmosphere and had never been terraformed, but was crisscrossed with lonely mining roads and dotted with a handful of little mining colonies that glowed white and yellow, like tiny bubbles in the frosting or pustules on the planet's skin.

Samson finally caught up to the leading pack as they approached the surface of Iapetus. Killian had been playing chicken with anyone who tried to move into the lead, slowing the pack down. Many of the other top racers had apparently decided this slower pace, and bottling up of the pilots, would be to their advantage. Samson cruised in below, and passed them.

"Where have you been, Ford?" Killian said casually into the com, as he and the other racers opened their throttles to catch up.

Samson's racer sunk into a long, aggressive dive at the moon's surface, and the other racers followed instantly, like a flock of sparrows changing direction.

"Your ship's fast, Ford. Why did it take you so long to catch up?"

"He's a cocky little shit, isn't he," said a racer named Magnus, who often finished third or fourth behind Killian in the races.

Samson maintained his aggressive dive into the canyon. Long, icy walls hurtled at him furiously, the sharp turn ahead was invisible. He switched to reverse thrusters and his racer howled in protest and shook violently, giving him a mild concussion. The ship pulled angrily around the corner and Samson accelerated through the end of the U-turn that marked the first checkpoint in the race. Killian swung through the turn behind him, rebounding around it in a sort of rubber-band maneuver, rather than breaking and accelerating through it the way Samson had.

"You push your ship too hard, Ford," Killian said. "That's going to get you killed eventually."

Samson switched off his com and wove through the twisting canyon aggressively They were not allowed to rise above the canyon surface until clearing the last checkpoint, which was a rock tunnel at the bottom. Killian kept right behind him, but the other racers fell farther back, unwilling to navigate the tricky canyon channels at such speed.

"Any slip and you're dead, Ford," Killian said ominously into his com.

Killian hit his boosters and careened at Samson, who spun underneath him and hit his own boosters as well, barreling seamlessly into a dive for the tunnel that was the final checkpoint. Killian dove too, and they plunged through the tunnel almost on top of each other, with Samson just in front. He gassed his thrusters, spraying a vapor cloud behind him and forcing Killian to fly by sensor. They cleared the tunnel and Samson rose gradually, beginning the loop around the moon's surface. He checked his GCU status, it was running to spec, but hot. Killian climbed above Iapetus more acutely, building for a long descent that would give him a maximum gravity slingshot.

Samson switched his com back on.

"Hey why are you flying so high, Killian?" he asked grimly.

"What do you mean?"

He switched the com back off and Killian's flight seemed to lose a touch of confidence. Samson opened up his throttle and circled along the big moon's surface. Behind him he saw Magnus' bright orange ship rise and follow Killian's path. It was too late. Samson knew he wouldn't win. He had given up as soon as they exited the canyon. He wouldn't make the gravity slingshot at all, he wouldn't risk it. He would take a heavy loop around Iapetus and hope that his GCU held up, and not stress it enough to kill himself even if it failed. Killian and Magnus had fallen behind, but as they entered their dives for the gravity slingshot each of them caught up and easily passed him. He flexed his hands against the control wands bitterly.

"Learn how to fly, you cocky shit," Magnus said as his ship flashed past, but Samson's com was still off.

He finished the race in fifth.

AMSON CLIMBED OUT OF HIS cockpit slowly. He was drenched with sweat. The crowds in the stands applauded him, but mostly they cheered Killian, who was already approaching the winner's platform. Samson's legs shook and cramped as he climbed down the rungs.

"Ken, I need electrolyte water," he said loudly, over his shoulder, as he slid the last few feet down to the tarmac.

He let go of the ship and turned around. And was surprised to see Stephanie in front of him. He reached out his arms for her.

"Stephanie!"

"I can't believe you," she said, slapping her palms into his chest and sending him stumbling backwards.

He glanced into her eyes and looked down. She was really angry. He had never imagined her beautiful, huge, dark eyes could look like that. Even so, he almost couldn't help laughing at her imperious body language. He wanted to hug her more badly than ever.

"It's not only yourself that you could kill up there! I can't imagine how a grown human being could be so irresponsible," Stephanie continued, her voice rising. "You're lucky to be alive, if that even means anything to you. Even if you don't care whether you live or die, did you ever consider that other people do, did you even stop to think about anyone other than yourself or what the ramifications of your actions might be? This race means nothing! This isn't even an important race!! How can you be so reckless, flying around with a broken GCU. I thought at any moment you were going to be dead and we'd see your blood and guts all over the news and on the 'net for the next fifty years, telling what happened when a natural born man was actually allowed to fly in the top circuits he was so stupid he flew a race with a broken gravity control unit and got splattered inside his own cockpit!"

Kenichi tried to approach with the bottle of electrolyte water, and Stephanie glared accusation at him. His face turned grey. She grabbed the water bottle out of his hands and thrust it at Samson before continuing her tirade. Samson took the bottle from her gently, gratefully, and leaned back against the dusty, white framework of his ship.

"I heard Ben wouldn't even come to the race, but do you care about your friends at all? Hell no, why would you care about your friends? So what if he's going to sit back in that hangar watching the coverage of the race on pins and needles, sick to his stomach, for hours. Do you even think about anyone other than yourself—"

He lurched forward and put his tired arms around Stephanie, leaning on her. She stood stiffly in his embrace, and her voice broke a little bit, and she continued to berate him.

KILLIAN STEPPED ONTO A LITTLE elevator dais that lifted him to the trophy platform. Cindy was gone, but in her place was a tall, spectacular girl with huge breasts, pink skin, and an impossibly small waist. She tried to hold his hand, but Killian brushed hers away, and she stood behind him uncomfortably. Killian shook everyone on the platform's hands, and they all grinned, and the President of Titan put a huge, golden medal around his neck and handed him the giant trophy. He held up the trophy with both hands, and they all began spraying champagne, and Killian set down the trophy and picked up two bottles himself, de-corking them neatly with his thumbs, and sprayed them at the people on the platform. He turned around and finally lavished his attention on the pink skinned girl, making sure she got completely drenched. He put down the bottles, and everyone laughed, and he pulled the wet, pink skinned girl in front of him as if she were shielding him from the cameras. She grinned charmingly. He rubbed the phallic tip of the trophy between her legs and made a comical thumbs up gesture for the cameras, and the girl laughed, and the old men on the platform nudged each other with their elbows. And the audience cheered.

Scamp pricked up his ears over the roar of the people cheering from the stands. He tried to hear what Samson and the girl were saying to each other. He was dressed up like a mechanic, with a big grey hat on, sitting behind a fuel trolley watching them, about twenty yards away. Samson and Kenichi were both there, along with the girl. She was mad at Samson about something. Scamp wondered when he should confront them. He had already done most of his work. He couldn't really do anything to them here, in front of all these people. Just breathe down their necks a little bit and make them miserable, let them wonder what was going to happen next. Next week, next month. Maybe he could get away with one punch, maybe he could crack Samson Ford's face open. He hoped he could, he'd have to start a fight with him and get all hell to break loose, then he could crack Samson Ford's face open in the melee. Lucho didn't want Samson Ford hurt too badly yet. Scamp sighed, remembering how Samson had conned him and smashed him with the ship at the casino.

"Lisa Maui," Killian said loudly as he and his pink companion descended back to the tarmac floor, "you beautiful little girl. I thought you said Samson Ford could beat me."

Lisa tried to pretend she was too busy with her work to notice.

Killian slapped the pink skinned girl on the butt loudly, handed her the trophy, and told her to wait there for him. He walked across the tarmac as if it were his living room. Racers landed here and there around him, finally finishing the race.

STEPHANIE STOOD IN FRONT OF Samson, gesticulating. He sat limply on a stool at the mechanic's bench beside his racer.

"I can't let you go off flying alone again after seeing a display like that," she said. "I'm going to join up as part of your crew. You need me, I'm a good mechanic. I'm staying with you guys from now on, I'll bunk on the Junket and work as a mechanic for you for the rest of the season. And keep you from killing yourself."

He watched her, mystified. He didn't know what to say, and Stephanie took this for an assent. It was the only answer she was accepting.

"WELL HELLO, FORD—"

"Hi Samson, you son of a bitch—"

Killian and Scamp managed to confront Samson at exactly the same time.

"Don't interrupt me, you great ape," Killian snarled. "Walk away while I speak with Samson Ford, then you may return."

Samson and Kenichi stared at Scamp in shock. Stephanie looked back and forth between the various men, completely confused.

"You shut your mouth," Scamp said, turning to Killian angrily, "or I'll shut it for you."

"You fucking orangutan," Killian said, squaring up to Scamp even though the huge man towered over him.

"Kiss my ass, you ivory prick!!!"

"Good heavens, don't tell me that I was right and you really do possess orangutan DNA," Killian said nastily, smelling blood.

Scamp swung a devastating, bludgeon of a fist at Killian's

head and Killian ducked past it easily. The race security agents had taken notice and begun to move towards the commotion. Samson and Kenichi started packing as quickly as they could.

Scamp charged at Killian, and Killian circled around him. He aimed a beautiful kick at Scamp's temple, but Scamp caught his leg and threw him through the air. Killian landed on his feet, grinning, and clapped his hands. The cameras were on them now. The audience in the stands around the tarmac became hushed. Scamp charged again, in a fury.

KILLIAN DODGED SCAMP'S BLOWS AND lunges with astonishing reflex and coordination. He had expected Scamp to tire quickly, which wasn't happening. Titan police officers moved in to separate the two.

"Stand down, men," Killian told them, and the bewildered officers backed up.

Scamp aimed another blow at Killian's head, and Killian dodged it awkwardly, almost being hit. He leapt onto Scamp's back and tried to put him in a choke hold, but Scamp dropped precariously to the ground, like a fallen tree, and Killian spun away at the last instant before being crushed under the big man's weight. Scamp's red eyes flashed as he hopped athletically back to his feet.

Samson helped Kenichi and Stephanie stuff all their things into a rental van and then scrambled back into his racer. He watched the van speeding away. It stopped abruptly where Stephanie's pilot friend had just landed, she jumped out and helped him out of his ship, and kissed him on the cheek, and waved apologetically, and jumped back into the van. It sped away again, rising into the air cautiously to avoid any incoming pilots. Samson lifted off and followed it. On the ground, several police officers were finally trying to hold Scamp down. Scamp threw them off easily, and more approached. Two other officers weren't having it any easier pushing Killian away. Samson finally saw the humor in the situation and began to laugh. As he continued to ascend, the tiny figure of Scamp lunged at Killian again, while at least a dozen police officers tried to hold him back. There were camera crews and media everywhere, the president of Titan waved his arms from the perimeter of the melee, appearing for all the world like a tiny humming bird. The scene disappeared behind him and Samson laughed until he cried.

Ben sat by himself outside the Junket and watched the insanity on a small holo-screen. He noted Samson's abrupt departure from the racing stadium and wondered how much delay there was on the tv signal. They would be back soon. Probably Stephanie, too. At least a dozen police on the little tv finally piled onto Scamp and held him to the ground. Ben wondered what Scamp was trying to accomplish coming to the race. He felt against his pocket for the outline of the gun he now carried religiously, and looked over his shoulder, scanning the doors of the big, empty hangar. He wasn't angry with Samson for going through with the race, just happy that he was alive. Each race there were plenty of chances that Samson would die, this one wasn't so different in that regard. He'd just had to put his foot down, that was all. He just couldn't be a part of it this time.

The door on the other side of the hangar swung open, and he flinched. Stephanie stormed inside, and Kenichi followed behind her meekly, pushing their mechanics' toolsets on a large hovercart. Ben waved to Stephanie.

"Hiya Steph, so he didn't even die, eh?"

"I'm so mad. I could strangle that idiot," Stephanie said. Her legs carried her across the floor in long, even strides.

"All's well that ends well," Ben said.

He watched Stephanie curiously, wondering what her rush was about.

"I assume we're leaving right away," she said.

"What do you mean 'we'?"

"Are *you* leaving right away?" Stephanie repeated academically. "Because I'm coming with you, I'm joining the team."

"Samson told you to come with us?"

"It's no good arguing with her, Ben, she's a very determined woman."

Kenichi clenched his jaw and looked down as he finished the sentence.

"I told Samson," Stephanie said hotly, "that if he is going to be such an irresponsible child to go racing in a Grand Prix with a broken GCU, then I'm going to fly along with him from now on and be his nursemaid to make sure he doesn't manage to kill himself before he grows up."

Ben laughed. He reached out and hugged Stephanie warmly, and she hugged him back.

"Well hurry up and get your things. We could use another good mechanic, anyway. We can't pay you, you know. Not right now, anyway."

"I don't care."

"I know you don't. Well, gee, this is turning into one big happy family isn't it," Ben said, slapping Kenichi on the back. "You're right, we are going to be bugging out of here probably as soon as Sammy gets back, so put a rush on it. I'll make sure your bunk is cleared out and ready for you."

A buzzer rang through the hangar, warning them that a ship was waiting for the doors to open.

"Ken," Stephanie said, pointing to a terminal on the wall, "would you go let that idiot in."

Lisa laughed at the sight of police officers dragging Killian away from the commotion on the racing tarmac, but immediately regretted it. He looked directly at her from twenty yards away and made eye contact.

"Don't laugh so hard, kiddo," he called, eyes sparkling mischievously, "you make your pretty little breasts bob up and down."

Her face flushed, more from anger than embarrassment. She tried to say something back at him, but was too upset to think of a response. Killian relaxed completely and patted the two police officers on the back.

"Alright boys, I'm letting it go. Thanks for pulling me out of there. I'm taking my beautiful sex slave back and having a victory celebration now, but you boys are welcome to come party with us right now if you want."

The two officers let go of Killian and stuttered to find a response. Camera crews and media people, escaped from their cordons in the excitement, crowded around them like malfunctioning robots, some shouting questions aggressively.

"No, I know," Killian said quickly, in a booming voice, "you're responsible men with jobs to do here still. You boys on Titan are some of the finest police officers I've seen in the whole Solar System. Be sure to come say 'hi' to me at the next Titan Regatta, though, ok?"

He looked each officer in the eye quickly, but turned away before either could respond. The tall, gorgeous, pink-skinned girl was fussing over him, and he caught her around the hips and swung her over his shoulder, like a cave man carrying a wild woman back to his cave. She dragged the bottom of the trophy along the ground behind him, and Killian laughed. The President of Titan followed, sputtering, apologizing, hoping that Killian was ok.

"I've had a wonderful time on Titan, Mr. President," Killian said, turning and putting a friendly hand on the man's shoulder. "This is usually my favorite race of the year and I can't wait for the next one."

The pink skinned girl giggled and kicked her knees against Killian's broad chest. He ducked through the pilots' exit tunnel and ran with her down the hall.

SAMSON LIFTED STEPHANIE'S HEAVIEST BAG and started up the steps to the Junket's door.

"I'm really glad you're coming with us, Stephanie."

"Th-thank you," she said sheepishly.

The hangar intercom cracked on and a voice blared at them from the gate.

"Uh, Mr. Ford. Mr. Ford are you there? We have a guy out here who claims to be your brother. Kind of a tall, skinny guy. '*I am his brother you–*' Uh, he won't go away."

There was another crackle and the signal shut off. Samson looked up at the loudspeaker in the ceiling. He set his bag down on the step and squeezed past Stephanie.

"Sorry. I better go see about that."

Ben pushed his handgun into Samson's hand as Samson jogged past.

Outside, at the gates, Theodore was arguing furiously with two guards. He gestured at them with great sweeps of his arms, like a giant, mechanical scarecrow. When he turned to see Samson, his face beamed with affection and relief.

"Samson! Ah, at last I found you. Can you tell these two bullies that I really am your brother. You wouldn't believe how difficult it's been to track you down here."

THEODORE PESTERED SAMSON INSISTENTLY, AS he and the others rushed to load up the Junket for departure.

"Samson I have to tell you something."

"Are you going to fly with us?"

"Yes."

"Well can't it wait?" Samson wondered, pushing a cartload of tools up into the Junket's little hangar and strapping them against the wall.

"This is important," Theodore said urgently.

"Tell me what it is Theo!"

"In private," Theodore said, glancing at Kenichi and Stephanie.

"Fuck! Can't you see we're in a rush?"

"Why do you think I'm still on this planet?" Theodore asked pregnantly, and helped Samson secure the Junket's bay for takeoff. Samson rushed him into the Junket's main hallway, in the back of the bay, and closed the door behind them.

"Ok, what is it?"

"When you dropped me off at the station," Theodore said, in a hushed voice, "I noticed there was a man following you. So I followed him. And, to tell you the short version, you're being trailed by gangsters."

Samson's eyes got big as Theodore told him this. He chuckled and patted his brother on the shoulder.

KENICHI LIFTED OUT THE GRAVITY control unit with a grimace and held it up in the air above the racer. Stephanie and Ben coughed and plugged their noses. It was fried. Ben pulled the GCU out of Kenichi's hands and threw it down onto the hangar floor of the Junket with a crash.

"Jettison that," he said to Samson, who peered at the melted GCU curiously.

"It's not even good for parts now?" Samson wondered.

Kenichi stood up on top of the racer, his face black from the soot that escaped the GCU housing when he opened it.

"No, they're integrated units, Samson. There's nothing you can do with one that has been fried like that. They're somewhat toxic, too. It's the best idea to jettison it right now, definitely."

"I've never seen a fried one before," Stephanie said, grinning wryly. "That's not easy to do."

"It wasn't me!" Samson protested.

He lifted the GCU and dropped it into the garbage chute, then waited for the chute to seal and pressed a dirty green button to clear it. The GCU along with some random bolts and wires shot out into space and disappeared.

"No, that was a very sophisticated job," Kenichi said. "Someone powerful is out to get you Samson, and that isn't a joke at all. It's unlikely that even other race teams or betting mobs could have done a job like that; I've seen a lot of racing sabotage before, and this is another level of sophistication. This certainly wasn't the work of Lucho's mob."

"Maybe it was just a subtle manufacturing defect that we hadn't noticed before," Samson offered hopefully.

Ben and Stephanie both shook their heads.

"No," Kenichi said simply, and climbed down from the ship.

"Did we make enough money to buy a new one?" Samson wondered a few minutes later, sitting against the wall between the kitchen and the little dining area of the ship.

"Barely," Ben said. "We need to find some advertising sponsors."

"I can't believe you guys don't have more sponsors already," Stephanie said, sitting at the little dining table, finishing her food.

"We don't really have any," Samson said. "I mean, we could get some sponsors, but on the official circuits only blue chip sponsors are allowed. Trade guild members, major companies only. That's the problem, because they don't want to be associated with a natural born pilot."

"That's ridiculous."

"It puts us at a big disadvantage, because we've never had a strong financial backer behind us. It's just me and Ben."

"And me now," Kenichi said.

"And Ken now," Samson said, smiling.

Theodore walked barefoot into the kitchen, wearing some goofy old pajamas and a towel draped over his head. He poked around at the stove, lifting lids and smelling the food.

"What's for dinner?"

They all gradually became aware that Ben was holding his breath. He stared into a terminal screen excitedly, jaw gaping.

"W-wait, listen to this," he finally sputtered. "You can't believe this. We got a letter here, it just came in, ok. Here. 'Dear Samson Ford and His Racing Team, We are interested in arranging a major sponsorship deal with you. We would like to enter into a long term relationship as Samson Ford's exclusive racing sponsor, and are prepared to offer sponsorship terms similar to those enjoyed by other top racers, such as Pascal Jiminez or Killian Gideon. Please reply back as soon as possible, so that we can at least arrange a holo-conference to discuss the proposition. Sincerely yours, Albrecht Durer, Vice President of Advertising and Promotion, Midlothian Sports AIG, 'A Rothschild's Company' ' !"

They arranged a holoconference with the Midlothian executive immediately, altering course to a relay station in deep space. Albrecht Durer, on Earth, rose in the middle of the night to speak with them. His face was pale and grey hair barely coiffed, but he was dressed in a suit and his eyes were bright.

"We see you, Samson, becoming the next big folk hero, becoming a cultural and historical icon. Your genetic status combined with your racing prowess is a storybook ending waiting to happen. With our support, we think we can push you over that final hurdle, from finishing well in the biggest races, to winning them. Your story is the story of the unlikely hero, the unlikely champion, the boy who succeeded against all odds. It will be an inspiration to billions across the Solar System, and, as a business matter, we want to be the brand name on the face of that inspirational story. We want very much to be associated with your legacy.

"And, I have to say, the timing could not be more perfect. You have really captured a zeitgeist, Mr. Ford, you have really stepped into the eye of an incredible hurricane. The anti-naturals legislation on Earth will be coming up again at the next legislative session. Not only that, similar legislation is set to be introduced on Mercury, Venus, and Mars. It's horrible, of course, from a human standpoint, and we at Midlothian are absolutely against this legislation, but from a business standpoint it means that you will be at the center of an incredible publicity storm. You have not witnessed the half of it so far, your story is growing and growing. People are still trying to say your win at the Earth-Moon Grand Prix was a fluke, because Killian Gideon was not there, but when you win another major race or two, or perhaps if you win the biggest race of them all – at the same time the major planets on Earth are trying to segregate and isolate natural born human beings on the basis of their supposed inferiority – it will be one of the great stories of the Century, the exposure will be unbelievable.

"We want to capitalize on that exposure, Mr. Ford, on that publicity. We want to maximize it. This anti-naturals legislation is bad for our business, and we want to see it fail. By forming an exclusive partnership agreement with you and your team, we think we can kill three or four birds with a single stone.

"Now you see exactly where we are coming from, so let me get to my final point: We want you in the Solar Regatta this year."

THE FLICKERING FIGURE OF ALBRECHT Durer sat with his hands folded in front of him and, like the good salesman that he was, waited patiently for their response.

"The Solar Regatta," Stephanie said, seemingly the only one not at a loss for words, "you can't do that in six months! Your ship won't handle it! You need more time to prepare!"

Samson looked at her affectionately. He glanced at Kenichi and noticed a faint eagerness in his expression. He rubbed his hands. Theodore stared at the floor of the ship. Ben shrugged his shoulders and smiled.

"I like the way you think, Mr. Durer," Samson said. "I think we're really going to enjoy working together."

Theodore stood up and walked off the deck of the ship before they could see that he was crying.

ON THE OTHER SIDE OF the Solar System, Phillipe Bloodworth paced through a big Manhattan office, still furious that the filibuster had been successful. His paunch was concealed in a peculiar, black, silk suit with golden pinstripes. He chewed on an ever-present cigar, unlit. Cuban. Bloodworth owned the last cigar factory in Cuba. All of their cigars were delivered to him, personally. No one in the entire Solar System could smoke a cuban cigar unless Phillipe Bloodworth had given it to them as a present. He chewed his cigar with immense satisfaction, as always. It did nothing to dull his anger.

The Manhattan skyline towered around the office window like a giant forest. The window was invisible and covered the entire wall. In front of the window, one of Bloodworth's top executives sat at an enormous walnut desk. He had bright blonde hair, olive skin, and faintly asiatic features. He was a handsome man, like one of the old movie stars. They all were, all the men and women who worked in Bloodworth's companies. They had been constructed that way, after all. It was in their DNA. Bloodworth's companies did not hire natural born human beings, that was his corporate policy. He had implemented the policy a decade before, and the several hundred million natural-born employees of his corporation were replaced by their genetic superiors in the space of a year. There was, in Bloodworth's own words, "great weeping and gnashing of teeth."

"Don't let it bother you, Mr. Bloodworth," the handsome executive at the desk said. "They've only managed to delay the vote until the next assembly, we're sure to pass it then."

"Yes, thank you, Han. I'm sure you're right."

An aide came into the office and his footsteps on the floor's black marble tiles echoed through the room. He was a medium built man, good looking, not overly so. Average in every way. Unobtrusive. He had short black hair that was parted neatly on one side. He walked through the room with a confidence that hinted gently at authority.

"We have a preliminary report for you on Samson Ford, Mr. Bloodworth," the aide said, nodding his head down in respect.

"Excellent," Bloodworth said, and sat down in one of the plush chairs against the wall. "Read it to us. Please."

"Of course sir," the aide said, and opened up the folder he was holding.

"Samson Ford," he continued, standing in the middle of the room and reading the document in an even tone, "nickname Sammy. Twenty-seven years old. One brother, Theodore. Mother and father are Rosemary and Boris. He was born into the Magdalena Cult, and is thus believed to be the product of entirely natural breeding, without even vestigial genetic enhancements. Raised in the Magdalena settlement, he was a precocious child, often in trouble, rebellious. We don't have any specifics about that yet, but he had run away from home by age 15 and settled in Neo Vega which is the only metropolis near the Magdalena settlement. His brother, Theodore, incidentally, became a Magdalena shepherd, which is what they call their special agents who are sent out into the Solar System to bring back individuals who have left the cult."

Bloodworth chewed his cigar aggressively.

"In Neo Vega, Samson joined a circuit racing jet bikes. This was apparently a talent of his since childhood, and jet bike racing is known to be a popular entertainment in the Magdalena settlement lands. Unusually handsome, fit, and intelligent, it is not clear that anyone at the time even realized Ford was a natural born. Neo Vega is a popular destination for riff raff – criminals, dead enders – so it would not have been unusual for a 15 year old boy to show up on the streets there. Also, the number of runaways from the Magdalena settlement is quite small, the settlement is very insular. In any case, Ford was extremely successful as a jet bike racer and almost immediately became a local star. He was praised in the local racing circles for his supreme confidence, risk taking, killer instinct, and creative maneuvers. These are the same qualities that he is known for in the ship racing circuits today.

"After racing jet bikes on Neo Vega for a few years, Ford met Ben Johnson and the two quickly became friends. Johnson was thirty-eight years old at the time, a veteran racing hustler who had worked in many different capacities on the smaller racing circuits, and who owned a small cargo ship."

"Faggots?"

"Not as far as we have been able to ascertain, sir."

"Carry on."

"Ford and Johnson joined forces to form their own racing team, with Johnson acting as Ford's manager and chief mechanic. In spite of their close relationship and Johnson's lack of notable female companionship, they don't seem to be homosexuals, as far as our research has uncovered. Johnson is thought to have taken a sort of father role in Ford's life, and his background is generally clean and unnotable, although there is a small indication he may have been involved in smuggling, and our research is still active exploring that possibility.

"After they formed their partnership, Ford and Johnson moved to a larger, interplanetary jet bike circuit, "The United Jet Bike League", the largest jet bike racing circuit in the Solar System. Here, Samson continued to be successful, however our researchers note that even for the most successful jet bike racers the money available is relatively limited. For this reason it is not clear how Ford and Johnson were able to acquire a first-class cigarette racer, but within the next year they had acquired one and had switched from jet bikes to spaceship racing circuits. This is the same racer that Ford still uses today, and it is considered an integral part of his success. Research into the origins of the racer, or how Ford and Johnson acquired it in the first place is ongoing.

"After switching to ship racing, Ford and Johnson slowly climbed their way up the ladder of racing circuits over the next several years, beginning with local open races and gradually qualifying for more exclusive circuits. Today, as you know sir, they race in the top racing circuit in the Solar System and Samson Ford is regarded as one of the 'young pilots to watch' by every current racing publication. Ford and Johnson are well respected in racing circles, but are regarded as loners or mavericks, they do not seem to be well networked within the racing community, and our racing experts believe Samson Ford has been underexposed throughout his career, or, in other words, he could already have been a much bigger star than he is today if his career had been handled better from a business and PR perspective.

"However, thanks to consumer and political pressures on the large corporate sponsors, and to your companies in particular, sir, Ford has been unable to obtain any major sponsorship deals. Thus, his team's income is still substantially below the income of most similarly successful racing teams, and it is believed they are barely scraping by financially.

"Returning to the subject of sexuality, Ford seems to be circumspect. He has a reputation for being popular with the ladies, but seems to have been more focused on his racing ambitions than his sex life, dating only occasionally and rarely maintaining long term relationships. Regarding his temperament in general, Ford is reputed to have a quick temper and susceptibility to brawling. There is a rumor that he had a run-in with the Martian gangster, Lucho Gonzalez, after one of Ford's races this year, and we are continuing research on that subject. Ford is reputed to be a formidable opponent in a fight, which would not be surprising considering his racing success.

"With regard to personal vices, Ford has been known to drink to excess, especially after successful races. There is no indication of any drug habit.

"That is all, sir," the aide concluded, closing the folder.

Bloodworth rubbed his smoothly shaven chin.

"Interesting. Very interesting. I assume we are taking pro-active measures to thwart this Ford's success, not merely conducting research."

"Absolutely, sir."

"Good. Good. Make sure he doesn't win any more races. We can't allow this little piss-ant to become some sort of figurehead that could sway public opinion about the naturals."

"Yes, sir."

"Keep digging," Bloodworth concluded, "and keep me informed. This business is my top priority now."

C H A P T E R 29

SCAMP HUNG HIS HEAD IN shame. The veins at Lucho Gonzalez's temples throbbed out of his skin like blue, overheated engine lines, pulsing, threatening to burst.

"All I asked you to do was make contact with them, deliver a little message, maybe rough them up a little bit. Instead you fucking get arrested. TWICE!!!!"

"I'm sorry, sir."

"I had to reel in a lot of favors to get you out of there, Scamp. Do you even appreciate how I stick my neck out for your constant fuck-ups? Son of a bitch! YOU CAN'T EVEN DO A SIMPLE JOB?"

"It won't happen again, sir," Scamp said meekly, folding and unfolding his huge hands.

"You're damn right it won't!"

Lucho stood up and walked around the big wooden desk. He reached straight up with his arm, all the way above his head, and squeezed the big man's neck fiercely.

"Alright, old friend," he said, though his eyes still flashed with anger, "I'm glad we got you out of that mess quick, even if it was your own fault. You got the cockroach onto their ship anyway, didn't you?"

"Yes sir."

"That's the most important thing."

He backed up and sat down on his desk. Scamp began to relax and watched his boss with hard, appraising eyes.

"I'm not at all happy with this Samson Ford, and Kenichi," Lucho continued, "with these fucking pricks. Their whole team is going to suffer now. As far as I'm concerned, their whole team is going to disappear from the scene, just vanish off the face of the Earth. But are we going to kill them? Oh no. No, no, no, no, no. We're not going to kill them. Twenty, thirty years from now, we'll let 'em back out into the public. Just dump them on a street corner somewhere. With their bodies ravaged, and their eyes vacant, their minds gone. All of them together. And people can wonder about it, what happened. It'll be like an urban legend.

"That's how it's going to be. I want you to take a team of men and go get all these pricks, everyone on Samson Ford's racing team, and bring them back here."

Lucho fished in his pocket and pulled out a thin black card.

"Here, take this card, there's a million credits on it. That should be plenty to get the job done. If for some reason you need more, let me know."

"Yes sir. Thank you, sir," Scamp said, taking the card and sliding it into his pocket.

"Alright, get out of here. Tony will brief you on the rest of the details from our end, but this is your job, Scamp, you do it your way brother, and I know you'll do it right."

"Thank you, sir."

Scamp turned to walk away. As he walked through the long, narrow office to the door, Lucho said his name again. He turned back.

"Eh, just one more thing, if for some reason you aren't able to capture these guys, at least make sure they're all dead. I just want to make sure we're on the same page."

"Absolutely."

SAMSON LAY AWAKE ON HIS bunk, staring out through the small window in his cabin. Stars and planets drifted slowly towards him. Ever so slowly. If you watched close you could pretend to yourself that you could see it, that their sizes had changed. The universe was so bright. It sparkled in front of him, undamped by the sun's rays shining at the Junket's back. It glowed like infinity, like God's hand. God. Samson never got tired of it. The thrill of the universe never wore off for him. It was why he loved to fly, to fly in space, to be part of it. It was like touching God. No one believed in God anymore. That seemed sad to him. More than anything else about the world outside Magdalena, the complete absence of faith seemed like an enormous loss. For them. For him, he never regretted it. He never regretted leaving.

No one believed in God. He watched the sparkling universe through his little window and it seemed strange to him. God was right there, right in front of them, you could feel him inside of you. Couldn't you? Couldn't everyone? He sat up in bed and rubbed the sweat off of his face. He didn't even believe in God himself. Why did he pray before every race?

He got out of bed and wandered quietly through the Junket's corridor. Kenichi had been making modifications to the insides of the racer and he wanted a chance to look at them by himself. He reached for the door to the hangar. Anyway, he couldn't sleep.

The bright, white hangar lights outlined the door brilliantly and blinded him as Samson pulled it open.

"Who's out here?"

"Oh, Samson!" Stephanie said. "Are you up too?"

He closed the door quickly behind him and hoped that nobody else would wake up. Stephanie was sitting on top of the racer's housing, with one of the panels removed, fiddling at it with a wrench and calipers. She was dressed in her usual mechanic's suit and looked like she had been there for a while.

"Don't you ever sleep?" Samson wondered. "You'll make yourself sick."

"Oh, not that much. I only sleep a little. And I always have perfect health."

He walked to the ship and smiled up at her.

"Well, it would be good to have some company, anyway."

"I was hoping you would wander in here," Stephanie said.

"Why is that?"

"Hmm? No reason."

He climbed up onto the ship and sat opposite her beside the open panel.

"I would have hoped that you would be out here to keep me company since I can't sleep," he said, "but I would never expect to be that lucky."

Stephanie pulled several unsecured wires together inside the panel, bound them, and hooked them into a holding bracket. Her hands moved rapidly, sure and fluent. There was something breathtaking about it, just the way her body moved. Fast. Almost superhuman.

"Don't be silly," she said. "You're the luckiest person I know."

She re-fastened some bolts inside the panel while Samson watched her.

"Lucky?" he said. "Haven't you noticed I've got people trying to kill me?"

"Oh, that's just a sign of success," Stephanie said lightly, and a thin smile cracked her lips.

She looked up slowly, almost nervously, and stared into his eyes for a long time. Stephanie was an unusually beautiful woman, but it was a quiet sort of beauty. The longer Samson watched her, the more beautiful she became. The more of her exquisiteness he noticed and appreciated. It was always this way when he watched her.

"Is this... done?" he wondered, and they both reached for the sealing wrench at the same time.

Their hands touched and the electricity of her flesh stung him. Stephanie dropped her eyes demurely, and Samson pulled the wrench out of her hands and fastened the panel cover back in place.

"I was actually–" Samson continued. "Uh, I had an idea to come out and look at all the work Ken has been doing tonight."

"He's been doing some amazing work," Stephanie said.

Her body seemed to lean towards him, as if there were some physical force pushing it, pushing against her shoulder, forcing her to lean. Her eyes were fluid, black pools lit up brilliantly by the glaring shop lights. Samson slid closer and sat beside her.

"I don't think I understand some of the changes he's been making. It makes me uncomfortable, like I'm not in control."

He put his arm around Stephanie and squeezed her tight against him. She caught her breath.

"I've been studying his work tonight," she said weakly. Then with more confidence, "It's amazing, Samson. It's incredible stuff. He really is a genius."

"I shouldn't worry?"

"Ben and I are keeping a close watch on Kenichi's work. We're all really scared after that sabotage incident, I'm still upset about it. Of course, Ken was the one who found the problem."

"I know. But sometimes I think– I don't know, like there's something not right about him."

"Yeah–" Stephanie said, and there was a long pause.

Samson squeezed her hand and rubbed her fingers.

"Actually, there's something that I wanted to show you," she said. "I've been doing some research on Ken, looking into his background more. There's some stuff that you should see."

Stephanie pulled up the reports she had saved at the terminal in her cabin. They were old investigators' reports telling about Kenichi's racing scandals. Not only had he bet against his own team, he had bet against them consistently for years. Whenever he was known to have placed a bet against them their racers had crashed out of the race with mechanical troubles. Two of the pilots had been badly injured. The investigators believed that Kenichi had sabotaged many more races than the several incidents they were able to prove. In the most famous and shocking case, one of the ships under Kenichi's care had a catastrophic GCU failure in the middle of a gravity slingshot attempt, killing the pilot instantly. Prosecutors on Earth had planned to prosecute Kenichi for manslaughter in that case, but he had disappeared before they had a chance, and was eventually presumed to be dead.

Samson didn't know what to think of it. He had a strong instinct that Kenichi was a genuine friend, and he always trusted his instincts. But, still. He didn't know what to think.

He looked out at the stars through the little window in Stephanie's cabin, and thought of God again. Did God have a plan for him? Was this part of it? He didn't even believe in God. But he felt it. Something.

Stephanie stood at the terminal, poring over the documents again. The light in her cabin was dim, and her body stood silhouetted against the twinkling stars. Her body curved so beautifully. She stared at the screen with a particular intensity, as if it terrified her. Samson put his hands around her hips and pulled her away from the screen. She turned her head tensely, and his kiss landed on the corner of her mouth. She caught her breath, and turned her face back towards him, and he kissed her on the lips, savoring the taste of her. He squeezed their bodies together, and kissed her long, black hair, and breathed her in deeply, not understanding how a human being could smell so good. Could smell beautiful.

Stephanie shivered in his arms and Samson pushed her back against the bed. Her eyes glittered as she looked up at him, he kissed her lips again, and she whispered something that he couldn't hear. Only the tone in her voice. Tender. She was so tender. He leaned back to look at her, keeping their hips pressed close. Stephanie was smiling, her eyes were huge, she looked like she could cry. He ran his hands along her arms, and kissed all over her face, but she pulled back from him. She slid the peculiar green ring she always wore off of the ring finger on her right hand and dropped it into a bowl on the little metal table beside the bed.

"What, I can touch you, but not the ring?" Samson said hoarsely, pulling her back to him and rubbing her hands. He rubbed her finger where the ring had been.

"It's... It's a sentimental thing. I can't really explain it."

THEY LAY NAKED TOGETHER, AND breathed softly, quickly, waiting for their hearts to slow. Inhaling each other. Avoiding eye contact, and then looking with huge eyes together, and being startled by it, and avoiding eye contact again. They rubbed each other's bodies affectionately, as if neither one had wanted their love making to end.

Stephanie put her head on Samson's chest, and listened to his heart, and rubbed her hands along the muscles of his arms, wiping away the sweat. He kissed the top of her head gently, and brushed the long, black strands of her hair off her back, sliding his hands up and down her rib cage, massaging circles into the little dimples above her bottom.

"You, uh, did you ever sleep with a man like me before?" he wondered self-consciously.

"There aren't any other men like you," Stephanie said, and turned onto her side, staring at his face, smiling.

"I mean a natural born man, one who hasn't been enhanced," Samson said, and the nerves inside of him made his hands tense against her body.

"I haven't slept with very many men, Samson," she said awkwardly, looking offended, and he caught her hand and kissed her lips.

"No, that's not. I don't care about that. I mean, it's good you haven't. But I don't care, that's not what I meant."

He kissed her again and squeezed her tightly. Stephanie was amazed at how little catharsis Samson had gotten from their love making. He was still anxious inside. She squeezed his hand as tightly as she could, and kissed him back, realizing how deeply rooted his demons were. Realizing that she loved him. Her eyes shook ever so slightly.

"It's," her voice cracked, "it's, you're a great lover, Samson. I don't know—"

"Is it better with an enhanced man?"

She tried to squeeze his hand tighter, to show him how she felt, and relaxed her body into him, as if to show that he possessed her.

"No," she said seriously, looking into Samson's eyes. "It's... different. With you it's more... organic. It's like sex is more than a mechanical equation with you. ...It's better."

Samson ran his fingers along the beautiful, sculpted curves of her rib cage. He rested his hand on top of her heart, touching her breast.

"Am I– Is it different with me?" Stephanie wondered, suddenly self-conscious too. "Have you only slept with natural women before?"

"No. I have."

"Have you slept with lots of women before?"

"No. I'm– no, I don't believe in that. Not many."

He lay back on his back and pulled Stephanie up, so that her head was resting in the crook of his neck.

"Don't dodge the question," she said, starting to sound upset. "Is it different?"

"It's different with you," Samson said. "Maybe it doesn't have anything to do with any of that. Maybe it's who we are that makes it different. It's better with you. It's because of who you are, not any of those physical things."

"Oh," Stephanie said musically.

"Don't you think?"

"Yes."

Samson ran his hand along her forearm, across the perfectly turned bones of her wrist.

"You're incredibly beautiful, though."

"Ooh," she said, and rested the crown of her head against his cheek, and tried to exist in that moment forever.

"WHAT WAS IT LIKE GROWING up with the Magdalenas?" Stephanie asked, as they were lying there together.

"I don't know."

"Samson, you know."

"I left for Neo Vega when I was 15. I guess I didn't like it very much."

"Why didn't you?"

"What was it like for you growing up?

"Oh, it was ordinary. The Magdalenas are something unusual."

"Not unusual to me, how you grew up would be unusual to me."

"Humor me," she said beseechingly.

"Ok. ...Well, the Magdalena settlements are really insulated. You grow up there and you don't know much about the rest of the Solar System, only what is happening in the settlements. The stuff outside, even a city like Neo Vega, which is nearby, it's like, it's not even real, you don't really know about it, it's more like myths and legends. You hear these rumors about what the outside world is like. Like, when you are growing up, on the playgrounds at school, you hear these rumors.

"It's not like it is really harsh – like, you can talk about what you want – but it's more like social norms. Like, no one will come throw you in jail for talking about the outside world, but everyone will look down on you for it and ostracize you.

"So when you hear about this stuff, cities where the people have been modified and everyone is tall and beautiful and stuff like that, it's not really real. You know what I mean? You don't see any of that on tv. So when you're growing up you just have a really different perspective about life, and those things outside the settlement are cloudy and vague and mysterious. It's a small world in Magdalena. I always felt claustrophobic there, like it wasn't big enough for me, that's why I wanted to really see what the rest of the Solar System was like, even from when I was really young. When we would talk on the playground about Neo Vega, I would always say I wanted to go there, and the other kids thought I was crazy."

"Wouldn't they teach you things at school?"

"No. I mean, the schools in Magdalena are really good, Magdalena isn't backwards like you might think. They teach you science and technology, and about the Solar System and everything, but a lot of the context is left out of it, the history and, like, what the rest of the Solar System is like, in a human context. It's hard to describe the way it is, it's really different from what almost anyone outside of Magdalena has probably experienced."

"So you just ran away when you were 15, that's like you," Stephanie said, rubbing her hand across his chest and squeezing up to him for warmth.

"I did, but, my brother, Theo, he went right into the liaison corps, which is really prestigious in Magdalena. He was a brilliant student and very devout, and he was the youngest man ever admitted into the liaison corps. So he was already learning about the rest of the Solar System, and had even been out on some missions outside of the settlement territory, all the way to Mars actually, like, when I was a teenager. He told me a lot about Neo Vega and the rest of the Solar System, which he probably regrets, so it wasn't like I was going out completely blind, I had a reasonable idea of what I was going to find there. And I was already racing by then, so I really wanted to race, and Theo had told me about the big racing circuits in the Solar System, the spaceship racing and stuff like that, so that is what I wanted to get out and explore for myself, and see what it was all about."

Lisa lay on her bed, listless, and hummed the tune to a recent pop song. She ordered the music of the song to play, and ordered the volume down until it was soft. She had her terminal projection put onto the ceiling and checked her messages as she lay there on her back. There was a holographic message from Killian Gideon, it was certified.

"Play."

"Hi Lisa," the image of Killian leered at her. "Since I saw you at the race yesterday I can't stop thinking about you. You're so interesting, such a spunky, different sort of girl. I can't stop thinking about the amazing things I could do to your perfect little body. Are you going to be at the next Grand Prix? Message me back, perhaps we can figure out a way to see each other soon."

The holographic Killian smiled and blew a kiss at her, then disappeared.

"What an ass," Lisa said. "Save."

Another holographic message came up, this time it was a mischievous looking woman in heavy make-up.

"Lisa Maui? This is Charlene, from Gossip Unlimited. You've probably seen me on tv or something like that, ha ha. We want to do a piece on you, we want the inside story. Is it true that you are dating Samson Ford? That's very interesting business, Lisa. We're willing to offer you a lot of credits for the details. This is about *you*, and *your* image. So get back to me, honey, ok? Ta ta."

"Delete."

There was a note there from Samson that had already been read. Lisa pulled it up again, and the words displayed on the ceiling.

Hey Lisa, thanks for your note. I had a good time with you, too. I hate to say it, but I might try to take you up on that offer

Lisa smiled a soft, satisfied smile at the ceiling. She hadn't had a chance to write back before the race. She wished they had gotten to talk a bit on Titan, and wondered what she should write back now. It made her nervous to think of what to write. Maybe she would just wait until the next race and talk to him then, she thought. She switched the terminal off and stared at the blank ceiling, and hummed along with the quiet drumbeat of the pop music for a while.

In the evening, she sat in the living room with her grandparents and listened to them talk. Her grandparents always talked. They didn't watch the tv very much. They were intellectuals. Lisa's grandfather had been a successful genetics engineer before abruptly retiring at the age of fifty-four. He had spent the rest of his life writing philosophical and religious treatises that few people read. Her grandmother was his great foil, the touchstone for all his ideas. She was an adventurous woman who had been the natural child of two highly genetically modified parents, and had always felt a sense of loyalty to the natural borns, even though she, herself, could blend in perfectly with the higher classes. They would sit and talk until late in the night, and Lisa would sit and listen to them. She always had. Sometimes she would venture into the conversation herself, or the two of them would invite her into it, but mostly she just listened, and let the ideas percolate around inside her mind. This suited her. She formed her own ideas on her own, and didn't need to talk to anyone about them. Her grandparents understood, and they liked it when she listened.

"It's because they don't have religion," Lisa's grandfather was saying. "They don't have any reason to care about other people."

"Everything's about religion to you," her grandmother said.

"Everything *is* about religion, exactly!"

"Then why is it dead?"

"Look, ok, wait let's stay on the other subject. People with religion had a framework, a schema, an idea of the universe that was bigger than themselves. It put their lives into a perspective and gave them something to believe in, something to aspire to that was more important than their own personal pleasure. Without that schema of the universe, whatever schema it was, take your pick, but without that schema, we have a world where we're all just rats, we're just nothings, just meaningless, worthless nothings, scampering around meaninglessly in the universe. And it doesn't matter how much propaganda you use, and it doesn't matter how much you say 'love your neighbor to make the world go round', at the end of the day people who believe they are just little rats, little meaningless nothings, random aberrations in the fabric of the universe – people who *feel* that about themselves, will treat each other that way. And we do! And we don't even have to be conscious of it, because we feel it, it's what's inside of us."

"Everyone isn't killing each other."

"Aren't they?"

"Oh hardly. The worst slaughters in the world still happened in the 21st Century, so we must have evolved since then."

"And what about this business with the naturals, this could be a hell of a lot worse than that."

"They're talking about relocation and isolation, not slaughter."

"And that's what they talked about in the 21st Century, too! But when you start to treat people like commodities, or like animals, then the line between relocating your so-called problem and just annihilating it becomes a very fine line indeed."

"I hope not, honey."

"I hope not, too. But that's the point. It's only hope that separates us from the most nasty eventualities. Take a man like that Phillipe Bloodworth – to a man like that, it's no difference whether these human beings are moved to a separate planetary colony of their own, or whether they are all killed. He wants to move them to a colony because he thinks that is the easier solution, but if they were all killed he wouldn't lose any sleep over it. They're just worms to him, just as he himself is just a worm, because he believes in nothing profound, in nothing beyond himself and his own selfish pleasures, and this is the same small, perverse excuse for a belief about the universe that we have all been led to have."

"He wouldn't care, I'll give you that."

"Not many would care, but the old taboos still have a little bit of power over us. Only a little bit. We have not commodified ourselves completely yet. But if you want to look at an example, look at the racing, Lisa can tell you about that. These men are killing each other all the time. Do you know what the average lifespan of a pilot in the top racing circuits is? Five years. Five years, and then splat. And the audience cheers, they love it."

"What do you think about it, Lisa?" her grandmother wondered.

Lisa blinked her eyes.

"Well," she said after a moment, "it is horrible when they die. But the best pilots don't die as much. We're all going to die, so– It's not like they don't know what they are getting into, all of those pilots are really happy to be on the circuit, I mean really happy."

"Exactly," her grandfather said, "we're all going to die, so what does it matter? Exactly, I couldn't have said it better than that. So these pilots, it's not all an accident you know, a lot of the time when a pilot dies it is because another pilot nudges his ship and intentionally kills him."

"That's true," Lisa said.

"And the audience loves it, that's their favorite part of all. That's when they cheer the loudest, when one of the pilots dies, and they all say what a brilliant move it was by the pilot who killed him."

WEAT DRIPPED OFF OF PHILLIPE Bloodworth's angry, grunting face. A yellow light flashed on the floating, wall sized, monitor, which beeped insistently over his bed. He finished humping a bizarre little creature in a frenzy, then pulled out and slapped it hard across the ear.

"Eee, don't!" the creature squealed, and scampered away. There was slime and ooze all over the bed.

Bloodworth stood on the bed with his feet wide apart, content in his own superiority. His suddenly limp member hung almost down to his knees. He snapped his fingers impatiently and one of the little servants ran forward to hand him his cigar. He switched on the com and the aide in charge of the Samson Ford investigation appeared on the screen.

"Yes, what is it?" Bloodworth said, chewing the cigar.

"I hope we're not disturbing you, sir," the aide said politely, betraying no emotion.

"No, not at all. I trust this is about that Samson Ford investigation? Out with it. Don't dilly dally."

"Of course, sir. We have made an unexpected discovery. Ford's racing team has a new engineer. A man named Kenichi Iwahara. It took us a few weeks to identify him, because he was banned from racing twenty years ago and disappeared."

"Kenichi Iwahara," Bloodworth said distantly, "the saboteur..."

"Your memory is comprehensive as always, sir."

"Don't flatter me, son. So what are you saying, this Iwahara is alive?"

"He appears to be Samson Ford's new chief engineer, sir. We can inform the racing league officials of this and it is a near certainty that Ford's team will be banned."

"No. That's not good enough."

"Perhaps as a temporary solution, sir. While we pursue other avenues for a more permanent one?"

"No," Bloodworth said. "Listen, Iwahara, I remember that business. He's no good. We can turn him to our side, get him working for us. Let other people figure out who he is and ban Ford for it; if nobody else does, we still have that card in reserve, we can play it whenever we want. You need to be more ambitious. Iwahara can be useful to us. He killed his pilots for money once, let's get him on our side and have him do it again."

"Yes sir."

"Can you get in touch with him and set that up?"

"Yes sir."

"If you don't know how just say so, and I can get Thatcher to use an agent who specializes in these sorts of things."

"Oh no, sir. This is my speciality. That is why Mr. Thatcher assigned me to the case."

"Good. Well, see to it."

"Yes sir."

"And make sure the people know ahead of time where Samson Ford is going to be. You know, the people who don't like his kind. So they can give him a welcome wherever he goes."

"Yes sir."

KENICHI USED A TORCH AND a force-hammer to smooth out a tiny ding in the paneling on Samson's racer. He finished it off with spit and a rag, it was a labor of love. He had put Ben and Stephanie to work carving out a new ion-jet channel he had developed that would increase the ship's thrust efficiency by 0.3%. There was polish and a fine brushing system that Kenichi could use, but mostly he polished the hull this way. For some reason it gave him a sense of satisfaction. It made him feel closer to the ship. He almost cried when he thought about it, and would run his hands up and down the wings framework, admiring his creation. He thought he had lost her forever. So, he didn't need any polishing machines. When he got a little nick or ding worked out of the hull he would polish it off with his own spit and the power of his own body. Because it was his, and it made him feel good to do that.

The racer was Kenichi's masterpiece, it had been his prototype design for a Solar Regatta racer. Cigarette racers had never been successful in the Solar Regatta before then. Now they were a little bit more common in the race, but still rare. This racer would have won the Solar Regatta, he was sure of it. He couldn't believe he was re-united with the ship again. It was like fate had placed it in front of him. It was like the god was real, and wanted him to be here, wanted his life to have gone this way. As he polished the long, white racer, to him it was a thing of beauty. A work of art. An infant, his baby. It was the last great thing in his life, the last beautiful thing, before everything had gone bad. Working on his prototype racer again, polishing it with spit and a rag – he felt like he had traveled back in time. Like he had traveled back to the time that he had wanted to go back to.

He pulled at his long, grey hair, and looked at his wrinkled hands. He watched Ben and Stephanie, working ever so carefully carving the ion-jet channel. Stephanie was bent over the pinhole torch, with her butt up in the air. She made his body ache. He didn't understand how she could know so much about ships, and engineering, and racing. She was one of the smartest people he had ever met. He wondered if Samson and Ben appreciated how smart she was, and concluded that they probably didn't. Stephanie was the kind of woman that he would have liked to marry, he wanted to grab hold of her, to pull her to him. He pulled at his grey hair. It wasn't supposed to turn grey, his parents had bought a DNA sequence with hair that didn't turn grey. Maybe it was from the stress. She was so beautiful. He hadn't touched a woman in so long.

Samson was fucking her. That's the way it went. Guys like Samson would fuck girls like her, guys who weren't smart enough to understand her. Guys who were exciting. And guys like him would sit in a prison for twenty years and their bodies would hurt every night, painful and alone. Without a woman to miss him. Fucking Samson. Kenichi wanted to kill himself when he thought about it. There had always been a Samson in the life of every woman he had ever loved. Or all but one. He hated Samson. No, he didn't. He polished the ship more, and watched Stephanie's body at the same time. He loved to watch her move, she moved so exquisitely, she must have extremely advanced genetics. She was very guarded about her past. Stephanie looked up and made eye contact with him, and smiled kindly, and Kenichi tried to smile back, but instead looked back down at the racer and polished harder.

"You're doing a good job over there," he said. "You guys are really great."

It wasn't Samson, Kenichi knew, admonishing himself. Samson was actually a good man. He wasn't even one of "those" guys. Samson was actually a damn intelligent man, too, and he probably did appreciate how special Stephanie was. It was just himself, it was just all those lonely years, and how Stephanie underlined it for him. Samson and Stephanie were a great match, actually. What kind of match would she be with an old man like him. Twenty years in a gangster's jail, and it wasn't like he didn't deserve it. Actually, it was better than he might have gotten from the law. But it hurt him. He watched Stephanie's body, the long curves of her legs, the graceful silhouette of her waist transforming into hips and chest. Maybe he should take a few days off at Neo Vega and visit the brothels there. Samson hadn't paid him anything yet. They hadn't even talked about pay. He'd been locked in a prison for twenty years, he didn't think they could resent him a little bit of free time in the city and a little bit of cash for all the work he had done. Whores. He watched Stephanie's gentle, serious face as she polished the new channel with a xenon filament and felt vaguely ashamed of himself. He scrubbed at the ship more vigorously and tried to imagine that he was twenty years younger again.

In the Junket's dining room, Samson and Theodore contested a game of Overchess. It was a virtual set, projected out of a tiny key ring. Theodore always kept the set with him.

"Why do you ever want to play against me?" Samson wondered. "When was the last time I ever beat you at this game?"

"You've never beaten me at this game," Theodore said haughtily.

"Oh, so that's why."

"I take immense pleasure in cutting my little brother down to size."

"That never works," Samson said.

"No. My brother is an extremely arrogant and willful person. Maybe that's why it's so much fun."

"I'm not arrogant."

"Aren't you?" Theodore wondered. "That's not a hypothetical question."

"What, is it because I think I'm too good for the Magdalenas?"

"How about: because you still think you have a chance to beat me at this game."

"That's not arrogant, it's just wishful thinking."

Samson moved one of the pieces on the board, and Theodore immediately captured it. His position was beginning to look grim.

"Well that's not very nice," he said.

"You don't think you're too good for the Magdalenas," Theodore said, "you think everyone is too good for them."

"That's true."

"You think I'm too good for them."

"Of course."

"And yet, here I am, your brother, a man who loves you with his whole heart, more than life itself, a man whose family misses you at Christmas every single year, who toast your name, who keep your picture on the wall and dream that you will come back to us."

"Theo..."

"Well, I'm saying, look at me. Here I am a man who has devoted his entire life to bringing back the lost sheep of the Magdalenas, our own children who have wandered away from us. That is what I devote my life to, because I believe in it. Because I love our people and what we are, and who we are. And you say that I'm too good for them."

"I just don't believe in all that stuff. The Prophet and his mysteries. Look, I don't want to say things to offend you, we've been through this before."

"No, no," Theodore said. "It's ok, please speak your mind."

"I still believe in God, Theo," Samson said, emotion creeping into his voice.

"I know you do, that's why I'm here."

"Let's talk about something else."

Theodore drummed his fingers and stared down at the board from an acute angle, his long spine perfectly straight. Samson started to move a piece, then hesitated, then put it back.

"Your friend Kenichi was quite upset when I beat him," Theodore said casually.

"You beat Ken? I bet he was upset."

"It must burn him up to lose to a natural born like me," Theodore continued with a smug smile.

"I don't think he's biased," Samson said, making his move. "He's just really smart. It would make him mad to lose to anyone in a game that seems to reflect on his intelligence."

Theodore watched the board quietly for a while, and Samson wondered if he had made a good move. Then Theodore reached out and moved his empress aggressively across the board.

"Checkmate. Good try, brother."

KENICHI SAT ALONE IN HIS room that night, and brainstormed new modifications to the racer on a sketchboard. The others were sitting and talking on the ship's bridge. Stephanie had been sitting in Samson's lap. It was nicer here, alone. He could focus. As he sketched out thoughts for new components, or new modifications, he would model them in three dimensional space in the holographic projection from his terminal. Then he would work and re-work the idea, or throw it out and start over, and sometimes, if it seemed promising enough, he would run it through simulation tests and see if it was worth saving. None of the ideas had seemed promising enough tonight.

There was a knock on his cabin door.

"Yes? Come in, please."

Samson opened the door and poked his head in.

"Hey Ken, uh, we're passing a relay link, and we actually have a call coming in for you."

Kenichi stared at Samson in amazement, and the color began to drain from his face.

"A— a call for me? Are you sure?"

"Have you even set up your terminal addresses yet?" Samson asked.

"No, I have not. How would anyone even know where I was?"

"Weird. Yeah, well, I'll transfer him to your terminal in here, ok? Let me know what it's about."

Samson closed the door again, and after a few minutes Kenichi's terminal projected the holographic image of an unassuming looking man with short black hair, parted neatly on one side.

"Do I know you?" Kenichi wondered.

"Mr. Iwahara," the man said soberly, and there was something strangely compelling in his voice. "This is a private call and I would prefer to speak to you on an encrypted channel if you don't mind."

"Ok," Kenichi said slowly, and punched at his terminal to activate the encryption.

"Thank you, sir. This is a long-chain quantum communication, so I want to get straight to the point. I represent an important businessman who wants to meet with you at your next port of call to discuss a private contractual proposition. We would appreciate it if you don't discuss this matter with anyone else until after you have heard the nature of our proposition. After that, of course, you will decide for yourself whether you want to work with us or not."

"I don't really understand," Kenichi began to say.

"To demonstrate our seriousness, I am transferring 50,000 credits onto your terminal card. Please spend them however you want, these are only a gesture of good will."

Kenichi quickly checked the account balance on his card and found that the 50,000 credits were there. They had been transferred through a highly certified and irrevocable process from one of the largest banks on Earth.

"Yes, well," he said, already imagining how he would spend the money. "Well, thank you, perhaps we can do business together. I will be in Neo Vega a few days from now, would it be possible to meet and discuss it there? In public."

"Of course. We will be in touch with you on Neo Vega, then. Please don't tell anyone else about the nature of our conversation until we have had a chance to talk. It could spoil the business plan, which would be a shame, because there is a lot of money to be made for all of us."

The holographic image flickered and disappeared. Kenichi removed his card from the terminal and held it in his hand excitedly, savoring the feeling of having money again, of being a free man. He didn't care what their business was, the credits transfer had been certified and irrevocable. Legally, it was a gift.

He slipped the card into his pocket, zipped the pocket closed, and walked out onto the bridge to tell Samson. He said that an old employer had spotted him on the coverage of one of the races. The man had been saving Kenichi's last paycheck in a bank account all these years, ever since he disappeared, and had just wired him the money! Even Theodore grinned in amazement.

"Oh yeah, we need to start paying you something!" Samson said. "We should have some money once this Midlothian sponsorship gets ironed out. Let's discuss business in a few days when we get to port at Triton. Can we wait until then?"

CHAPTER 32

Triton was Neptune's largest moon. It was a cold, desert planet, the farthest place in the Solar System that could be considered hospitable to human life. Not very hospitable. It was a backwater. Neo Vega, Triton's only major metropolis, was more famous than the moon itself. The Magdalena settlement territories on Triton were also quite famous, although hardly anybody knew anything about them. They were myth and fable. Other than that, there wasn't much there. Most people said that the terraforming of Triton had been a waste of energy. But human beings were awash with energy, they could afford to waste it.

Stephanie climbed into a big, black hovercar and sat down opposite her escort, by the tinted windows of the door. Samson and Theodore got in on the other side and slid over next to them. Theodore tried to smile at everyone, as if he could set them at ease. Stephanie smiled too, exuding friendliness and positivity.

"Do you have many visitors here, Angela?" she asked the escort.

"No."

Angela was a frumpy, stocky woman in her late 20s. She had arrived at the outpost in a huff, an hour after the rules and boundaries of Stephanie's visit had been agreed upon. She was dressed extremely conservatively, in a cream colored smock and long, grey skirt, and wore a funny, square hat on the top of her head. Her hair and eyes were the ancient, mousy color, the dull brown. Stephanie had rarely seen this color of hair and eyes before, and never in a woman.

"You must have visitors sometimes," Stephanie offered politely, "or you wouldn't have any use for escorts."

"It is rare," Angela said.

Samson and Theodore raised their eyebrows, and Angela smiled at them politely then swung a critical gaze back at Stephanie, scrutinizing her. The car rose into the air and they began to move away from the little outpost at the edge of the Magdalena territories, towards the big city in the distance. Stephanie smiled at Angela curiously. Angela frowned. Stephanie's hair was pulled back in a severe pony-tail, she wore fitted jeans, a thin, black, shiny leather belt, and an elegant black blouse that buttoned in the front. Angela seemed unwilling to be friends, and Stephanie turned her attention to the countryside passing below them.

The Magdalena territories were dry and dusty, like ancient Mars had been before it was terraformed. Colder. Plant life seemed limited to cactuses and occasional brushy desert weeds, but the landscape was punctuated by huge greenhouse bubbles and round buildings, with great pipes running between them and along the roadways. The giant greenhouses bloomed lush with vegetation.

"So your food is all produced in the greenhouse domes?" Stephanie wondered.

"That's right," Theodore said. "Obviously we get little enough sun here, even with all the solar radiation collectors orbiting Neptune, so the greenhouse glass and atmospheric controls are essential."

Angela glared at him.

"These things aren't a secret, Angela," Theodore said. "It's all the same on Neo Vega, you know."

"It still looks exactly the same as when I left," Samson said distantly.

"The city is much bigger, brother. That will surprise you. Anyway, Stephanie, there is a substantial amount of water on Triton, but it is pooled under the crust and doesn't generally rise to the surface. It is sort of like the crust is floating on top of the water. So the water has to be piped like this to the greenhouses and the farms and little communities out here away from the city. So even though the land is dry, there is actually a lot of water down there; basically people have as much as they want, even out here in the desert. In the city, of course, we have irrigation systems, canals, and it is not dry like it is out here. See, you can see the shimmer in the air over the city, there is much more vapor in the air."

"I see that. Interesting."

A battery of armored vehicles moved in formation on a desert plain in the distance.

"What are they doing out there?" Stephanie wondered, "All those, they're tanks aren't they?"

"Yes, they—" Theodore began.

"Military training," Angela said, cutting him off. "We are always prepared to defend ourselves and our way of life."

"Yes, but Magdalena has never been in a war," Theodore said quickly, and Samson slid up against Stephanie on the seat and pointed out different features of the landscape to her.

MAGDALENA CITY WAS LOCATED NEAR the center of the Magdalena territories. It was a small metropolis, with a population of about one million people. The total population of the Magdalena settlements was about five million. The city was bright, dense, tall. Nearly all of the buildings were white, and the architecture was based on cylinders. The streets were paved with a peculiar pink stone, like a cross between soapstone and granite, and punctuated everywhere by canals and fountains. At the perimeters of the city, houses and estates fanned out in swaths across the countryside, becoming sparser and sparser until they became the little farm settlements with their greenhouse domes, and villages that dotted the desert.

The hovercar cruised through downtown Magdalena, past

the big towers, temples, and judicial halls, just above rows of palm trees that lined the main avenues.

"Oh, it's beautiful," Stephanie said, glancing in every direction as they passed, afraid to miss something.

"Do you think so?" Angela said.

"Of course. I had only seen a few photos of Magdalena before, it's different than I imagined it. Look at all the people, only natural skin and hair. It's very organic. It gives the city a different feel, it seems more virile somehow. Maybe healthier."

"No one in Magdalena has had any genetic modifications at all," Theodore said. "If you compare it to Earth, for example, even the natural born people on Earth will usually have had some designer genetics that have crept into their bloodlines from generation to generation. In the rest of the Solar System it is actually very rare to find a human being with entirely natural genes."

"Yes. Is it actually impossible for an outsider to join, then?"

"Outsiders are not welcome here, they bring only corruption," Angela said blankly, as if she were repeating a common epithet.

Samson glared at her.

"It isn't strictly impossible," Theodore said, "but it is quite rare. For any person with modified genetics it is impossible. There are still some individuals, and some small communities, in the wider Solar System whose genes are entirely natural, and there is a process of conversion and resettlement for them."

"I see."

"Not a very welcoming place, is it," Samson said sarcastically, and Theodore looked hurt.

"Theo and Angela have been very nice to me," Stephanie said. "There are always limits to hospitality when you are trying to preserve something that you think is important."

"It's just funny that Neo Vega accepts outsiders more

graciously than they do here," Samson said.

Angela caught her breath and stared at him as if she had been struck. Theodore slid across the large seat to the opposite side of the hovercar and gazed out the window silently.

"Samson Ford," Angela said, "don't think that your people here in Magdalena have forgotten about you. Twelve ministers gather to say a prayer for you every day in the Temple, they have prayed for you every day since you left us."

"I'm sure they feel very righteous."

"They pray first of all for your safety and welfare, and secondly they pray for the day of your return. Even now they are offering a sacrifice of thanks at the altar in the desert."

Samson looked at her coldly.

"I won't be staying, I assure you. My brother convinced me to come back and visit our parents, that is the only reason I have returned."

Angela watched him silently, face etched with disgust and, more vaguely, pity.

"What are the streets paved with?" Stephanie asked, changing the subject.

"Pinkstone," Samson said, putting his arm around her and glancing at Angela rebelliously. "It's a kind of rock they have all over Triton, kind of like granite or something like that."

"It is a kind of granite," Angela said, looking down and smoothing out the wrinkles in her smock.

"They are calling it granite now, Sammy," Theodore offered.

"Well, it's not like Earth granite anyway," Samson said, leaning across Stephanie to look down at the street below them.

"It's beautiful," she said.

"How is it not like Earth granite?" Angela wondered.

"It's– the granite on Earth is coarser, and harder."

"Always?"

"Perhaps there is some granite similar to this on Earth,"

Stephanie said, "but the color is unusual. By the way, I have to tell you I have never seen a hat like that before, Angela. It's very pretty."

Angela looked confused, and raised her hand to her hat self-consciously. It was a little, square hat that sat on the top of her head, as if it had been pinned into her hair. The hat was white and finely embroidered, with little peach colored beads that hung down around it. As Stephanie looked at the hat more closely, she realized that it resembled the tops of the tall, cylindrical towers they had passed in downtown Magdalena City, which were all crowned with funny little polished cubes.

"My hat?" Angela said. "Yes, it is the Magdalena hat. Women wear them here, it is a mark of our devotion to God."

"You have to wear them?"

"Not have to, but choose to. Some women do not wear this hat."

"It's very pretty," Stephanie said again. "The embroidery is beautifully done."

"Thank you," Angela said nervously, and finally smiled. "I– I made it."

"Oh, you must be very talented with your hands," Stephanie said brightly. "I have tried to learn to embroider, but I can't do anything like that."

"It all comes with practice," Angela said. "I'm sure your embroidery is very beautiful too."

"Oh, no. It's not."

They rode in silence for a moment.

"I feel bad for drawing you away from your husband and family so suddenly," Stephanie said, as if it had been weighing on her. "I didn't mean to be a burden on anyone here."

"You're not a burden," Samson said, irritation in his voice.

"No. This is my job," Angela said. "It is my pleasure to be your escort."

"Do you live in the city here?" Stephanie asked.

"You want to know where I live?"

"Yes, do you live here in the city, or in one of the other settlements?"

"Yes, I live here," Angela said. "In an apartment. There."

She pointed to a tower a few miles away from them. It was a tall tower, with many rows of shiny, silver windows. The base of the tower was round, in the shape of a cylinder, and at the top the cylinder became a square and was crowned with one of the little, white cube structures. Nearly all of the buildings were shaped the same way. They were all white and glossy. If the sun had not been so distant, the effect would have been blinding.

"Why do some of the men carry guns?" Stephanie wondered, and Angela choked.

As they walked up the path to Samson's parents' home, he tripped over his feet and nearly fell. He kept his arm around Stephanie as they approached the door. The house was a big, circular, single-story building, with a courtyard in its center and little gardens surrounding it. White, of course. The windows cast an inky yellow reflection as the diffuse light from Neptune's solar collectors faded slowly in the afternoon. The air smelled pungent and lush.

Theodore's wife greeted them at the door. She gasped when she saw Samson, but leapt straight past him into Theodore's arms and embraced him wildly. She was a bright, strongly built, attractive woman with earthy skin and red hair. After embracing Theodore for an awkwardly long time, she turned to Samson and grabbed hold of him, too, trapping him in a sort of bear hug.

"Mr. Samson Ford, it's a pleasure to finally meet you," she said, with a melodious and faintly accusing tone.

She let go of him, and motioned them all inside.

"I'm sorry it's taken me so long, Maria," Samson said sheepishly. "I really have been looking forward to finally meeting you."

"Oh, don't worry. Hurry into the courtyard, your parents are waiting."

Maria pulled Stephanie aside and introduced herself, as Samson stepped through the house's semi-enclosed entranceway. By the time they caught up to Samson in the courtyard, his parents were standing away from him, with their hands on his shoulders, crying happily. Samson smiled back tensely, and seemed to withhold himself from their deeper emotions.

His parents were tall, elegant people. Stephanie could easily see him in them, or Theodore. He introduced her to them and they greeted her politely, but with little warmth. He called Stephanie his "friend". Theodore suggested that perhaps Stephanie and Angela should wait in the sitting room while the family caught up with each other, and, after a long pause, Samson agreed.

He squeezed Stephanie apologetically.

"It's not because of you," he whispered. "It's Angela. We can't speak openly around her."

Stephanie helped herself to a sandwich on a tray in the sitting room. She offered one to Angela, who declined. The sitting room was a little library, with two wooden bookshelves filled with books on engineering, farming, and religion. The religious books, especially, caught Stephanie's eye, many of them she had never heard of before. She poured herself a glass of grape juice from a pitcher on the table and inspected three unopened bottles of wine that had been left for them. The labels indicated a local vintage.

"You have vineyards here?"

"Yes. Like Tuscany," Angela said proudly.

Stephanie sat down beside Angela and nibbled at the sandwich. It was rye bread, with chicken, mayonnaise, and tomatoes.

"You should eat, Angela," Stephanie said protectively. "You must be hungry by now."

"No. Thank you."

"The sandwiches are very good."

"I'm sure they are good. But, you see, I do not eat between noon and sundown."

"You fast?"

"Yes, I fast. For half of every day."

"So you are accustomed to not eating during this time, it doesn't bother you."

"You understand," Angela said gratefully. "For me, to see food in the afternoon, it doesn't affect me at all. I never feel, 'ooh, I would want to eat that', because I never eat during this time. It is not a possibility for me, and so I do not regret it."

"I see. Then, after sunset you will eat again."

"Yes, a big meal," Angela said smiling, and made a large circular motion in front of her stomach.

Stephanie took another bite of her sandwich, while Angela watched her eat.

"Gosh, I'm hungry. You must have enormous willpower to fast like that every day."

"It is not hard," Angela said, "when it is for the right reason."

"It is a sort of sacrifice for God, when you fast?"

"Do you believe in God?" Angela said, and rubbed non-existent wrinkles out of her skirt.

"I don't know."

Angela looked sad. Stephanie could not help staring at her dull brown hair and eyes, her blemished, natural skin. She was like a little, wild mouse, Stephanie thought, compared to the perfect little pet mice that they sold in pet stores.

"Not many people, outside of Magdalena, believe in God?" Angela asked slowly.

"No, not many."

"How many is it? Only one in ten people?"

"No," Stephanie said gently. "No, it isn't one in ten people, it's less."

"One in one hundred?" Angela's eyes were big.

"No, perhaps only one person in one thousand," Stephanie lied, inflating the number, and Angela caught her breath in horror.

Stephanie ate her sandwich and they sat in silence for a moment. The garden outside the sitting room window was beautiful, with a little fountain in the center of it. There were two small fruit trees, and orange and yellow flowers that Stephanie had never seen before. She looked up at the copper and orange sky of Triton, and reminded herself how incredible it was that people had built a living world here in the far reaches of the Solar System.

"Do you have children?" she asked Angela.

"Yes, two. A boy, the older, and a girl. And what about you?"

"Oh, no. I don't have any."

"No?"

"No."

"And do you want children?" Angela asked.

"Yes."

"In– Out there," Angela said awkwardly, "many women do not have children. Their babies are made in a machine. Is it true?"

"Yes, that's true," Stephanie said.

"How can this be?"

"Well, what do you mean? The technology?"

215

"Don't you want your baby to grow inside of you, to be a part of you?" Angela asked, touching her stomach reverently. "How can you make your baby in a machine?"

"Yes, it must seem very cold," Stephanie said.

"What about you, will you make your baby in a machine?" Angela asked accusingly.

"I don't know, Angela," Stephanie said. "Are all the babies conceived naturally here?"

"Of course."

"You've never even seen a gene weaving machine, or an incubator?"

"No," Angela said. "We make chickens in an incubator."

"How old are your children?"

"The boy, Peter, is seven. The girl, Maria, is three years old."

"They must be beautiful children."

"I think so," Angela said, and smiled.

"I am sorry to keep you here, away from your family," Stephanie said. "I'm sure they are missing you right now."

"No, it is my job. We do not have visitors here very often, you see. It is a special occasion to be here with you. For me, it is a special honor to have the responsibility of your escort."

Angela stood up and poured herself a glass of grape juice from the pitcher. She picked up another little sandwich from the tray and set it on Stephanie's plate, then sat back down next to her again.

"Eat more. You are hungry."

ANGELA HAD BEEN GIGGLING, TELLING Stephanie about her husband when Samson walked back into the sitting room and told Stephanie that they needed to leave. He was angry. His parents peered into the room behind him, pained expressions on their faces, and Theodore tried to reason with him.

"We have to leave now," Samson said conclusively, pulling

Stephanie along with him and pushing past his parents.

"Sammy, please stay with us for one evening," Theodore said. "It's been so long since you were here, please don't be this way. We're so happy to see you and have you here."

"It's so good to finally meet you, Samson," Maria said and smiled, but looked on the verge of tears. "You don't have to leave so soon."

"You haven't even met the children yet!"

Samson rushed out of the house as if its walls were closing in around him and Stephanie allowed herself to be dragged along, not knowing what else to do. Theodore continued to plead with him as they walked out through the gardens to the big hovercar with the tinted windows. He stopped talking suddenly. Two officious looking men in crisp, white suits were blocking their path to the hovercar. The chauffeur shrugged.

"Hello, Mr. Ford," one of the men said to Samson.

"What do you want?"

"The Prophet desires to meet with you. Both of you."

"Now?" Samson glared at them.

"In two days."

"We're leaving tonight. Maybe he can link up with us on a holo-conference or something."

"I'm afraid we can't allow you to leave the city until you meet with The Prophet two days from now," the man said.

Angela stared at the ground.

"So you want us to wait here?" Samson asked, sounding defiant.

"Not exactly, Mr. Ford."

NEO VEGA WAS A GIGANTIC city. A wild, seedy, dangerous place where almost everything was legal. Except stealing. But where stealing was common, where everything was common, where anything could be bought and humanity was cheap. If you could have gone back in time to Earth in the 1970s, and combined Times Square, New York with Las Vegas, Nevada and Central, Hong Kong and Kabukicho, Tokyo and isolated it all in a claustrophobic petri dish and let it acculturate for about fifty years, and then deposited it in the middle of the American Old West, you'd just about have Neo Vega. It was a great place to lay low and buy Gravity Control Units.

Kenichi sat in a sitting room in an enormous brothel called, "Madame Coochie's". It had thick, pink carpets and vagina shaped chandeliers. The walls flickered and crawled with moving pornographic images.

"Could you turn that off please?" Kenichi said. "The images on the walls."

"Of course," the Madame Coochie's manager said, and waved her hand. The images disappeared and the walls became a soft, glowing white. The manager was a short woman, with huge breasts and a tiny waist. Her face was distorted, it resembled the face of a child, but with deep lines around the eyes that were not quite concealed with make-up, as if she were wearing a mask over her real face. "So, will Abebe do for you?"

A pretty woman with soft green, glittery skin, neon blue eyes, and a grotesquely exaggerated hourglass figure stood in front of them hopefully.

"No, she won't do. She won't do at all."

"She has an advanced lactation capability," the madame said in a syrupy voice.

"I don't care about lactation."

"Well, she has everything else. Lubrication enhancements, orgasm potential, you do want her to orgasm don't you?"

"Yes I want her to orgasm," Kenichi said with some irritation.

The madame motioned for Abebe to go.

"We have girls who don't. We have something new that I'm sure you've never seen before. A girl with luminescent skin. Gorgeous. Her skin glows like a light bulb. She's had to wear sunglasses her entire life."

"No."

"What exactly are you looking for, Mr. Iwahara?"

"I don't know."

"You're not being an easy customer to help. You want me? I'm afraid you can't afford me, though. Those days are in the past..."

"I don't want you."

"Alright, honey. Alright. No need to be rude."

There was a long pause, and the madame sighed heavily.

"Ok," Kenichi said, "I want a woman who is more natural looking. Nothing extreme. Twenty-eight, twenty-nine, thirty years old. With black hair. Beautiful, but nothing extreme. Tall. Pale skin, white skin, no colors. Dark eyes."

"Well that's very specific."

"Do you have a girl like that?"

"I think I might have just the girl for you. Wait here, I'll go and get her."

The madame walked out of the room and returned a few minutes later with a tall, long legged, raven haired woman. Her skin was faintly silver, but pale, and her eyes were a dark, navy blue. Her body was willowy and more naturally proportioned than what was popular. She smiled at Kenichi dully. She was wearing a short, red dress.

"Well?" the Madame said, as if this were his last chance.

Kenichi leaned forward in his chair.

"Pull down your panties, I want to see between your legs."

"Mr. Iwahara," the madame said, "that doesn't happen for free."

"Well how much? Just for a quick look. If I like it I'll take her for the night."

"200 credits, Mr. Iwahara. For a quick look."

"Fine."

The madame nodded to the girl, who pulled down her panties nervously, a weak smile on her face. Kenichi squatted on the floor inches in front of her, and peered up between her legs.

"Spread wider, I can't see."

"Mr. Iwahara, that's enough. Glynis put your panties back on."

"She's so worn out," he said with disappointment, and Glynis' shoulders sank under his gaze.

"We do have some virgins, Mr. Iwahara," the madame said icily, "but I doubt you can afford them."

"I don't want a virgin."

"Will Glynis suit you, or should I ask you to leave now?"

"Fine, fine. She'll do. I want her for the night."

Phillipe Bloodworth leaned forward over his enormous desk, as if it would bring him closer to the person on the screen.

"Did you meet with Iwahara?"

"Not yet, sir. We have a meeting scheduled with him on Monday. On Neo Vega."

"Good. Get him on our side. Whatever means necessary, you understand?"

"Mr. Bloodworth," another voice chimed in on the com, "you have an incoming call from Simon Okunle."

"Put him up."

Bloodworth chewed his cigar nervously.

"You tried to fuck me, Simon!" he said as soon as Simon Okunle appeared on the screen.

Simon folded his hands in front of him, completely relaxed and composed.

"Phillipe, what are you saying?"

"You went against me on the vote on the goddamned kinderfucks, don't you think I'd find out about that?"

"It's only business, Phillipe. We don't want that legislation passed, we think it's bad for our bottom line. The natural born are 35% of our customers."

"Fuck business. Fuck your bottom line," Bloodworth said, "Don't you understand what's happening out there?"

"What's happening out there?"

"A revolution, man! A chance for humanity to move forward, man! A chance for a bigger, brighter, wealthier, more glorious future. Natural born? It's an anachronism, my friend. The world doesn't just march into the future whistling koombaya, it has to be dragged there, it always has to be dragged. And I'm doing the dragging."

He allowed a slight pause before continuing beseechingly.

"I need your help."

"Phillipe, we feel like you are trying to undermine our companies."

"What?"

"We don't think this legislation is in anyone's best interest, and it undermines our business positions quite dramatically."

There was a long pause, and color slowly drained out of Phillipe Bloodworth's face. He set his cigar down on his desk and flattened it with the palm of his hand as he stood up in his chair and leaned forward.

"Simon," he said quietly, "are you saying you want war?"

"Of course not, my friend," Simon said, unfolding his hands calmly and setting them in his lap. "But we support the status quo."

"I'm sorry to hear that."

C H A P T E R ³⁴

AMSON PULLED AT THE DOOR angrily, and kicked it for the dozenth time. It was extremely solid.

"At least it's nice here," Stephanie said, sitting down on one of the big leather couches in the main room of the suite. "It's like a nice hotel."

"A nice prison," he said sourly, and walked into the shiny, stainless steel kitchen.

He started to fill a glass with ice, thought better of it, started to get water out of the tap to drink, thought better of it again, and finally tore a sealed bottle of water out of a dusty, unopened carton in the back of a cabinet.

"How long do you think they'll make us wait here?" Stephanie wondered.

AS THE TIME PASSED THEY developed a sense of ease with their confinement. The suite was nice, even luxurious. Samson was suspicious of the food that had been provided them, but he couldn't complain about its quality. The kitchen was completely stocked. Big windows looked out onto Magdalena City. It occurred to him that this would actually be pretty nice if it were really a hotel room, if it had a terminal and if their com cards weren't blocked... and he were stuck there alone with Stephanie. They talked for hours. Samson stretched out on the couch luxuriously to wrap his arms around her hips, and rest his head in her lap, and Stephanie ran her hands through his hair.

"Have you ever met The Prophet before?" she asked.

"No."

"Do you think they're monitoring us right now?"

"Probably."

"What do people think they'll learn from monitoring each

"

other?" Stephanie asked philosophically.

"That we're human beings like them, with feelings, and ideas, and insecurities I guess," Samson said, sliding his hands up onto the skin of her waist where her blouse had come untucked. "That's what they're afraid of."

"But aren't they afraid that we're not like them, that we're different, or not that we're different, but that they're different?"

"Maybe it's a sort of paradox," Samson said. "When somebody wants to spy on other people, they want to discover what those people's secrets are, and they get sort of both irritated and relieved to discover that those people are pretty much the same as everyone else."

"You're not the same as everyone else," Stephanie said.

"No, neither are you."

"So they must be having a lot of fun monitoring us, since we are so different."

"Or feeling really bad about themselves."

"Because you're so great," Stephanie said, "it might make them feel bad by comparison."

"Exactly. You don't understand how beautiful you are, how smart, and in Magdalena there aren't any women as beautiful and smart as you."

"Oh, thank you."

He sat up and put his chin lightly on Stephanie's shoulder, holding her close and staring at her face.

"You'll make me self-conscious if you stare at me like that," she said quietly.

"I don't think you have a problem with self-consciousness," he said, and she smiled.

"Why were you angry at your parents?" she asked, and Samson relaxed his grip on her unconsciously.

"It's, uh–, look weren't we just talking about being monitored here?"

"Oh, true."

"I don't want these goons to know about our family business, but obviously, I haven't been back home since I was a teenager. My parents feel pretty bad about that, and it really upset them when I said I was only staying for a few hours."

"Oh."

"That's just the general thing, I don't want to get into it too much, circumstances being what they are and whatever."

"But you could stay more than a few hours," Stephanie said, "it's something special to be with your family like that, especially after so long."

"I don't want to talk about it here."

"No. Well ask me about me, I don't care what they hear."

"Whenever you tell me about yourself I never feel like I actually learn any more about you," Samson said.

"Really?"

"You're a very mysterious person."

"Well, I– There are some things I also can't talk about," Stephanie said, and she slid back on the couch and rested her head in Samson's lap, looking up at him. "But tell me what you want to know."

"Where were you born?"

"On Earth."

"Where on Earth?"

"In Manhattan."

"Ah, I guess that makes sense," he said, and undid the top button on Stephanie's blouse.

"Do I seem like a Manhattanite?"

"No. You seem like someone who was born in Manhattan."

She laughed.

"Did you grow up there?"

"No."

"Well, where did you grow up?"

Stephanie closed her eyes and rolled onto her side, so that her face was facing away from him.

"All over."

"You grew up all over?"

"Yes."

"See, that's what I'm talking about."

"Well it's true..."

"See I haven't really learned anything about you now."

"You can still ask more questions."

Stephanie rubbed the tops of his thighs and got up off the couch.

"Let's open up one of those bottles of Magdalena wine they have," she said. "It's like Tuscan wine, isn't it? That's what you like."

"I'm afraid to eat or drink anything here," he said skeptically.

"I think it will be ok," Stephanie said. "We're at their mercy here, they could have hurt us if they wanted to. And, one way or another, we'll have to eat eventually."

She held out a bottle of wine and Samson jumped up off the couch and hopped over to her, spinning the bottle in his hand and examining the label.

"And besides," Stephanie said, "I have a sixth sense about these sorts of things. And I'm never, ever wrong."

Samson laughed.

"Well, that's the sort of sixth sense that I like," he said.

He cut the wrapper off of the bottle's top, and held the bottle up to the light, examining it carefully, scrutinizing the cork, shaking it, trying to discover any evidence of tampering. Stephanie pulled the bottle out of his hand and uncorked it rapidly. He took the two wine glasses she had selected and rinsed them out with some of the bottled water and shook them dry.

"You're quite meticulous," she said pleasantly.

"Lots of people try to fuck with me," Samson said with a wry smile.

"So I've discovered."

They went back to the big leather couch and sipped the wine. It was very good wine. It really was like Tuscan wine, which surprised Stephanie. She didn't know what she had expected.

"You can still keep asking me questions if you want."

"Oh, I want to," Samson said. "I've got about a million questions."

"We probably won't have time for a million," Stephanie said. "At least, I hope not. I guess we don't really know how long they're going to keep us in here."

"Where do your parents live?" he asked.

"My parents don't live."

"Oh, I'm sorry."

"It's ok. My mother died when I was young, I can't remember her very well. And my father died a few years ago."

"Were you close to him?"

"Yes. We were very close," Stephanie said distantly and paused for a while. "It was really unfair, I don't have any brothers or sisters either."

"I'm sorry."

"It's hard for me to understand," she said, "when I would do anything to spend time with my father or my mother again, and you have your parents here and you want to leave as quickly as possible."

"Yeah."

"What if your mother or your father died, wouldn't you regret that, that you didn't spend more time with them?"

"Yeah. I don't know, Stephanie."

He downed his glass of wine.

"I'm sorry, Samson."

"Don't be sorry." He squeezed her hand. "You don't offend me, Stephanie. I like it that you're direct like that."

"Do you?"

Samson poured himself another glass of wine.

"Yes, I do. I like almost everything about you."

"I'm not so direct with everyone, you know."

"I know. I bet your Father was an amazing man. I wish I could meet him."

"Oh, he was," Stephanie said. "I wish you could, too. He would have liked you."

C　H　A　P　T　E　R　35

Kenichi pushed Glynis' shoulders down onto a big hover bed. Her huge, navy blue eyes stared past him distantly and she pulled her face into a smile, as if she were smiling at him.

"Don't– Don't smile like that," he said, and Glynis stopped smiling.

"Don't you like me?" she asked.

Kenichi put his hands on her body and started taking her clothes off. He rubbed her breasts in what he imagined was an affectionate way. Her skin was very silver, it was starting to annoy him more and more.

"Oh yes, that feels good. Yes," Glynis said hollowly.

"Stop talking please," Kenichi said with unmasked irritation.

"Why don't you want me to talk?"

"Just stop talking!"

He finished taking her clothes off and ran his hands again and again through her long black hair. He turned her over and caressed her hair, and rubbed her back, but the silver skin seemed to shine at him. He turned down the lights so her skin would appear more natural, more porcelain white. He made her lay on her back again. Glynis was tense.

Kenichi rubbed her long legs and started having sex with her, but whenever he looked into her face he would stop in exasperation, and run his hands through her long, black hair again, and pull it across her face. She started to cry. He pulled all her hair together and wrapped it around her face so that he could barely see her. Glynis sniffed quietly and was completely limp on the bed. He tried to thrust into her again, but his body was reluctant. He couldn't stop noticing her silver skin. He could still see her navy blue eyes through the curtain of hair. He slumped down on top of her, his face pale and dripping sweat, and breathed a long, frustrated, angry sigh.

White-suited Magdalena security agents knocked on the door of the suite on the second day that Samson and Stephanie were imprisoned there. Samson stared at the door and, as the knocking continued, finally opened it bemusedly.

"Oh, is this unlocked now?" he said.

The agents instructed them to collect their things, and led them through the Temple to meet The Prophet. Magdalena Temple was a bright, airy, enormous building, with incredible vaulted ceilings, as if it were built into the sky. It was filled with stained glass windows and old fashioned tapestries that featured white birds and crosses, hourglasses, crescent moons, and ten pointed stars. The halls of the temple were very quiet, so that one's footsteps echoed through them loudly, as if they went on forever.

The Prophet's quarters were like a separate mansion built into the Temple. The rooms had an old-world, medieval European sensibility to them, as if he were some ancient king or archduke. The security agents led Samson and Stephanie to The Prophet's den, a large room with plush red carpets, filled with books. A wall of windows looked out onto a huge courtyard of flowers and fountains. The ceiling of the den was an intricately framed oval window that looked up to the sky.

The Prophet stood up when he saw them and smiled magnanimously. He shook out his robes. He was a pasty, ordinary looking man, with the exception of huge, grey eyes that seemed to shine from his face like beacons of light. He stepped forward and embraced Samson in an enormous hug.

"Samson, child," he said, "you have returned to us at last."

Samson returned the embrace stiffly, unsure of what to do, until The Prophet finally let him go.

"And you, madame," he said. "We do not often receive visitors here in Magdalena. It is my honor to have you here in our lands."

He grasped Stephanie's hand warmly between both of his and kissed it.

"Thank you," she said politely. "Please call me Stephanie."

"I am very sorry to have detained you both," The Prophet said, "I have only just heard that you were planning to leave. Please forgive my people, I had told them that I wanted to meet with you and they tried a little too hard to make sure that it happened."

"These things sometimes occur, and there was no harm done," Stephanie said smoothly, before Samson had a chance to reply.

"Thank you, Stephanie, you are a gracious woman. Please come in, come into my little office here, both of you."

Samson and Stephanie walked into the room and The Prophet motioned them towards a couch in the center, behind a fine, black, coffee table.

"Coffee?" he offered, picking up an intricately engraved golden pitcher.

"Do you grow coffee here, too?" Stephanie asked, sounding impressed.

"Oh yes, I couldn't live without it. I would really be in a fix. We grow fine, hybrid beans to produce the finest Turkish coffee. It is my great vice, and my great pleasure."

"We would both love to have a cup, I think," Stephanie said, looking at Samson.

"Yes, sure," Samson said. "A cup of coffee, but we need to leave soon I'm afraid."

"I'm sorry to hear that."

"We do have lives of our own to lead, I'm sure you can understand that," Samson said. "I need to meet up with the rest of my team in Neo Vega, they're waiting for me and we're losing days."

"I'm sorry to have delayed you, Samson. I hope you have had a chance to visit your family while you were here?"

"Yes, I saw them."

"It was such a joy to me when I heard that you were returning to us at last. I had hoped, even if it was only a wishful hope, that you perhaps had returned to us to stay."

The Prophet brushed away moisture from his eyes, and sniffed his nose conspicuously. He selected three small, golden bowl-like cups and poured the coffee into them.

"I'm afraid not," Samson said. "Just for a visit this time."

"We will still pray for you. You are our child here, and our brother, and we have twelve priests who pray on every Sabbath that you will return to us."

"Thank you, sir," Samson said. "It is hard to respond to that, but I do have a different life out there that I have to return to."

"Of course. You have Stephanie. A beautiful woman. That's why we don't like for our people to leave, because it can be so difficult to extricate yourself again and return to home after you have become involved in a life away from your home."

"Yes."

The Prophet sat down in a chair close to them and all three sipped quietly at their coffee.

"I have heard about your life, Samson," The Prophet said, "out in the Solar System. You have been making a name for yourself."

"Thank you."

"You are a famous racing pilot now, we're very proud of you."

"Thank you, sir."

"You can do a lot of good for the world with your racing."

"I hope so, sir."

"Have you thought about that, Samson?"

Samson gulped his coffee and it burned his throat. He looked at The Prophet skeptically. He was an older man, perhaps in his sixties, with white hair. He wore white and purple robes. There was something about him that Samson found repulsive. More so than he had expected. The Prophet watched him with an easy, patronizing superiority, as if watching a very stupid child.

"I'm not sure what you mean."

"You're becoming very famous. You're becoming a representative of natural born people everywhere."

"I don't really think I'm a representative of anyone," Samson said uncomfortably. "I'm just a pilot."

"Billions of people watch your races, Samson."

Stephanie sipped her coffee silently, and Samson set his cup down on the tray on the table.

"Well, I plan to keep winning races, if that's what you mean."

"What are your plans for this year?" The Prophet asked eagerly. "Will you race in some of the biggest races?"

"I've just found out I'm going to be racing in the Solar Regatta at the end of the year," Samson said. "Nobody else knows about that yet, it's a secret, but it is the biggest race in the Solar System."

"Your role in life is very important, Samson," The Prophet said, setting down his own cup. "The natural born people in the Solar System need a figurehead right now, a symbol and an example, to give them pride in themselves and to show them what they are capable of. And that is the role that God has chosen for you, for you personally. You have been selected."

Samson started to respond, but The Prophet held up a finger quieting him.

"I'm sure you've heard of the legislation on Earth that they are trying to pass, the quarantine of natural born people. These are grave times, my son, very dangerous times. In the Temple we have been watching the outside world with open eyes, observing the currents of the Solar System, the ebbs and flows. We're worried. Similar legislation is set to be introduced on Mars and Venus, as well. All of our welfare is imperiled, and you might be our only hope."

"With all respect, sir," Samson said weakly, "I don't think there's very much that I personally can do."

"You're very wrong, Samson," The Prophet said, staring at him intensely. "By winning races, and by living a life of example, you can demonstrate to billions of people the value and equality of the natural born. You have the power to change the tide of public opinion all over the Solar System. I don't have that power. Kings, and presidents, and corporate lords across the Solar System don't have that power. But you do. You have been given a blessing and a talent by God, and put into this position, to make a difference for all of humanity. That is why I wanted to speak to you today, to impress upon you that you have been selected by God, and what a great joy and what a great responsibility that is."

Samson didn't know what to say. He stood up, and Stephanie stood up with him, and they walked around the coffee table as if it were time to leave. The Prophet stood up as well, and walked over to them, watching them both curiously.

"I don't know if we believe the same things, sir," Samson said, "but if you want me to keep winning races then you could say we are on the same team."

"Yes, Samson, we are on the same team, absolutely. Here in Magdalena we are behind you completely."

"Thank you."

"It does worry me to hear you mention the Solar Regatta,

though. You are a special gift to our community, even if you don't consider this your home right now, and we would hate to lose you."

"The races are always dangerous," Samson said. "I have a knack for staying alive."

"God watches over you! Your success in the Solar Regatta would be a wonderful thing for the world, Samson. If you could place, let us say, in the top 10," he lifted his eyebrows, "it would be of enormous benefit to natural borns everywhere. Even that by itself could be enough to keep this vile, hateful legislation from passing."

"We're not aiming for the top 10," Stephanie said, an edge of irritation creeping into her voice, "we're going there to win."

Samson put his arm around Stephanie's shoulder, surprised at how possessive she sounded about the race.

"Winning would be the best thing of all," The Prophet said. "And that is where I want to help you. I know that racing is very expensive. And here in Magdalena we want to support Samson as much as we possibly can, even if he is our *prodigal* son. We want to help you financially, Samson. I want to give you a financial gift to help with your racing efforts."

Samson squirmed.

"Thank you, sir. That's very generous. We really couldn't take advantage of you in that way, and our racing team has secured a new sponsorship just in the past week. We're fully funded for our efforts in the Solar Regatta."

"Don't be so rash, Samson, your success is important to me. Let me help you. This will be only between you and me, it won't be for the public. It will be money 'under the table', as they say."

Samson tried stubbornly to reject the gift, but The Prophet was insistent. Fearing they would not be allowed to leave, he finally allowed The Prophet to transfer a sum of money onto his card. The Prophet took Samson's card and transferred 500,000 credits onto it from a Geneva bank, as if he performed such transactions all the time.

As he embraced them both and finally allowed them to leave, The Prophet pressed a solid gold coin into Samson's hand. It had likenesses of The Prophet himself on both sides.

"A token of my appreciation, Samson," he said, smiling brightly. "Perhaps you can send it to your mother or your brother as a gift sometime. I'm sure it would be a special treasure for them."

A CHAUFFEURED CAR FLEW SAMSON AND Stephanie to a small, independent settlement near the Magdalena border. It was a town with a daily shuttle to Neo Vega, a general store, dust, and not much else. The town served as a transportation hub for the rancheros, prospectors, Magdalena agents, 'lost sheep', and criminals who inhabited the Triton badlands. Samson and Stephanie sat on metal benches near a door in the mostly empty terminal and waited for the shuttle to arrive.

Neither of them was in a good mood.

"I can't believe that asshole locked us up like that," Samson said, "and then we had to play nice with him."

"I'll never understand what can drive people to worship such shitty human beings," Stephanie said. "Maybe it is actually a good thing that religion has been wiped out."

"Yeah, I don't know."

Samson was surprised by the venom in Stephanie's voice. It made him forget for a moment about his own anger and mixed up emotions over their whole visit. He scanned the other people in the terminal. A stubbly-chinned old, prospector burnout in one corner whispered excitedly to himself. His eyes sparkled as if that long awaited gold vein would open up right then in front of him. A couple of farmers were talking to the clerk. A Magdalena agent, dressed neatly in an old fashioned suit, sat by the main entrance, stiff, and ignored everyone else. Samson watched him for a minute and concluded that the man had nothing to do with them. He looked down at the swept clean, concrete floor and kicked gently at the soles of Stephanie's shoes.

"Yeah, I don't think it's a good thing," he said. "Even if religion has a tendency to get hijacked by lunatics and assholes, I think there's something to it. I don't really know what I believe about it, but, I really feel on some level, somewhere deep inside myself, almost like a fundamental knowledge of self kind of feeling, like as much as I know anything in the world – anyway, I feel like the reason I don't die when I race is because God is protecting me."

Stephanie sniffed sourly.

"Men like that shouldn't be allowed to spread their poison and pollute people's minds," she said.

"Wow, I don't like The Prophet, but you really hated him," Samson said.

"It makes me crazy to play nice with men like that."

He looked at Stephanie curiously, she was almost shaking with anger. Her whole body was taut and her eyes bored into the space in front of her as if she were watching images play out in her mind. He put his hand on her back and rubbed it bracingly.

"A powerful man should never be so arrogant," she said, blinking back tears in her eyes and turning her face away from him. "It's disgusting."

IN NEO VEGA THEY FOUND protesters outside the hangar where the Junket was parked, holding signs that said things like, "Monkeys go home!" and "Ford should be banned!" The fact that the protesters knew where they were bothered Samson much more than the protesters themselves. There were reporters there, too. He asked their cabbie to turn on the tinting in the cab's windows and they pulled through the security gate at the hangar without incident. Ben was relieved to see them when they got inside. He tried to ask them about the visit to Magdalena, but pulled at his beard distractedly.

"Where's Ken?" Samson asked.

"He left," Ben said rapidly. "I didn't want to say it on the phone just now, but Ken left as soon as we got here. He had a bag all packed and walked out the door as soon as we set down in the hangar. He said he'd be back, that was the only thing he said, and when I followed after him he just said he had business to take care of and couldn't talk about it. Acting really weird. I haven't heard anything since then."

Samson raised his eyebrows and wondered if Kenichi could have had something to do with the protesters.

"Yeah, I don't know," Ben said, as if reading his mind.

KENICHI SAT IN A BATHROBE in his hotel room and stared at Phillipe Bloodworth's agents. They were sitting in chairs across the room. The unassuming looking one who did all the talking was the brains, Kenichi decided. The other guy was just muscle. They were trying to set him at ease. He finished cutting a thin line of powdered cocaine with a razor blade on the glass table in front of him and looked at it lovingly with a small metal pipe in his hands. His eyes were red.

"The two of you don't mind, do you?" he said. "It's been twenty years for me."

"Of course not," the brains said, straightening his tie and smoothing out his hair in the reflection of a wall mirror. "Enjoy. Please."

Kenichi snorted up the line of coke, sniffed in the air a few times for good measure, and caught his breath. He put a finger under his nose and held back a sneeze.

"It's pretty silly that they still ban cocaine on Earth," the brains said. "They try to make you feel like a criminal every time you need a hit."

"Is cocaine still banned on Earth?" Kenichi asked, letting out his breath. "I thought they would change that by now. When I was younger."

"Things change slowly on Earth," the brains said.

"Yes."

Kenichi set the little pipe down on the table and leaned back in his chair. He sipped from a glass of ice water and watched the spinning fan on the ceiling. His face had two days of stubble accumulation on it, his long hair was greasy and hung in strands.

"Oh, would you two like a drink or something?" he asked absentmindedly. "I'm sorry not to offer you any of the coke, that was the last I had."

"That's alright, Ken," the brains said. "We don't need any-thing, we're still on the job. This is Neo Vega after all, we'll go out and party later tonight, make an adventure out of it. We'll get some coke then. You're welcome to come if you want."

"No. No, thank you," Kenichi said.

"Yes, well we're sorry to disturb you, Ken. Let's get down to business. We don't want Samson Ford to win any more races."

The muscle unfolded his wallet and shuffled through it as if he were looking for a card. He was a handsome, perfect man, with soft yellow eyes. A typical Bloodworth man. He checked the meter tucked into his wallet to make sure the mind control device in his briefcase was turned on, and pulled out an old fashioned business card and set it on the table in front of Kenichi.

"That's Mr. Bloodworth's card," the muscle said.

Kenichi picked the business card up and examined the layers of embossing. It wasn't really like the old business cards they used to use, it was almost a mockery of them. It was almost a work of art. He sniffed and smiled. Phillipe Blood-worth had been a powerful man in the Solar System twenty years ago. He was a lot more powerful now. He was one of the leaders of the legislative push on Earth to have the natural borns quarantined. He had more money than the Bank of Manhattan. He had more money than the gods. He was a fat, disgusting troll. His goons had killed a racing engineer thirty years ago because Phillipe Bloodworth thought the design he commissioned from her was mediocre and she told him he was an idiot. Kenichi took his card out of the terminal beside him and ran his finger across it, there was a flashing orange signal. He slid it into his pocket.

"Samson doesn't have to win," he said finally. "It's an economic question. He is good enough to win, and unless something unexpected happens he will continue to win races. The economic question comes down to the fact that by winning races he is going to make a great deal of money. As an important member of the team, a share of that money will be mine. That is the economic question. For me, I like Samson, so there is an additional element to that, because, everything else being equal, I would prefer to see him win races. If you want to do a deal, first of all I can't guarantee anything, because he has two other good mechanics in his team and they are both scrutinizing my work closely. So you can understand what the situation is now."

"But you will try to help us," the brains said.

"We can calculate an arrangement that will be suitable to us both," Kenichi said. "You have it within your power to change the economic dynamics of this situation for me, and I probably have it within my power to prevent Samson from winning any more races in the near future."

"There would be a substantial bonus involved if Samson were never able to race again," the brains said, and watched Kenichi closely without appearing to be watching him.

"That's an intriguing proposition," Kenichi said, and sniffed, and smiled, and watched the circular patterns made by the spinning fan blades on the ceiling.

C H A P T E R ³⁷

CAMP SAT IN THE CAPTAIN's chair on the deck of a deep-space battleship. It was a rental. A couple of technicians worked at the ship's controls, but the captain had wandered off to bed. It was a big ship that had been built for war. It came equipped with huge cannons and an official registry that claimed they had been de-activated, which they had not. In the deep, dark, empty spaces of the Solar System, it was a ship whose cannons were still used regularly. For the right price.

He filled up the captain's chair completely, and it was uncomfortable, but Scamp stubbornly refused to move. It was a stubbornness against the world, against fate. A way of refusing to be different. He watched the moon turn slowly below them. They had been orbiting Triton for two days.

THE MAIN DINING ROOM IN the battleship had orange walls and was lined with metal tables and benches. Three of Lucho's soldiers sat in the dining room alone and talked. They all wore shorts and old, ribbed tank tops, they were relaxing. They laughed easily, and spoke furtively, conversation punctuated with shouts and whispers. They were muscular, beautiful men. They were scarred men, and vaguely misformed, with faces that spoke of difficult lives and bodies that spoke of genetic manufacturing gone slightly wrong. They were factory seconds, close-out specials, that were for all practical purposes just as good as the real thing.

"What's his story, anyway?" asked the youngest man, who had only recently become a member of Lucho's gang.

"Oh, fuck you, you must have heard."

"I heard some rumors and shit, but people seem afraid to really talk about it."

"They are afraid. He tore a guy's head off. That's not a rumor, I was there. When I was first working for Lucho. Some asshole said some shit to him in front of a bunch of guys and Scamp grabbed him and tore his fucking head right off of his shoulders and dropped it on the floor."

"Holy fuck."

"Oh, bullshit," said the third man. "I never believed that story."

"Hey, I was fucking there. He grabbed the dude and ripped his head fucking off. It was like a fucking comic book, you can't even imagine, like what do you think you do, you're all standing there, standing around, and all of a sudden some huge dude rips another guy's head off and there's blood all over everything and he just dropped the dude's head on the floor and walked out of the room."

"Holy fuck."

"And that's when Lucho promoted him, I guess Lucho didn't like the dude either."

All three of them laughed.

"Oh shit, that's funny. I still don't believe that shit."

"No? I got pictures, I can show you. I got pictures of the head on the fucking floor."

"No shit?" the third man said, laughing more than before. "Holy shit, I gotta see that."

"Yeah, you gotta keep it under wraps, though. I don't want to get on that fucker's bad side."

"What about the other rumors?" the first man said again.

"What, that he's part dog and part fucking chimp? Were you born yesterday or something, look at the dude. It's not that hard to tell."

"But all those fucking hybrids were supposed to be exterminated."

"Yeah, well. Welcome to life, kid."

"Shit."

ON A SUNNY SATURDAY AFTERNOON on Mars, Lisa sat on a stool and transcribed documents in a little room outside the office of the marketing director of the Inter-Planetary Racing Board. His regular staff had been contractually required to take the weekend off, and he had recruited the interns out of desperation. It was boring work, and she wished she had a proper chair.

Her mind drifted off, and Lisa wondered if the administrative side of the racing business was where she belonged. Perhaps working on a ship's crew, like Stephanie did, would be better. She tried to make herself keep typing. She was checking individual racer registration data against two databases and correcting the inconsistencies.

Killian Gideon suddenly walked past the doorway and Lisa caught her breath. He glanced inside as he walked past, but didn't stop, and she breathed a sigh of relief. Then the sound of the trailing footsteps reversed abruptly, and he turned around and walked back to the office. Lisa stared at the terminal screen, trying to continue her work, paralyzed.

"Lisa!" Killian said genially. "I was just thinking of you."

"Hello," she said flatly, and tried not to make eye contact.

He walked through the room and sat down heavily on her desk, on top of all the papers that she had spread out there, so that his leg was almost touching her. Lisa slid her stool back several inches, and he slid closer to her again.

"What do you do to be so beautiful? Is there some cosmetic or something that makes your skin so smooth and your eyes so bright and luminous? Because I want to try it."

"I'm trying to work here."

"It's ok. I'm here on business, too."

He was dressed in a brand new, blue racing suit, but did not appear to actually be planning to fly. Lisa slid the stool back another inch and didn't say anything to him.

"What's the matter?" Killian said, pretending to be hurt. "Didn't you get the note that I sent you? I'm really excited to see you and get a chance to talk to you, and you are treating me very coldly. Even if you don't like me, you don't have to be so rude, you could just try to be polite."

"I'm sorry," she said, still avoiding eye contact with him.

"It's ok," Killian said brightly. "So what are you doing, are they wasting your time working on tedious stuff? You're far too exceptional to be working on tedious stuff."

He stood up and stepped slightly behind and to the side of her. Lisa slid the chair back closer to the terminal screen and pointed at the different databases.

"I have to go through these registration databases and make sure they all match."

Killian put his hands on her shoulders familiarly, and she caught her breath. He began massaging her shoulders and neck. Lisa cringed, and started to pull away, but his hands were strong and held onto her naturally. His touch felt so good. She hesitated. His hands nurtured away the tension in her muscles with magical dexterity. It was unlike anything she had ever felt. She hated him for it. His hands were touching her, and she hated him, and she wanted to pull away, and it seemed like forever. And it felt so good to her body, and her mind cringed.

"I hope you're not abusing our interns, Killian," her boss said, peering into the room.

He took his hands off of Lisa's shoulders, and patted her on the back, completely comfortable and relaxed.

"What?" he said, walking away. "Of course not. Lisa is an old friend of mine. Let's hurry up and do those photos."

As the two men walked off down the hall, Lisa slumped forward on her stool and exhaled a long sigh of disappointment and relief.

KENICHI PEERED OUT FROM THE back seat of a taxi at the crowds of protesters. There were at least 100 of them, split into two different sides that chanted and screamed at each other angrily. A common, apparently mass-produced, sign on one side read, "Go Home Kinderfucks!" Signs on the other side said things like, "Natural is Beautiful", "Just Let The Man Race", and "Samson Ford's A Total Babe." The pro-Samson side was now the larger of the two, after friends and allies of the Magdalenas had heard about the protests against him.

As the cab approached the gate leading to the hangar, protesters ran up and surrounded it on either side. The cab driver complained bitterly, and Kenichi left him a large tip. Kenichi squeezed the door open and wove his way around and through the crowd, holding his hands open in front of him placatingly. When he finally got through the security gate, he found Samson, Stephanie, and Ben in the big hangar, installing a new gravity control unit into the racer. They were more upset with him than he had expected.

"I was held in prison for twenty years," Kenichi said finally, after several minutes of arguing and angry accusations. "I had to take care of some personal business, what do you want me to apologize for?"

He reminded them that they needed to leave Neo Vega and get the sponsorship with Midlothian ironed out as soon as possible, so that they could begin preparations for the Solar Regatta at the end of the year. Samson agreed, and they loaded up the Junket and left Triton that day.

LATER THAT NIGHT, AS THEY cruised back through space towards the inner planets, after Stephanie had gone to bed conspicuously early, Samson checked his personal messages at the terminal in his bunk. There were lots of notes and messages from reporters and from fans who had somehow

managed to get ahold of his terminal address. He didn't like
the reporters, they were greasy. He had a new note from Lisa.

Dear Samson,
*   How are you doing? Are you going to be racing on Mars in*
the Grand Prix? I'm here, working on the preparations for the
race. I hope I see you. If you're around Mars sometime soon, we
should get together. It would be really good.
*   XOXO, Lisa.*

He thought about Lisa. He hoped she wasn't too hung
up on him and wouldn't be hurt if he ignored her note. He
wondered why Stephanie had been distant from him and gone
to bed early, and drifted off to sleep and dreamed about her.

EVERYONE WAS SLEEPING WHEN THE Junket's alarm sounded, a bright red wailing sound that poured itself coldly over their dreams. Samson tumbled out of bed in his boxer shorts, struggling against the soup of sleep hormones that still circulated in his blood. There was a warning message, it repeated a few times before he could wrap the words around his brain.

"Warning! Unknown ship approaching. Warning! Unknown ship approaching. Warning! ..."

He glanced reflexively out the window of the little cabin, confirming that they were still in deep space. He hazily remembered Stephanie's penchant for deep space ship transfers.

"Can't be."

He grabbed a pair of pants off of the floor and sprinted for the deck. Ben was already there. His face was grey and he looked old. He had turned off the warning and was punching frantically at the ship's controls.

"What's going on?"

"I don't know," Ben said. "Pirates maybe. It's a big ship. They've jammed the com."

The Junket shook.

"Shit! They're hooking us. Get on the arm and see if you can cut the line."

"On it," Stephanie said behind them.

She was already strapped into a chair. A holographic panel appeared in the air in front of her, modeling the space around the arm. She guided it around the ship, looking for the tow cable.

"It's on our belly," Ben said.

Samson tried to get some kind of link up on the com, either to the other ship or anyone else, and slammed the control board in frustration. Stephanie's holographic panel lit up white, and the Junket shook from an explosion.

"What was that?" she said.

"I don't know."

"Oh shit," she said, "they shot off the arm."

"Are you sure?"

"I can't see anything."

The ship shook again with another explosion, this one larger.

"Our engines are out."

The Junket rocked violently up and down as the larger ship towed it in. They could see it through the bridge windows now, parts of it. A battleship. Samson turned on the automatic distress signal and sealed off the ship's hull. He stood up and waded across the stuttering deck to Stephanie's chair, unhooking the safety straps.

"Let's go, they're boarding."

Stephanie stood up nervously. Ben looked grim. Within seconds they were sucked into the larger ship's hull and the shaking stopped.

"Where's Ken?" Samson said, as he pushed Stephanie back into the ship's corridor and Ben sealed the bridge.

Kenichi was standing in the corridor, completely petrified. Samson pushed him forward, back the other direction.

"I was – trying to stop their jamming signal," he said, as Samson stepped past him and ran forward through the corridor.

Samson started to tell everyone what they needed to do. A hull panel between him and the others suddenly exploded and the corridor filled with smoke and dust. He coughed violently and covered his mouth with his sleeve. He tried to shout. He couldn't hear anything. Just ringing. A man with a gun stepped through the hole in the ship's wall and Samson rushed him. He blindsided the man and tackled him, knocking the gun out of his hands. It clattered down the corridor and Stephanie picked it up. More men flooded in. Samson wrestled with the first man, he rolled into a good position on top of him and started slamming the man's head with elbow punches. There was a gunshot. He could tell more from the shaking of the air than the sound. He glanced up and saw Stephanie through the smoke, backing away down the corridor. One of the pirates was holding his stomach and bleeding all over. Samson's man was unconscious, but someone else was on his back. They weren't pirates, they were gangsters. Stephanie kept pulling the trigger of the gun, but nothing was coming out of it. She disappeared in the smoke. Ben swung a large wrench at somebody. It was Scamp. He caught the wrench in his hands, as if Ben were a child.

The man on top of Samson pushed him heavily into the ground, and Samson tried to throw him off. Kenichi clattered into them both at a sprint and sent the man sprawling across the corridor. Someone else grabbed Kenichi and pointed a gun at him, but he spun out of the man's arms and stumbled away through the smoke and confusion. Samson grabbed for the man's gun, but Scamp was suddenly on top of him. He picked Samson up and threw him into the ground. It felt like his shoulders were out of socket. He could see Kenichi slump against the wall of the corridor, eyes boggling. Scamp held Samson down and beat him severely before locking his wrists in restraint ties.

 gangsters, holding the gun in front of her, pulling the trigger, hearing it click, click, click. Her ears rang like crazy, and the air made her eyes water. The surging adrenaline in her blood made everything exaggerated and surreal. She threw the gun down in front of her and ran into a storage corridor. The gangsters chased her. She leapt into a dusty storage locker and tried to slam the door. One of the gangsters kicked it open against her, knocking her backwards onto her butt.

"You shot my friend, bitch," the man said as he stepped into the room.

Stephanie stood up and backed slowly away, into a corner against the wall. There was no where to go. The man leered at her.

Two more men stepped into the room. They had pistols out. The first man had put his away. He advanced towards her slowly, teasingly, filling up the space between Stephanie and the door.

"Hey, you're real pretty. You're a real pretty bitch. Why are you trying to run away?"

CHAPTER 39

STEPHANIE WATCHED THE GANGSTERS INCH towards her. They said horrible things. She watched the first one, the one in front. She had a look on her face, not fear. The men leered, enjoying her vulnerability. Disgust.

When the first gangster lunged, Stephanie brought her hands together and twisted the peculiar green ring that she always wore. The air cracked and her body was suddenly enveloped in a haze of orange and pink. Angry tendrils of energy exploded over the gangster's skin as he collided with it in mid-lunge. It threw him back across the room and filled the air with the smell of burning hair and flesh, and plastic where his clothes had melted.

"What the fuck is this?" said one of the other men, redrawing his gun.

He fired at Stephanie's suddenly tranquil body through the orange and pink haze. The bullet seemed to splash, evaporating at the edges of the haze in a tiny puff of precipitation. A lightning bolt exploded back at him, striking his heart. He fell awkwardly, without a word, and his chest spilled ash onto the storage locker floor.

"H-holy shit!"

As the third gangster fled, the orange and pink haze with Stephanie inside of it glided slowly out into the middle of the room, like gelatinous fluid running to the center of a bowl. Her body turned gently within the energy field, until she was horizontal on her back. It was as if she were sleeping there, floating in the air within the field, eyes closed, her breathing slow and steady. Tranquil. The energy radiated from the little ring on her hand in faintly discernable, cloudy, waves. The waves shimmered, and twisted, and sheared around her, like imperfectly mastered chaos. Like a miraculous cocoon.

SAMSON WAS WATCHING DOWN THE corridor where the girl had run. Both his eyes were cut and swollen to tiny slits. He was mumbling something to himself. He continued to mumble, quietly, and put his forehead on the floor. Scamp took his foot off of Samson's back. His friend was tied up, but wouldn't stop screaming. Swearing at them, squeakily, through the blood in his mouth. It was amusing to the men, but Scamp didn't like it. He rolled the man over with his toe and the man spit blood at him, but it all just splattered back into his tangled beard, and he started swearing again. Scamp stepped on the man's nose, rubbed his boot back and forth smashing it completely, then put his foot on the man's beard and slid his foot down, holding the jaw open. Blood ran into the back of the man's throat and he started to cough violently.

"Shut up," Scamp said in slow, distinct syllables.

He rolled the man back over onto his stomach. Kenichi was curled up in a ball in the corner. He flinched when Scamp made eye contact with him.

"Hey, you idiots, put some cuffs on that one," Scamp said, pointing.

One of his men who had chased the girl came running back along the corridor. Anand. He was pushing others back, pushing them out of the way, telling them not to go.

"Hey. Nando! What's wrong with you?" Scamp said. "Where's the girl?"

"Don't go there!" Anand sputtered hysterically. "There's something, she released something—"

The other men were staring at him and moving back away from the corridor where the girl had run. Anand was young, his face was drained and sweaty, he was shaking. Scamp put his hand on Anand's shoulder and squeezed it hard, until he stopped talking.

"Ok, take this lot to the brig," Scamp ordered. "Now where's the girl? Show me what happened."

One of the men who had chased Stephanie, Nails, crawled out into the corridor, a mess. His skin was all melty, black and peeling.

"She's back there," he said slowly, eyes dripping water to the floor. "She's – surrounded – by some – kind of – thing."

"Jesus," Scamp said. He turned to his best lieutenant, "Gilly, get him to the medical room. Frank's dead, shot. Get some of these fucks to carry him out of here. Where's Paco?"

"Dead," Nails said. "The – stuff – killed him."

Scamp felt the adrenaline rising in his blood again.

"What? Shit. Stuff? Shit. Ok, I gotta go look. She doesn't have a gun, does she?"

"Don't touch it," Nails whispered, as they carried him away.

SCAMP DRAGGED ANAND DOWN THE main corridor with him. Anand kept protesting that he didn't want to go. When they got to the storage corridor where the girl had run he started crying. He pointed to the end of the corridor where a faint glow emanated from a storage locker.

"It's down there, in that room," he said nervously. "See where it's glowing? It's in there."

Anand turned and jerked his shirt out of Scamp's hand.

"Hey! Get back here, godamnit."

Scamp walked into the little corridor by himself. It was low, his head almost touched. He crouched a little bit. None of them were following him. It was spooky, like some old ghost story. The corridor was dark, steel. He tiptoed towards the glowing doorway at the end, until he was standing outside of it. He thought he could feel the orange glow on his skin. Half of an arm and a hand stuck out of the doorway.

The hand was clenched. Scamp bent down and felt it. Dead. He felt for the gun on his belt, but didn't draw it. He looked at the hand again. Must be Paco. The orange glow seemed to pulsate and move. Scamp noticed it more and more as he stood in the dark of the little corridor, hunched over, thinking about peeking through the doorway. The light pulsed, and turned, and glowed, like a thing, like an it, an entity. He wanted to see it, but didn't want to cross the sight threshold of the door. He wanted to see it, but he didn't want it to see him. He watched the light from the door drift slowly along the steel walls, pulsing brighter and softer. He held his breath.

Lisa sat at the terminal table in her little hotel room on Mars. She had papers, files, and brochures piled around her, advertisements about the big race. She looked into the holographic imager, then stopped it. She stood up and brushed her hair in the mirror, and looked at herself, and smiled, trying to find a good expression. She sat down at the terminal and peered into the holographic imager again.

"Hi Samson!"

"It's Lisa. Well, you can see that. I saw you are listed for this race. I can't wait to see you. Can we meet up when you are here? I really want to see you. Everyone says you guys got some big sponsorship deal that you are going to unveil. That's great. You wouldn't believe the press here, they're waiting to mob you guys. I don't know what else to say."

She blew a kiss nervously at the lenses of the machine and turned it off.

A SMALL IMAGE OF LUCHO GONZALEZ peered out of the back of Scamp's terminal card. Scamp pointed the tiny lens of the card at the orange and pink energy field, which glowed menacingly in response. The hairs all over his body stood up. The air in the little storage locker still smelled like burnt hair and flesh.

"See that boss?" he said. "I've never seen anything like it before."

"And what happened to Paco?" the image of Lucho asked, in a miniature voice.

"It's like, there is like a hole through his chest where everything is turned into charcoal. It went right through his heart."

"God damn."

"This is some heavy shit, boss."

"God damn."

Scamp walked out of the room, ducking through the little storage locker door and back into the corridor.

"I don't even like to be in there with it. The other guys won't even come back onto the ship."

"Fuck me, Scamp," Lucho said. "This must be one valuable girl. This is – I've got a really good feeling about this, a really good feeling."

"What are we going to do with her, though?" Scamp said. "We can't even get near her."

"But, Scamp, use your brain. We've got Kenichi back. We've got our genius engineer, he'll figure this all out."

"Yeah," Scamp said.

"If he doesn't, I'll cut his dick off! Ha Ha."

"That's true. He knows the girl, too."

"Of course, of course. Just bring them all back here. Bring everything back here. You've done well, my friend. I'm grateful to you."

KENICHI'S FOOTSTEPS ECHOED ACROSS THE long dark floor of Lucho Gonzalez's office. The bright blue and reddish-green surface of Mars loomed over him triumphantly through the transparent glass ceiling. The new anklet chafed against his right leg as he walked. His arms hung limp at his sides, shoulders slumped low, defeated. Exhausted. Lucho looked up and smiled coldly.

"Kenichi, how is your work progressing?"

Kenichi looked down at his feet. He stood well back from the desk, as far away as he thought he could stand and get away with it.

"We figured out how to move her using magnetic fields," he said meekly, "and have moved her into a lab in the casino."

"Excellent. Excellent."

Kenichi turned slightly, as if he were hoping to leave.

"Why are you standing so far away?" Lucho said. "Come closer, walk over here. Look at me when I'm talking to you, dumb faggot."

Kenichi walked forward, but watched his feet meekly.

"You're smart, but you're also like one of those retards," Lucho said.

"I'm sorry, sir."

"So what is this thing?"

"The thing?"

"The stuff that's protecting her, don't play dumb."

"Oh, sorry, we still don't know what it is."

"You must know what it is."

"It's an extremely exotic technology, I have never encountered anything like this before."

"Really?" Lucho asked, sounding pleased.

"It is some kind of energy field," Kenichi continued, "but it seems to have an element of artificial intelligence."

"How did you know how to move it?"

Kenichi rubbed the fingers of one hand.

"It was just by chance. I noticed that the field shifted when a strong magnetic force was applied nearby."

"So doesn't that tell you something about what it is, Kenichi?"

"No."

"It must," Lucho said with irritation.

"I'm sorry, sir," Kenichi said meekly. "We only figured out how to move her today, perhaps I have not had enough time to think about it yet."

"I trust you've had time to think about who the girl is," Lucho said malevolently.

"I have thought about it often, sir, but I don't know anything else about her."

"Bullshit."

"I'm sorry, sir. She was a very secretive person."

"You know I kept Samson Ford alive on your behalf, Kenichi," Lucho said. "Maybe if I cut one of his feet off and have it force fed to you you would remember more about who this girl is."

"Her name is Stephanie," Kenichi said rapidly, "she's a ship's mechanic, excellent, brilliant, she never told us anything about her past. She doesn't have a last name."

"I find that hard to believe."

Their conversation was interrupted by an incoming call to Lucho, which his secretary said was urgent. An image of Simon Okunle appeared in front of Lucho's desk, looking drawn and very grim.

"Yeah, who are you?" Lucho said.

"Hello, Mr. Gonzalez," Simon said. "My name is Simon Okunle, I believe you are holding a woman who belongs to me."

"I don't know what you're talking about."

"I'm sure you know what I'm talking about, Mr. Gonzalez. The woman I am seeking to recover would be surrounded by a protective energy field that is extremely difficult to deal with."

"That doesn't sound familiar to me," Lucho said. "But I could make some inquiries. What kind of money are we discussing here?"

"What do you mean?" Simon asked, ice cracking in his throat.

"I'm sure you know what I mean," Lucho said.

"The girl does not belong to you, Mr. Gonzalez."

"I don't know who she belongs to," Lucho said. "But I'm pretty sure for a girl like you are talking about that there would be a significant finder's fee. Something like, I don't know, 100 million credits?"

"Do you know who I am, Mr. Gonzalez?" Simon asked.

"Do you know who *I* am?"

"As a matter of fact, I've made myself quite familiar with you," Simon Okunle said. "I know all about you, your casino, your gang and the different rackets you're involved in."

"Well who the fuck are you then?"

"I am the Chief Executive Officer of The Rothschild Corporation."

Lucho's face suddenly went stiff. He swallowed hard.

"There will be no negotiation, Mr Gonzalez. Either you will return the girl to me immediately and we will consider overlooking the fact that you attacked her, or you will suffer the consequences of my displeasure."

A vein throbbed in Lucho's forehead. He stared into the com lenses angrily, breath coming faster and faster. He sputtered, unsure what to say. Finally, when he did speak, it was through a cloud of meanness and anger.

"The girl inside that thing – she looks to me like a beautiful woman. A real unusually beautiful woman. A real peach. The truth is, I'd like to stick my dick in her. In fact, I was planning on doing that, and I really want to. So here's the deal, Simon. The price just went up to one billion credits. You know a lot about me, so I'll give you only 24 hours to wire the money into my accounts. After 24 hours, if I don't get the billion credits, I'm going to have to have a few parts of her brain removed to make her nice and docile. Don't worry, I'll parcel those to you. We'll use her as a prostitute here until that expensive, peachy body is used up, probably for only a few years. Although, if she's equipped with some special, designer genetics, which it looks like she is, she might be more durable than most. A few years is just a guess, but her body might be good for longer, it's hard to say about these things. After that, eh, you can have her back."

Simon tried to say something in reply, but Lucho shouted over him, grabbing the com microphone on his desk and blowing spit into it.

"ONE BILLION CREDITS. 24 HOURS. DON'T TEST ME!"

He pulled the plug on the com and Simon Okunle's image disappeared.

THE IMAGE OF SIMON OKUNLE still seemed to crackle in the air, as if it hadn't gone away. As if it shouldn't have. Kenichi stared at Lucho weakly.

"We don't even know what that field is yet," he said.

Above his head, through the transparent ceiling that looked up onto Mars, something huge materialized in space. All that could be seen was hardened, armor alloy, glass resin panels, and black structural bolts the size of a small cargo carrier. It was an enormous warship, a huge super-cruiser, larger than the entire casino station. A small moon constructed by men, a small spaceship larger than a small moon – black, and slate grey, and green, and ominous. It was just empty space and then the ship was there. Its gravitational pull shook the Casino's floors.

"What the f–"

Lucho's words stopped, suspended in the air. He stood motionless, muscles taut. Every cell in his body frozen and un-yielding. It was the same for every living creature on the casino station. Their brains, even their mitochondria on pause. It was the same for Kenichi. The synthcats tumbled stiff cartwheels across their oval race track, limbs snapping, until they rolled to a stop, frozen in mid-stride.

Rothschild Company soldiers flooded onto the casino, at least a thousand of them. They secured Lucho's office in less than one minute, and located Stephanie in less than three. They secured the whole casino space station in less than ten. They were professionals. It was the most important mission of their lives.

The soldiers cried at the site of Stephanie. They had realized who she was. A goddess to them, she was radiant and floating in the air, untouchable and perfect. The warship's dispatch coughed hoarsely when she announced to the bridge that Steph-anie was unharmed. She called her 'Our Mistress', she didn't know who 'Stephanie' was. Tears rolled down her cheeks and she held her breath reverently when the soldiers beamed back pictures of 'Our Mistress' floating in her protective shell. They all cried, even Simon.

An admiral led Simon onto the space station as soon as it had been given the all clear. They walked through the casino quickly, past all of its waxy patrons. Some were toppled over on their heads. The roulette wheels were still spinning on their magnetic tracks, the tiny balls bouncing back and forth from black to red. They walked as quickly as they could, back through the gangsters' corridors, through halls that became concrete tunnels. Tiny doctors' offices, a surgical stadium, and finally a little laboratory on the inside of a cargo ship hangar.

Stephanie was there, floating serenely, surrounded by the warm, embracing, glowing orange and pink cloud. It pulsed through her as if it had become her heartbeat. Simon confirmed with the officer that the room had been scanned for cameras and monitoring devices and they had all been removed. He ordered everyone to leave the room and closed the door. It was a windowless room. He was alone with Stephanie and the orange and pink glow, the little cloud of protection that surrounded her. He locked the door and walked calmly through the cloud, and twisted the ring on her finger carefully to turn it off. The energy slowly evaporated, like clearing fog, and Stephanie's body drifted gently to the ground as it disappeared. Simon slid his jacket under her head as she came down, and held onto her hand. She opened her eyes.

"Samson!"

"Easy, child. You're alright."

Stephanie sat up and looked at him. Her face was very pale. Her deep, dark eyes seemed to protrude out of her skull. Her hair suddenly matted, lips dry and cracked. She squeezed his fingers.

"Simon, where are Samson Ford and the others?"

She hugged him. Simon lifted her to her feet, and she leaned on him. She was dizzy. Her lungs felt stiff.

"I do not know, Mistress. You were with them when you were attacked?"

"Yes."

Stephanie's mind passed in and out of phase, like rising above water and then sinking back down, and rising again and trying to stay on the surface. She struggled furiously to focus her thoughts.

"Simon, you have to help them. Find out what happened. Samson Ford and Ben Johnson and Kenichi Iwahara. Oh God."

"Of course, Mistress. We will make sure of it."

She leaned on him heavily. She could barely stand. She was coughing and her breath was a struggle. Simon kept his arm tight around her waist and opened the door. He led her out into the ship's hangar. The soldiers all bowed their heads reverently in front of her.

Ben's Junket was in a corner of the hangar. It was damaged. Stephanie was slowly knitting her memories together.

"We're on Lucho Gonzalez's space station."

"Yes, Mistress."

"That's the ship over there," Stephanie slowly raised her arm to point. Simon pushed her arm back down admonishingly. "That's the ship we were on when they attacked us."

"I understand."

He turned to his admiral and ordered him to inquire into the welfare of Samson Ford, Ben Johnson, and Kenichi Iwahara who were all on board the ship with "Our Mistress" when she was attacked. The admiral assured him that inquiries were already underway and they would make the status and welfare of the three men a chief priority.

Simon led Stephanie gently, quickly, back through the

corridors, through the casino, to the warship. She needed to walk with him, to walk back onto the ship, to appear virile and strong. It was a better thing to walk leaning on him than to be carried on a stretcher, although her body was cold and seemed to have been sapped of every last fiber of energy. She leaned on Simon desperately, and he tried not to show any effect from the weight. He tried to hold her up, so that it looked like she was standing on her own. The soldiers kept their heads bowed as she passed. Some of them placed their hands over their hearts.

"Simon, you have to find out about Samson," Stephanie struggled to whisper. "I have to know if he's alright."

"I will tell you as soon as I find out," he said. "I'm sure he will be alright. Samson Ford is a valuable person, one of the best pilots in the Solar System. The gangster wouldn't just kill him."

"Oh, God."

"Your people are working very hard to locate your friends and secure their welfare, Mistress. Do not despair. We will not leave here until then."

As they approached the space-lock onto the warship, Stephanie's eyes closed. She tried to hold them open. She realized that she was shivering.

"I don't want to leave them, Simon."

"I know. I'm sorry."

CHAPTER 42

Lisa stood on the Martian racing tarmac and went through the checklists for the various racing teams, ensuring that all the required regulations had been met. She tried to avoid Killian. She had made sure that another one of the interns was the one checking off his team. Samson wasn't there. She was worried about him, and felt let down. And she was sort of happy that he wasn't there, since it might mean he had a good reason for not replying to her messages. People on the racing teams kept saying 'hi' to her, and Lisa tried to smile at them and be cheerful. She loved the noise and commotion of the races before they began, the tension and excitement in the air, the engine dust that filled up your nostrils, and the beautiful racing men who were so brave and hopeful, brash, and confident, and determined, who were all caught in the midst of the intensity of life.

She hadn't dated any of the pilots other than Samson. She really wished he was there, and was relieved that he wasn't at the same time. He was different than the other ones. She didn't know if she wanted to date any of them, she just liked watching them and being around them. Not because of Samson, but just because. They were going to die, and it didn't seem to mean anything to most of them. She kept checking for Samson whenever she was at a terminal, hoping he had showed up at the last minute, even when it was too late for him to race. Killian never looked at her, and she was relieved and vaguely disappointed. One of the racers snapped his finger in her face, "Hey, hey! Stop daydreaming."

"I'm not daydreaming."

Lisa pointed him towards one of the race supervisors, and wondered if this was the right business for her to be in after all. She watched the ships shake and sputter, warming up their engines, and the pilots looking up at the big, clear sky, or closing their eyes and moving their hands gracefully through the space in front of them, and wove her way with the big 'paperwork' tablet through all the men and women darting back and forth on last minute errands, and smiled, and couldn't wait for the race to begin.

"GET ON THE GODDAMNED SHIP!" The young lieutenant shouted into Samson's face, where the bruises were slowly beginning to fade away.

He was pointing at the Junket. Ben and Kenichi were already inside and the ship was running, floating inches off the ground. Two other soldiers stood close by Samson, they had their guns out and kept stepping up against him, trying to herd him towards the ship.

"Where's Stephanie?"

"That's no concern of yours. Get on the ship, you have to leave."

"I'm not leaving until I find out what happened to my friend."

One of the soldiers pushed him in the back, and Samson circled away from them, away from the Junket, his face set stubbornly. They were beginning to attract attention from soldiers all over the hangar.

"Who are you guys?" Samson said.

"That's no concern of yours, get on your ship. We're running out of time."

Another officer walked over and looked at Samson sternly. He opened his mouth to say something, but stopped, cocking his ear to one side, and turned around and held a conversation with someone through a com link. Samson looked around the hangar, no one other than the soldiers was moving. They were all frozen in place, like wax figures or mannequins – inanimate, imitation human beings. It was eerie.

The officer turned back around. He motioned the other soldiers to back up, and led Samson several steps away where they could talk in private.

"Here," he said, pulling out a small com screen and punching in a code before checking that it was connecting properly and handing it to Samson.

Stephanie came on the screen. She wasn't sitting up straight. She looked weak and very pale. She stared out through the screen with dark, sunken eyes.

"Samson, you need to leave as soon as possible," she said, without preface or greeting.

He clutched the communications tablet intently, pulling it closer to his face.

"What happened to you," he said, "are you ok? Where are you?"

"I'm fine, I'm on my ship. Listen, I can't explain all this. The stasis has left me weak. I'll be in touch, ok? Hurry and leave."

The officer was watching Samson impatiently, edging forward as if he would take the tablet away.

"Don't tell me what to do," Samson said into the screen, turning away from the man. "You're hurt, let me take care of you."

"I'm sorry, Samson. Hurry and leave please. You don't have a choice."

Stephanie slumped down farther in her chair.

"Goodbye," she said, and the com shut off.

The officer snatched the little tablet out of Samson's hand.

"If you don't leave now we're putting your ship out to space without you," he said, and motioned for the soldiers to escort Samson to his ship.

Ben came out to help them get Samson onto the Junket. His nose was still swollen, but had been repaired.

"Come on, Sammy," he said, with his arm around Samson's chest, dragging him backwards towards the ship. "She'll be ok."

THE JUNKET LOOKED THE WORSE for wear and had a large hole in its hull, but it could still maintain atmospheric integrity with its field walls. All the main things were working. Kenichi had somehow managed to make sure the engines got repaired while he was analyzing Stephanie's protective field for Lucho. It was safe, but the ship looked terribly forlorn, floating in space like a little, broken tub, between the space station and the titanic war ship. The war ship was beautiful, they had never seen anything like it. It was frightening.

Samson insisted they had to follow it. They couldn't seem to make any contact on their coms. Ben and Kenichi watched the warship nervously, sweating. Samson was distraught.

"Follow it! Get closer!" he said, as the warship drifted fractions of a kilometer away from them.

Ben inched closer, tacking along beside it. They weren't even following movements, they were just following its drift.

After a little while, the ship simply disappeared. They felt a tiny jerk as its gravity impression evaporated.

"What– Where is it?!"

"Cloaking," Kenichi said simply.

"They can't be cloaking."

"Samson, that ring that Stephanie had, that field thing that was generated around her: *very* advanced technology."

"You can't cloak a ship that big," Samson said stubbornly. "And it would violate every space law."

"You apparently can."

"I'm sure we'll get to talk to Stephanie again," Ben said, pushing him down into a seat. "Right now we need to get out of here."

That night, on the television, they watched Killian win the Martian Regatta. After landing his ship, he raced across the tarmac and embraced Lisa Maui, who blushed deeply and blinked at the flashing cameras in embarrassment.

C H A P T E R ⁴³

THE LITTLE CARGO SHIP CHUGGED tenaciously through the deep space of the Solar System, like one of those ancient, under-powered trains that rolled on metal rails. Pilots called it deep space, and travelers did. But they knew that none of the space in the Solar System was technically deep space. It was space between planets, near the sun; it was tiny, shallow, claustrophobic space. If you stood by the window on the side of a spaceship facing away from the sun, and looked out into the starry, glittering, endless black, you would call it deep space. If you cruised for days through that nothing. And yet, you would know that out there, out past the farthest asteroid belt, between the sun and the nearest kindred star, was true empty blackness. What the astronomers would call deep space. Where there was nothing for endless years of flight, where you could cruise for a decade at 100,000 km/hr and watch yourself on a map, and not notice that you had made any progress towards the nearest star. And yet, the astronomers knew, this was not technically deep space, because the truly endless vacuums that existed between galaxies were such interminable planes of nothing as to make the space between stars microscopic by comparison. Space.

There were many pilots who wanted to explore the universe. Men and women who fancied themselves a latter day Columbus, who dreamed of discovering a New World. Ships would fly past the outer asteroid belts on endless voyages, hopeful and insane. They were rarely heard from again, but occasionally a ship would return. Stuttering along mindlessly, years or decades later, filled up with mummies and dusty, crumbly hopes.

Where were the aliens and space invaders? Out in that huge, scattered, friendless, empty void. Where an electron could travel a thousand light years to find a mate. Only microbes and explosions, and endless rocks, and endless nothing. It didn't seem fair to the men. To the people. They had been sure that they would find something. They had been sure that they would find friends. Or even enemies. Some other face in the universal sands. Some something that would cast perspective on their lives, their worlds, something to help them not feel so alone. They couldn't even travel there. They could look at some of it. They could send out their little probes and wait a hundred years. And hope that some of those signals would be returning soon. And when they did they found grainy images of empty rocks, tumbling endlessly through endless empty spaces. The rocks looked so beautiful when you looked at them from far away. The people hoped that out there, out in the nothing, in the tiny specks between the nothing, there were other bits of dust like theirs, like themselves, sending out little probes and hoping to make contact. It must be awfully hard to travel there. None of them had ever traveled here. But the pilots, and the travelers, even the astronomers, sat by their windows shielded from the sun, and looked out into the endless, cold, glittering nothing and hoped that they were out there. Whoever they were. And that they were looking and hoping for someone too.

KENICHI RAN HIS SCANNER PAST a large bolthead for the dozenth time. It clicked, faintly. There was a feedback of 0.03. Almost nothing, but consistent. He examined the bolthead carefully with an optical lens. It was one of the bolts that held the Junket's frame together. It seemed fully intact and untampered with. He ran the scanner over it again, click. 0.03.

It had taken him two days to build the scanner. To design and build it, but the design went very fast. Ben had been scouring the ship with more conventional means, a traditional feedback-loop scanner, and mostly just by eyeball. Looking for any little robot or tracking device that could have broadcast their location to tell the gangsters where they were. There must have been something. Kenichi had been scanning for half the day, and the bolthead was the first anomaly he had found. He wiped sweat off of his brow with a greasy hand and sat down on a hard metal bench in the corridor. What a hassle.

"Ken," Ben called excitedly from down the hall, "check this out. Look, I found it."

He held up a walnut sized, ant-like, electronic device. It was dead.

"Wedged into a crack on the outside of the ship."

"You de-activated it already?"

"Yeah."

Ben handed Kenichi the little robot, and Kenichi turned it over in his hands. Its shell was black, coated steel, and it had little retractable legs and a broadcast antenna that looped around its body. He twisted it in half at the main joint and pulled the wire guts apart.

"This looks like a pretty standard tracking bug."

"Yeah."

"It must have attached itself to the ship when we were on Titan and Lucho's gangster showed up."

"That's what I'm thinking."

Kenichi twisted the guts of the little robot in his fingers and looked away.

"Well, look what I've found here," he said, pointing to the big bolt head. "Watch when I run the scanner over it. You hear that click?"

"0.03," Ben said, watching the readout on the back of the scanner.

"Exactly, it's very faint."

"It's just static, isn't it?" Ben said. "That bolthead is huge, it holds the whole ship together. It probably picks up a lot of random noise from all over the ship."

"That is possible," Kenichi said, peering closely at the bolthead like a jeweler examining a diamond, "but I have covered perhaps 20% of the ship already and there have not been any other false positives."

"Spooky."

STEPHANIE LAY IN AN ENORMOUS, downy, four-poster bed constructed from carved ebony planks, with gold and silver filigree threads entwining into and around it. In the little ceiling of the bed's frame, magically illuminated as if sunlight shone over it diffusely from no noticeable source, was an original 17th Century Dutch masterpiece, an oil painting, showing a woman in a yellow and blue dress pouring milk into a bowl on a small table set with bread.

Stephanie's shoulders were propped up by several cottony, feathery pillows. She lay limply in the bed, as if her muscles lacked the energy to set properly, and her face was wan. A pretty, robust maid, of about Stephanie's age, with brassy hair and smooth, faintly golden skin, tended to her. She lifted Stephanie's arms and massaged them, and rubbed lotion into Stephanie's hands and manicured them. Stephanie smiled at her weakly.

"Look at your hands, mum," the maid said, squeezing Stephanie's calloused fingers. "You don't take good enough care of yourself out there."

"Thank you, Cylla."

"The effects of the stasis will take at least a week to wear off," said Simon Okunle from a little waiting table near the bed.

"I'm so exhausted, Simon," Stephanie said quietly.

"You don't feel sick otherwise?"

"Only exhausted, that's the only thing."

"The stasis impacts every cell in the body. It is an enormous load for your system to recover from, but it should not do any permanent damage. Lee Xian says all your scans have come back normal and that your system is functioning in a sort of slow motion, gradually speeding back up."

Stephanie watched Cylla massaging her hands. It was hard to concentrate on anything.

"We did something a little bit harsh, Mistress."

She raised her eyes to look at Simon, but her head and face did not move.

"What did you do?"

"We removed Lucho Gonzalez' testicles and altered his brain in some regards."

She watched him for a moment, as if she couldn't hear.

"Oh," she said finally, very quietly.

"I know you disapprove of such measures, but a display of force was necessary in this case. He will be terrified of us, but his brain now lacks the capacity to seek revenge. He will probably attempt to placate us and make amends for his behavior. He will not bother your friends again."

Stephanie looked down at the beautifully embroidered quilt that covered most of her body. It was patterned after ancient Japanese paintings, with tall mountains, great waves, waterfalls, and little solitary houses in the wilderness, created with bright blue, red, and black silk threads. The ocean waves in the quilt seemed to engulf everything else.

"Ok," she said quietly. "That's good, Simon. Good work. I don't know what I would do without you."

"Thank you, Mistress. It is only my job. We were all so worried about you when we got the beacon. Cylla nearly had a nervous breakdown."

"I did, mum," Cylla said, folding her arms tightly and tearing up. "What would we do if something happened to you?"

"Oh, Cylla. I'm sorry. Stop that. I'm ok. Nothing is going to happen to me."

"In any case," Simon continued, "that ring is worth every penny your father paid for it. Truly remarkable."

Stephanie leaned forward and patted Cylla's knee soothingly, although it took enormous effort to do so. She looked up at Simon with a grateful, affectionate expression, and tried to smile at him, but rolled onto her side in spite of herself and fell back asleep.

SAMSON LAY ON TOP OF the grey blanket in his bunk thinking about Stephanie. He closed his eyes and tried to say a prayer for her, but didn't know what to pray, and just said he hoped that she would be ok and hoped that there was a God that heard it. He thought that she probably was ok, and it made him angry to think of her treating him so distantly, running away from him and talking to him curtly on a little screen, and still not sending him any messages about her whereabouts or well being. He remembered how little he knew about her, how she had always dodged any questions about her past, and he felt manipulated. Then he imagined she was really hurt, or in trouble, and the thought crushed him under its weight.

He sat up in bed and leaned his back against the cold rivets that ran up and down the ship's hull. The rivets pressed into his skin and caught it with a tacky suction, and he leaned forward again off of them and slid over to lean against a smooth section of the hull.

He thought about the signaling bug Kenichi had found implanted into one of the boltheads in the frame. Sophisticated. Nearly indetectable. He wondered how much he trusted Kenichi, and wasn't sure. Someone in the racing circuit could have done it, perhaps. He was beginning to doubt Kenichi. Stephanie wasn't there anymore to help keep an eye on Kenichi's work.

He sat down at his terminal and checked the messages on his card. It was flooded. Messages from the media, mostly. Some proposed sponsorship deals from before he missed the race on Mars. Midlothian had just sent a new message wanting to meet and finalize their agreement, and put their logos on the ship. That was good. They didn't even ask why he had missed the race. The organizers from the Martian Grand Prix had sent him several notes and holograms, the latest of which were angry and accusing.

He found the message from Lisa and added her to his list of important people, so that he would find her messages more easily in the future. He smiled at the image of her nervously blowing a kiss at him. There was something unusually cute about her. He was sorry he had missed her at the race, and suddenly wanted to see her again.

He tried to compose a message to send to Stephanie, starting and stopping, and deleting what he had written. He switched on the holo camera and tried to send her a hologram, but deleted it each time. After a few hours, he had finally composed a note.

Stephanie, I hope you're ok. Get in contact with me as soon as you can, I'm worried about you. -Samson

C H A P T E R ⁴⁴

THERE WAS A DIFFERENT ATMOSPHERE on the streets of Manhattan than before. Samson thought it was different. He had only been there a few times. It was cleaner, a lot of the riff-raff was gone. The people all seemed tall, and beautiful, and exalted. They exuded pride, and a faint suspiciousness, a kind of mean, happy, vigilance. There weren't many of them with natural skin and hair tones. He stood as tall as he could, and puffed out his chest, walked quickly, and hoped that his metallic red beard and hair looked genuine. He glared at a natural looking man suspiciously and enjoyed the feeling of superiority, and didn't do it again. The man's teeth had been clenched and his eyes darted nervously back and forth as he walked down the street under the many-gazing glare. Samson could tell immediately from the eyes that the man was not natural born. They were too big, too cloudy, milky blue – and too raw and haggard to be contacts. All the peacocks on the street wouldn't notice those things, they wouldn't want to notice, they wanted to believe he was a natural born man, hiding out, trying to pass for something he was not; they wanted to have someone to feel superior to, and to be offended at, and to hope that someone would catch him soon.

It was always busy in Manhattan. So many people. Cars weren't even allowed on the streets here, they buzzed overhead like endless bees around a busy hive. Like endless gnats. Their computers navigated the chaos effortlessly. A man on the street was hawking the New York Post. A car had malfunctioned causing a wreck and eight pedestrians were flattened under the fall: "Eight Squished in Soho Traffic Squash". Read all about it. Unfathomable seas of people engulfed the spaces between the towering buildings and Samson wove his way through them balletically, at a quick walking pace. He loved the crowds. It was funny that they would throw him out of here if they could. He smiled mirthfully at the strangers who glanced his way. It was a funny world. He turned into the entrance way of the Midlothian building and walked through the big revolving doors into a large, brass walled lobby. The security guard looked at him suspiciously, but Samson had an appointment.

In the elevator on the way up he tried to focus on what he was here for. The sponsorship. Money. He was a famous racer now, he could demand a lot. He couldn't just accept the first offer they made to him, he would have to negotiate, to play hard ball. He wondered what hard ball was. This was big business, he was out of his element. He had to appear relaxed and confident or the Midlothians would rip him off. But he needed the money, so he had to get a deal. "Just refuse the first offer," Ben had told him. "Try to hold out for at least a million. Just take whatever they offer you and counter back with 50% more, and try to get them to meet in the middle." Ben didn't know either. He was a mechanic and a race hustler, that's why he didn't want to come himself. Or not as much as Samson. They couldn't both come. They don't know that we don't have any other big offers on the table, Samson told himself. They probably think that we do. Just don't accept the first offer. He wished that Stephanie was with him. Something told him this would be easy for her.

SAMSON HADN'T TOLD THEM THAT he was coming personally. The executives at Midlothian had naturally assumed he would send someone else. They thought he would send Ben, and Samson used Ben's name at the front desk. This was fun. A pretty secretary walked him to the meeting room, where several executives were sitting around a large table with Albrecht Durer at the head.

"Mr. Durer, Ben Johnson is here," the secretary said, motioning Samson inside.

Albrecht Durer looked at him curiously.

"Hello," Samson said, waving, and glanced around the room.

He took off his sunglasses and waited for someone to recognize him, forgetting about the fake beard and wig.

"You sir," Albrecht Durer said coldly, "are not Ben Johnson."

Samson grinned.

"Oh. You've got me there. But," he said, and pulled off the rest of the disguise, "I'm probably still the person that you want to talk to."

Albrecht Durer stuttered in amazement.

"Y– Y– W– We–, Samson Ford! We didn't expect– Well, this is a surprise!"

He stood up from his chair quickly and walked around the table to shake Samson's hand.

"I didn't realize you were a man for such grand entrances. Imagine, coming here yourself in these troubled times. Your valorous reputation has not been exaggerated."

He ushered Samson deeper into the meeting room and furtively closed the door.

"Not at all," Samson said. "This meeting is important to me."

"Yes, well let's try to keep your whereabouts here as quiet as we can, nevertheless. I like the wig and the beard. Very convincing."

Samson sat down and the Midlothian executives discussed their ideas for the sponsorship with him. The terms of the plan. Logos to be placed on the ship, and racing suit designs for Samson to wear. They were all excited and the mood was infectious. He kept wondering why they didn't discuss money, but the executives seemed to consider their reaching an agreement to be a forgone conclusion. It made him suspicious. Were they trying to low ball him? He really needed to get out of here with as close to one million credits as possible. The executives were worried about all the other details, especially their logo placement on the ship and obligations for Samson to appear in an advertising campaign. They had already done a lot of planning. Albrecht Durer, in particular, described their plans with bubbly excitement. Every few minutes Samson thought they were going to start discussing the financial terms of the contract, and every few minutes they shifted to another subject entirely. His stomach knotted up more and more.

"Ok, let's talk money," Mr. Durer said abruptly, a couple of hours into the meeting.

"Ok."

"Forgive us for waiting so long to get around to it, we've been so excited to have you here, personally, in front of us. We've really gotten carried away with the details and put the cart before the horse, as it were."

Don't take the first offer, Samson kept telling himself. Try to hold out for a million.

"Ok," he said.

"We were discussing figures this morning," Mr. Durer said, "and we were thinking ten million credits."

Samson swallowed hard. He waited for Albrecht Durer to say something else, but the man sat perfectly still, staring impassively at him, waiting for a reply.

"Did you say ten million credits?"

"That's right. It seems to match up with the sponsorship deals of some of the other top pilots in the circuit."

"D– do you think we could make it 10.5 million credits?" Samson said meekly. "Instead of 10."

Albrecht Durer smiled.

"10.5 million credits. I think we can do that, Mr. Ford. Let's call it a deal."

"WHAT DO YOU THINK ABOUT Manhattan?" Lisa's grandfather asked Samson.

They were sitting at the dinner table, eating pork chops, carrots, and green peas. Drinking fine Ninkasi beer from Oregon. Samson, and Lisa's grandmother, and Lisa's grandfather. It was hard to believe that they were Lisa's grandparents. They were so sophisticated. Samson hadn't spoken to Lisa in a few months. He suddenly wished that he knew her better.

"I've always loved Manhattan," he said. "Whenever I've been here. I love the crowds of people, all the humanity squeezed together in such a little space, it creates a special energy. I can almost feed off of it, I can soak it up. Is that what you mean?"

"Yes, but it's different now."

"I guess it is."

"The atmosphere is different, don't you think?"

"It seems very different to me," Samson said. "Although, I've only been here a few times before. There is still that same intense energy on the streets, though."

"There are still a lot of people squeezed together in a small space."

"Yes."

"Do you feel out of place here now, Samson?" Lisa's grandmother wondered. "On the streets I mean."

"Yes and no. I never– I've always been able to blend in with genetically engineered people pretty easily. At the races, in my line of work, there usually aren't any other natural borns. So, I can see the difference on the streets compared to what it was before, but it doesn't feel that strange to me."

"But you have to wear a beard and a wig, just to protect yourself."

"That's true."

"It makes us sick."

"You're good people. Thank you for letting me stay here, by the way."

"Not at all."

"We're pleased to have your company, Samson," Lisa's grandfather said, "You're an unusual person."

Samson chewed his food thoughtfully.

"I don't really feel unusual," he said.

"Don't you?"

"I don't know. Does anyone?"

"Most of the racing pilots do, from what I'm told."

"Most pilots aren't very nice people," Samson said.

"That's what Lisa says, too."

"Well she's right."

"But you were born in Magdalena, that's unusual."

"Magdalena doesn't seem unusual when you were born there," Samson said.

"No, I suppose not. But it is."

"Yes."

"Lisa told us that you believe in God, Samson," Lisa's grandmother said. "That you pray before every race."

"I– That's not exactly common knowledge," he said defensively. "I don't know how she knew that."

"From watching you, no doubt," Lisa's grandfather said.

"Well do you believe in God?" Samson asked them.

"No," Lisa's grandmother said.

"I want to believe," her grandfather said wistfully. "Sometimes I almost think I do. I think it's important."

"But you don't believe."

"I don't know if I do or not."

"I don't know either," Samson said. "The people in Magdalena do. They talk about God all the time. They pray to God, like, it's as if they are having a constant conversation with someone, they are always praying. That's the center of Magdalena. Well, no, The Prophet is the center, but God was supposed to be the center, in theory. And everything is about God there. Outside of Magdalena, I almost never hear anyone even mention God. You both might be the first."

"God was the last of the great myths," Lisa's grandmother said. "They don't mean anything to people anymore. They talk about God in storybooks for children, in the cartoons. Like wizards and witches, it's just a fantasy."

"They don't have any wizards or witches in Magdalena," Samson said.

SAMSON CRUISED AT SPEED BETWEEN the dwarf planets Pluto and Haumea. His ship sparkled a bright, clean white, with crisp red highlights from the new Midlothian logos. The space was colder out here, you could feel it. It was one of those things that wasn't supposed to happen, the difference for a ship in the far Solar System or in the inner Solar System shouldn't have been so much. He couldn't remember why it was, something about planetary heat radiation, and an uneven diffusion of solar radiation, and just the vast distances out at the edges of the Solar System. Or maybe it was psychological. The temperature in his cockpit was the same as it always was. He leaned forward and felt the glass bubble of the cockpit with the knuckles of his hand. The glass was warm, and hummed with the pleasant vibrations of a well tuned engine. It always felt cold out here, maybe it was the overwhelming darkness of space, how small the sun looked, or maybe it was the appearance of the big ice station on Pluto. He didn't know how people could live there. At least on Triton they had their great solar reflectors and a semblance of natural life. He was cruising fast, accelerating steadily but slowly to avoid the relativity effect. It was a long race. He could see Killian's racer as a speck in the distance in front of him, not far. They were leading the pack.

Samson switched on the ship's auto-cruise at the current trajectory and took his hands off of the control wands. They snapped out into the space in front of him and quivered back and forth in the air. His hands ached, and he rubbed his forearms. He tried to lean back in the harnesses. There were no other ships nearby and he had to get rest where he could. He bicycled his legs in the air in front of him, and tried to ignore the pain where the straps of the harnesses dug into his shoulders. They would rub raw wounds by the end of the race, but that was part of it. He pulled at the straps to let the blisters breathe. He hated long races.

His mind wandered to Lisa. He missed Stephanie. He wondered if it was right for him to see her, he didn't want to hurt her. But he liked Lisa. He was seeing her after the race. She didn't seem in danger of getting hurt. And Stephanie was gone. And all the racing whores were horrible. Lisa was sweet. He was excited to see her. He wondered if he would ever see Stephanie again. She had finally called him on the com link, and they had talked for a few minutes. She was cold, and unapologetic. She wouldn't explain anything. She told him to focus on his racing, that it was important. Bitch. When he asked if they would see each other again, she said she didn't know.

Samson knew that Stephanie was not a bitch. He was worried about her. He reached out impulsively and caught hold of the control wands and spun the ship in a perfect barrel roll.

"Don't waste your energy, Ford," Killian said through the com. "If you don't finish in the top ten, the magazines will crucify you."

Samson peered ahead, blinking against the faint glare of the sun. Killian was just a speck in the distance still. He switched off his com. He double checked his sensors, but none of the other racers were gaining on him.

He worried about Lisa. She was just young. What did Killian want with her? He thought about her grandparents. Strange people. What was it her grandfather had said? "The fate of the world could very possibly rest on your shoulders right now." He hoped not. An image of Lisa's quietly transparent, guarded, smiling face seemed to fill up the endless vacuum in front of him. She was just young still. He wondered what she wanted from him. She probably didn't know either. She was young, even for being young. She probably thought she was old for her age, she was young. It was only when you got older that you realized how young you were. Maybe he could help her somehow, maybe that's what he liked so much about her. She wouldn't want him to. It was easy to get messed up when you were young.

Samson remembered his first girlfriend, from racing bikes on Triton. They hadn't even made love. She was young, and sweet, and lost. Genetically engineered and beautiful. Worked as a whore now on Neo Vega. Last he heard. Maybe she turned her life around. She'd believed somebody's lies. She'd wanted to believe them. Lisa was smarter than her.

A SHIP PULLED UP BEHIND as if to pass. Samson didn't mind. He didn't recognize the ship. Some kind of saucer deal. He didn't even bother to turn on his com. When they came up close and swerved, he rolled silkily, avoiding collision. And caught the hammerfist edge of his wings framework above their engines and torqued them out of alignment, sending them cartwheeling insanely out through space. Assholes. He hoped they had good inertial dampers, but didn't care enough to watch and see if they ever pulled out of the spin. He raised his acceleration a fraction and slowly began to cut out the distance between himself and Killian. Killian had been setting an easy pace. Probably waiting for Samson to move up alongside him.

SAMSON INCHED UP TOWARDS KILLIAN as if to pull up beside him, then opened his throttle further to shoot past. Killian spun an aggressive cartwheel at him, and he curled easily around it, leaving Killian racing to catch up. Samson's ship was fast. He kept his com off and focused a hard, straight line into the Haumea orbit. Haumea would provide a small gravity whip. Killian lit his boosters wastefully, and Samson pulled inward, to a tighter curve around the planet, as Killian blasted back past him. Killian waved from his cockpit, and Samson plunged towards Haumea in the tightest possible curve, until the pressure on his back felt like it would crush him. At 150,000 km/hr he seemed to be blasting into the little planet's surface.

"Ohmygod, Ford's got it wrong!" one of the tv announcers screamed.

Samson's racer shot past Haumea in a puff of vapor, meters above the giant, icy rock. Spectacular. The announcer cheered and crowds and individuals all through the Solar System screamed excitement at their screens. Samson turned hard and switched on his GCU. He blacked out for a few seconds, but his muscle memory took over – the bright white racer whipped around the planet like an explosion. Samson blinked rapidly at the starry, empty space as his head slowly cleared. Killian was behind him.

The bright, white racer screamed through space like a lightning banshee. Samson knew that Killian could not afford to waste his boosters again to catch up. The race was his to win now, he could visualize himself on the winner's podium already. If he could stay ahead through the asteroid field he would win. Through the field, around the buoy, then a sprint back to Pluto. Easy. Several racers died in the asteroid field every year. More than a few had cursed their luck for being born in a period when Pluto and Haumea were orbiting so close. Otherwise, this race would be impossible. The planets' orbits kept them apart for decades at a time, for centuries. The crowd loved these races. In a few more years the distances would be too far and this race would be only a memory. Maybe he could watch it revived again from an armchair when he was an old man.

The asteroids were the problem, they were chaotic and

unpredictable. There weren't actually that many asteroids in the Kuiper belt, in the outer asteroid belts of the Solar System. There wasn't much of anything at all in the Kuiper belt, you could have a hard time hitting an asteroid if you tried. It was all so spread out, across unimaginable distances. Tiny distances. Everything in the universe was relative.

The big objects like Pluto, Haumea, Makemake, even Neptune when it came close, plowed through the Kuiper emptiness leaving gravity wakes. Trailing particles, and rocks and ice, pulling on comets, creating a series of waves. The waves would wash over each other, multiply each other, or cancel each other out, or clash awkwardly to create chaos and confusion. Over the thousands and thousands of years, the billions of years. And the little planets that collided, and the big ones, and their clouds of rocks and ice, of dust and debris. But there was nothing out there, it was so empty. The waves would interact and carry their bits of stuff, and in the chaos, somewhere in the interaction, were the peaks and troughs of their movement. Holes of true emptiness punched into the pattern, and spaces filled up with matter of every sort, where the waves had multiplied and drawn everything together up onto a crest, and sucked in an exploded dwarf planet or two. The thickest of these was the asteroid field. It was dumb luck that it happened to be so close to Pluto and Haumea. Dumb luck. The Racing Board had stared open mouthed when it was discovered. When they had finally heard about the discovery. Years after the discovery. It was so perfect for them, as if it had been placed there. As if fate was on their side. A great cloud of dust and rocks and ice spinning through space. Perfect. Put a buoy on the other side. Tell the racers to fly through it and round the buoy. Perfect.

The distances in the outer Solar System were vast, even when planets' orbits brought them close together. The races were long, a trial of endurance, with great stretches of cruising, of flying straight, where the pilots could push the limits of their ships, push up to their true maximum speed. 500,000 km/hr, 600,000, 750,000.... It was a function of how much time the ships had to accelerate, how much energy they could store. And, of course, the relativity effect. 768,250 km/hr was the record, it had been reached in the Solar Regatta fifty years earlier and was the fastest that any person had ever flown. Most of the racing pilots who had pushed the envelope past 600,000 km/hr did not survive.

The relativity effect was a strange thing. A mystery of physics, or not quite one. It didn't make any sense to Samson. He thought they didn't know what they were talking about. They couldn't predict it very well. He flexed his hands on the control wands, remembering what it had felt like. Or not remembering. Foreign, wrong, indescribable. They said that it felt different to every person. They said it could do things to you, that it could rearrange the protons in the atomic structure of your body, that the atomic particles could get swapped out, jumbled up. That you would look the same, but different, and your body would become like some mysterious substance that the doctors tried to isolate in their labs and study, that your mind would be pulled out of your brain, severed from your body, like severing the connections of a computer network. Like death, but different. Some of the survivors had told strange tales.

It wasn't the maximum speed, really, that was the problem. That was part of it. If you went fast enough, it would get you eventually. Nobody knew why the one dumb fuck had survived 750,000. Most pilots would be overtaken by the effect as they pushed past 600; 500 if they were unlucky. The ships were less sensitive. Machines could pilot a ship up to 1,000,000 km/hr or so. That would ruin any living creatures on board, but the machines would be ok. Not quite the same as brand new. Corporations were developing metal alloys with the relativity effect now. You could buy some amazing stuff. But the problem was that no one could predict it. It was a crap shoot. So they would fly a ship up past 1,000,000 km/hr, filled with steel alloys and other junk, and cross their fingers and bring it back and see what happened, and they would have new metals that had never been seen before, and sometimes they were amazing. Expensive. You couldn't afford them, they went to research labs. The good stuff did. Maybe some of the top pilots had a little bit of it in their ships, maybe some of the guys like Killian. But not a lot.

Of course, 1,000,000 km/hr was just a rough gauge, the relativity effect could hit hard and unexpectedly at 800,000 or 900,000, the ship could spin out into the outer Solar System lost in space, what was left of it. Whatever it had become. It could be unsalvageable. It could be radioactive. It wasn't the speed so much, but the acceleration that was the problem. That was how the relativity effect could really sting you. As a pilot you were rarely going to be pushing above 500,000 km/hr anyway. There were only a few races where you had a chance to build up that kind of speed. But if you accelerated too fast between 200,000 km/hr and 250,000 km/hr it could be a problem. It all depended on gravity fields and points of reference. The fabric of the universe. They said that's why the relativity effect was so unpredictable, that it was like an intricate structure that formed suddenly out of the chaos. It was dictated by the will of the universe itself, by subtle influences and variables which could not be ascertained. They quoted the uncertainty principle, and quantum paradoxes. They just didn't know what they were talking about.

It wasn't usually a problem. The racing ships' ability to accelerate peaked at the lower thresholds of the relativity effect.

Dumb luck. If the technology got much better, pilots would fry themselves with relativity all the time. As it stood, only the very fastest ships could even push the envelope. Few of them had experienced the relativity effect at all. The beginning stages of it. Of course, it was a spectrum. They said everyone was experiencing the relativity effect at all times. That it was inherent in the nature of being, that it was only a question of magnitude. They just didn't know what they were talking about.

Samson's bright, white racer cut through space like a ray of light. Edging up towards 600,000 km/hr. Killian's ship tore a blue streak through the universe behind him, keeping pace, pushing, trying to catch up. Samson cursed him and pressed the outline of the cross against his chest. Killian was a calculated racer, but seemed to enjoy taking risks. He was fearless. It was part of what made him so good. They were coming up onto the asteroid field soon, they would have to slow down. Otherwise, Samson felt sure, Killian would keep pushing him faster until one of them was dead.

It must have irked him that Samson's ship was fast enough.

Samson smiled. He turned on the com and Killian's voice came through in mid-tirade.

"–even listening to this, you fuck? Is your com off? Hello? Where did you get a ship that fast you two-bit outskirts, fresh off the deck, dust plains of shitsville, faggot."

Samson switched the com back off. The asteroid field was coming up fast and he began his deceleration. This was by far the most dangerous part of the race. Even Killian would take it slowly, even if he was behind. Some of it would be luck. It would depend on how the asteroids came at you, and what kind of clouds you had to edge around or fly through. How well your ship could weather the beating. If you tried to shoot through it quickly you would wind up dead. Of course, you couldn't go too slow, either.

The twinkling, bright patch of space grew larger and larger until it was the only thing in front of him, until it began to surround him. The larger asteroids and the clouds of dust, and gas, and debris began to take shape.

There were ships here from the Racing Board. Referees, and a great, hulking salvage ship. Buoys marking the the space they had to fly through. A cold shiver ran down Samson's back. Other people. It was a strange feeling how lonely space could be. He imagined flying through these dark reaches truly alone, without even Killian and the other racers. It was so empty and cold. One of the referee pilots tipped a casual salute with his fingers as Samson's racer slid past and he chose his point of entry into the denser section of the field. A large asteroid hammered through the jumbly cloud and he dropped in behind it, angling slowly forward, using it for a shield. Tiny rocks and sand peppered the ship, and the sound filled up his cockpit, like a hailstorm on the roof of a car. Killian had chosen a different point of entry. Boulder sized rocks and chunks of ice careened past, and Samson dodged them as he moved deeper into the asteroid field. The space behind him closed up tight with dark purple, rocky gas. He followed the path he had chosen, as if he were crawling through a narrow hole. A shower of softball sized rocks flew at him, and Samson climbed to avoid them. One of the rocks deflected off the edge of the wings framework, and the whole ship vibrated like a gong.

Something popped. The sensors went crazy. Samson blinked his eyes in disbelief. He punched rapidly at the buttons in the cockpit, and craned his neck to make a visual survey of the ship. It shuddered. There was a tremendous, nauseating, wrenching sound of steel grinding on steel. He switched on his com. Static.

"CYLLA," STEPHANIE SAID GENTLY. "WOULD you leave please? I'd like to be alone for a while."

"Of course, mum," Cylla said, and began walking away.

"Please take the afternoon off."

"Yes, mum."

Cylla curtsied quickly as she disappeared through the door, leaving Stephanie alone in her bedroom. It was a large, second story room, with vaulted ceilings and enormous windows that looked out onto a deep blue lake shore. The windows were punctuated with intricate stained glass. Stephanie switched on a large television projector as soon as Cylla had gone. Samson was still in the lead. She watched the race nervously, sipping at her coffee. Twisting up the edges of her embroidered silk robe until the tips of her fingers turned white. The pilots were approaching the asteroid field. Samson was slowing down. Killian was close on top of him, and a small pack of racers followed a few thousand kilometers behind them. The asteroid field looked particularly foreboding this year. It had filled up with purple clouds of ice and vapor. The racing announcer was breathless. He went over the latest betting odds.

Some idiot had already died crashing into Haumea. Stephanie didn't run the replays. The first pilot to die was a favorite betting angle. He had been a 150 − 1 shot, and the news stations were trying desperately to secure an interview with one of the handful of individuals across the Solar System who had bet big on him and scored.

One of Killian's tirades into the com was played back and the announcing team laughed uproariously. They played it again and again. At the end of the loop, Killian said, "I'm going to kill you, Ford." Each time it repeated, Stephanie's face ticced. She switched to another audio channel and listened to the chatter of the racers in the leading pack. Samson flew into the asteroid field. He slipped in behind a large asteroid that tumbled past him and rode its wake. He never talked much on the com.

The view of Samson crackled with static as a cloud of tiny robotic cameras tried to follow him through the field. Stephanie saw his ship lose power and shudder. Something was wrong. She held her breath and stared with huge eyes at the screen. She switched back to the announcer's commentary.

"What the hell is Samson Ford doing?"

Samson's ship lurched underneath a hail of small boulders, and the screen blinked as one of the cameras was obliterated and the view switched to another one. A boulder careened off the wings framework of the racer.

"I think there's something wrong with his ship, Paul."

"What bad timing. At the worst possible time. Can he get out of there?"

"No, he can't turn around, he's too far in. It looks like he might have a loss of power, he has to try to ride his momentum through."

"Oh-my-god."

The announcers held their breath as Samson's ship lurched jerkily through the field, struggling to get out of the way of the large boulders and gas clouds that tumbled past. One of the cameras got a close-up angle on him through the cockpit glass. His face was white and streaked with sweat.

"I mean, turning around or not, let's be honest," the first announcer said soberly, "he's a dead man now."

"He might be–"

"Nobody can survive that–"

"Hey, look at this, Killian Gideon's turning back around."

Stephanie bit her lip. Her left fist was clenched, and she pressed the china coffee cup into her chin. She couldn't smell the coffee, only space dust and engine fluid.

The screen divided in two, to show Killian's ship circling back towards Samson through the asteroid field. The asteroids seemed to flash past Samson's crawling ship. They were moving too fast. A small, cantaloupe sized rock exploded into the side of the racer, leaving a dent in the hull and a cloud of dust around the cockpit. Killian's ship wove neatly through the flying boulders and debris, until he was nearly on top of Samson, gliding in above him and behind.

"That's just not right," one of the announcers said. "I just can't agree with that. Killing a racer that is already disabled."

"He's liable to kill himself, too."

"There's just no sportsmanship in that."

As Killian's ship flew in over the top of Samson it seemed almost to pause. It seemed almost to stop.

"LEAVE HIM ALONE, YOU–" the words contracted painfully in Stephanie's throat.

But Killian didn't stop. His engines kicked up again, and he flew past Samson's ship without touching it. There was a tiny, wry smile on his face through the cockpit, and he seemed to bring his hand up in salute to Samson as he cruised away. Samson's ship continued to worm its way slowly through the asteroid field, seemingly on the verge of obliteration at any moment.

"It's a crying shame we can't get any com link up to hear what they said to each other."

"Don't worry, it will be on Killian's vocoder."

"But how is he– Wow!" the announcer exclaimed as the edge of a large boulder caught the wings framework and sent Samson's racer spinning about its axis like a drill bit. Even as it spun, the ship pulled into a turn around the path of another boulder, and slowly righted itself.

"Woah! Amazing. He's not, I mean, he doesn't have any computer on board that can take over that piloting for him."

"Oh no, the ship systems are checked very thoroughly. They're very, very careful about that."

"You know, this is a real pity, this guy, Samson Ford. I mean, say what you want about his genetic background, but this guy was one hell of an exciting pilot."

"He's not dead yet, Paul."

"No. He thinks he can make it through. And who are we to say he can't. Don't blink folks, don't even breathe. We're not going to take our eyes off of Samson Ford. I can't believe he's still alive!"

"He's a hell of a pilot."

"How long can he keep this up before one of those big boulders obliterates him?"

"He's got– Killian Gideon is almost through the field now, by the way. He's got, at this rate, probably about an hour to get through to the other side. It's just so hard at such a slow speed, you're just a sitting duck."

"You wouldn't have wanted to test that against yourself."

"When I was racing?"

"Yeah."

"Hell no, are you kidding? I would have been dead already."

The announcers laughed. Samson's ship pulled up around the path of another boulder and shivered slowly along the edge of a big gas cloud. Killian was soon through on the other side, rounding the buoy and rocketing away in a straight shot for Pluto. Other racers passed Samson. A young pilot approached the field too quickly and obliterated himself against an asteroid. The announcers couldn't believe that Samson was not the first racer to die in the field, another popular betting angle. He continued. Only one of the cameras following him was left. His face was ashen, sunken in, eyes big, peering back and forth rapidly like quivering spotlights. He had been in the asteroid field for half an hour. He was more than half-way through to the other side. Many more racers passed him. Several more miscalculated and were annihilated in great explosions within the field. Samson piloted stubbornly forward, apparently unaware of the fact that he was supposed to be dead. His ship disappeared in an icy cloud of gas.

"It's not the gas that will kill him, it's the loss of visibility, the clouding of your sensors. I just don't see how he can survive now. Can you see his ship still? It's so dark in there."

Racing fans throughout the Solar System held their collective breath. Stephanie held her breath. The last of the little robotic cameras finally blinked out.

"OHMYGOD, IS THAT—?" SOMETHING WAS moving at the edge of the asteroid field. Something with intention, something that flew. The announcer's voice rasped awkwardly from the overwhelming emotion of genuine shock.

"Can we zoom in on that, can it possibly—? Ohmygod."

The ship was just a blur at first. A dot amid the tumbling debris. Slowly, slowly, it drifted out of the asteroid field and into view. It was battered and dirty, you could scarcely tell that it had been painted white.

"Ohmygod! He's alive!!"

Samson's face looked gaunt through the dusty glass of his cockpit windshield. He piloted out to the big space buoy and stopped there beside a little group of broken racing ships with blinking lights. He switched on his own racer's distress beacons, and collapsed forward in the cockpit harnesses.

"We've got a cockpit readout on his vitals folks, he's going to be ok. It looks ok. We'll get a doctor to look at it in the next few minutes, but it looks ok. This is a miracle. This almost wants to make you believe in the old religions doesn't it? What are the odds. What a hell of a pilot. How did he possibly fly through all that? I can't believe it."

Far away from Samson, far from the race announcers on the ice station at Pluto, far on the other side of the Solar System, Stephanie's face was stained with tears. Streaks of them that had already dried. And fresher beads of the damp, salty, drops. She took the first deep breath she had taken in hours and pulled a blanket on top of herself to stop from shivering.

A BIG, YELLOW TOW SHIP with white checkering and flashing orange lights pulled up beside Samson's racer.

"How you doing, Ford?" a woman's voice asked.

"I've had better days."

"Are you good for a tow, or do we need to get you into an air lock on the hospital vessel?"

"No, I'm— A tow would be fine. I'm ok. A tow would be good."

"You sure? That's what they're here for."

"No, no. A tow, please. As long as you're going to be the tow pilot?"

"I sure am, sir."

"That's perfect," Samson said into the com, remembering how nice it was to talk to a friendly human being. "Let's get back to Pluto. Hook me up."

The big, checkered ship reached out two robotic arms and attached a series of cables to the back of Samson's racer. The arms pushed and pulled at the battered wings framework, making sure that it was secure. In less than ten minutes they were underway.

"That was a hell of a performance back there," the tow-ship pilot said.

"What's your name?" Samson asked.

"Cindi."

"Cindi. What do you mean a hell of a performance?"

"That's some of the best piloting that I have ever seen."

Samson exhaled impatiently into the com, as if he were irritated.

"Who, Killian?" he said.

"What?"

"You're talking about Killian's piloting?"

"No. No, of course not. I mean you, piloting through that asteroid field on low power, silly. Everyone thought you were dead."

"Oh."

"That's probably going to be one of the all time moments in racing history."

Samson pondered this thought, but it didn't make him feel any better. He was being towed back to Pluto. He was in last place. He thought he should be happy to be alive, but he wasn't. He was irritated and angry at not having won. He punched one of the control wands in front of him and it bounced back and forth sympathetically.

"You ok, Ford?"

"Yeah," he said, failing to keep the weariness out of his voice. "Yeah, thanks, Cindi. I think I'm gonna take a nap here for a while. I'm really tired."

"I think you should. That sounds like a good idea."

SAMSON SLEPT LIKE A STONE, and when he awoke two hours later he felt positively rejuvenated. He looked down at the racing IV trickling two thin streams of fluid into his veins. The blue stream was for nutrients, the clear one for hydration. The drip was very slow now. The IV worked on a bio-feedback loop to the ship's computer, which regulated it automatically. It was essential for long races. When he had been in the asteroid field, the valve on the IV had opened completely, flooding his veins. It left him feeling puffed up.

He activated a mirror in the cockpit's windshield and looked at himself. His face was a little swollen. He looked like hell. He switched off all the lights in his cockpit, and leaned back in his harnesses, and stared out into deep space. The stars were diminished by light from the tow-ship's engines, but they were still bright in this distance, so far away from the sun. You didn't have an opportunity to really watch them when you were racing. Not to just sit back and watch. All those other planets, all those other galaxies. There must be such in-credible things in the universe. Such amazing, unimaginable things. Such endless reaches to explore. He sat perfectly still, and breathed deeply, and watched the star trail behind him in its beautiful infinity.

"Hey Cindi, who won the race?"

"Hey honey, are you awake again already?"

"Yeah."

"Killian Gideon won it, damn him."

"Ah."

"Disappointing huh?"

"I hate that guy."

"Well if it makes you feel any better, honey, nobody's really talking about him. Everyone's talking about how you managed to get through the asteroid field."

"Really?"

"We all thought it was a death sentence. I was watching it, too."

"Crazy, eh?"

"What went wrong?"

"I don't know," Samson said. "It wasn't anything that came up on my diagnostics. It wasn't from an impact or anything, it just happened all of a sudden, something just failed."

"Weird."

Samson was silent for a while.

"Well I'm glad you survived, honey. You're my favorite racer."

"Thanks, Cindi. You're my favorite tow pilot."

"Get out of here."

"No, it's true. I mean, I don't know a lot of tow pilots, I have to admit. But you're my favorite."

"I was really hoping they'd send me to pick you up," she said.

"So what's the news around the Solar System other than racing?" Samson wondered, changing the subject.

"Oh, all the same old crap. They're just going on and on about a war between Rothschild's and Bloodworth's now. I don't watch the news that much."

"A war? It's not a real, fighting war I hope."

"No, no. It's just a trade war. It isn't enough for them to run the universe, they have to bicker with each other, too."

"Crazy."

"You scored a big blow for the Rothschild's side today."

"Did I?"

"Well, I mean, you're sponsored by Midlothian now aren't you?"

"Yeah."

"It's the whole division between the two companies, isn't it? I mean, they chose sides. It's all about the naturals legislation and stuff."

Samson leaned his head back silently.

"I'm sorry I brought it up," Cindi said sheepishly. "I didn't– Me and my big mouth. My brother's a natural born, you know. I don't want you to think– I mean, I'm all about that, I'm totally, like, on your side."

Her voice trailed away as she tripped nervously over the words.

"I'm sorry," Cindi said, when Samson continued to be silent.

He shook the thoughts out of his head and responded quickly into the com.

"No, not at all. I hear what you're saying. I really appreciate it. I was just, you got me thinking about it in a different way, I never thought about Bloodworth's and Rothschild's choosing sides like that. I guess I'm caught in the middle of it all now."

"Oh what do I know," Cindi said.

"No, no. I'm sure you're right."

"They want to take my brother away from my parents on

Earth, can you believe that?" she said, with an angry strain in her voice.

"It's insanity," Samson said.

"But you showed 'em, honey. You showed 'em today. They all must have been so happy when you were trapped there in that asteroid field, up in their big old boardrooms in Manhattan and Delhi, but you put on a master class. You showed 'em that you're the best pilot in the world. You're better than Killian, you're better than all of 'em. Ohgod, my heart almost broke when I thought you were dead."

"I don't know if they'll see it like that," Samson said.

"Of course they will."

"I bet a lot of the papers will say I'm a joke, that I couldn't even finish the race."

"Oh... pish."

"You know they will."

"Oh, it won't matter what the papers say, everyone was watching. We all saw it on tv. Even I did, in my ship. It was beautiful. You won a lot of fans today, this was the most exciting thing to happen in racing for a long time."

"I hope you're right," Samson said.

"I'm always right. You'll see. I always pick the winner."

ONLY A FEW RACING FANS had the resources and inclination to make the trip all the way out to Pluto. It was mostly locals in the audience at the big hangar base that had been temporarily converted into a racing stadium, transient workers who would sign up for six months or a year, or three, and hope to survive it and return home. Many of them had stayed behind to wait for Samson, and when Cindi finally unhooked him and he set his racer down at dry dock he could hear cheering through the thick glass bubble of his cockpit. It took him by surprise.

The tarmac was empty, most of the other racers had already

gone. His right arm ached as he unclipped the IV connection to his veins and slowly unsealed the cockpit. It took him fifteen minutes to climb back to the ground, with the help of Ben and Kenichi. A small contingent of racing reporters crowded around them, asking questions and getting in the way. The workers in the stands were still cheering. Samson lifted his aching arm and waved to them, and Ben pushed him over to a bench to sit down on, and ran the medical scanners over him. He untaped Samson's arm, pulled the needle out, staunched it with fresh cotton, and taped it again as quickly. Samson felt dizzy and hung his head over the ground.

"How did you survive in the asteroid field after the loss of power?" a woman reporter shouted insistently, shoving a microphone into his face. Ben pushed her away.

The cheering gradually subsided, and what was left of the crowd began to dissipate from the stands. Samson stood up unsteadily and looked at his ship. It looked almost as bad as the day he had pulled it out of the junkyard.

"Did you think you were dead when your ship malfunctioned?" one of the reporters asked, as Ben caught Samson under the arm and steadied him.

"No."

"What about when Killian Gideon flew back and was right above you?"

"I had something for him if he tried to bump me."

"Would you all please get back," Ben said, glancing around for the race security, who were supposed to keep the reporters off to the side in a separate cordon.

"What went wrong with the ship?" Kenichi asked a few hours later, with the racer safely loaded onto the Junket and the journalists being herded away outside.

Samson stared at Kenichi hard.

"I don't know."

"But, what did the diagnostics say?"

He glanced from Samson to Ben, who was actually glaring.

"The diagnostics didn't say anything," Samson said. "I couldn't see anything on the outside of the ship either."

"Well that's extremely unusual," Kenichi said.

"Yes."

"You just suddenly lost power, without warning of any sort?"

"I'm really curious to find out what it was," Samson said. "There was just this pop all of a sudden, and the ship started shivering, and I lost everything from the main power supply. But the diagnostics said nothing was wrong and that the power was still full, which it obviously wasn't."

"This sounds like some kind of sabotage," Kenichi said slowly.

"It sure does."

Ken's face flushed. He stammered and looked at the ground.

"I HAVE TO GO FIND Lisa, we're supposed to go on a date," Samson said, after taking a shower. "What time is it?"

"You're going on a date? On Pluto?"

Ben looked incredulous.

"They have a little arcade."

"With the kid?"

"She's not that young," Samson said defensively.

"She's young."

"You know Lisa, she's a sweet girl."

"So don't dick her around," Ben said.

"I never do that," Samson said lightly. He grabbed Ben's arm and pulled him up next to him before continuing in a whisper, "Hey, you worry about the ship. I want to know what went wrong and I don't want to have to take Kenichi's word for it."

"Right," Ben said grimly.

"Right-io," Samson said, opening up the Junket's deck door and walking out onto the steps.

"Hey Samson," Ben shouted as Samson reached back to close the door behind him.

"Yeah?"

"I'm glad you're alive, brother."

Samson looked up and they made eye contact, and he noticed how much older Ben's eyes were than his.

"Oh, I wouldn't die," he said. "You know that."

He waved, and closed the door, and raced down the steps to go and look for Lisa.

"Why don't you go away, I don't like you," Lisa said nervously as Killian followed her down the hall. She wondered resentfully where Samson was, only vaguely worried about him.

"Of course you like me," Killian said, wrapping his arm around her shoulder.

Lisa squirmed in his grasp, but it felt good.

"I'm always sweet to you aren't I?"

"I don't know," she said, without looking up.

He took his hand off her.

"Of course I am."

Killian seemed to glow, as if the brilliance of his racing victory had been captured and reflected inside of him. His body was relaxed and well oiled, a few hours rested, but still pumping on overdrive from the effects of the race. There was a faint, omnipresent sheen of moisture on his skin. He was beautiful.

Lisa didn't look at him.

"Well, what about that girl you were with?" she said.

"What about her?" Killian looked confused.

"Isn't she waiting for you?"

"She's not as sexy to me as you are."

Lisa walked away from him again, and Killian followed her step for step, watching her body rakishly.

"Please leave me alone," she said, and hurried through a door out into a lobby area where there were mechanics and other racing staff.

"She's just happy to be here," Killian said. "She doesn't mind waiting. She'll do what I want."

Samson strode hawkishly through the lobby, nodding to people who stood up and applauded as he walked by. He spotted Lisa and Killian almost instantly.

"Hey, Killian!" he said with hostility, and everyone turned to stare.

"Why Samson Ford," Killian sneered, "congratulations on finishing the race, my friend. Many pilots find it a difficult course to complete."

Samson walked past him and put his arm around Lisa, who had been staring into space. She suddenly looked relieved, and wrapped her arms around his waist and embraced him tightly. Killian's nose twitched.

"Why don't you leave Lisa alone, asshole," Samson said loudly, making sure that everyone could hear. "I think she's asked you enough times."

While Killian sputtered, Samson turned on his heel and hurried her away.

"Do you want to have sex with me?" The words floated out of his brain like bubbles of music. Almost like sound. It was hard to understand if they were even words. His eyes were closed, covered. But he could see her in his mind. Or, if not her, something like her. Some combination of his own imagination and her mental image of herself. As if they were sharing the same dream and equally in control. As if their brains had been wired imperfectly together. Which was exactly the promise, and what they had paid for.

"No."

Her response came to him as a thought. Like a thought within his own mind, but that he had no control over. He could feel the emotion of it. Her thoughts had a quiet emotional reserve, not as a reaction to himself, he realized now, but simply as a part of her nature. This was her personality. A very slow fuse. The question neither upset, amused, excited, nor offended her. It evoked only response and gentle curiosity, soft and quizzical.

"You're not attracted to me?"

"Of course I am."

He could see himself as she saw him, or a ghost of himself as she saw him, an impression of it. He could feel himself touching her, and how good it felt to her, and then a stop. Then a nothing, as if she didn't know what else she might want him to do. And her mind reacted to his own thoughts, and there was dissonance and static, like a crackling inside their brains.

"Woah."

"Calm down," her mind seemed to massage his own. "Don't move so fast."

"But, if you're attracted to me– I don't understand."

"You don't."
"I'm trying."
"It's ok."
"There's someone else?"
"No."
"But–"
"Wait."

It was a pleasant sort of sensation to wait while Lisa thought. To feel the impressions of her thoughts washing over him. It was like melody, and dancing, but different – passive, internal. He wondered what anger, or irritation would come through as. It was hard to believe they were not even in the same room. Lisa never seemed to become irritated. It was one of the things that was very endearing about her.

"My Grandmother told me a story once," her thoughts came through as ideas, and words, sensations, and feelings, "that many years ago, in ancient history, there were men and women who never had sex with anyone until they married them. That they never shared that experience until they had already committed to love and cherish that person. And that for these people sex was so special, because it was only shared between the two of them, it was this amazing bond and uni-fying experience, like a symbol of their joined lives. Because they loved and cherished each other, sex between them was an action of loving and cherishing each other. It was like, they believed that if you had sex with other people it cheapened and interfered with that bond between you and your husband. And people would live their whole lives and only have sex with their husband or wife, and nobody else. It was like it was sacred, like it was a holy thing, like the things that were in the religions. Isn't that amazing?"

"You mean you want to wait until marriage to have sex?"
"Yes."

The directness of his thought seemed to strike through Lisa's dissonantly, like a hammer on water.

"You mean, you're a virgin?"

"Well, yeah."

"Wow. Even the Magdalenas don't believe in that."

"I believe it."

"I think you're very special."

"Thank you."

"I think you should stay away from Killian."

"I will."

"I can't believe what happened in the race today."

"The race is over, you need to stop thinking about it. I hate Killian."

"You're so beautiful, I can't believe how innocent you are. Killian almost killed me, I was going to bring him down with me if he did."

"I know you were. Thank you. Can't you stop thinking about it?"

"Didn't you worry about me?"

"I don't, really— When they said you were going to die I felt bad. Lots of racers die, lots of friends of mine have."

"You're different."

"I'm better at this than you."

"I've never done it before."

"Do you think it's the future?"

"I don't know. If I died you wouldn't care?"

"I like you. I don't know."

"You really are young."

"I know."

"Someone sabotaged me."

"Who?"

"Someone in my camp. Kenichi maybe. I don't know."

"The old guy who works for you now."

"Yes, no. Maybe. Yes, him, but I don't know if he did it."
"Report it to the race officials."
"No."
"Why not?"
"You don't understand."
"I know."
"I don't know if I like this."
"I like it."
"It's for kids."
"I'm not a kid."
"You are."
"Sort of. Then you're an old man."
"No."
"No, I know. You're not."
"A lot of people are trying to kill me, you don't care?"
"I... care about you, but. No, I don't know. I don't think about you that much."
"I don't either."
"About me?"
"Yes."
"I know. We don't love each other."
"No."
"But that's ok."
"You're so serious, I didn't know."
"Don't worry, I'll find my boy and marry him."
"You will."
"You think so, don't you?"
"I'm sure you will. You're special."
"Thank you."
"Are you sure he couldn't be me?"
"No."
"We have fun together."
"Yes."

"Can we get out of this, it's making me crazy."

"Yes."

"Meet in the hall."

"Yes."

Samson pulled up the visor covering his face, and jerked the sticky sensors off of his temples. He stared at their silver foil connectors and wondered how they worked. He felt nauseous, and wondered if it was a physical or psychological reaction. The little pod was claustrophobic. He climbed out of it and pushed open the door, and sucked in the fresh air in the hall. A moment later, Lisa came out of her room. She was bright and smiling, and Samson hugged her tightly and kissed her on top of the head.

"You really think that's fun?" he asked, as they walked past a young employee at the exit and back into the main section of the arcade.

"Of course!"

TEPHANIE HAD SENT SAMSON A message on his com. It was an audio message. He frowned, wondering why she wouldn't send a hologram.

"Hi Samson, it's Stephanie."

"Hi," he said into the empty air of his cabin on the Junket.

"I was watching the race on Friday, you scared me to death. I'm so glad you're ok."

"Me too."

"Is everything alright? This isn't good, you need to be winning races. If you don't place well in the Solar Regatta the press are going to turn you into a joke. I don't know what the problems are, but if you need to hire a security service do that. Flying well to avoid death and then finishing last place is not going to be good enough at this level. And if you end up dead that looks even worse."

Samson stared at the metal wall of the ship.

"I'm sorry, this is just— I can't say the things I want to say, but you need to get it together and start flying your best again, ok?"

There was an edge in Stephanie's voice.

"Don't screw this up. Take care of yourself, I wish I could see you. I have to go. Bye."

"Delete."

SAMSON AND BEN SAT AT the counter of a little coffee shop in the Venutian city of Mamito. They were dressed casually, in linen slacks and loose, white cotton, short sleeved shirts that buttoned half-way up the front. A popular style on the sunny, breezy planet. Samson also wore large sunglasses and a brimmed, straw hat. The coffee shop was long and narrow, with a big, glass counter that ran its length and little booths on the side. It had windows at the entrance where the bright, Venutian sunlight streamed into the dim interior, creating a painful contrast of light that divided the room.

The barista set coffee cups in front of them.

"You can take the sunglasses off if you want," she said. "You're in the shade."

"Oh, it's– I need to keep them on, I have a problem with my eyes," Samson said.

"I'm sorry," she said. "Hey, you know, your voice is familiar."

"Is it?" Samson smiled skeptically.

"Do people tell you that?" she asked.

"People say he sounds like some jerk on tv," Ben said.

The barista smiled slightly.

"Well, I think it's a nice voice," she said, and walked away to help another customer.

Ben and Samson sipped at their coffee silently for a while. It was very hot, and served in heavy ceramic cups with no handles. Mamito was famous for its exceptional coffee. It had an exotic, un-Earthly character that resulted from the unique mineral content of Venus' soil. Coffee growers around the Solar System tried to duplicate that soil quality, and most of the brands of 'Venus' coffee were not actually from Venus anymore.

"What do you think about the race?"

"Ken's gonna kill me this time."

Ben laughed.

"We could fire him."

"We can't win without him," Samson said.

"Winning isn't everything."

Samson wrapped his hands around the thick, stony coffee cup, and enjoyed the heat against his skin. He lifted the cup in both hands, like he was making an offering, and up to his lips and sipped it slowly. The coffee in Mamito was infused with small amounts of coca.

"Neither of us trust him," Ben said. "It's a kind of insanity."

"Yeah."

"I've been watching him really closely, and I put up cameras everywhere in the shop."

"Good."

"Let's just fire him, Sammy. We can get another good engineer."

"Not that good," Samson said. "I want to win. Besides, this is his ship."

"It's your ship."

"It's– As far as an engineer goes, it's his ship. He built the damn thing. He designed it. He's not replaceable."

"But you don't trust him, either."

"I have a feeling that Ken is being straight with us," Samson said. "But I don't trust him."

"Won't that mess your racing up?"

"No."

"You can just turn it off in your mind?"

"Yes."

"Ok."

Ben tapped the fleshy tip of his finger on the counter.

"It's going to suck if you die," he said.

"Aww, it's bound to happen eventually."

Samson took off his sunglasses and rubbed his eyes.

"Maybe not," Ben said. "If you win this race you can retire."

"It's going to be great if I win," Samson said.

"Yep."

SAMSON FORGOT TO PUT HIS sunglasses back on, and a few minutes later one of the other patrons recognized him.

"Hey, aren't you that racing shit they keep showing on tv?"

"No."

"Yes you are, you're that kinderfuck pilot that's stirring all the retards up."

"Fuck off and mind your own business," Ben said murderously.

"You fuck off."

Samson and Ben turned back to their coffee and tried to ignore the man.

"Yeah, that's you right there," the man said, holding up a projection from his card. "Samson Ford. The kinderfuck."

"I told you to mind your own business," Ben said, standing up.

"Hey, that is him," another patron said. "That's Samson Ford!"

There was a stir in the coffee shop. People began to crowd around them. Ben, in a rage, tried to push his way through to the first man, but Samson hooked an arm around him and dragged him towards the entrance. People outside peered in through the glass, trying to find out if it was really true. Samson pulled Ben out through the door and walked across the sidewalk to hail a cab.

"Ok, ok," Ben said, slapping away his arm. "Shit, do you see any cabs?"

"No."

Dozens of people crowded around them on the sidewalk, like leaves clumping together on the bank of a stream.

"Excuse me, sir, can I please have your autograph?" a young man implored, holding out an old fashioned pen.

"I don't have time," Samson said distractedly.

"Fuck you, kinderfuck," someone shouted.

"Hey, fuck you!" the man with the pen responded angrily, glaring at the edges of the crowd.

Ben and Samson squeezed farther and farther out into the street. They finally spotted a cab and hailed it down.

"Quick, drive quick," Samson said as he pulled open the door and the crowd surrounded them.

"Oh shit, man," the cabbie said.

"Quick, hurry."

The cabbie, a dark, natural looking man, raised his sunglasses and squinted at Samson in the rear view mirror. He spun to face them, and disbelief on his face disappeared into a wide smile.

"Oh shit, you're Samson Ford. I love you, man."

"Get us out of here."

Someone banged on the window of the cab, and Ben clicked the door lock.

"Of course. I'll get you out," the cabbie dropped his sunglasses into place and pulled the cab into ascent. "I'm getting you out right now. Samson Ford, man. I can't believe this. This is the best day of my life."

As they pulled away from the crowd, Samson heard someone yell, "He's in there, in the cab!" He turned around and a handful of cars were following them. Men leaned out of the windows of the cars holding cameras.

"It's no problem, Mr. Ford," the cabbie said happily, "I'll lose them."

The cab leapt forward as he pushed its accelerator to the floor.

"You see," the cabbie said, sliding around the corner of a building and plowing haphazardly through a stream of traffic at the neighborhood's edge, "I try to drive my car like the way you drive your space ship."

The news cars stayed tight behind them, filming the entire time. One of the men with cameras flipped out of the window on a turn and banged against the side of his car, dangling precariously from a harness cable. He pulled up his camera, which was attached to himself with another cable, and began filming again immediately, while a colleague pulled him back into the car.

"I like the way you drive," Samson said politely.

"Salvador. Call me Salvador, please."

"I like the way you drive, Salvador. I'm glad we got into your cab."

It occurred to Samson that this was what Stephanie would have said.

"Haha, yeah, man," Salvador said cheerfully, turning in his seat and whipping the cab dangerously close to a building. "We'll lose the rats. I'll leave them in the dust, man. Just like you would do. I know this city like the back of my hand, man."

Five minutes later, despite Salvador's best efforts, they had not lost the rats. Several more news crews had converged on the chase.

"Salvador, I have an idea," Samson said, as they cruised over a huge stretch of lawns and forest. "Why don't you pull up here, above this park, and trade places with me. I think I can lose them."

Salvador looked back.

"You want to drive my cab?"

"Let me show you a few tricks," Samson said.

"Oh, man. Oh yes, man. I'm stopping right here."

The cab lurched to a halt, throwing Samson and Ben forward against the front seat, and was quickly surrounded by the news cars, whose camera flashes snapped against the windows violently. Salvador slid over and Samson scrambled into the driver's seat.

"Put your belts on," Samson said, strapping in.

Salvador smiled at him and watched.

"I'm serious, man," Samson said, "put your belt on."

"What? Ok."

No sooner had the latch clicked than Samson dropped them into a sharp, high-G dive. Salvador and Ben both screamed as the cab rocketed towards the ground underneath them, and Ben caught vomit in his mouth as Samson pulled them up lurchingly short of the ground, bending into a throttle-open sprint along the edge of a large business area.

"Where's a tunnel?" he asked, looking at Salvador.

"Up, to the left," Salvador said, grinning.

Samson spotted the line of traffic and aimed for the tunnel entrance.

"Samson Ford driving my cab," Salvador said gleefully. "This is the best day ever. The best!"

The news cars were above and behind them, following closely, but avoiding Samson's sharp curves and acceleration.

"There's a lot of traffic there, man," Salvador said, as Samson approached the entrance of the tunnel without slowing down.

"I hope so."

Some of the news cars had realized what was happening and were diving and accelerating to catch up. Samson spun the cab onto its back and shot in along the tunnel roof. Air brakes and horns squealed angrily and seemed to fill up the tunnel as he passed. Ben held his breath, perfectly white. One of the news cars hit the ceiling and crashed into a wall behind them, but the others continued pursuit. They fell slowly behind as Samson piloted a perfect line through the tunnel, just above and between the traffic on either side. A car swerved in front of him, and he dove under it automatically. Salvador caught his breath, then pumped his hand in the air.

"Fuck yes, man. Yeeeeehaaawwwww!"

By the time they had exited the other side of the long

tunnel, the news cars were no longer visible. Samson saw a police patrol car approaching from well down the block. He accelerated into a crowd of buildings and turned left, right, left sharply, then continued to accelerate for another mile, and turned right, left, right. On the last turn, both Salvador and Ben passed out. Samson slowed the cab to driving speed and joined a heavy stream of traffic through the outskirts of the city. Salvador shook his head and sat up. He spun and looked behind them.

"Holy fucks, man. Are they gone?"

"They're gone."

They cruised out of the city uneventfully, and Samson chose a nice hotel in an expensive suburb and asked Salvador to drop them in front of it. Salvador refused to accept payment for the cab ride, and Samson shook his hand and autographed a racing poster for him that he happened to have in the glove box. Samson and Ben walked into the lobby, hats and sunglasses pulled firmly down, and chatted with the woman at the front desk for a few minutes until Salvador had left. Then they walked back outside and Ben negotiated a ride with a limousine driver to take them back to their space dock.

Stephanie flicked through the news channels and saw the name 'Samson Ford' pass on the screen. She clicked back. There was footage of him in a taxi cab, trading places with the driver.

"...and treated these reporters to an impromptu display of driving skills this afternoon. We followed the cab, now driven by Samson Ford, as closely as we could, but in an amazing display of driving prowess, he accelerated and – well, the footage speaks for itself. Thanks entirely to his own incredible abilities, this racing pilot's location remains – a mystery."

C H A P T E R 50

PHILLIPE BLOODWORTH SAT IN A tiny, but ornate little office with two of his most trusted executives, a man and a woman. They were all staring at a holographic projection screen against the wall. A surly looking man in a trench coat stared back at them through the holo-screen, nostrils flared in excitement.

"We've found her identity, sir."

"Her? The Rothschild's heir is a she?"

"She, certainly is, sir."

"How do you know?"

"Family photos, sealed contracts, a DNA match to the dead Baron."

"You've obtained her DNA?"

"Enough for an identification, sir," the man said huskily.

"Well, don't dawdle," Bloodworth said cheerfully, "show us a photo of our competitor."

There was a pause while the man fiddled with his card terminal.

"What's her name, Golan?" the female executive said.

"Anastasia Leizu Stephanie Rachel Elizabeth Marie de Rothschild."

A photograph of Stephanie appeared on the screen, taken from a distance through a telephoto lense. She was getting out of a large car in front of Rothschild Palace. On the opposite side of the car was Simon Okunle.

"But, wait a minute, I know this girl," Bloodworth said.

"Do you know her, sir?" the man, Golan, said through the holographic screen.

"But, she's one of that Samson Ford's crew members."

The male executive furrowed his brow.

"Is that possible?"

"Show us another picture," Bloodworth said.

Another photograph of Stephanie appeared on the screen. His eyes began to twinkle.

'BREAKING NEWS! BREAKING NEWS!' Huge capital letters flashed across holo-screens throughout the Solar System. Phillipe Bloodworth's news stations were the first to carry the story, but everyone else had picked it up within the half hour. Even the Rothschild's stations ran it, although they tended to cast doubt on the story's veracity.

"We're breaking into our regular programming, ladies and gentleman," a dour faced newscaster said into the cameras, "to bring you an important and rather strange piece of news which has just hit the wires. Several journalists tonight are alleging to have uncovered the identity of the Rothschild's heir. Viewers will surely recall that when the Baron de Rothschild died the identity of the heir to his fortune was kept a secret. The Rothschild's business empire is one of the largest in the Solar System, possibly the largest, and it has been estimated that the Rothschild's heir controls as much as 10% of the Solar System's economy. Several sources are reporting tonight that the Rothschild's heir is a woman. Here is her picture, if our sources are correct. The wealthiest and most powerful woman in the world.

"Her full name is Anastasia Leizu Stephanie Rachel Elizabeth Marie de Rothschild, and she is, we are being told, the only child of the late Baron. Here is a photo of her getting into a limousine with Simon Okunle, well known Rothschild's chief executive. Her identity has been a closely guarded secret within the Rothschild corporation, and the release of this information now is believed to be related to the ongoing business war between Rothschild's and the corporations of mega-tycoon Phillipe Bloodworth. The story was first broadcast on Bloodworth's news stations, but we have confirmed it with several independent sources.

"There is a strange twist to this story, ladies and gentlemen, it is a subject which we are hesitant to enter into, and yet, it is an important part of this news story. It has been reported that the Rothschild's heir was recently working as a racing mechanic for the well known natural born racing pilot, Samson Ford. Phillipe Bloodworth has publicly accused the young heiress of miscegenation, and questioned her competence to control such a large part of the Solar System's economy. He has also accused her of wielding her influence to prevent the passage of quarantine legislation on Earth and in the rest of the Solar System."

The next afternoon, Simon Okunle held a press conference. The journalists were tense, aggressive, frothing at the mouth, but Simon was as relaxed and ambivalent as ever.

"I have no comment to make about Mr. Bloodworth's accusations," he said. "I can only say that here at Rothschild's we're pleased to keep the identity of the Rothschild heir a closely guarded company secret, a trade secret if you will, which prevents our owner from being unduly burdened with some of the less savory pressures that come from leading a large business empire. Mr. Bloodworth is keenly aware of these pressures himself, and it is sad to see that he would attempt to pile them onto the back of a young, unsuspecting girl, as he has done in this case. You know, Phillipe Bloodworth is an old friend of mine. Or, at least, he was. Today, I worry about him. Here at Rothschild's it is our guiding policy to make the world a better place for all human beings, however so great or humble, and I wish that Phillipe would see the beauty in that, the transcendent power of that idea, and infuse it into his companies.

"This is what built Rothschild's: the love of humanity. This is the seal of our brand, our guarantee. It is the thing that has made Rothschild's the most trusted company in the Solar System, and we are not about to walk away from that principle now."

At the hangar on Venus, Samson watched Kenichi work feverishly on the racer. Kenichi's work was obsessive. He started on the racer as soon as he woke up in the morning. He fiddled with parts while he was eating his meals. When he took a break, he talked about the racer, about the Solar Regatta, about engineering ideas, and how they could make sure that Samson would win. He was pale and losing weight, he seemed to be tuning the racer with the lubrication of his own blood, investing it with his very life force. It was difficult to believe that he could be working to sabotage them.

Samson helped with guidance as Kenichi floated the engine out of the racer for the thousandth time. The central firing rods needed reshaping according to a new theory Kenichi had developed. They should have an oval cross-section, not perfectly round. Samson watched him rapidly disconnecting heavy cable wires and removing bolts, the engine lurched as Kenichi released a vacuum valve. Any little thing that was amiss could kill him when it was all put back together. Kenichi would know exactly what to leave amiss, if he wanted to.

"I can't practice flying if you always have the engine taken apart, Ken," Samson said.

"I know, I know, but this is important, believe me. This will give you increases in fuel efficiency and speed. We will have you running again by tomorrow."

"Did you see this shit that's on the news?" Ben called.

He was sitting at a table against the wall, staring at a small holo-screen.

"What?" Samson said.

"You gotta see this. Look."

Ben enlarged the size of the projection and turned up the sound. Phillipe Bloodworth looked out through the holo-screen from a press conference on Earth. He was standing triumphantly in front of rows of reporters, and holding up one giant photo of Stephanie after another.

"Stephanie! Hey, that's Stephanie," Samson said, "what is he–"

"Ohmygod."

When Kenichi said it, it almost sounded reverent.

SAMSON SAT ON THE BED in his bunk and dialed Stephanie's card over and over again. For hours he dialed it. Finally someone picked up. His heart quivered.

"H-hello?" a feminine voice said.

It was her.

He didn't know what to say to her. He didn't know what he did say. They talked. She would sound like she was going to cry, and then her voice would harden and she would seem distant from him, and then her voice would soften again, as if she were sorry. She couldn't come to help Samson, or work on his ships anymore. She wanted him to visit her, she begged him to come. He tried to explain to her that he didn't have time, that the Solar Regatta was coming up so quickly. He tried to explain it to himself. She sounded like she was going to cry again, and her voice didn't harden up this time.

"Please come," she said. "I need to see you."

LISA SAT BY HERSELF ON the couch in her grandparents' apartment and watched the news. They kept showing photos of Stephanie and saying how important and powerful she was. Lisa didn't know Stephanie well, she was just a nice woman who sometimes worked as a mechanic at the races. Lisa had chatted with her a few times, and liked her. It didn't seem possible that Stephanie could really be the Rothschild's heir, that she was the person who owned and commanded the Rothschild's empire. Everyone loved Rothschild's. It was like being in charge of the world. They kept showing pictures of Stephanie and Samson.

"So, basically," a woman with huge pink eyes was saying on the tv, "the Rothschild's fortune is passed on to the Baron's only daughter, who turns out to be some dumb bimbo who likes to hang out around races, a racing groupie, and she just ignores all her obligations and responsibilities, even when the state of the Solar System rests in her hands, she ignores all that to go shack up with some dumb racing pilot, and a natural born racing pilot with no genetic enhancements at that! It's a perfect picture of humanity isn't it, it's—"

"Now, hold on Ingrid—" her male co-host tried to interrupt her.

"No, you let me finish. It's a perfect picture of humanity, just go back and read through history about young women, it's the same pattern of the dumb, irresponsible bimbo squandering whatever she has, even if all she has is looks, or all she has is youth, even go back to ancient Earth and the story of Don Quixote, now wait let me finish, Don Quixote you will see over and over again it was the same thing, some dumb young tart squandering the family fortune and lusting after some semi-moronic troubadour, and the point is, look, the point is this: this girl 'Stephanie', the Rothschild's heir, look her full name is Anastasia Leizu Stephanie Rachel Elizabeth Marie de Rothschild, and–"

"We know what her full name is."

"Would you let me finish! Anastasia Leizu Stephanie Rachel Elizabeth Marie de Rothschild, ok, she's the heir to the biggest fortune in the history of the universe, ok, and she must have had all the most enhanced genetics that money could buy, she must have tricks in her DNA that the rest of us haven't even imagined yet, and look she's still this dumb human tart lusting after the nearest brainless, witless, neanderthal troubadour in the vicinity. And that's the most amazing part of this story, it makes me embarrassed to be a woman."

"Oh, I'm sure that's not true."

"Well of course it's not true," the pink eyed woman continued between rapid breaths, "but it makes me embarrassed for *her* to be a woman, and it makes me worry about the fact that someone like that is in charge of the Rothschild's empire. I mean, can you imagine? And we all thought so highly of the Baron and thought he was a man of impeccable judgment, but then he gives it all to some dumb tart of a daughter whose life ambition is to hang out in greasy arenas and have wild sex with flash in the pan, soon to be dead, racing pilots of the lowest intellectual order–"

"Well thank goodness for Simon Okunle."

"Thank the old gods of the universe for him, I just hope he's the one who is really steering the ship. Isn't there something we can do, some legislative thing or something that some of the planetary governments can do to take this power out of the hands of this girl who is so obviously unsuited to wield it? It's like we're going back in time and there's all these lords and monarchs again, and some dumb bimbo has managed to become queen in the midst of–"

Lisa changed the channel. The next station was showing a photo of Stephanie and Samson standing together in front of his racer. She was dressed in an old mechanic's suit that hugged her body tightly, and Samson had his hand around her hip.

Lisa wore a quizzical expression on her face. Her eyes seemed to change color, from green to silver to blue, as the clipped light from the holo-screen carved her features into shadowy relief. She looked like a child. She watched the television intently, curiously, without any sign of being upset. Her grandfather came into the room and sat down on the couch beside her. He watched the tv with her in silence.

"Your friend Samson," he said after a moment, "did he let you down?"

"No," Lisa said emotionlessly, and continued to watch the floating images.

AT THE SOLARIUM, LISA AND the other interns ran errands for the racing league directors, or whoever the directors assigned them to. Lisa's director was a fat, black haired, violet hued man named Copernicus Brown. People called him 'Copper'. He was a pleasant person, an easy boss, well liked – a schmooze. He waddled around the racing arenas genially, chatting and gossiping with anyone and everyone who was involved in racing. Accomplishing little work. Copper must have been handsome before the flesh piled onto him so heavy, before he fell in love with food. If there ever had been a before that. Lisa didn't understand why he wouldn't take pills or get surgery to fix that problem. The fat. There was no need to be fat anymore, it didn't matter how you lived. He could afford not to be fat. Maybe he thought that the pills or the surgery were unhealthy. Maybe he had some other health problems that complicated things.

Copper waddled up to her with a smile spreading across

his lips. He seemed perfectly healthy. He motioned Lisa over to a table and spread a set of large engineering blueprints out on top of it, pressing his meaty hands into the paper and rubbing at the creases where they had been folded.

"They're the newest blueprints for the first Solar Regatta obstacle. Aren't they beautiful?"

"Yes."

Lisa stared at the blueprints curiously, but didn't know what to make of them.

"See, the tunnels here," Copper said, pressing a finger into the paper.

"Right."

He wanted Lisa to make copies of the blueprints and deliver them to Shia Herrman, the chief engineer who was supervising construction out on the arena floor.

"Joseph Ilunga, Gideon Killian's manager was here earlier today. He thinks that these obstacles are going to be very exciting."

Lisa frowned. The obstacles were supposed to be a secret.

"Is that... normal?"

Copper smiled.

"Oh yes, don't be surprised. It isn't a big deal. Things aren't always the way they look on television, Lisa. Most of the top racers will find out what the obstacles are, one way or another, before the race. Keeping them secret is more for the suspense of the public, more a part of the show than of the competition."

"Oh."

A SINGLE SECTION OF A race obstacle filled the huge arena working floor. The two obstacles in the Solar Regatta would be much larger than the arena itself, of course. Construction crews fabricated one massive section at a time, which were picked up immediately and towed into space. Each individual section towered above the stadium like a giant skyscraper, and crews were usually able to construct several sections a day. It was noisy and dangerous. Lisa wore protective headphones and walked as quickly as she could, trying not to be crushed or run over.

Shia Herrman barked orders into an electronic com system, and sometimes at workers on the floor through a megaphone. He was wearing a bright orange construction helmet and was hard to miss. He looked angry and exhausted, and glanced at Lisa resentfully as she approached. He tried to ignore her.

"Excuse me, Mr. Herrman," Lisa screamed.

"WHAT?"

"EXCUSE ME, MR. HERRMAN."

"WHAT DO YOU WANT?"

Lisa held the stack of blueprints out in front of her, and he pulled them out of her arms.

"COPPER TOLD ME TO GIVE YOU THESE."

He flipped through the enormous pages and ran his index finger across some of the drawings and figures, then shoved them all back at Lisa and turned away again.

"I DON'T NEED THESE," he said as an afterthought, and brought a yellow com talkie up to his mouth and started shouting orders into it again.

"I'LL JUST GET RID OF THEM, THEN," Lisa said.

"YEAH, DO THAT."

Herrman turned his back to her and walked several steps away, pointing and shouting as a truck drove by filled with enormous metal fittings. Lisa folded one copy of the plans up neatly and slipped it into her bag as she hurried back out of the construction zone.

IN HER HOTEL ROOM THAT night, she dialed Samson on her

card. She was surprised when he answered instantly.

"Hello, Lisa?" Samson said quickly.

"Hi."

"How are you doing? What's going on?"

He sounded rushed and distracted. Lisa could hear clanking and shuffling in the background, as if he were packing something up while talking to her.

"Hey, I saw you on the news," she said.

"I guess everybody's seen that, huh?"

"Is it, um, true? I mean, are you and Stephanie, like, together?"

"I don't know. We were. Not when I met up with you. It's been kind of off and on, I don't really understand it. But I guess Stephanie has this whole secret life that she was keeping secret. You know. Do you know Stephanie?"

"Not really."

"Ah, so yeah. It's kind of confusing, but I think maybe we're going to be together."

"Oh."

"But that doesn't bother you, does it?" Samson said. "I thought we kind of like, had realized that we weren't the right match for each other, right?"

"It doesn't bother me," Lisa said. "I guess we just shouldn't see each other anymore."

"Yeah, I guess not, Lisa. You're still my friend, though, right?"

"We can still be friends."

"Ok," Samson said.

There was an awkward pause on the line.

"Well, I have to—"

"I have something for you," Lisa interrupted him. "It's the blueprints for the first obstacle in the Solar Regatta, I'm transferring them to your card now."

Samson stuttered into the phone.

"Well, I've got to go now," Lisa said. "Goodbye. Don't get killed in the race."

"Ok Lisa," he said rapidly. "I'll see you at the race I hope. And thank you."

"Ok."

She hung up the line.

C H A P T E R ⁵²

Samson took his card out of the cabin terminal and stared at it in his hand. The blueprints to the obstacle were there, inside it, waiting to be read. They were stored. He wished for a moment that they weren't there, that he didn't have them. He didn't want to win the race and not be satisfied by the victory. To have a taint on it. If he did win the race. Maybe he wouldn't look at the plans anyway. He rubbed the palms of his hands together around the thin, black, computer and blew on it, as if it were an ancient rubbing stone, a talisman of luck. He probably would look at the plans. Would it be better to not look and lose the race? He didn't have to decide now. There was plenty of time to decide. He didn't even think about deleting them.

He threw the bag he had packed onto his bed and went out to the Junket's hangar to see what Kenichi was doing. Ben had taken a shuttle into the city and wouldn't return until the afternoon. Samson trusted Kenichi now. He had to, and he did anyway, and he felt like there wasn't any purpose served worrying about it. They weren't getting rid of Kenichi. Ben had quietly installed a specialized program of checks and diagnostics into the ship's computer and that was the end of it. Now they were a team again, just preparing for the race.

"Hello Samson," Kenichi said, as Samson walked out into the little hangar, "come look at what I'm building for you."

"Hi, Ken. How's it going?"

"You won't believe this."

"I'm going to have the best ship in the race."

"Undoubtedly."

Samson walked around the racer to their electronics bench. Kenichi's long hair was tangled, and his face was smeared with grease. He was fabricating a pattern of copper lines around a hollowed out steel cube.

"What is it?"

"What it is– What it will be," Kenichi said. "A quantum replicator. Are you familiar with the idea?"

"No."

"Well, they didn't exist before, as far as I know. But the theory was that the synchronization of a ship's booster engines could be controlled perfectly with a device like this. Do you see what I mean? Perfectly, in the literal sense. It will mean smoother control and more stability when you use your boosters. There is an idea, as well, but I don't know whether it is true or not yet, but there is an idea that by using a quantum replicator for synchronization one can delay the onset of the relativity effect when accelerating with boosters."

"Wow," Samson said, "that sounds great."

"Do you know how it works?"

"What, the quantum replicator?"

Samson pulled a stool over and sat down at the bench next to Kenichi. The tracing oven had finished painting copper lines onto the cube and popped open. Samson took it out and turned it over in his fingers.

"I can explain it to you," Kenichi offered.

"Ok."

"It's not finished yet, of course, this is just the core. I still have to program a controller for it and install it into a housing, and fit it with optic tunnels that will feed in from the booster stream."

"Ok."

Kenichi spent the next twenty minutes explaining the concept of the quantum replicator. Samson tried hard to follow the explanation. He couldn't make any sense of it. He thought that the synchronization of the boosters was already more exact than he needed it to be. Delaying the onset of the relativity effect could be a big advantage in the race, but it sounded unlikely. Kenichi tried to explain the intricacies of quantum sampling and how mirroring could be used to circumvent the old uncertainty principle and supply a stream of perfect data to the microchip that controlled booster synchronization. Samson frowned.

"It will be interesting to try it in the ship, and see if I can tell any difference," he said.

"Absolutely. I think you will be surprised. It might seem like such a small degree of difference between the high synchronization supplied by the traditional drivers, and what this new replicator can supply, but I think you will be surprised what the difference feels like in terms of actual control of the ship."

An image of Stephanie flashed across a small holo-screen behind the electronics bench, and Samson reached forward to turn up the volume.

"They're still talking about her, huh?"

"Yes," Kenichi said, looking away.

The program was a rehash of all the news about Stephanie that they had already seen.

"Do you think she is really the Rothschild's heir?" Samson wondered.

"Oh, yes."

"Yeah, I think so too."

"She is, umm," Kenichi's voice was hoarse and he stared straight ahead as he spoke, "she's a very special woman, Samson."

"Yes."

"In any event, I–"

"It's really terrible that they did this to her," Samson said. "Exposing her in the public like this, I mean."

Kenichi's face turned red.

"Yes."

BEN PUSHED OPEN A DOOR and the air outside hit him like a blast furnace. He stepped out of a sterile, blue, climate conditioned shop and blinked up at the bright Venutian sun. It irritated him that he had had to park a block away. He walked down the street purposefully, with a stern set to his face. The brown box under his arm made him nervous. A new, state of the art, processing core. It had been extremely expensive. He wiped the sweat off of his brow as he came up to his little shuttle-car. Sometimes on Venus he was tempted to shave off his beard.

The trunk in the back of the shuttle was reinforced, and probably the safest place. Ben unlocked it and placed the box gingerly inside, and breathed a sigh of relief as he slammed it closed. He looked up and made eye contact with Scamp.

"Shit! Shit!"

He dropped into a crouch behind the shuttle and drew his gun. It felt like a dream. Heart pounding. Hoping to wake up.

"It's ok. I come in peace," Scamp said in his huge, intimidating voice.

"Fuck you."

"Don't shoot me, I need to talk to you. Lucho sent me here to apologize in person, and to give you a message of peace and friendship."

"I will shoot you," Ben said committedly.

"Look, people are staring," Scamp said, and it sounded like he had backed up, farther away.

Ben stood slowly and peeked around the car, holding the gun in front of him. Scamp had moved back to the opposite side of the wide sidewalk, standing parallel to the front of the shuttle. He was holding his hands up in a gesture of peace. Some of the passers by on the sidewalk were staring at them. Ben cleared his throat, and slid the gun back into its holster. He moved around to the front of the shuttle, eyes on Scamp, and began opening the driver's door.

"Please wait and talk to me," Scamp said. "This is important."

Ben watched Scamp across a little table in the nearest coffee shop. He kept his chair backed up warily, as far from the table as he could. He should have simply left, and he didn't understand why he hadn't. Scamp leaned forward across the table, seeming to engulf it. You couldn't get used to how big he was. It was the way he had pleaded, the way Scamp had pleaded with him to stay. There was something pathetic about it. Maybe he had taken pity on Scamp.

"Lucho sent me to apologize and to try to make up for everything he owes you guys," Scamp said, pulling a scrap of paper out of his pocket and reading off of it. "Lucho wants to send his thank you to Stephanie and Samson for being so lenient with us."

Scamp leaned back in his chair, and the legs quivered underneath him.

"I was hoping to talk to Samson personally," he continued, "but my instructions are to speak with whoever I find in person first."

"Ok, I'll tell Samson about the apology," Ben said. "How did you find me?"

"When we captured your ship, we installed trojans on your and Samson's cards, they phone home and tell us where you are."

Ben glared at him.

"We didn't put one on Ken's card," Scamp said quickly, "because he would have found it. Anyway, here."

He slid a chip across the table.

"This program will take the trojans off. You can get Ken to check it out. Or anyone you trust."

Ben picked the chip up between his thumb and forefinger and looked at. The waitress kept staring at them, at Scamp. Everyone was staring at them. Ben had chosen a table away from all the other people.

"That's fine," Ben said. "I'm going to leave now."

"There's something else. Lucho has learned, through some of his connections, that there is going to be a hit on Samson soon."

"What?"

"We don't know much, but this is a gesture of good will. Lucho thinks it's going to be some of Phillipe Bloodworth's agents, they've been keeping tabs on you guys for a long time."

"Phillipe Bloodworth – the tycoon?"

"He hates naturals. It would be Bloodworth's worst nightmare if Samson won the Solar Regatta. The rumor underground is that they're the ones who sabotaged you guys out on Pluto. Samson was lucky to survive that."

"Don't tell me who's lucky," Ben said resentfully. "Big ape."

"Hey, now. I'm trying to help. The point is, one of the guys in the hit team was shooting his mouth off. He said they know where Samson is going to be, and that he's going to have an accident. You know, the kind you don't recover from."

Ben looked at Scamp skeptically. He reached forward, and grabbed his untouched coffee cup, and gulped it down without taking his eyes off of the big man.

"I'm here to offer you my personal services as a bodyguard and security agent," Scamp said.

"No."

Ben sounded annoyed.

"I'm the best," Scamp said. "You need me."

"No chance, son. I don't trust you at all."

Scamp looked at him eagerly, trying to think of what to say to make Ben change his mind. He realized there was nothing.

"Ok, but listen," he said quickly, as Ben started to stand up, "this hit is for real. You need to get some real security for Samson, because these guys aren't playing around. Wherever he's been planning to go, he better not go there. You guys need to change up all your plans, starting right now."

"Shit. I gotta go find him."

Scamp pulled out his card and fiddled with it.

"He's still on your ship."

C H A P T E R ⁵³

A SHINY, DARK VIOLET SHUTTLE GLIDED up to the Junket ominously. It was a large shuttle, a private transport ship, it was larger than the Junket. Samson watched the shuttle through the bridge windows and slowed the Junket to a standstill, allowing it to come alongside and establish an airlock. Both ships shook as the lock was made, and a clank of metal clamping together echoed through the corridors.

"Hey Samson, a ship is alongside us," Kenichi shouted, running down the hallway towards the Junket's bridge.

"It's ok, Ken, they're picking me up. I have to go on a trip for a little while."

Samson walked off of the bridge and straight past Kenichi in the hallway. He grabbed a large duffle bag out of his cabin and headed for the airlock doors.

"But – where are you going?"

"I can't tell you that," Samson said.

He punched the button on the doors and they slid open, revealing the tiny walkway that connected the two ships. There were uniformed men waiting on the other side, and Kenichi stared through the hallway in confusion.

"Don't fly off anywhere," Samson said, as he crossed the threshold of the Junket, "I'll be back in a day or two."

He nodded to the men on the violet ship.

"All ready, Mr. Ford?"

"Hi. Yes, let's hurry."

The airlock sealed off with a hiss, and the door in the Junket closed up automatically. Kenichi stammered at the door in confusion and peered out the window to see the big, violet shuttle pulling away.

"It's good that you decided to let us pick you up, Mr. Ford," a weathered looking shuttle commander told Samson when he got to the violet ship's bridge. "We've received a tip that there's a hit out on you and they will be watching for your racer."

Samson raised his eyebrows.

"I couldn't take the racer anyways," he said, "we're still fitting it up for the Regatta."

BEN GOT BACK TO THE JUNKET a few hours later.

"He did what? They said they know where he is going to be!"

Kenichi was drenched with sweat.

"He must have told you something," Ben said accusingly.

"I don't understand any of this," Kenichi said. "This big shuttle showed up and Samson left right away. He already had a bag packed. He wouldn't tell me anything."

Ben told Kenichi about meeting Scamp, and everything that Scamp had said. He watched Kenichi closely while he relayed this information. Kenichi was flustered, upset. He didn't seem to want to make eye contact. With Kenichi's help, Ben was able to analyze the tracking virus and track Samson's location. Kenichi insisted that he could do it faster himself, but Ben wouldn't let him. They pulled the Junket out of orbit around Venus and accelerated after Samson's shuttle.

"There is a very good chance that this has something to do with Stephanie," Kenichi said, as they sat on the Junket's bridge.

Ben watched their progress on a chart, checking and re-checking the relay signals that told them Samson's current location.

"That's a definite possibility," he said.

"But I cannot understand why he wouldn't tell me what he was doing," Kenichi said.

"Maybe he doesn't trust you."

It took them 12 hours at full acceleration, and after using both of the Junket's booster tanks, to finally make a com connection with the big, violet shuttle. The shuttle was traveling unusually fast. Ben's Junket had only gained slightly on them, for all of his efforts, and it was more of a lucky relay connection that allowed them to signal the shuttle and establish a com link than that they had actually gotten closer to the ship. Not that the shuttle responded. Ben hailed them again and again, insisting that he had an urgent message for Samson Ford.

After more than an hour, he set the com to auto-hail every thirty seconds, and sat back in his chair trying to think of some way they could catch up. The Junket simply wasn't fast enough. The little shuttle he had taken down to the surface of Venus was even slower, and not outfitted for long space flights anyway. That left Samson's ship. Ben had only ever flown it a few times, and the racer's engine was currently removed.

A hailing signal finally bounced back from the big transport shuttle. Ben opened up the com and a blocky picture of Samson appeared on the bridge's holo screen.

"Samson!"

The audio was garbled. Samson's image moved awkwardly in stops and starts. He frowned at them through the camera.

"I can't hear you," Ben said, as Kenichi tried frantically to adjust the signal resonance.

The picture became clearer.

"–some weird shit going on here. It makes me nervous," Samson said.

"What?"

The signal went bad again, then the image of Samson blinked out and disappeared completely.

"Shit!"

"I can't get it back," Kenichi said. "The shuttle is pulling away from us again."

Ben slammed his fist into the control panel. Everything was going wrong. He glared at Kenichi and raced out of the bridge. Kenichi was confused for a moment, then suddenly jumped out of his seat and raced after him.

"Ben, what are you doing? Ben!"

He was already in the hangar, already installing the engine into Samson's racer when Kenichi caught up.

"What are you doing? Are you crazy?"

Ben ignored him. After he got the engine installed and ran checks on the racer to be sure it was ready to fly, he plugged into a terminal to the ship's main console and set the Junket to autopilot. He programmed it to follow the path of the racer. He then punched-in several strings of code to lock Kenichi out of the ship's controls.

"What are you doing?" Kenichi demanded. "The racer is not ready to fly."

"It's ready," Ben said, climbing up and strapping into the racer's cockpit. "I've been keeping a close eye on it."

SAMSON STARED WITH ANNOYANCE AT the little cameras and the blank holo-screen in front of him. He hoped that Ben had heard enough of his message not to worry. The shuttle that Stephanie had sent was extravagant. They had shown him to a private communications chamber to receive the call. The chamber was wood paneled, and sound proof. It had its own, fully stocked bar. He walked back out to the main corridor and up onto the bridge. The crew were staring at an old, rusting space hulk projected onto the bridge's main screen.

"Hmmm...," the commander said warily, "I don't like the look of that. Shields up, boys."

"It's just space junk, Captain."

"Something not right about it," the commander said distantly. Then with authority, "Steer us away from that space junk. And call into the station and order us a fighter escort. And send someone out to look at this thing."

"Yes sir."

INSIDE THE RUSTED SPACE HULK, behind a mirrored blind, with an insulated suit on that masked his heat signature completely, sat a man with an electron-laser sniper rifle. The rifle was long, and black, and clamped into two enormous tripods. There were several huge scopes mounted to it, green, and pink, and orange. He shifted his eye from scope to scope while he watched the dark, violet ship. It wasn't what he had been told to expect.

He breathed deeply, and slowed his heartbeat nearly to a stop. He zoomed in with the big green scope to try to see who was on the ship's bridge. In the windows. He could almost make them out. He drew a crosshair on the most prominent man, and stopped his heart completely, and waited for them to come into view.

The violet ship's windows suddenly became opaque, and it pulled away, changing direction.

The assassin's heart suddenly beat very fast. He breathed a long sigh into his glassy, ventilated helmet.

"What did they see? I can't stay here for long now."

SAMSON'S RACER ARCED THROUGH SPACE past the rotting hulk. A laser shot punched a single hole through the cockpit glass. Through Ben Johnson's head. The racer spun out of control, like a deflected bullet, then slowed itself to a stop and began to emit emergency beacons. The rusting space hulk fired up engines and cruised away.

Hours later, Ben's Junket slid to an obedient halt in front of Samson's racer. Kenichi sat on the bridge of the Junket, helpless, locked out of the ship's controls. He didn't under-stand why the racer had stopped. He couldn't even radio Ben to see what was happening. And then he didn't need to. The racer was right in front of him, right in front of the bridge's window. He stared open mouthed, in horror. A pool of blood floated in the air beside Ben's head like a little, red balloon.

C H A P T E R 54

THE ROTHSCHILD PALACE WAS A small, moon sized planet that orbited the sun in close proximity to Earth. Or the palace was on the planet. The planet, technically, was named 'Rothschild', and had been built by Stephanie's ancestors a century before. It was a private paradise, a personally held world. The palace on the planet was grand indeed, and seemed to dominate Rothschild, so that most people said 'Rothschild Palace' whether they meant the planet itself or the building. Stephanie called it 'home'. Whether she meant the planet itself, or the building.

The palace was a bright, chalky, marbly white, and had blue, tiled roofs. It was filled with fountains and gardens, punctuated by tall spires and impressive courtyards – larger and more magnificent than any of the palaces on Earth had been. That was important to Stephanie's ancestors. The little planet, and the palace itself, were unprecedented achievements in human ingenuity and engineering. To live and work on Rothschild was a cherished aspiration of the company's employees throughout the Solar System.

SAMSON'S SHUTTLE FLEW LOW OVER a huge, turquoise pool lined with tall, white, roman columns. It passed a little ridge and the earth opened up beneath them into a big, airy transport hangar that stood in front of and off to the side of the palace's main grounds. Samson couldn't help noticing the security presence as he was escorted into the palace. There were soldiers at every entrance, and robotic monitoring beacons tucked inconspicuously throughout the area.

The lavishness of Rothschild Palace amazed him. He had been expecting a lot, but the reality was luxury and opulence on a scale that was difficult to absorb. A guide, or escort led him up the hundreds of steps of the palace's main, grand entrance. Half-way to the top, the steps leveled out to engulf a large, golden fountain. Bubbly champagne ran down to the fountain from the top of the steps along a series of channels. The main bowl of the fountain, perhaps thirty meters in diameter, was inset with elaborate mosaic scenes of angels and gladiators, deer, lions, sparrows, and birds of prey.

"We don't really need to walk all the way there, Mr. Ford," the man escorting him said. "I just wanted to give you a chance to see some of the grounds."

He was a formidable looking, but mild mannered man. He wore a black uniform with a thin, creased, grey hat.

"It's an amazing place," Samson said. "I wish I had more time, but we should hurry."

"Of course, sir."

The man snapped his fingers and a floating platform descended from the top of the steps and stopped in front of them. He motioned for Samson to step on, and the platform carried them up into the palace in a rush. They floated down several large halls before the platform came to a rest in front of more intimate, private quarters.

"Where is Stephanie?"

"I'm sorry, Mr. Ford. We're almost there."

The man led him through an elaborate hall whose walls were covered with painted murals and bas-relief figures. The figures were exotically perfect men and women, representations of the things that genetic engineering could do for humanity. Some of the men and women had wings, some had gills in their necks. Their skin seemed to radiate sunlight back at a dark, solid gold disc inlaid into the wall.

An aide ran past them at a sprint. He glanced at Samson as he passed, then stopped in front of a large set of doors and whispered excitedly to the soldiers standing there. The soldiers looked taken aback, and said something into their communicators. The doors opened up and the aide ran in. When the doors closed, Samson could hear a commotion from the other side. The soldiers glanced at him, and looked down guiltily when he met their gaze.

"What's that about?" he asked, motioning towards the door.

"I don't know, sir," the man escorting him said. "Must be some urgent business. Those are Simon Okunle's offices."

The doors opened up again and another man dashed out into the hall. He glanced at Samson in surprise, and started to say something, but caught his breath and ran the other direction.

"They seem to know who I am," Samson said, striking a quick pace as they walked on.

"Everyone knows who you are, sir," his escort said. "I mean, everyone everywhere. I hope you don't take that as an insult, sir."

"No, it's ok. So she really is the Rothschild's heir."

"You mean you don't know, sir?"

The man led him into a little garden, behind which was a beautiful manor house built into the rest of the palace.

"Do you know?" Samson asked.

"These are our Mistress's personal quarters," the man said quickly. And then continued, "I'm afraid that I am forbidden from speaking on that subject, sir.

Samson looked irritated.

"I'm sure she– our Mistress, will be happy to talk to you about it this time, sir," the man said placatingly, and blanched.

"You don't have to call me 'sir'."

"I do, sir."

"Why?"

"Samson!"

Stephanie sprinted down the stairs from the entrance of the manor house. He leapt to meet her, fearing she would fall, and she crashed into his arms impetuously. Samson felt a shockingly strong arm suddenly push forward on his back and prevent him from tumbling down the steps. He embraced Stephanie tightly, and she cried into his neck, and out of the corner of his eye he saw the man who had escorted him walk backwards from them in a pose of reverence. He hugged Stephanie still more tightly, until her body was imprinted against him, and his eyes began to sting. He inhaled deep breaths of the scent of her.

"Stop, stop, I can't breathe," Stephanie gasped, and held onto him more tightly still.

She pushed her brow against his, and they blinked together, and she kissed him as if she had been waiting there to kiss him all of her life.

"I missed you so," she said, and grew faint in his arms.

Samson held Stephanie upright, and turned, with his hand around her hips, until they both faced upwards on the stairs. When she had steadied herself, he gripped her hand tightly, tracing the lengths of her fingers with his thumb. Their heads bent together like little birds.

"I'm so sorry, Samson," she said softly.

"You don't have anything to be sorry about."

"I am sorry," she said, and he set his hand on her neck, pulling their faces together, and kissed her temple.

"Should we go upstairs?"

"Yes."

An aide came and told them in Stephanie's visiting room. Stephanie and Samson were sitting together on a couch, catching up with each other. Talking. The aide rushed into the room and tried to draw Stephanie away. She told him to speak in front of Samson. The man protested, and Stephanie became irritated with him. He glanced between her and Samson nervously, and cleared his throat and held his breath before continuing.

"Mr. Ford's ship and his racer have been found adrift in space, Mistress."

"What?"

"We're still piecing together what happened, but – you see, mum – it's hard to say this, but–"

"But what? Say it."

"It's your friend Ben Johnson, Mistress. He was found in the racer. He's dead, mum."

Samson stood up.

"What are you talking about?"

"I'm sorry, sir," the aide said, trembling. "We have ships and investigators there now trying to figure out what happened."

STEPHANIE ORDERED THE RACER AND the Junket towed to her little planet and placed in the palace hangars. Samson didn't know the codes that Ben had used, and it took Stephanie's engineers hours to disable the ship's engines and cut the door out. Kenichi was beside himself as he emerged from the ship. He ran forward with his arms out, trying to hug Samson. Samson stepped away from him coldly.

"What the hell happened out there, Ken?" he said.

Rothschild's soldiers stepped forward.

"What?"

Kenichi's eyes shifted to Stephanie, who looked down at him imperiously, face grim.

"What the hell happened out there, Ken?" Samson repeated.

"What? But, Samson, there wasn't anything I could do! Ben locked me out of the controls of the Junket, it was set on autopilot. I tried to stop him from going."

"You God damn son of a bitch."

"What?" Kenichi spit the words, and gesticulated. "You can't think I had something to do with this? Are you crazy? Ben was my friend. I told him not to take the racer."

"Because you knew," Stephanie said.

"No!"

"Why did he lock you out of the ship's controls?" Samson asked, open hostility in his voice.

"Samson! I don't know why. He said– Wait," Kenichi held his hand up at the advancing guards. "He said that Lucho Gonzalez sent word that there was a hit put on you by Phillipe Bloodworth and that they knew where you were going to be. When Ben found out you left, he went crazy. We were chasing to warn you."

Stephanie motioned the soldiers forward.

Samson's racer had been secured in the cargo hold of the big tug that towed in the Junket. A group of soldiers carried a long, round, metal box down a creaky metal ramp and set it on the ground beside the tug. It was a beautiful, sunny day. Most days at the palace were. A breeze swept gently around the trees and grass and played across their skin. It was such a beautiful day. Samson held his hand up, blocking out the sun, and marveled at the crystalline blue and white of the sky. It didn't seem possible that Ben was dead. Stephanie put her hand on his shoulder and squeezed it hard.

"Do you want to see the body?"

He realized that she was squeezing as hard as she could. He looked at her. Her huge, dark eyes were cloudy with the reflection of unspent tears. They were supposed to be happy tears this time. He touched the hand on his shoulder, and pulled her forward with him towards the metal box.

"Yes, let's look."

She tried to wrap her arm around his shoulder more tightly, but Samson turned out of her grasp, and wrapped his own arm around her, and held her close to him while they walked. The soldiers that had carried the box stood politely away, and stared straight ahead respectfully. It was an old, pot metal, soldier's coffin. There was the shape of a cross pressed into the front of it. Stephanie was shivering in the bright sun. Samson rubbed her arm vigorously, and let go of her, and reached forward to unlatch the top half of the coffin. He wrapped his fingers around one of the flimsy, plastic handles, and the metal squealed angrily as he lifted the lid open. Sunlight poured over Ben's face. Over what had been Ben's face. And was now dead.

There was a hole there, right through the left eyebrow, through the center of his head. Stephanie caught her breath. Ben was so pale, he needed the sun. He would have. The hole was remarkably clean, it wasn't gory at all. As if he had been made of plastic and had had a red hot, metal pin poked through him. Samson reached out and put his hand on his friend's face. It didn't seem possible that this was Ben. The skin was cold and indifferent, like waxy rubber. The beard already didn't feel like real human hair. Stephanie pulled his hand away.

"I'm so sorry, honey," she said thickly.

He closed the lid of the coffin.

"It's ok."

He pulled Stephanie away and walked back in the direction of the palace. He didn't know where he was going, just straight ahead, just in that direction. She stood close and followed with him, just walking.

"We always knew that we would die in this business," Samson said.

"No."

"I just always thought I would be the one to die first."

"No."

She was squeezing his shoulder again.

"I don't mind dying. Ben was terrified of it. I wouldn't mind. It's not right that he died before me."

"No."

C H A P T E R 56

THERE WAS A SOFA IN the room where they put Kenichi. There was a little bathroom, and a television. It was a nice sofa, a big, grey sofa. It was comfortable. He recognized the room for what it was immediately. A cell. He had spent so many years in jail. This one was just nicer than most. Lucho's cells were nicer still, if you were a prisoner on his good side. A jail could look like a lot of different things. He could hear the voices of the guards outside the door. Not what they were saying, just their voices, just the resonance of speech.

He sat down on the comfortable, grey sofa and thought about the situation. It was a little bit too comfortable, the sofa. He sat down on the floor, on a rug pushed up against the wall. He tilted his head back against the wall and thought. It was concrete. He tapped the back of his head against the wall, it was cold and stable.

They must know about his past already, that was why they were so suspicious of him. He had wondered why they hadn't confronted him about it before. He thought they must have known for a long time. They were too smart not to know. Stephanie, especially. That's why they were so suspicious.

The sabotage from Bloodworth's men hadn't helped. Kenichi finally realized that they must suspect him of that as well. It seemed stupid of them to suspect him. If he had done the sabotage there would have been no mistake with it. If he was trying to kill Samson, Samson would be dead. He thought they would know that. He wouldn't screw up, and they wouldn't catch him. He banged his head against the wall.

They still didn't understand how brilliant he was, he realized. They still didn't appreciate him. He didn't understand why people didn't appreciate him, how good he was. He was the best, he was smarter than everyone else. That's why they suspected him, because they still didn't understand how smart he was. But they should have known that he wouldn't screw up or make foolish mistakes, that if he was sabotaging Samson he would succeed and leave nothing to chance. He could easily change Samson's computer to overload the engines and blow the ship up. They would never find it, they would never find out what happened. It was so stupid to suspect him. He thought they were smarter than that. He looked at the polished, sterile floor, and imagined the blood that had been mopped up here. The horrors that had occurred in this pleasant, little prison cell. He thought about Stephanie's dark side. She must have one. With that much power. He wondered about the tortures and depravity that had happened on this tiny, private world, the destruction of human beings here. Samson and Ben thought that Stephanie was such a sweet person. They were fools.

No, he liked Samson and Ben.

He saw Ben, mouth open, floating in the cockpit of the racer, tangling up with the bubble of blood. He couldn't get the image out of his mind. It made his stomach hurt. The hole in Ben's head was so perfectly smooth and precise. He tried to block the image out of his mind. He felt with his hand along the cold, concrete wall.

The problem was, how to gain Samson and Stephanie's trust again. At least enough to get released. Which wasn't good enough. He wanted to finish his work on the racer. To win the Solar Regatta. Stephanie would do what Samson wanted. He had to gain Samson's trust. Samson would come and talk to him. Samson was inclined to trust him. Samson was a friend. If it was Stephanie he would be here forever. He had to think of what to say before Samson came.

The problem was Ben's death. Everything else didn't matter. If Samson believed that he had nothing to do with Ben's death, then it would be ok, it would be workable. Samson wanted to trust him. They knew that they needed him to win. The outfitting and modifications for the Solar Regatta were not yet complete. They couldn't bring in another engineer and still finish on time. So it was all up to Samson. He had to think of what to say to Samson.

BARON DE ROTHSCHILD WALKED ACROSS his palace grounds. He enjoyed walking, it helped him think. The lifts and platforms were nice when you needed them, but it didn't do to become lazy. He leapt into the air and snatched a peach from high in the branches of a peach tree as he walked past it. It was an heirloom tree, from an ancient seed. Some of the fruit had worms. They used to call trees like this 'organic'. A long time ago. The fruit tasted good.

He smiled at some of the groundskeepers as they walked past, and they bowed to him. He didn't require them to bow. He wondered how that had gotten started. He jogged down the little dirt road in the sunshine, to the top of a small hill, and looked out across his planet. It was beautiful. It was good. He was like the god. It was good. His people were working everywhere, and seemed happy. It upset his security chief for him to walk around like this alone. Gunther kept getting an ulcer. The doctors couldn't understand why it kept coming back, when their antibiotics should have cleared it. Well, security chiefs were born to worry. Anyway, protection is what the robots were for.

He looked down the hill at the big spaceship hangar where his daughter liked to play. Maybe they'd tweaked her engineering quotient a little too high. They'd given her everything. Why the ships and racing and mechanical things appealed to her so particularly was a mystery. That was the good thing about life, it was always a mystery. No matter how much you controlled it, you couldn't control it. A paradox. Some of the best philosophers said that reality was an adaptation to consciousness, that it was inconstant. Maybe the nature of life was like that. Forever evading your grasp, so that when you learned to control a part of it that part stopped being important and it was the other parts that you couldn't control that seemed to determine everything, and there were always other parts. He brushed his peculiar, copper hair out of his face as a gust of wind blew over him. The air was so perfectly clean. He tried to always bear in mind what a privilege it was to live in paradise.

Stephanie was covered with grease and fiddling with ship components as usual. Her face lit up when she saw him.

"Hi Daddy!"

"Hi Angel."

She was already getting tall, 5' 8", she was already becoming beautiful. The maids had a terrible time cleaning the grease out of her long, black hair. She looked like a more natural version of her mother.

"Has Ebeneezer been teaching you interesting things about the racing ships?"

"Oh, yes, Daddy. They were letting me help to install the engine in that big carrier today. Well, it's not a racing ship. Ebeneezer's just wonderful. He's really a very good teacher. Cylla doesn't like him, though."

Stephanie's servant playmate, Cylla, sat on the ground nearby and looked on resentfully.

"He's ok," she said fairly. "It's true what the miss said that he's a good teacher. He's a sweet old man, anyone could tell you that."

"Cylla just doesn't like *mechanical* things," Stephanie said. "She likes to do *imaginative* things, like playing, or riding horses and telling each other stories about it."

"Well what's wrong with riding horses?"

"Cylla's a good friend to you," the Baron said. "You have to remember to think about how the people around you feel, and be good to them."

"I know, Daddy."

"Imagination is an important part of your mind, and it has to be cultivated."

"Even when I'm as old as you?"

"Especially when you're as old as me."

The Baron put his arm around his daughter and pulled her away from the mechanic's work bench.

"The maids are going to have a terrible time getting you cleaned up tonight."

"Oh, they always complain, Daddy."

"Come take a walk with me, it's a beautiful day."

"Can Cylla come too?"

"I think that Cylla should go ahead of us to the stables, and we'll catch up with her in a little while so that you two can ride horses. Is that alright Cylla?"

The little girl smiled brightly and looked up, but was afraid to make eye contact with the Baron.

"Thank you, sir," she said. "Stephanie will come along soon, sir?"

"You don't have to call me sir, Cylla. Stephanie will walk over there in a little while and she will ride with you."

"Thank you, sir! Oh, boy. I get the blue pony today, Stephanie!"

"Hey!"

Cylla walked away giggling, and then broke into a run, and then walked again, and then ran, and waved back at them with a smile and ran some more. The Baron led his daughter out of the hangar and they walked down to a little path that ran in a circle around a green, mossy lake.

"What do you want to talk about, Daddy?" Stephanie said.
"Oh, I don't know. I just want to talk."
"Ok."

He didn't know what he wanted to talk to his daughter about, but he always talked to her. And he always remembered her mother when they talked, in a way that felt good to him and not bad. And day by day, his daughter became very much like him, until she was the one that knew him best, until people called her 'the little advisor' and said she was the Baron's better half. She was so smart. He wished his wife could be there to see her. She would have been so proud. And he went on long walks with his daughter, and talked to her about his thoughts and ideas, and what it meant to lead people and how to be in charge of so many things, how to wield power without being destroyed by it. And she listened to him, didn't understand much of it at first, and talked to him about childish things, and helped him to remember his wife without realizing it, and helped him to remember that the world could be a better place than it was.

C H A P T E R ⁵⁷

IT WAS THE GIRL WHO helped Kenichi to convince Samson of his innocence. The girl he had loved, who had saved him before. He couldn't believe it. It was his girl, her, he couldn't remember her name. She saved him again. Some time ago he had stopped remembering. He had tried to be honest and tell Samson everything that had happened. He thought that might work, but it didn't. Samson didn't believe him. He had said everything and Samson had heard none of it, and he didn't know what else to say. And then he remembered the storage vault. He hadn't thought of it for so many years. It was his only part of himself that he still had, his only secret. The only bit of him that he had, that was concrete, that he could prove and that nobody else had. He didn't want to look into it and see her again. He didn't know if it was still there.

But he punched in the address and it was. He entered the old passwords, he didn't know how he could still remember them.

Samson had watched him suspiciously. He didn't understand what Kenichi was doing, what he was trying to show. He was about to kick Kenichi off of the console when the first picture came up. It was an old picture.

It was a picture of a handsome young man and a beautiful young woman, both of them highly genetically engineered. There was a light in the woman's eye, as if she was very smart and very happy, and the young man stared into the camera lense magnanimously. Samson didn't understand why Kenichi was so taken with the picture, why he was watching the picture and holding his breath, and pulling his hair. Samson had to look for a long time before he realized that it was a picture of Kenichi himself. He looked so different, so healthy and happy. His hair was cut short, and his eyes were bright and friendly. Arrogant, but friendly. It didn't look like him at all.

The next picture was a picture of just the girl, in the spring season on Earth, standing beside a blossoming cherry tree in Japan, wearing a yellow dress. Samson started to get angry, but then he heard a strange sound, like a walrus snorting. It was followed by a long, excruciating sob. Kenichi. He didn't seem to know that Samson was there anymore.

And that was what it was, that was what had changed Samson's mind, just more and more pictures of Kenichi and the girl. Just lots and lots of pictures of the two, young, happy people. And Kenichi crying hysterically and forgetting that Samson was there. At one point he fell forward onto his knees and touched the screen and watched it sparkle around his hand as he tried to touch the girl's face.

"Phillipe Bloodworth killed her," Kenichi said finally, and snorted mucus back into his nose. "She had designed a ship for his personal racing team. He told her that the ship was mediocre, and she told him that he was an idiot. To his face, see, she called him an idiot to his face, and because of that he killed her."

"I'm sorry."

"We were supposed to get married that spring, on Earth, in Japan. That was— but, he killed her, and that was all. That was all there was to it."

"Phillipe Bloodworth had her killed?"

"See," Kenichi said angrily, "you can't even understand how powerful these people are, you have no clue about it. Your girlfriend Stephanie, and I like Stephanie, Samson, but she's just like Phillipe Bloodworth, these are the people who run the universe, and you know nothing about any of that, you are like a child."

"Stephanie's not like Phillipe Bloodworth."

"Even back then," Kenichi said, "it was our dream to design a new kind of racer and to win the Solar Regatta. That girl and me, that was our big dream that we had together. Do you know that I can't even remember her name? As if I erased the memory out of my own mind. Do you have any idea how strange it feels? I loved her so much, and I can't remember her name at all."

"I'm sorry, Ken."

"Do you see what I want to tell you? That was my ship. That was our dream, she was the reason I built that ship after she died. And you're my chance to win the race. It would help. If I realized our dream that we had, it would help. I would never sabotage you, not on anything, not on this. You winning that race with my ship is all I care about. Do you see how hard I've worked? You can beat Phillipe Bloodworth. Do you see what I mean, Samson? All my dreams, my whole life, everything that I loved and wanted, it all comes to rest on your shoulders. I depend on you. What could I do about Bloodworth's men, tell them to fuck off and then they would kill me? Everything in my life depends on you, I'd let them kill me if it meant that you could win this race with my racer and beat that fucking piece of shit. That son of bitch mother fuck shit eating–"

His voice descended into an incoherent garble and he clenched his fists together hysterically.

"It's ok, Ken," Samson said, and put his hand on Kenichi's shoulder. "It'll be ok."

Kenichi slowly collected himself.

"I would die a happy man if you won that race flying my ship."

"Ok."

Kenichi looked up at the screen again. He had closed the last photo, it was just a bunch of files and folders.

"Everything is there, you can look at it," he said. "Our letters to each other and everything. I don't want to see them.

I don't want to remember her name. Isn't that a strange thing? You can read them. You can look at all of it. There's naked pictures of her in there, too. I don't want to see those. I don't remember what else is in here. All my private stuff, all that is left of it. You can look at it, that's all. If it helps, so you can believe me. I understand how you feel, and you can look at all of it. I don't even have to be here. I mean, I can give you the passwords, you can look at it all and take your time, on another console or anything."

Samson looked down at Kenichi with pity in his eyes. Kenichi didn't understand why it didn't bother him. Pity. He always hated pity. Now it didn't bother him. He pulled back up the picture of the pretty girl wearing a yellow dress, standing beside a blossoming cherry tree in Japan. He stared at the photo and didn't mind Samson. For some reason it was ok for Samson to pity him. He didn't care.

"It's ok, Ken," Samson said distantly, as if he were whispering from across the room. "I think I've seen enough."

Stephanie insisted that they stay and finish the race preparations there at the Rothschild Palace. Her investigators had linked the assassination attempt back to Phillipe Bloodworth, and everyone agreed that the Rothschild facilities were the safest and most convenient option. She put Kenichi in a suite near her best hangar and assigned a team of mechanics to help him with his work. Samson stayed with her in her own quarters, and they lingered together over the time that they had. Not as much time as they would have liked. Samson was kept busy working with Kenichi on the race preparations, and Stephanie came to help out again when she could, but she was the busiest of all, attending constant meetings and briefing sessions, finally taking control of her empire.

"Don't you miss your parents?" Stephanie wondered on the first night that Samson spent with her there, when she couldn't sleep, after they made love.

Samson held her, with the bridge of his nose against her cheek, and his breath blew across her neck when he talked.

"No."

"I would do anything to have my father back," Stephanie said. "Or my mother."

"Maybe I miss them sometimes."

"They seemed like nice people," Stephanie said. "I would like to meet them again."

"Ok."

"But that was the only time you have seen them in years and years."

"Yes."

"Don't you miss your brother?"

"Yes, but– Theo comes and tracks me down every couple of years anyway. So I see him."

Stephanie was silent for a long time. She stared up at the darkness and imagined the outline of the painting above her. The woman pouring milk. Sometimes she thought that she was that woman, that her life was to pour out sustenance and provide it for other people. The woman in the painting wasn't a part of the family of the house, she was caring for people who weren't her own. Stephanie felt where Samson's hand was resting on her ribs, and underneath it there was an ache, an ache inside of her for a family of her own, an ache to care for and provide for her own, and not to have to worry about everyone else. She hated to think of everyone else, and to worry about them. It was too much.

Samson felt the rise and fall of her anxious breath, and rubbed his hand back and forth on her skin.

"I was never close to my parents," he said. "I could never

see the world the way they saw it, even as a child. It always felt like I was born into a foreign land, like I was snatched out of the place that I belonged and put somewhere else. I never felt at home until I ran away to Neo Vega."

"And then you felt at home?"

"No. Maybe. It was more like, not like I found my home, but I felt like I belonged there. When I met Ben, and he kind of adopted me, when we teamed up and started traveling around to the races together, that was when I really felt at home. On the Junket."

Stephanie felt a tear from Samson's face against her cheek and held her breath.

"Ben had a little brother who was my age, did you know that?" Samson said. "He died in a race accident when Ben was still a teenager. In the crowd, when a ship crashed."

"I didn't know that."

"I still think he's here, you know. Like he's still working on the ship and I'll meet up with him tomorrow or something and we'll talk about our plans for the race."

Stephanie rubbed Samson's hand, and he squeezed her fingers tight.

"It just doesn't seem possible that he's not here anymore," he said.

SAMSON AND STEPHANIE WALKED THROUGH her gardens together one afternoon. She almost always wore the same clothes, well fitted jeans and a tailored blouse. Expensive clothes, but simple. Practical. The blouse was always a solid color, a violet or blue or black. She was so beautiful. The gardens were exquisite, and Stephanie was remarkably at home in them. More relaxed than Samson had ever seen her. She described the different exotic plants to him, the beautiful flowers. There was a long, violet and yellow, trumpet shaped flower that shook and whistled if you blew on it, or if the wind caught it just right. It had a resonant, melodic sound, like a wooden flute. Peach and green love birds would come to investigate the sound, and shake the flower, and twitter at each other. Stephanie could get the birds to land on her hand.

"I'm so sorry I dragged you into all this mess," she said to Samson regretfully.

"You haven't dragged me into anything. You saved my life."

She smiled at him sadly.

"No, I have to apologize, I should have been honest with you and told you who I was."

Samson sat down on a bench and looked at her. She was standing in front of the whistling flowers. The lovebirds on the bush squawked and chirped at her furiously.

"You couldn't have told me," he said.

"Maybe I could have. I could have trusted you. It's not that I don't trust you. I do trust you. It's not that—"

"It's ok."

She sat down beside him, and he put his hand around her hip and scooted her over until their legs were touching.

"It's just that I didn't want to be who I am, you see. I wanted to know you without, everything else, getting in the way. And see what would happen."

"It's ok," he said, and squeezed her hand. "You're still the same woman..."

He kissed her cheek.

"...that I love."

Stephanie breathed quickly and looked uncomfortable. She didn't tell him that she loved him.

"It's very lonely to be powerful," she said after a moment. "Most people who try to become powerful don't understand how lonely it is. They aren't able to deal well with the loneliness, they get lost in it. You have to be able to cope with it, or it consumes you. I couldn't have been friends with you if you knew who I was. I couldn't have even gone anywhere alone, outside of this palace."

"Don't you love me?" Samson said.

She blinked her eyes rapidly, and looked down, and sighed. Samson put his hands on her face and and tried to turn it to look at him, but she wouldn't let him.

"No?"

Her silence seemed to last for an eternity.

"Yes, of course I do, but I shouldn't."

"Of course you should."

Stephanie stood up, and Samson stood up next to her, and held her hand and watched where her eyes were looking. He put his arm around her and pulled her off balance, so that she was leaning into him. Stephanie laughed.

"Come on, I'll show you something," she said excitedly, and grabbed his arm and sprinted away, dragging him with her.

She ran through the garden, hopping over a stream and splashing through a shallow fountain. She pulled him through dense hedgerows, scraping up both of their skin, until they emerged into a tiny, hidden, clearing. There was a single, pale pink, rose bush in its center. Stephanie stretched out her arms and walked backwards around the clearing, looking at Samson and looking up at the vivid, blue sky.

"Isn't it wonderful?" she said.

"Yes. It is."

"I used to come here when I was a little girl. This was my special, secret hiding place. I would come here and read books, and write diaries, and paint pictures. Of course, Daddy knew all about it. He had tabs on me at all times, to make sure I was safe. But as far as I knew, this was my secret, and this was where I would come to be alone."

"Your father kept tabs on you at all times?"

"See this flower," Stephanie said obliviously, "I planted it here when I was fourteen. Souvenir de la Malmaison, an ancient rose."

She stopped and smiled at Samson so brightly and so affectionately, and for so long, that he realized he was standing in the most wonderful place in the world.

"The rose was named in honor of Empress Josephine, the wife of Napoleon in ancient France. She was six years older than him, did you know that? Malmaison was the name of her estate, a wonderful French mansion that she purchased early in their marriage while Napoleon was away at war. They couldn't afford it, and he was furious with her when he got back, but it ended up becoming their cherished home. Josephine filled Malmaison with the most beautiful gardens in the world, and it was particularly famous for the rose gardens she planted there. She was divorced from Napoleon, and caught pneumonia and died, but they say that when the English finally invaded France and won the war, they were ordered to protect Malmaison from damage because the gardens were so exquisite. She was the most beautiful, and most beloved rose gardener, and Souvenir de la Malmaison was the most beautiful of the roses in France."

She produced a tiny knife and snipped off one of the flower's bulbs.

"Some people say," Stephanie said mischievously, holding the flower in front of Samson's face, "that Souvenir de la Malmaison is especially beautiful to men, because it resembles the most intimate parts of a woman's body. What do you think?"

Samson breathed in the heady, myrrh scent of the flower, touched one of the softly pink petals, and looked into Stephanie's eyes. She laughed, and pulled the flower back, and tucked it into the hair behind her ear.

"It's not a rare or expensive flower. But it's just wonderful, isn't it?"

C H A P T E R 58

T HE SOLARIUM DURING THE SOLAR Regatta was another
world, another universe. Reality ceased to exist. Everything
was larger than life, colorful, more percussive, joyous, and
intense. Everyone was on a high, on top of the party, even if
they weren't using any drugs. Most were using. The best, the
wildest ones, the new designer formulas, were always on sale
at the Regatta. Classics were the main thing. Alcohol and cocaine, the mainstays. Live music was everywhere. Competing,
amphetamined, intoxicated bands riffing fast rhythms, filling
up the air with sexual, heady, primal sound. Dancers followed
the bands in outrageous, feathered, miniature outfits. Or led
the way in front of them, with exotic animals in tow – a pair
of de-fanged, purple lions perhaps leading a procession, or a
winged, flightless unicorn. It was ecstatic chaos. Hips churned,
feet stamped, voices sang, cried out and chanted, arms twisted
apart and wove together like mating snakes. The sweaty fervor
led inexorably to Solarium brothels and the thousands of poor
girls and boys that had been flown in from all over the Solar
System to meet demand.

Phillipe Bloodworth and Simon Okunle were both there.
They sat and brokered power in the Icarus Club, which was
crowded for once, and quietly refused to acknowledge each
other's presence. Stephanie stayed home and worried, and
waited for her ring to be fixed, yet knew that even then she
would never again travel freely through the Solar System as
she had done in the past.

Her people shepherded Samson onto the Solarium in secret. His absence was the source of constant speculation in the
media. Bloodworth still believed that he was dead, and quietly
enjoyed the 'mystery'. He wondered why they were keeping
the death a secret, but assumed there were business reasons

connected to Samson's sponsorship contracts.

On the shining white floor of the racing stadium hundreds of ships were lined up in orderly rows, but concealed beneath opaque, blue energy fields that guarded them from prying eyes and tampering. Only the ships being worked on by their engineers and mechanics were visible. Blue shields were up at the designated place for Samson's ship, and no one in the media could seem to confirm whether the ship was actually there or not.

Lisa was at the Solarium too, and very busy. She could hardly pay attention to the festivities. She was faintly disgusted by the revelers, and fascinated with them, and tried to avoid them as she crisscrossed back and forth through the Solarium's streets on endless, last minute gopher assignments. When she wasn't rushing from one side of the space station to the other, she was cooped up in an office with another intern, doing clerical work. But it was still exciting to be there, she could feel the energy and adrenaline slowly rise in the people around her as the days led up to the race. And in herself. She worried about seeing Killian, and tried to make sure not to, and worried about Samson occasionally and wondered what had happened to him and if he would be there. And there was a boy intern who had taken an interest in her, and she thought about him a lot of the time, and wondered if she was interested in him or not.

Killian, for his part, was unusually focused before the race. He locked himself in his quarters and trained, visualizing the victory, bringing his body – his entire life – into line with a strict regimen and schedule. He avoided female contact entirely, having convinced himself that this hardship would give him the cutting edge he needed to ensure success. On the day before the race, he found himself aroused by an ancient photograph of a fat woman someone had projected as a joke onto an enormous viewing screen in the park outside his apartment. He smiled and sealed the windows, confident in his rampaging libido, certain that he could now conquer any obstacle in his path.

The night before the race, Samson sat in an immaculate cabin aboard Simon Okunle's private transport ship, which was parked on a private dock in a wing of the Solarium leased exclusively by The Rothschild Corporation. He held his card between his thumb and forefinger and flipped it into the air again and again, as if he were flipping a coin. The black, plastic computer reflected the light sharply, but was virtually identical on both sides. Samson stopped and plugged it into the terminal. He pulled up the obstacle plans that Lisa had given him, he hadn't looked at them. He had been afraid to taint the satisfaction of victory. He was still afraid of that.

The first obstacle was not much different than what he had expected. It was a cave-like, honeycomb structure, like the inside of a bee hive, a maze of tunnels, filled with twisting paths that doubled back upon themselves and abrupt dead ends. Most of the tunnels eventually converged into larger channels that were color coded to tell the racers whether they were on the right path or not. Racers had to find a large yellow channel and follow it to get to the obstacle exit, although some of the unmarked tunnels were shortcuts to the exit themselves, tempting racers who wanted to try their luck for an extra edge. The honeycomb structure surrounded two large, empty halves, like the halves of an hourglass, that held the entrance and the exit of the obstacle.

Samson wondered what the second obstacle would be like. He plotted a course through the honeycomb maze of tunnels that would keep him near the front of the racing pack and not arouse suspicion, and spent the next half hour committing the course to memory. Then he tried to bring Stephanie up on his cabin com, but couldn't reach her, and went to sleep thinking about the tunnels and visualizing his course through the first obstacle, and dreamed about her.

Early the next morning, Samson rose to begin his race day rituals. He started calisthenics, but stopped. His muscles felt weak. Everything was grey, the light, the room. Something wasn't right. He felt sick, the ship's cabin seemed to suffocate him. He was in an alien environment. He wanted to be back on the Junket. Ben was supposed to be here. Stephanie wasn't here, and Ben was gone. Dead. He looked down at the ham and potatoes and eggs that he was frying, and took them off the burner and set them in the sink, nauseous A cloud filled up the apartment and enveloped him. He searched for ventilation fans and gasped for air.

"Samson?" Kenichi banged on the cabin door. "Are you ready? We have to check in for the race."

Samson burst through the door and choked in air from the ship's corridor. He looked terrified.

"Are you ok, Samson? What's wrong with you?"

"There's, something in the air. In my cabin. It's all grey."

Kenichi kicked the door open cautiously and peered inside. He took his card out of his pocket and looked at it. The card glowed with a soft, benign green light.

"I don't see anything," Kenichi said.

"I just," Samson glanced up and down the corridor, there were people passing by, "I, it must be me. I felt like I was overcome by this grey cloud, like everything became grey. Something's wrong with me."

"This ship has an advanced medical room with a high density gravometric medical imaging scanner," Kenichi said practically. "Let's go have you checked out quickly before the race."

"How much time do we have?"

"Check in is in thirty minutes, let's hurry."

Samson pushed Kenichi away and put his hands against his temples. People at the end of the corridor were staring at him.

"No. No. I'll be ok, I just," he walked back across the threshold of his cabin and began to close the door behind him. "I'll meet you on the gangway in ten minutes."

He closed the door, and Kenichi shouted in protest, but Samson ignored him and rushed to force himself under a cold shower.

"Damnit Ben," he said, the cloud around him evaporating, "the one time you try to fly my ship. You mother-fucker. I needed you here. You fucked it all up."

HUNDREDS OF MAGNIFICENT RACING ENGINES purred against the polished, white floor of the Solarium's stadium. Glossy, painted ships as far as the eye could see. They were grouped in packs, according to how much success they were expected to have. Most of the ships had the simple goal of survival. Only a dozen or so were given a realistic chance of winning the race, and only a few of these were favorites. Samson was considered a dark horse.

A murmur ran through the crowd when the hazy blue shields around his racer came down and revealed his ship, shining white and new – at least it looked like new – with Samson already strapped into the cockpit and ready for the race. The news echoed quickly around the Solar System, and media cameras zoomed in tight to confirm that it really was Samson Ford in the cockpit.

Lisa had helped him to keep a low profile while signing in and getting ready for the race. They were so successful that Samson had even been removed from the betting pools. Now, moments before the race began, bookmakers were giving even odds for Samson to survive, and 99-1 for him to win. Stephanie, watching the start of the race from her private quarters before going to sleep, ordered her maid and confidant, Cylla, to call in a heavy bet on Samson at 99-1, and the odds on offer shifted down almost immediately to 50-1. There was a high volume of betting against him to survive.

A series of enormous glass plates floated into the starry air above the stadium, which faced out onto the side of space away from the sun. The plates were illuminated by star-like, multicolored globes. A man dressed all in black suddenly rose through the air below the plates, floating on a dais of pearl white and gold. The hundreds of thousands of spectators in the stands held their collective breaths as the man rose high above the stadium floor. He raised his arms to the heavens, revealing a long, silver conductor's baton, and as he brought the baton down in a commanding arc the plates and globes began to move. The plates were hundreds of meters in diameter and their surface seemed to course with water or liquid, which melted away into vapor as it fell around the conductor and down to the stadium floor. As they turned slowly through the air the plates began to hum melodiously, thousands of tons of ringing, perfect glass. The sound was transcendental, it seemed to fill up the air in the stadium, to surround and permeate you and encompass your whole being. Against the background of the stars, it seemed a sound that must overflow through the universe itself. People gasped and cried, their salty, unfamiliar tears splashing on the ground. The conductor's black suited body swayed in slow, hypnotic circles, and his silver baton painted patterns of rhythm across the air.

"Ohmygod!" a woman screamed, as thousands of spectators fell onto their knees, and raised their arms instinctively, moaning, sweating, in a kind of worship.

Samson revved his engine and cursed angrily as the angelic noise threatened to overwhelm him. He could feel the racer begin to vibrate with the cadence of the plates, and cut his anti-gravity and set it down hard into the stadium floor, hoping to damp the vibrations.

The conductor raised his wand and held it still in the air, expectantly, and the melodious vibrations of the glass plates were slowly joined by another sound. A harsher, earthier sound, filled with static and electronic noise. But beautiful. The colored globes circled the plates in an esoteric dance, pulsing steady rhythm, louder and louder until the vibrations of the plates were overcome, drowned away, yanked from people's chests, and the audience screamed out in exhilaration at the sound, and noise, and overwhelming music that seemed to have taken to life inside their flesh. Suddenly the globes exploded, and there was a tremendous, deafening crash. The plates shattered and fell towards the stadium floor. Cries of terror rang from the audience as glass rained onto them only to puff into mist and disappear, leaving a faint, silvery sheen that sparkled on their skin.

The conductor bowed his head, and the audience rose to their feet in a unison of hysterical applause. The race was set to begin.

CHAPTER 59

"I THOUGHT HE WAS DEAD!" PHILLIPE Bloodworth shouted incredulously in a private viewing suite perched high above the stadium floor.

"It is strange, Mr. Bloodworth," an executive at his elbow said. "We're trying to get to the bottom of it. We can, of course, still have him disqualified – on the basis of Mr. Iwahara's role in the team."

"Not yet. Give him a chance to die first."

He watched the black-clad conductor rising on his podium through the glass with a look of disgust on his face.

"But what if he is winning, sir?"

"He won't be winning," Bloodworth said coldly. "Have you gone mad too, Raymond? He's a goddamned kinderfuck! Look at these plates. I'm glad we got the soundproofed suite this time. Look at all these animals raising their arms. They're disgusting little creatures aren't they?"

"Inferior genes, sir. They are biologically inclined to an attitude of worship."

"It's sad isn't it, Raymond? Camilla?"

"Pathetic, sir," said a tall, unusually beautiful woman who was staring intently at the spectacular, vibrating plates, with her hand pressed up against the glass.

"Even after so many years," Bloodworth said, "after generations – all our work for humanity – and even here at the Solarium. So many rats still infesting the ship. It would be better if they were never born. Think it through. Think how beautiful the Solar System would be. Look at them clap and shout. Horrible little viruses."

"I sometimes wonder why you even bother, Sir."

"Business! You don't actually think the racing matters. Do you? Stunt jockey pilots, dead tomorrow. Jesuschrist."

A LARGE GLOBE FLOATED INTO the air above the stadium floor and changed colors from red to orange to green. Samson pressed the wooden cross into his chest as the colors changed. He needed God now more than ever. If there was a God. For the first time in his racing career he was afraid of dying. As if it would be a big loss if he died, as if it had become a monstrous shadow looming over him. Stephanie flashed across his mind as the colors changed, and he wondered if she was watching him. He wished she could have come to the Solarium, and pressed the cross into his chest until it seemed like the impression would stick. Then, in an instant, he shut everything out of his mind and waited for the light to turn green.

The beginning of the race was easy. Samson's racer was one of the fastest. He quickly caught up to the vertical lift vehicles that had roared out of the stadium in front of him, and eased in among the lead pack. Fifteen or twenty ships jockeyed for position in a swarming sprint for the first obstacle. It came early in the race this year. In most Solar Regatta years it was placed so that the racers would reach it near the end of the first day.

Samson kept an easy position near the back of the leading pack, and avoided any confrontations or entanglements with the other racers. Killian and the usual top racers were here. And a few others. The most formidable was Giuseppe Chang, a near-legendary racer who only competed in the Solar Regatta, and had won it twice before. Chang was feared and respected, and he was flying a new model of large, wedge shaped racer that must have been manned by a crew. He seemed to easily keep pace with the smaller, more agile ships that made up most of the lead pack and everyone kept their distance from him, even Killian.

THE FIRST OBSTACLE LOOKED FROM the outside like a giant, enclosed cube. The walls weren't all solid, but they looked it. A mixture of actual fabrication and projected energy fields. There was an entrance at the bottom of the front side of the cube, and an exit at the top of the back side. What was in between was supposed to be a surprise. The pack of ships slowed down as they approached the entrance to the obstacle, and Samson mentally rehearsed the path he would take, automatically rolling under a careening orange ship as it flew out of control and maintaining his place in the tightening pack.

"Are you worried about the obstacle, Ford?" Killian's voice crackled across the com system. "I know this is your first time."

"Fuck you."

"You sound worried."

The ships curled up into the obstacle entrance like water poured into a spout and filmed upside down. There was atmosphere inside, and Samson could feel the jerk at his back when his wings framework finally caught it and delivered extra thrust. The inside of the obstacle was a giant, black and grey honeycomb of twisting tunnels wrapped around an enormous hourglass of empty space. In the distance the racers could see the glow of the exit for the obstacle, through the center of the hourglass and on the opposite side. It was possible to fly straight through, to avoid all the tunnels and the maze and fly straight to the end. But the passage was tiny, scarcely large enough for even the smaller ships like Samson's cigarette racer to pass. Worse, a pair of tight laser grids floated back and forth in front of it, effectively barring the path.

Samson separated from the pack with confidence and flew into the tunnel that he had planned. He could see some of the other racers through transparent sections in the maze, like ants in an ant farm, and not many of them had slowed. No one else had chosen the same tunnel as himself, there was no one at his back. He negotiated the tunnel's twists and turns as quickly as he could. It was like flying through a cave system. Dangerous. He almost exploded against a sharp, 135 degree turn. The hair on the back of his neck stood up and his adrenaline surged as he scraped past the corner into a long, curving, boxy corridor filled with columns. This wasn't what was on the plans. He adjusted his iv drip to even out the effects of the adrenaline. His hands still felt smooth. He slalomed quickly through the columns and made another sharp turn, then raced down a long, straight pipe. He could see through the gaps that some of the other racers were getting ahead of him. They were flashes of color in the distance, across the empty hourglass space. He accelerated.

Around another bend there was a blank wall. It came too fast. Samson cut his engines and hit his reverse thrusters and looked for someplace to turn into. Negative Gs almost pulled his eyeballs out. Blood vessels in his eyes exploded and he couldn't see. He caught his breath and flung his hands across his face. Thhhhhunk!

The racer bounced and crunched to a stop against the tunnel wall, the carbon-fused glass of the cockpit barely withstanding the impact. He blinked his eyes blindly and stretched his arms out in front of him to feel the cold of the glass against his skin. He switched some morphiate-amphetamine into his IV mix and ran an audio diagnostic. No cracks. After a few more seconds his eyesight came back, with sharp pain, like needles thrust into his head, until the morphiate kicked in. He touched the cross at his breast, and grabbed the racer's control wands, and slowly turned the ship around. He was breathing fast, hyperventilating. He tried to hold his breath and slow down.

Reversing and coming back out of the tunnel took longer. He flew as quickly as he could, but was forced to hug the tunnel edges in order to avoid any incoming racers who might have chosen the same path. A boxy, blue and black racer shot past him, and cursed into the local com and slowly decelerated to turn around. The light of an explosion in a nearby tunnel flashed through the wall gaps, and Samson's racer shook from the concussion wave. He wondered if it was anyone he knew, and was disturbed by the thought. It wasn't the right thing for a racer to think about during a race. It wasn't anything Samson had ever thought about before during a race. A lot of the racers were going to die and there wasn't any reason to care about them. None of the people here mattered in his life.

He finally exited back into the hourglass space at the beginning of the obstacle. A few dozen other ships circled indecisively, apparently having chosen dead end paths as well. An occasional explosion flashed in the hive-like network of tunnels around them, showcasing other racers who had lost their way. Samson felt disgusted by it. Not disgusted by how poor the other racers were, which he knew was the way he should have felt. He felt disgusted at the racers dying, at the loss of life. As if that mattered. Maybe he was getting too old to race. Maybe he was losing his touch.

"You too, Ford?" an unfamiliar voice said into the com.

Samson brought up the telescopic plate on his cockpit bubble and peered through the tiny, center channel of the obstacle into the opposite half of the hourglass. A couple of racers were already on the other side and heading for the exit.

"Fuck off," he said, and pulled his racer up abruptly.

SAMSON'S CIGARETTE RACER TURNED AND accelerated at the tiny path that divided the two halves of the hourglass. Stephanie was at home, watching on the holo-tv. A salmon colored, silk blanket was wrapped around her, its edges clenched in her hands.

"No, don't."

"Ohmygod!" the announcer exclaimed. "Ford's going for it!"

"No! Don't!"

Samson's racer turned on its rocket thrusters and exploded at the floating laser grids. Stephanie's heart stopped beating. The other ships seemed to slow and watch.

"Ford's making the shoot! He's gonna die!"

"No!" she screamed at the tv.

The laser grids slid into an overlap as the ship flashed through them into the narrow passage and out onto the other side.

"OH-MY-GODDD!!!"

She couldn't breathe. She turned off the announcer's voice.

A line of other ships circled towards the tiny passage that Samson had flown through, following his lead. A tiny, yellow racer accelerated to the front of the pack fearlessly and plunged into the laser grid. And exploded. The other ships pulled away and flew back to the edges of the hourglass to find a new tunnel to try.

"WHAT IS THIS SHIT?!" PHILLIPE Bloodworth shouted, apoplectic.

The racing announcers sputtered breathless superlatives in praise of Samson's audacious maneuver. Bloodworth grabbed an antique lamp and hammered, red faced, at the lenses and speakers of the tv system until the holo-video crackled opaquely and the audio changed to a noisy hiss.

"Get me Lukovich on the phone," he said, suddenly breathing calm. "I'm having him disqualify Ford right now."

"BUT PHILLIPE, WE CAN'T JUST disqualify him," a queasy looking old man said, and then flinched away from the receiver at his ear. "Yes, b-but, we have to do this in the proper way. The committee will have to meet. M–, but–, most of them are here right now! Don't worry. Send me the information that you have, we'll see to it. Well the race won't end tomorrow, Phillipe! Yes. I apologize, forgive me. We'll see to it as quickly as possible. Yes, of course. Thank you, Phillipe. I'm sorry to hear about this, too. We'll take care of it."

The mood in the room was apprehensive and pregnant, like an interrupted party. Every face pointed at the stammering director of the Racing Board, Abou Lukovich. He put down the receiver slowly and collected his thoughts.

"What is it Lukie?"

Abou cleared his throat and raised his face, but avoided eye contact with anyone in particular.

"There seems to be a small problem. Several racing teams are, or will be, submitting evidence that Samson Ford's chief engineer has been the subject of a lifetime ban from racing. They are requesting, or will be requesting, that Ford be disqualified from the competition."

Several gasps.

"What?"

"I will convene an emergency meeting of the board in two hours to discuss this situation. I trust you all will be there."

He walked quickly out of the room.

SAMSON PULLED UP ALONGSIDE KILLIAN at the front of a pack of more than a dozen ships. The horizons of their vision were engulfed by the enormousness of the sun, which spit angrily at them, a turmoil of yellows, orange, and red. Its blinding white was tempered by special coatings on the pilots' cockpit windows. Most of the other ships in the leading pack were larger racing vessels, ships with a small crew. Killian was the only single pilot other than Samson, and he was not flying a regular cigarette racer, but a similar looking, black and pink ship that was more than double a cigarette racer's size.

"Where'd you come from, kid? I thought you took one of the dead end tubes back there."

Killian's voice crackled noisily on the com, distorted by the intense background radiation.

"Fuck you."

"And I thought *my* ship was small," Killian said. "I can't believe you're flying a cigarette racer in a course like this. You know the race lasts for several days, right? If you live through it."

Samson ignored him.

"We need to clear out some of these big, fat ships," Killian said after a few minutes.

His black and pink racer dropped back, leaving Samson in the lead, and pulled up above one of the larger ships, an enormous, grey hulk. For the first time, Samson noted a large, phallic spike protruding two feet out of the bottom of Killian's ship. The much larger ship tried to drift away from Killian's racer without slowing down. It began to perform rolls and evasive maneuvers, dispersing much of the pack. The black and pink racer continued to buzz around the huge, grey ship, like a fly on the butt of a cow.

"Hey, look on top of their ship," Killian croaked gleefully, "there's a little red and white box. Do I know what that is?"

"Fuck you, Killian," the ship's commander said.

"It's a control power coupling, a pretty big one, too. Oooh, your designer screwed up. I'd say without that coupling your ship will lose power and sink right into the sun."

The grey ship shifted back and forth and rolled more frantically, while Killian continued to maintain his position above its roof.

"You'd better drop back a ways or I'm going to take that white and red box off."

"Go to hell."

"You think I wouldn't do it."

"I'm sure you would, you bastard, that's why I said go to hell."

"You silly people," Killian said, addressing the ship's entire crew, "there is no hell. We're all just food for the worms. You must know that, don't you?"

The racing pack spread further apart, away from Killian and the grey ship, but their pilots were silent. The grey ship continued its evasive maneuvers and refused to fall back. Killian's racer swooped down and tore the ship's power coupling box out with the small spike on its body – a maneuver of astonishing skill. Screams of the ship's pilot and crew cracked over the com for a split second and then cut off as it lost most of its power. The huge, grey, hulk fell off course, and began a long, slow, silent descent into the sun.

All of the other racing ships except one pulled away from Killian, spreading out as far as they could without being drawn off course. Some formed into tentative, defensive groups of two or three, eyeing their now make-shift allies as suspiciously as Killian himself. Samson throttled up a little more and tried to stretch out his fragile lead over Killian and the rest of the pack.

A large, wedge shaped, red and yellow ship drifted closer to Killian rather than away from him.

"We've got something for you too, Gideon," the voice said dangerously.

"Ooh, I'm scared," Killian said, but kept his distance from the red and yellow ship. "You won last time, don't expect a repeat, Chang."

"That was four years ago, I can't even remember it. Wait, wasn't there a kid in that tournament? A funny little, purple-eyed boy that everybody said was going to win," Chang laughed. "But he didn't even get into the top ten, that's the only thing I remember."

Killian's racer seemed to waver nervously.

"Come on, Samson, your ship is fast isn't it?" he said, punching up his boosters and accelerating away from Chang. "Let's leave these big, slow, whales behind."

The black and pink ship shook ominously as Killian accelerated up to Samson, passed him, and moved slowly away from the pack. To everyone's surprise, Chang's ship pulled forward too, keeping pace with the reckless acceleration. It shouldn't have been possible for a ship so large. Samson kept his distance and let them pass. He stayed with the larger pack, conserving his fuel and boosters, waiting to make his move.

THE SUN BURNED EVERYWHERE AROUND them, as if they were adrift on a molten ocean. The racing ships cut across its surface at their hundreds of thousands of kilometers per hour. Slowly. Against the unfathomable backdrop of that plasma ocean they hardly seemed to move. They tore forward, inch by inch on the holo-screens, like explosions wrapped tight and trapped. The sun took on an orange or yellow cast from the cameras' tinting, and the racers stretched across its surface in trails of white. While the viewers watched, a long finger of plasma might flick out into space, and cast the great velocity into relief. Years before, an especially large flare had wiped out half the racing field. As a pilot, you had to watch for them, for days on end while holding tight to your trajectory and jockeying for position with the other racers. You had to know what to look for as they formed, so you could change course. Some were better at it than others. Some of the scientists said it couldn't be done.

The IV drip, drip, dripped into Samson's blood. It gave him the sugars and stimulants that he needed to live through the race. There was no resting. By the end of the Solar Regatta, even the supermen like Killian were empty shells. Used up. It would take months to recover. Drip, drip. Everything hurt, that's what the opiates were for. The straps cutting into your shoulders. They would leave scars. The vacuum tube attached to your anus, chafing the skin until your cockpit seat was a sticky mess of blood. Samson twisted uncomfortably back and forth, trying to ease his circulation. Every tiny lump, or groove in the foam seemed to bore into his back. He opened and closed his aching hands on the control wands and blinked protesting, red eyes furiously. The opiates would help, but you didn't want to use too much. They clouded your brain and slowed your reaction time. You could only use a little. Just enough to get by. Just enough to dull the pain, but not to stop it.

Killian and Chang were still in front of him, but Samson was solidly in third. He aimed straight for the horizon of the sun, cutting an angle that would be incredibly close. Aiming for a much tighter turn than the one that Killian and Chang were taking. The gravity slingshot around the sun was much more dangerous than around the planets. The forces involved were immense, and it was easy to blow out even the sturdiest GCUs with the maneuver. And the closer you went to the sun the more intense the radiation would be. Which was harder on your ship in every way. And tended to make things fail, like the GCU. Your coatings could melt off, or your ship's temperature regulation could be overloaded, and you would disappear in a single, intense spark like a mosquito landing on an inter-continental power line. If your GCU failed instantly your body would burst like a balloon inside your cockpit under the sudden forces of acceleration, but if it only burned out slowly you would live through it and your ship would sink into the sun, having pulled too close for your engines to escape.

Killian and Chang jockeyed for position for hours on end, wearing each other out. Then they would take a break for a while, then they would start again. It made Samson exhausted just to watch them. He didn't know how they could keep at it. Or maybe it was better than the monotony of cruising. Days spent skittering across the sun, alone with your thoughts. As you came into the bend, the radiation was too strong for any communication. Every signal obliterated in the noise. It was silence. You were alone in the universe. It seemed as if the radiation from the sun would wipe out your thoughts, too, but all you could do was think. Hold your course, and think. If you didn't have to fight with any of the other racers. Which you wouldn't, if you were taking the bend around the star close enough. Which Samson was.

His life played back and forth in front of him, and he tried to make sense of it. To fashion a story. If there was any sense to be had. If it wasn't all just random. Sometimes he thought it all was just random. Dumb luck. But if he thought long enough there seemed to be a pattern to it. It was the days awake, watching the sun, scanning for flares, the torture of your body and its adrenaline used up, and the synthetic adrenaline and the opiates holding back the anguished tide. The IV stopped for a moment, and Samson was overcome with indescribable horror. He shook the drip tube desperately, and it started again, and the feeling went away. It was a feeling of what hell must be like. If there was hell. It felt worse than anything he could possibly have imagined. Then more hours and hours of cruising. You couldn't listen to music. The speakers only hissed.

There was something poetic about the Solar Regatta. The race of humans against each other, against the unforgiving backdrop of the sun. Samson realized that his whole life had been a part of this race. A part of being here, of getting to here. That he had had to win more races than he had ever realized, or dreamed. He wondered why he had won them. What was it that had made him better, that had kept him alive, and allowed him to surpass all those other men? Was it the God? Men with their genetic engineering, superior bodies, stronger and more beautiful than him. He had beaten them so many times. As if he were meant to beat them. As if that was the way that it was supposed to be.

He wondered if he would die and thought that he didn't care now. If he lived through the slingshot it would catapult him into position with Chang and Killian. Maybe past them. He wondered about his parents, and Theo, and Stephanie, and couldn't remember what they looked like. For some reason he could remember Lisa's face. It made him laugh in the crinkly, hot, emptiness. He didn't care about Lisa. It seemed ridiculous to remember her. He couldn't remember what Stephanie looked like at all.

THE CRUSHING PULL OF THE sun seemed to envelope him. It made the racer heavy. Diving towards it helped to mitigate the burden of gravity. He was approaching the apex horizon, the point on the turn when he would switch the GCU back on and pull away. He was close. The white layers of radiation coating on the racer looked wet. They were turning to grey. The glass of the cockpit windshield crackled. Samson touched the back of a fingernail to it and pulled his hand away in pain. He was close. Pushing through the turn, still accelerating. Gaining ground on Killian and Chang. He could feel the wobbly beginnings of the relativity effect. The sun's gravity made it worse.

He reached a finger up to flick on the GCU. He scanned the surface of the sun. Something there. A bubbling, dark grey spot. It could be a flare. He put his finger against the switch. It didn't matter. This was the only way to catch up.

Samson flicked the switch on the GCU and his body snapped violently against its harnesses. He lost consciousness. He blinked his eyes open and checked his position. The GCU was screaming. Only a few seconds. It was hissing angrily, like an old tea kettle. There were warnings all over his instrument panel. The GCU temperature was going into melt down. As long as it didn't completely fail. The ship was shaking. A sudden lurch sent his teeth together painfully, and he clenched his jaw. The sun was falling away behind him. Ever so slowly. He was closer and closer to Killian and Chang.

The gravity load began to fall off, and the GCU temperatures dropped. When it cooled down enough he flushed it out with liquid nitrogen. It was burned out pretty bad. Less than 50% functionality. He felt for the cross against his chest. It would be enough for the rest of the race. There was no surge of exhilaration or excitement in him. His body had already used its chemicals up.

He watched the racers behind him as they came out of the bend. Some of them didn't make it. He could see a distinctive quiver run through a ship when its GCU blew out. As if it had died, like rigor mortis. Down they would go, suddenly lifeless mechanical hulks. Engines overwrought and churning, snapping angrily against fate. Down slowly, softly, gently burning up into the sun.

Lisa sat in an empty conference room with some of the other interns, double checking the racers' entry forms and insurance status. Quite a few of the racers had already died. Several that she knew, but not any of her friends. She started to wonder if the racing wasn't a bad thing, and cancelled the thought from her mind immediately, unwilling to contemplate it. They were working so hard, they didn't get to watch very much of the race. There was a projection on silently in a corner of the room, but it was difficult to follow without the commentary. If they had time to look up and watch it. Last she had heard, Samson was catching up to Killian and Chang. She had never met Chang. Hardly anybody had.

One of the Racing Board's vice presidents burst into the room and grabbed an attache case off of a corner table.

"Did you guys hear the news yet? Samson Ford is being disqualified!"

"What?!" Lisa blurted loudly.

"Lukovich is announcing it on tv now. It's going to get crazy. Hurry up finishing that stuff, we'll need you guys today."

The vice president ran out of the room and Lisa watched his back as he disappeared, doing nothing to disguise her emotion of disgust.

"You did go out with him, didn't you," one of the other interns said conspiratorially.

"Maybe."

Lisa smiled faintly and bit her lip, and looked down at the terminal in front of her. There was a hard knot in her stomach.

"FOR THIS REASON, WE HAVE been forced to disqualify contestant Samson Ford from this year's Solar Regatta."

Phillipe Bloodworth muted the sweating figure of Abou Lukovich fumbling with his cards, and laughed. He laughed loudly, wagging his fat index finger, and grinned at the handful of executives that were sitting in the exclusive box suite with him.

"That's finally dusted, then. Too bad he didn't die, but nobody likes a loser and a cheat."

"He's a laughingstock, Phillipe," said the woman who had pressed her hands up against the glass of the viewing box during the musical show at the beginning of the race.

She topped off his drink with an ancient whiskey, and poured some for herself. Bloodworth gripped her low around the hips.

"It will be rich to see the look on that shit's face when the racers catch up and get the announcement," he said.

"You become such a touchy-feely man," she said, "when you're destroying another person's life."

"Watch," Bloodworth said with a croak, pulling down her pants to reveal her curving, white, bottom, and jamming his hand aggressively into it. "Watch what happens when they show his face on the screen while he hears the announcement."

The woman caught her breath, and the other executives

looked on with amusement. Bloodworth twisted his fat index finger inside her bottom.

"Oh, don't do that, Phillipe," she said coyly.

"You like it."

"I'm not one of your monkeys."

"Aren't you?"

She grabbed his hand roughly and twisted away. Bloodworth giggled, raising his finger to his nose and sniffing it extravagantly for the benefit of the crowd.

"No, I'm not," she said flintly, without looking at him, and stormed out of the room.

Phillipe Bloodworth laughed and laughed. Another female executive said, "Good show, sir," but choked on her words when he glared at her. One of the youngest executives raised his glass in the air.

"Here's to Camilla, a spitfire for sure."

"Here, here," Bloodworth said. "She's one of my best."

Then he laughed again, harder than before.

CHAPTER 62

SAMSON WATCHED CHANG AND KILLIAN in front of him. He was close enough to catch up to them if he wanted to. They had stopped jockeying against each other several hours before the turn round the sun. He didn't say anything to them on the com, and they were silent too. Cruising straight for the second obstacle. He stayed close behind them. Far enough to avoid conflict. Close enough to catch up easily when he wanted to make his move.

Chang pulled off tightly, without warning.

"Shit," Samson said under his breath.

He scanned the sun frantically. It looked normal. Killian flew straight ahead. Chang continued to veer farther off course. Maybe his ship was having a problem. It looked like evasive maneuvers. Samson glanced back and forth between the two other ships. Chang was falling behind. He swallowed hard and raced after Chang.

"You alright, Chang?"

There was no response. Samson felt nauseous. Chang continued to veer off course, but his ship looked like it was going somewhere, not like it was rudderless. Killian got further and further ahead of them. He'd lost. Killian was going to win. Samson clenched his jaw angrily and began to steer back to the straight path towards the second obstacle. He felt a low rumbling run through his body, and stared in shock at the sun. Something was wrong. Chang hit a short booster, and Samson hit a booster too, following him. Killian's ship seemed to waver. Samson looked at the angry surface of the sun. Something was there.

"This is a big one, Ford," Chang said suddenly on the com, startling him. "Hold tight, you were smart to follow."

The rumbling increased to a crescendo. Samson didn't

understand why he could feel it. The sun was, by now, pretty far away. It wasn't even his ship that was shaking. It was just his body, maybe only in his mind – a strange feeling that sparked like electricity through his nervous system. The sun was opening up. Killian turned to a ninety degree angle and flew directly away. Straight away from the sun. Hitting his boosters. The solar flare exploded right at him. It was massive. Samson and Chang accelerated past it as quickly as they could, but both of their ships were flung haplessly aside, like boats in the path of a tidal wave. Samson's radiation meters lit up like a light show. He tried to hold course as much as he could while his ship twisted and rolled.

Stephanie watched the solar flare in horror. She couldn't close her jaw. It was a century-class flare, it covered everything. You couldn't see any of the racers in the first half of the pack. Half the field must have been wiped out. Her eyes trembled, and she hoped against hope for Samson. She wished there was more that she could do than hope.

Chang had seen it coming, he had made an evasive maneuver. Samson had followed Chang. It could have saved them. The flare was blowing out equipment all the way to Mercury. The Racing Board were apologizing and calling it technical difficulties. They were using telescope videos of the sun, which made the flare look like a balloon that had been blown up until it popped. It was beginning to fade.

She held her breath. Hazy pictures were coming back. Samson and Chang's ships looked damaged. Were they flying? The picture flickered in and out. The announcer said they were flying. You couldn't tell. How would he know? Another camera angle came on, crisp. They were on course for the second obstacle. She let out an enormous sigh and sank down into her couch. Both ships were intact. She wished she could see Samson's face. The radiation was still too strong to get signals back from the ships. She thought that he was very smart to have followed Chang. So many of the other racers were dead. Killian had survived they said now. He had used all his boosters. His ship was damaged.

All of the other top pilots were dead. Stephanie felt like she would cry. She knew it must be that bad, but still couldn't believe it. The announcers were excited. At least fifty ships had been destroyed, some of them incinerated so completely that not a trace was left behind. Racers who had not been in the top 100 were now in fourth and fifth place. Stephanie's heart was racing and she curled up into a ball on the couch. She didn't want Samson to finish the race, she just wanted him to come home. She'd been watching the race too much, she'd been so depressed. She'd been working so hard and needed to work harder. Everything was a struggle, a fight. Bloodworth and his allies were aiming for her throat. She needed Samson to win. She didn't care, she wanted him to stop now and come home. She could feel his arms around her, and smell the smell of him. Her beautiful, dark eyes were clenched shut, and had sunk deeply into their sockets.

Samson watched Chang's ship and tried to push the shock out of his mind. His teeth were chattering, and he wished Chang would say something on the com. Say anything. The emptiness of space began to overwhelm him. He added a slight sedative to his IV drip. Chang must be feeling the same way. Although, Chang had a crew. All the broadcast channels were still static, it might be minutes before they could get the newest signals from the Racing Board, it might be hours. They approached the second obstacle warily. It was a huge, black cube, just like the first one. Impossible to guess what was inside. Often in the past it had been highly technical flight through dangerous hazards. This would give Samson and his smaller ship an advantage. Sometimes the racing organizers got creative. At the previous regatta, the racers had been forced to navigate a constantly shifting, generated gravitational field. Samson tried to peer in through the obstacle entrance as they approached, but it was opaque. He slowed ever so slightly to let Chang go in first.

As Chang's ship crossed the threshold of the obstacle, it seemed to be swallowed up in grey smoke. Samson frowned as his own ship plunged in behind, and became engulfed in sandy, grey fog. The ship chattered noisily and vibrated from the patter of rusty sand against its hull. Visibility was low, less than 100 feet. Smaller than some of the ships. Like being caught in a slow, impenetrable storm. Chang's lights disappeared in the haze. Suddenly, like they were flicked off. Samson looked at his sensors tensely. Nothing. Jammed. He turned an evasive maneuver, then thought better of it and slowed to a complete stop. Flying blind. Diagnostics all checked out. The atmosphere was coherent enough to hear the rumble of Chang's ship, further and further away. Scanning the space around him, the entrance to the obstacle could no longer be seen. Samson's blood pressure dropped as he realized that he had lost orientation. He didn't know which way was up, which way was back. In which direction the exit lay. He was entombed.

One of the racing channels had opened up on the com. Not a broadcast channel, an automated message from the cube.

"Greetings, racers," an irritatingly cheerful voice chimed. "Follow the green lights to get to the exit of the race. Your sensors will be of no use to you here. Good luck!"

He turned his ship slowly, looking for the first light. At least he had the tomb to himself. He hoped he could still see the light from wherever he had drifted to. He turned slowly in 360 degrees, then spun in a half twist and turned the ship about the other axis. He wondered how far behind him the next racer was. The searching seemed to take forever. Finally he saw a flicker, traveling through the grey, rusty haze like a far off wave. It was the green light. It was dim.

He piloted the racer forward slowly, at almost a walking pace. The path was tortuous. Strewn with cables and floating space junk. The green light seemed to move back and forth, blinking off for minutes at a time. He drifted forward as the light blinked out. A wall appeared suddenly in front of him. He turned past it awkwardly. A hundred feet of visibility. If that. It could take all day to get to the exit. He wondered how far ahead Chang had gotten. These obstacles should be harder for Chang, but he had motored straight into them with confidence.

A warning signal wailed at him from the instrument panel, and Samson twisted the ship. An enormous, crackling cable passed inches in front of the cockpit glass. He breathed deeply and looked at the instrument panel. Everything was jammed. He punched and scanned through the sensors. There were dozens of minor ones that he rarely used or even looked at. Click, click, click. All jammed. Click, click. Wait.

One of the sensors was online. Samson looked at it curiously. Background velocity, sub-acoustic imaging. Why would it work? He brought the read-out up and a three dimensional, real time map of the space around the ship flashed onto the cockpit glass in front of him. He immediately sped up. Samson didn't understand why this sensor would be unblocked, it was a common sensor. He hoped that Chang had not discovered the same thing yet, and cursed himself for not checking through all of his sensors in the first place. The sub-acoustic imaging wasn't as precise as most of the newer sensors that the pilots used, it was an old back-up in case other systems failed.

Then he remembered Kenichi's newest invention. A quantum signal feedback damper. He hadn't understood what it was. He'd been afraid at the time that it was some kind of sabotage device. Suspicious. But now he remembered what Kenichi had said, "It protects your eyes in a storm."

The pittering, grey atmosphere cloud was irrelevant now. Samson cruised through the obstacle faster and faster. It was only trying to follow the green light that slowed him down. When it would blink off or he would lose sight of it. The sensor extended his sight by several thousand meters, but was little use in plotting a course to the exit. And even at this increased speed it would probably take several hours to get there. Kenichi had been extremely proud of the signal damper he invented, it wasn't something that Chang could possibly have. There was plenty of time to catch up. And then Samson could pass him.

SAMSON WAS SURPRISED HOW LONG it was taking him to catch up to Chang. He flew faster, precariously. A recorded message rang through on the com, an official announcement from the Racing Board. Finally, communication. He wondered if they would tell him how bad the solar flare had been. If it had wiped out the entire race. Maybe only a few pilots were still competing.

"We regret to inform all pilots," said an officious voice, "that Samson Ford has been disqualified from the Solar Regatta. The Racing Board convened on the decision this morning. Mr. Ford, please remove yourself from the race and return to the Solarium. Thank you."

Unconsciously, Samson flew faster. He glanced at the speaker in disbelief, and played the message back again. Certified. Had the anti-naturals legislation already passed? Had prejudice infected the Racing Board? He tried to pull up a communications relay back to the Solarium, but there was still too much static. Could it be a trick?

His teeth ached, and he tried to relax his jaw. The race was almost over now. Couldn't be thrown off by distractions. Winning was the only thing that mattered. There were a million tricks to lead a racer astray. Everyone was against him. He just had to maintain focus. He had to win.

The racer burst out of the grey, sandy fog into a huge, open cavern in the center of the obstacle cube. All of his sensors came back online. An automated message blinked at Samson from the obstacle relay. He brought it up.

"Only one racer may exit this corridor every five minutes."

At the far end of the cavern, the wall was sealed, and a huge illuminated countdown read 4:15.

"Shit!"

Samson circled through the cavern impatiently, performing rolls and dives. At least now he knew how far ahead Chang was. The countdown seemed to take forever. With three minutes left, something unexpected happened. Killian Gideon burst into the cavern at a speed of thousands of kilometers per hour, and screeched to a slow, bitter stop in front of the blocked wall. Samson slid to the left of him to avoid collision as he passed.

"This is my passage," Samson said, "you'll have to wait your turn for the next one."

"You'd like that wouldn't you, faggot," Killian said.

His ship looked like someone had gone over it with a giant welding torch. The paint was ashy where it wasn't peeling off. Samson looked Killian in the eyes through the windows of their cockpits. The perfect white face was bruised and smeared with blood. He looked terrible.

"You're disqualified, anyway, Ford," Killian said. "Don't get in my way. I have to catch up with Chang. And I don't want to kill you out of respect for Lisa."

"Out of respect for Lisa? Are you joking?"

"Yes. But I don't have time for you right now. Consider

yourself lucky and fall back."

The clock was down to one minute. Samson let his ship drift above and in front of Killian's, pressed close against the wall.

Killian tried to say something into the mic, but his voice disappeared in fitful coughing and he cut it off.

"You're hurt, Killian."

"I'm going to kill you."

He suddenly rolled his ship and swung up towards Samson, trying to hook the smaller racer onto his spike. Samson dropped easily under the attack and tried to stay against the wall. Suddenly, both ships were thrown tumbling back across cavern, and an enormous voice reverberated through the air.

"Multiple ships are not allowed in the vicinity of the passage entrance. Please approach only one ship at a time."

"FUCK!" Killian screamed irately into the mic.

Samson watched as Killian's racer righted itself and accelerated towards him. The countdown clock had run. He flew towards the wall, hoping to get there first. When they got close, both ships were again thrown violently back. It was making Samson dizzy.

Killian tried to swarm around him like a wasp, but Samson's ship was quicker and more nimble. He tried to lure Killian away from the far wall, and then suddenly race to get there first, but Killian stayed close and they were thrown back again. The space in the cavern wasn't large enough to use his boosters.

"Why don't you just let me go first," Samson said.

"I was saving this for Chang, but I guess I'll have to use it on you."

Samson dove, and curled off towards the far wall. A round, black object dropped out of Killian's ship, sparkling with yellow fingers of lightning. Samson hit his boosters. Weapons weren't allowed in the race. The wall accelerated towards him. He could feel the yellow snakes of energy touching his ship. He braced to be thrown back from the wall, or to die, and exploded through it into a pepper of grey, sandy mist. The sensors all went down again, except the one. He didn't pause, or look back, but accelerated precariously through the murky passage, determined to catch up with Chang.

HALF AN HOUR LATER, SAMSON calculated that he was nearing the exit to the obstacle cube. He wondered how far ahead Chang had gotten. The racer scraped against the obstacle cube walls on a tight turn, and threw him hard against his harnesses, spraying sparks into the sandy, grey haze. The sparks looked like fireworks twinkling through a thick fog. He righted the ship without slowing down, pulse barely rising. A smell like iron permeated the cockpit. Like blood. It was beginning to make him nauseous. He wanted to fiddle with the IV settings, but couldn't relax his attention on the path ahead. He listened to the racer's wailing engines, and hoped that whatever dust and particles made up the haze were not doing too much damage.

An object suddenly flashed towards him on the sensor screen. Before he had time to realize consciously that it was another ship, he dropped low and rose, nudging the other racer's tail as it flashed past. The ship pitched off course into a spin as it hurtled out of the sensor's range.

He didn't slow. He tried to picture the ship in his mind. It had been Killian. A few seconds later the rusty clouds reverberated with a tremendous crash. Within a few minutes, Samson saw the light of the obstacle cube exit and flew back out into open space. His eyes caught the far off glint of Chang's racer. Not too far.

As he gave chase to Chang, he was surprised to notice Killian's ship emerge from the obstacle cube behind him.

C H A P T E R ⁶³

AMSON'S RACER MELTED AWAY TO a blur. It arced through space like a white falcon in a steep, predatory dive. His booster rockets left silver trails. He seemed to surf along the top of a lightning bolt. He was delirious. Chang's big, wedge-shaped racer ploughed through space in the distance ahead. Samson was closing the gap. It was still hours to the finish. There was plenty of time. Killian's battered racer dogged their heels stubbornly, but slipped further and further back.

The boiling, red ocean of the sun had finally fallen away behind them. They were like mariners splashing ashore and stumbling onto land. After so many hours, the presence of that perpetually exploding mass grew overwhelming. Claustrophobic. The deep, magnetic hum came to permeate every vein and tissue. Until you were sick with it. Until you forgot that it was there. And when you finally emerged it was like coming out of cold water, after your body had finally given up and forgotten that it was cold. It was jarring, and felt important. And for some reason you missed the hum. You could feel your heart beating.

Samson pressed at the imprint of the cross against his chest. He had survived the race. He could win now. Here at the end. His racer was faster. All the dangerous parts were behind him. And there was nothing that Chang could do. There was too much space. Endless, open space. He wouldn't have to come close to Chang to pass him. Not really close. It would look close on tv. But it would be kilometers. So many pilots had been lost, destroyed by the solar flare, but he was here, alive, his ship intact. Because he was supposed to be. Because he was supposed to win. It must be the God.

He looked at the meters on his IV dispenser. Almost out of stimulants. Almost out of everything. He thought he could feel the chill of the drips as they slid into his blood. He shouldn't be able to, they were regulated at body temperature. He wondered what he must look like in the mirror. Almost drained. Almost dead. You always saw the pictures of the racers after they finished the Solar Regatta. It was amazing what they did to themselves, how far they pushed their bodies. They never looked like the same men that had started the race. He wondered what it was like for the ships with a crew. Easier. They could even take shifts. Everyone but the pilot. It was good that he hadn't had to tangle with Chang. The race had gone perfectly.

The boosters were running out, and he pushed the ship's engines harder, until they screamed. His hands were clenched on the control wands as if his fingers had turned to stone and could never be released. At this velocity his acceleration could bring on relativity sickness any time. He only had to stay focused and keep his speed. The constant acceleration pressed against his back, and it felt good. It should have hurt. It was because the race was almost over, and because he was winning. Because he would be winning. Everything felt good. The hurt felt good. Far in the distance, like a star on the horizon, he could see the Solarium again.

"Hello, Mr. Ford?" a voice crackled through on a com relay. Samson blinked at the speaker, trying to place it. It was the head racing official. "Uh, you know that you've been disqualified from the race? Do you? Did you get the message, it should have been relayed while you were in the second obstacle cube. Hello? It just, it looks like you're still racing, and–"

Samson switched off all the com channels from the Solarium. He was closing the gap on Chang faster than expected. He was almost neck and neck with him, almost alongside. Chang's racer seemed heavy and precarious. Samson smiled at them as he sped past. He craned his neck to watch the big, red and yellow wedge trail away behind him.

It didn't trail away.

Chang's ship caught back up to him almost immediately. There was something weird about it. It seemed to shimmer and glow. It seemed to cut through space, for split seconds to flicker and disappear. And it had stopped leaving an engine trail. It passed him and began to pull away.

Samson jettisoned the elaborate wings framework of his racer. It drifted away in space like a cast off shell.

"You can't win, Ford," Killian's voice rasped at him through the com, with something like affection. "You're not even in the race."

"I don't care."

Samson activated his last booster, and the racer shook violently, but accelerated. It shook until he could barely keep it flying straight. Until he was blazing through space, straining all his muscles against the control wands. The cockpit panels blinked warnings at him. Until the impossible sensation of the relativity sickness began to close in around him. In the corner of his eye the IV fluid dripped more and more slowly.

He was catching up with Chang. He was passing him. Chang's ship shimmered and glowed, and began to fall behind.

"You idiot," Chang said through the com, "you're going to kill yourself."

His voice seemed puffed up, exploded. It had an other-worldly quality to Samson's ears. Then Chang's ship was in front of him again. Leaving him behind. It was glowing a sort of brass and silver now, it was cutting through space. Not traveling through it. It was unlike anything Samson had seen. The ship disappeared and reappeared in space. It was like laying underwater and watching a stone skip across the top of a murky pool.

Samson accelerated, opening the throttle completely, as

fast as his ship would go, but there was nothing he could do. Chang drifted away into the distance, leaving him behind. Sure to win. It was sure that he would lose. He wasn't even in the race. All was lost.

Then Chang's ship exploded with a flash of blue. It stopped shimmering and returned to normal flight, trailing flames. He seemed to pass it in an instant.

HE WANTED TO WATCH THE ship disappear behind him, but couldn't turn his head. He couldn't even look at the sensors. He had tunnel vision now. His hands were frozen around the control wands. He could only see the path right ahead of him. The finish coming up in the distance. Closer. He could barely see it. It seemed to be part of another place, of another world. It didn't seem to matter anymore, but he raced for it with every fiber of his being, as if it was the only thing that mattered in the world. As if his body and his mind had become separate. He could feel how hard his body was struggling to get him there, but he couldn't understand why. He had already won the race, or he would win it. It didn't matter.

It seemed like the whole universe was opening up for Samson, as if he would disappear into it. And then suddenly it was closed and he was alone in a place he didn't know, an empty place. Cold and empty, and he tried to look around him, but there was nothing, just empty blackness, without even stars in the distance. But somehow he could perceive it, the endless empty space. As if he were underneath the fabric of the universe, of universes, or as if he had become the universe. But it didn't seem curious to him, it just was that way, it just was.

Then he was cold again, with the world sucked in around him, as if it would suffocate him. As if he could feel the touch of every person he had ever met, simultaneously against his skin, but as if their fingers were cold, like corpses. More people than he had ever met. As if it was every person in the universe that was touching him. Their hard, bony, icy fingers seemed to press into him and crush his flesh.

If he had any flesh. Now he thought that he didn't. He wondered if he had won the race. He wished that Stephanie was with him. He thought of all the people like him on all the different planets, rounded up and herded. Or not. Quarantined. People like Killian and Scamp. At least he could beat them, at least he could have beaten them. They couldn't. He wished that he had tried harder. Hadn't he tried hard? He thought that he had tried so hard. He wished that Stephanie was there beside him, and tried to reach to her. And tried to slow his ship down. And wondered if he had won.

END